DON'T ASK

By Donald E. Westlake

NOVELS

Humans • Sacred Monster • A Likely Story
Kahawa • Brothers Keepers • I Gave at the Office
Adios, Scheherazade • Up Your Banners

COMIC CRIME NOVELS

Trust Me on This • High Adventure
Castle in the Air • Enough • Dancing Aztecs
Two Much • *Help* I Am Being Held Prisoner
Cops and Robbers • Somebody Owes Me Money
Who Stole Sassi Manoon? • God Save the Mark
The Spy in the Ointment • The Busy Body
The Fugitive Pigeon

THE DORTMUNDER SERIES

Don't Ask • Drowned Hopes • Good Behavior
Why Me • Nobody's Perfect
Jimmy the Kid • Bank Shot • The Hot Rock

CRIME NOVELS

Pity Him Afterwards • Killy • 361
Killing Time • The Mercenaries

JUVENILE

Philip

WESTERN

Gangway (with Brian Garfield)

REPORTAGE

Under an English Heaven

SHORT STORIES

Tomorrow's Crimes • Levine
The Curious Facts Preceding My Execution and Other Fictions

ANTHOLOGY

Once Against the Law (coedited by William Tenn)

DONALD E. WESTLAKE

DON'T ASK

THE MYSTERIOUS PRESS
New York • Tokyo • Sweden
Published by Warner Books

A Time Warner Company

Copyright © 1993 by Donald E. Westlake
Mysterious Press books are published by Warner Books, Inc.,
1271 Avenue of the Americas, New York, NY 10020.

A Time Warner Company

The Mysterious Press name and logo are registered trademarks of
Warner Books, Inc.

Printed in the United States of America

First printing: April 1993

10 9 8 7 6 5 4 3 2 1

Library of Congress Cataloging-in-Publication Data
Westlake, Donald E.
    Don't ask / Donald E. Westlake.
        p.   cm.
    ISBN 0-89296-469-3
    I. Title.
    PS3573.E9D66   1993
    813'.54—dc20   92-53721
                                                        CIP

Dedicated, in awe and admiration, to Robert Redford,
George C. Scott, Paul LeMat, and Christopher Lambert:
Dortmunders all, and who would have guessed.

DON'T ASK

1

Stuck in traffic on the Williamsburg Bridge out of lower Manhattan in a stolen frozen fish truck full of stolen frozen fish at 1:30 on a bright June afternoon, with construction out ahead of them forever on the Brooklyn Queens Expressway, with Stan Murch on Dortmunder's left complaining about how there *are* no decent routes anymore from anywhere to anywhere in New York City—"If there ain't snow on the road, there's construction crews"—and with Andy Kelp on Dortmunder's right prattling on happily about global warming and how much nicer it will be when there isn't any winter, Dortmunder *also* had to contend with an air conditioner dripping on his ankles. *Cold* drips. "My ankles are freezing," he announced. As if anybody cared.

"Nobody's gonna freeze anymore," Kelp assured him. "Not with global warming."

"I can't wait," Dortmunder said. "The bones in my ankles are getting all cracks in them. I got ice water from the air conditioner squirting all over my ankles *now*. I'm never gonna walk again. I can't wait for the globe to get warm."

"The thing about getting on a bridge," Stan Murch said, "once you're on it, you're *on* it. No changing your mind on a bridge. No

1

turning off, turning around, take a little detour. You're on a bridge, you're on a bridge, and that's it until you get to the other side, and, the way I see it, we ain't gonna *get* to the other side."

"Enough is enough," Dortmunder decided, and leaned forward to peer at the dashboard's array of controls. After one false start—the windshield had needed washing anyway—he found the knob marked A/C and switched it off.

Which didn't help. Apparently, the air-conditioning system had already collected enough frigid condensation in its innards to keep raining on Dortmunder's parade (or his tarsals, at least) well into the next century, which was how long Stan announced he anticipated they'd be stuck on this goddam bridge. Dortmunder twisted around to the right to hide his ankles behind Kelp's, but there wasn't really room over there, and in any event Kelp was a kicker, so it was back to the January thaw.

Inch by inch they crept across the bridge, among all the rest of the smoking, snorting, stinking traffic, Dortmunder only glad the interior of the truck cab remained cool enough (probably because of the ice water gathering in a tarn at his feet) so that neither Kelp nor Stan insisted on turning the air conditioner back on. Think what a cataract, what a cascade, it could produce if left on for the whole trip. But the sun was behind them, since they were driving east—or pointing east, anyway—so the truck cab was in the shade. A nice shady spot, with a waterfall.

The trip to Farport, on Long Island's southern shore, should have taken an hour and a half, max, but with most of the population of New York State fitted out in bright orange vests and told to stand around in the middle of every highway and byway and look busy, it was nearly four hours before the trio and their fish truck drove at last into the yard at the Ocean Deeps Processing Plant, where their load/loot would be commingled with fish brought here more conventionally—that is, by boat, from the ocean—and eventually driven back to New York in a similar fish truck and possibly even to the same fish wholesaler who'd been anticipating its arrival today.

Except, no. When George of Ocean Deeps snapped the lock and raised the big articulated door at the rear of the truck, the odor that came out was strong enough to plant beans in. *"Jesus Christ!"* George prayed, and yanked down the door, though not before two nonsmokers in the office across the yard fainted.

George backed away from the truck as he stared at his alleged suppliers in outrage and disbelief. "You turn off the AC?" he demanded. "On a day like this?"

"Oh," Dortmunder said, while eyes from both sides turned and did laser things to his cheekbones. "That's why the cab stayed cool."

The ride back to the city on the Long Island Railroad was a quiet one. They'd abandoned the truck a block from the station, and, when last they'd looked back, the thing had a kind of shimmery quality to it, as though it were just about to be teleported to another planet, or another time. Which wouldn't be a bad idea.

Dortmunder had too much dignity to try to alibi himself in front of his onetime friends—cold water, ankles, no assistance from *them*, A/C clearly marked on the knob—while apparently neither Kelp nor Stan trusted himself to speak, so the three sat in silence all the way to Penn Station. Dortmunder had paid for all the tickets—it seemed like he should, somehow—but nevertheless it was Kelp who was glumly looking at the glum suburbs outside the window and Stan sitting with his big brogans in the aisle and giving the fish-eye—pardon; staring back at any passerby who seemed to be considering a complaint, while Dortmunder was *still* seated in the middle. At least there wasn't any ice water.

It was well after seven o'clock in the evening before Dortmunder finally unlocked his way into his apartment on Nineteenth Street and walked back to the kitchen, where his faithful companion May said, "Good," got up from the table where she'd been reading "Seven Fast-Track Careers for *You*" in last month's *Self,* and hit the START button on the microwave Dortmunder had brought home late one night a couple months ago. "Dinner in four minutes."

"Don't ask," Dortmunder said.

3

May had no intention of asking. One look at Dortmunder's face told her the day had not gone well. "Beer or bourbon?" she asked.

"Definitely bourbon," Dortmunder told her, and went away to wash up.

On his return, she handed him a glass and said, "Tiny called, before. He'd like a meet tonight at the OJ, ten o'clock."

"He's got something?" Anything, Dortmunder thought, to erase the memory of those fish.

"I guess so." May sounded dubious, or confused. "He kind of chuckled and said, 'Tell Dortmunder, it's exactly his kind of thing.' Whatever that means."

"Nothing good," Dortmunder surmised, and the microwave beeped in agreement.

2

When Dortmunder walked into the OJ Bar & Grill on Amsterdam Avenue at ten that night, the regulars were discussing why the big annual automobile race called the Indy 500 was called the Indy 500. "It's because," one regular explained, "they run it on Independence Day."

Rollo the bartender was nowhere to be seen.

"They do not," a second regular responded. "Independence Day is the Fourth of July."

Dortmunder walked over to the bar to see what was what with Rollo.

The first regular reared back and stared at the second regular in aggressive astonishment. "What boat did *you* get off? The Fourth of July is the *fourth of July!*"

The duckboards behind the bar were lifted and leaning against the backbar, and the trapdoor was open. Dortmunder settled down to wait.

"And the Fourth of July is Independence Day," the second regular said, with the calm confidence of the well-prepared scholar. "They run the Indy Five Hundred on Memorial Day, if you want to know."

"They why don't they call it the Memo Five Hundred?"

"The *place* where they run it—" started a third regular; but, no. Not a regular at all, or he would not have allowed himself to be interrupted.

Which he was, by the first regular, still as calmly confident as ever, explaining, "The *reason* they call the Indy the Indy is because they named it in honor of the guy in *Raiders of the Lost Ark*. On account of what a terrific driver he is. Indigo Jones, nickname Indy."

"You know," mused a third regular, "it's only called the Indy Five Hundred *this* year." Yes; this is the third regular. "Next year," he informed the world at large, "it'll be the Indy Five Hundred and One."

Everybody paused to think about that.

"It's called the *Indy* because—" said the nonregular.

"Are you telling me," the first regular said to the third regular, "the Indy Five Hundred started in the sixteenth century? Are you sure they had cars then?"

"They used chariots the first few years," the third regular explained. "That's where the movie *Ben-Hur* came from. It's like the Super Bowl, with the numbers, ex-ex this and ex-ex that. Only they use American numbers. Five hundred. Five hundred and one."

"Indianap—" said the nonregular.

"It isn't Indigo," said the second regular.

The first regular reared around to confront this new challenge to his scholarship: "*What* isn't Indigo?"

"The guy's name," said the second regular. "An indigo is a kind of fruit, like an orange or a quincy."

"That's right," the third regular said. "My first wife made pies."

The first regular did another half turn on his stool to lower an eyebrow at the third regular. "Indigo pies?"

"And quincy pies. And rubabayga."

Rollo came heavily up the basement stairs, screwing the top onto a full bottle of Amsterdam Liquor Store Bourbon—"Our Own Brand." When he saw Dortmunder looking down at him, he pretended he wasn't screwing the top on, that the top had been on all along. "The other bourbon said you'd be along," Rollo said.

"Andy Kelp's here?" He's telling Tiny, Dortmunder thought, about the fish.

"*And* the beer and salt," Rollo said. "And two vodka and red wines."

"Two?"

"Your big friend brought another guy," Rollo said. He put the bottle of muddy brown liquid on the backbar, stooped with a *grunt* to close the trapdoor and drop the duckboards into place, then pretended to go through the process of opening a brand-new fresh bottle, using the bottle he'd just come upstairs with for the demonstration. He placed this triumphantly open bottle and a glass in front of Dortmunder and said, "I told the other one you'd bring it in."

"Thanks, Rollo."

The regulars were now discussing whether or not it was permissible for a person who'd only been married once, and was still married, to speak in terms of "my first wife." There were many opinions expressed on this topic. "Not in front of her," the non-regular advised, but of course no one listened to him.

Dortmunder picked up the bottle and glass and carried them past the regulars and down beyond the end of the bar and down the hall past the doors decorated with black metal dog silhouettes labeled POINTERS and SETTERS, and past the phone booth with the string dangling from the quarter slot, and on to the end of the hall, where the knob of the green door stymied him for just a second, until he figured out how to hook the glass with one finger of the hand holding the bottle, leaving the other hand free to open the door.

"—nobody ever *did* hear him cry for help. I guess he's still there."

Dortmunder nodded to the speaker as he entered the room and bumped the door shut behind him with his behind. The speaker, who looked mostly like a hillside brought to life by Claymation, was a man monster—or monster man—named Tiny Bulcher by someone with a grim sense of humor, or fast legs, or both. In the company of human beings of normal size and shape, Tiny Bulcher looked . . . different. He reminded most people of the thing they used to believe lived in their bedroom closet at night, when they were very very small, and they would wake up, and it would be really really dark in the whole house, and they would lie in bed and know just how small they were, and the closet door was the only thing in the entire vast universe they could see, and they just *knew* that inside that closet *right now*, reaching for the doorknob on the inside there, was . . . Tiny Bulcher.

"Hello, Tiny," Dortmunder said, and crossed to sit at the table near an aloof Andy Kelp, placing the bourbon bottle between them.

"Hello, Dortmunder," said Tiny, with a voice like a seaplane engine with gasket trouble. He chuckled, with a sound like small bones being crushed, and said, "I understand you went fishin. Only the fishin stunk."

"Heh heh," Dortmunder said.

The scene of this good-natured teasing was a smallish square room with a concrete floor. Beer and liquor cases lined all the walls, leaving a small open space in the middle, containing a battered old round table with a stained green felt top. Half a dozen chairs, all but one now occupied, stood around this table, and the only light came from one bare bulb under a round tin reflector hanging from a long black wire over the very center of the table.

The unoccupied chair had its back to the door; this was never a popular chair. To its right sat Dortmunder and to its left Stan Murch, who even without a steering wheel managed to look as though he were driving. To Dortmunder's right, Andy Kelp poured bourbon into his glass without saying thank you, and beyond him, facing the empty chair and the door, lurked Tiny Bulcher, in his massive paw a minuscule glass of what looked like cherry soda but was, in fact, a combination of vodka and Chianti that Tiny seemed to find restorative. And beyond Tiny, between Tiny and Stan Murch, was another one.

Another glass of noncherry soda. Another massive paw. Another man monster. Not quite as large as Tiny, but then, there are some villages out west that aren't as large as Tiny. But this guy came close.

It was mostly his shiny baldness above and the thick, heavy black beard below that made his face look like a boulder on a mountaintop. His shirt was black, with black buttons, and over it he wore a vaguely military tunic kind of thing, the Nehru jacket's homicidal cousin, in a dark olive green; exactly the color of an ornamental pond that hasn't been cared for right. The hands

8

emerging from the black loop–embroidered sleeves of this tunic were depressingly large and thick and knobbly, with rings embedded in them here and there. Up at boulder level, the eyes were small, dark, brooding, and too close together, under a single hairy black caterpillar of brow resting on the ridges of his craggy forehead.

Tiny made introductions: "Dortmunder, this is—" And he cleared his throat.

Dortmunder leaned forward, looking alert. "Say what?"

"This is—" Tiny repeated, pointing a fat thumb at the new one, and repeated the throat clearing.

"It's his name," Kelp said. "The best I can figure, it's Grijk Krugnk."

"Only wid an accent," said the new one, with an accent, "over da *cccchh*."

"Well, I'm still working on it, uh, Grijk," Kelp said, and said to Dortmunder, "He's not from around here."

"So you're talking to me," Dortmunder observed.

Kelp grinned and shrugged. "Sure, why not? What's a few fish between friends?"

"Now that you told the whole world and everybody."

"Aw, come on, John," Kelp said. "Isn't it better to have a funny story than a bitter secret?"

"I wish you'd given me the choice."

"Dortmunder," Tiny said, low and impatient, "you with us or what?"

"I'm with you, Tiny."

"And you met my cousin."

"Oh, he's your cousin? Grijk Krugnk?"

"Dere!" announced Grijk Krugnk triumphantly, pointing a weisswurst, or possibly a finger, at Dortmunder. "*He* can say it!"

"I can?"

"Yeah, my cousin," Tiny said. "From the old country. My long-lost cousin, you could say."

"I see the family resemblance, Tiny," Dortmunder said.

"Most people do. Anyway, the old country, they got a problem, so Grijk looked me up."

"Dat's right."

"So I figured, the country my grandparents had the sense to get out of, they got a problem, I gotta show some loyalty, am I right?"

Everybody agreed Tiny was right. (Everybody *always* agreed Tiny was right.)

Tiny nodded, agreeing with himself, and turned to Grijk. "Tell them about it."

Grijk nodded, his bald head sending semaphores. "We godda gedda bone," he said.

Dortmunder and Kelp and Murch all sat there, attentive, wanting more. But Grijk had no more to give. He nodded emphatically and consumed half his noncherry soda.

It was Dortmunder who pressed the issue, saying to Tiny, "Did he say a *bone?*"

"Yeah," Tiny said. "The femur of Saint Ferghana." (Oddly enough, he pronounced *femur* correctly, with the long *e* as in *female*.)

"That's a bone?" Dortmunder asked.

"It's a relic," Tiny explained. "From a saint. It's a bone from a saint, so it's a relic." He consulted his cousin. "Am I right?"

"Dat's right!"

"Now, the old country," Tiny went on, "what they—"

"Pardon me, Tiny," Dortmunder said, "but exactly what old country is this?"

"Well, that's kind of complicated, Dortmunder," Tiny said. "It's a very old country, but, on the other hand, it's a very new country, too."

"Does this country have a name?"

"Lately," Tiny said.

Dortmunder frowned. "Lately? That's its *name?*"

"No no," Tiny said. "You always complicate things, Dortmunder. It's called Tsergovia." And beside him, his cousin sat to attention at the sound of the sacred syllables.

"Tsergovia," Dortmunder said. "I never heard of it." He glanced at Kelp, who shook his head, and at Stan, who said, "If it isn't in the five boroughs, *I* never heard of it."

Tiny said, "This poor little country, it really got screwed around with over the years. It was independent for a long time in the Middle Ages, and then it got to be part of the Austro-Hungarian empire, and one time it was almost a part of Albania, except

10

over the mountains, and later on the Commies put it together with this other crap country, Votskojek—"

Grijk growled.

"—and called it something else, but now the Commies are out, that whole Eastern European thing is coming apart, and Tsergovia's becoming its own country again."

"Free at last," Grijk said.

"So it's gonna be a real different country," Tiny said, "from when my grandparents decided to get the hell out of . . ." He frowned, and turned to his cousin. "What was the name of that place again?"

"Styptia," Grijk said.

"Yeah, that's it," Tiny agreed. "My ancestral village home."

"A beautiful little willage," Grijk said, "nested in da crags a da mountains."

"My one grandfather was the village blacksmith," Tiny told the others, familial pride in his voice. "And the other . . ." Again he was at a loss; scratching various acres of his forehead, he said, "Grijk? What was my other grandfather? You never told me."

"Oh, vell," Grijk said. "Such a long time ago."

"Yeah, but what did he do before he left for the U.S.? One was the village blacksmith, but what was the other one?"

"Vell," Grijk said, reluctantly, "da willage idiot."

"Oh," said Tiny.

"Bud only because," Grijk hastened to add, "dere veren't d'opportunities in dot liddle place. Nod like here."

"Yeah, that's true," Tiny agreed.

"And nod like da vay it's gonna be, vid *your* help."

"Whatever I can do, Grijk, you know that," Tiny said.

Dortmunder said, "Tiny? What's the problem?"

"Well, the problem," Tiny said, "the problem is the UN."

Dortmunder absorbed that. He said, "You want us to go up against the United Nations? Us five here?"

"No, we're not goin up against the UN," Tiny said, as though it were Dortmunder who was being ridiculous. "We're goin up against Votskojek—"

Grijk growled.

"—which is a whole nother thing."

"Which nother thing?" Dortmunder wanted to know.

"The bone's in the mission," Tiny explained.

"Well, that makes sense," Kelp said. "You got a religious relic, you keep it in the mission."

"Not that kind of mission," Tiny said.

"Is this in California?" Dortmunder asked, expecting the worst.

"It's *not* that kind of mission," Tiny said, louder. "It's the Votskojek"—*growl*—"mission to the UN. Or it will be if they get the seat, which they ain't gonna get, because *we're* gonna get the bone." He turned to his cousin. "Isn't that right?"

"Dat's right!"

"Wait a minute," Dortmunder said, "I'm seeing some daylight here, I think. Either that or my brain's on fire. Tsergovia's a brand-new country, so they aren't in the UN yet, and in order to get accepted into the UN they've got to steal this saint's bone from this other brand-new country. The bone is like their admission to the UN."

Kelp said, "John, that's the dumbest thing I ever heard in my life. The *United Nations* lets you become a member if you got a *bone*? That's too stupid to even be a sentence."

"Nevertheless," Dortmunder said, "I bet that's the story here. Am I right, Tiny?"

"You're right, Dortmunder," Tiny said.

Kelp said, "He's *right*?"

"More or less," Tiny said. "And if you guys come into this with me, you'll be doin a wonderful thing for a little country never hurt nobody."

Dortmunder nodded. He said, "And?"

Tiny was not a subtle man. He could be seen pretending not to understand what Dortmunder meant. He said, "And? That's it, and. That's the story."

"Tiny," Dortmunder said, more in sorrow than in anger, "if we get this bone and turn it over to your cousin here, Tsergovia gets into the UN, don't ask me why. What do *we* get out of it?"

"Heroes!" Grijk cried. "A statue in the main square in the capital at Osigreb! Your pictures on stamps! Your names in children's schoolbooks!"

"That's kind of, uh, public," Dortmunder pointed out, "for a burglary. I mean, Tiny, we're talking a burglary here, aren't we?"

"Right up your alley, Dortmunder."

"What I like out of a burglary, Tiny," Dortmunder said, "no offense to you or Tsergovia, is not so much publicity as profit."

"Vot problem ve god in Tsergovia," Grijk said very sincerely, "is ve god nod enough hard currency."

"I know exactly how you feel," Dortmunder said.

"So vot ve could offer," Grijk went on more brightly, "is fifty tousand dollars apiece."

"Well, that's nice," Stan said, and he and Kelp and Dortmunder all smiled.

"In Tsergovia," Grijk finished.

They stopped smiling. Kelp said, "What do you mean? We got to go there and bring it back?"

"Vell, it vould be in draffs," Grijk explained, "nod in dollars, so you vouldn't bring it back, you know, you couldn't spend draffs anyvere bud in Tsergovia."

"That's what you call your money," Dortmunder guessed. "Draffs."

"D'exchange rate is wery good right now," Grijk told him. "It's, uh, I tink today it's two tousand six hundred fifty draffs."

"To the dollar."

"To da penny. *Tinka* all dose draffs! You could stay da best hotels, eat da best restaurants, ski da mountains, water sports da lakes, meet beautiful local girls—"

"I don't know," Dortmunder said, regretfully shaking his head. "Vacation travel hadn't actually been part of my plans, May and me, we thought we'd just stick around the city this summer."

Kelp said, "Tiny? Isn't there anything we could get for ourselves? Something valuable in this mission we could pick up while we're in there anyway? Crown jewels? Old master paintings on the wall? You know, Tiny, a little something for our trouble."

"Gas money," Stan said.

"They got a couple electric typewriters in the mission there," Tiny suggested doubtfully. "And, uh, Andy, you always like phones."

"Not enough, Tiny," Dortmunder said. "I can't speak for Andy and Stan, but—"

"Oh, sure you can," Kelp said, and Stan said, "Go ahead, be my guest."

"Okay," Dortmunder said. "In that case, Tiny, I got to tell you, we don't see it. We value your friendship, the nice professional

13

relationship we had in the past, we hope to work with you again in the future—"

"Naturally," Tiny said.

"But this time, I'm sorry to say it, Tiny, this time is a pass. You break and enter, you risk arrest and imprisonment—"

"A country's mission," Stan said, "probably they got armed guards."

"They do," Tiny conceded.

"Murderers!" Grijk shouted, thumping the table with his free hand. "Scoundrels!"

"So there's another risk," Dortmunder said. "And for what? For some guy's bone that I don't even know, that—"

"Girl," Tiny said. "Saint Ferghana was a girl. And it's her leg bone, the bone from the hip to the knee."

Kelp said, "Which leg?"

Dortmunder shook his head at his friend. "I don't think that matters, Andy," he said. "In the first place, she's dead. And in the second place, we're turning the job down."

"Well, that's true," Kelp agreed.

Tiny turned to his cousin and performed a massive shrug, like tectonic plates moving. "I'm sorry, Grijk," he said, "but there it is. I told you I'd give it my best shot, present the thing with the best spin on it, but the truth is, if I didn't have this feeling for the old country, if it was just a professional question, me, too, I'd give it a no."

Fiercely glaring into the middle distance, Grijk raised his glass of noncherry soda, drained it, threw the glass across the room, where it hit a wooden wine case and shattered (Rollo wouldn't like that), and cried, "Ve must nod stop!"

"We're not gonna stop, Grijk," Tiny assured him, "not you and me. But these fellas here, they're gonna stop. And I don't blame them."

Kelp said, "Thank you, Tiny."

"It's just that I have to keep in mind," Dortmunder explained, "what it says across the bottom of my family crest."

Tiny lowered an eyebrow; in fact, half an entire forehead. "And what's that, Dortmunder?"

" '*Quid lucrum istic mihi est?*' "

"Meaning?"

" 'What's in it for me?' "

2A*

$\mathbf{S}$aint Ferghana Karanovich (1200?–1217) was born into a family of murdering and robbing innkeepers in Varnic, a then-important stop for wayfarers to and from the HOLY LAND (qv), who had to cross the Carpathians from Karnolia to Transylvania through the Feoda Pass (much later to become the site of a signifi-cant tank engagement during the Battle of the Crevasses in WORLD WAR TWO [qv]).

For generations, the Karanovich family had operated an inn some little way off the beaten path, high in the mountains just north of the primary route (the beaten path) through the pass. Customers for the inn were few and far between as a result of this poor location, and for decades the Karanoviches, whose unre-lented interbreeding had made them nasty, brutish, and not very tall, supplemented their meager income by murdering and robbing the unwariest of the passing wayfarers.

By the age of eleven, young Ferghana, too, had become an active participant in these activities, which, even by the commu-nity standards of the time (early 13C), were generally considered

---

*Optional—historical aside—not for credit

unacceptable. Having no knowledge of the world beyond that imparted to her by her ungentlemanly uncles, Ferghana could not have known that in normal society it was deemed wrong for ladies of her tender years to introduce themselves into the beds of male strangers late at night so as to distract them until an uncle could surreptitiously enter the room with a club. Though eventually she would, with time and wisdom and patient instruction, renounce these activities, there are reasons to believe that until the age of seventeen she played her role in the family enterprise with unfeigned zest.

Ferghana's transmogrification from murderous accomplice to saint began when the family inn was chosen as a stopover by Archbishop Scheissekopf, an Ulm prelate on a pilgrimage to the HOLY LAND (qv). Though even the benighted Karanovich clan knew better than to try to rob and murder an archbishop by luring him to destruction with the wiles of a depraved NYMPHET (qv), there was a spontaneous nocturnal discussion between young Ferghana and the holy priest, in which the child's eyes were opened to the possibilities (and responsibilities) of a wider world.

When, the following morning, the archbishop departed the inn, he had no idea that hidden within a burlap sack putatively containing potatoes and lashed to his packhorse with hairy ropes there huddled concealed, in fact, Ferghana. Imagine the worthy gentleman's surprise at the end of that first day when, in lieu of potatoes, out from the sack rolled the innkeeper's daughter!

For six days, Ferghana traveled with this excellent ecclesiastic, during which time the good father instructed the child in diverse matters, ranging from the mundane (personal hygiene) to the transcendentally moral (killing people is wrong). Ferghana, undergoing an ecstasy of conversion, confessed to God's shepherd her unseemly part in the nefarious goings-on at the inn, and vowed henceforth to lead a cleaner—in every sense of the term—life.

When, on their sixth day together in the wilderness, the revered patriarch explained to the child the general situation of women—and particularly girls of her own age—at that time in the HOLY LAND (qv), Ferghana decided her wisest course was to return to her family in the role of missionary, dedicated to the conversion of her relatives from their evil ways and the turning of them onto the

16

paths of righteousness. Chancing upon a traveling troupe of acrobats from KLOPSTOCKIA (qv) who were heading northwestward toward the Feoda Pass, Ferghana made her emotional farewells with the learned reverend and joined the acrobats for the return journey, with further education and discoveries along the way. (Scholars differ as to whether the leathern purse of shekels she carried with her on the return was a gift from Archbishop Scheissekopf or had been filched by her in a light-fingered or lighthearted, certainly distracted, reversion to her previous ways.)

Though the exact circumstances of Ferghana's martyrdom can never be precisely known, it would appear the young saint-to-be lost some of her missionary zeal when face-to-face with her family once more, and did not at first make any of the impassioned pleas in favor of sobriety, decency, humanity, and godliness (see under "cleanliness") which she had rehearsed so fervently en route while performing pyramids and other architectural edifices with the acrobats. It was not until the child's refusal to enter the room (and the bed) of a musk-ox merchant named Mulmp that the family first discovered that the archbishop's influence extended beyond the leathern purse of shekels that she had, as a dutiful daughter, presented to her parents on her return from her travels.

That a reconversion, or deprogramming, effort was made, to rid the child of "furrin" influences and restore her as a useful family member, is known. That this reconversion attempt involved imprisonment, starvation, beatings, and other degradations can be inferred from family histories. That the attempt ended in murder and, regrettably, cannibalism, is known only because the saintly archbishop, some months later, on his return from the HOLY LAND (qv), stopped again at the Karanovich's inn and quite naturally inquired after the fair Ferghana. Being informed by the wretched child's mother that there was not *nor never had been* anyone of that name at the inn, the archbishop grew fearful that foul play might have overtaken the missing miss, and he made haste to the nearby castle of BARON LUNCH (qv), who held sway over the land where the inn was situate.

The Baron's stewards, investigating the activities at the inn and persuading by a variety of means several family members to divulge everything they knew about the case, soon dug up a number of bodies from shallow graves in ravines and arroyos all around the neighborhood, but nothing was found of Ferghana except her upper left leg, from knee to hip, which, having become gangrenous as a result of the family's deprogramming effort, had been left uneaten. Archbishop Scheissekopf was enabled to make a positive identification of the leg on the basis of a peculiar heart-shaped mole high on the inside of the thigh.

Returning to his cathedral in Ulm, armed with statements drawn—along with their teeth—from various family members concerning the conversion and martyrdom of the late Ferghana, Archbishop Scheissekopf recommended to the HOLY SEE (qv) at the VATICAN (qv) in ROME (qv), which was not then the capital of the not-then-existent ITALY (qv), the canonization of the poor mistreated child, and in due course Ferghana became beatified (1489) and ultimately sainted (1762).

Prayers to Saint Ferghana are said to have proved efficacious in a number of areas, particularly for those seeking inexpensive lodging. The hawthorne is associated with the saint, God knows why.

3

Stan Murch took a cab from the Long Island Railroad station to the Westbury Music Fair, but he didn't join the late arrivals rushing into the theater to see the superstars who would perform there this evening. All spring and summer every year, the superstars—the really important stars that play Las Vegas and Atlantic City and the Sydney (Australia) Opera House and even Sun City in South Africa—can be found at the Westbury Music Fair, less than an hour east of New York City. All of Long Island's most prosperous dentists and accountants and shag-rug dealers grab their wives and go to the Westbury Music Fair to be entertained, and some of them are too cheap to park in the Music Fair's parking areas, so they leave their cars on nearby streets. In fact, a lot of them do.

In a way, Stan Murch was a fisherman, and this time of year the Westbury Music Fair was one of his favorite fishing holes. He could go out there, wander around a bit, and in no time at all reel in a nice Rolls, pick up a Porsche, catch a Caddy, sometimes even land a Lamborghini. The catch of the day would then be driven to Maximilian's Used Cars, just across the Nassau County line into New York City, where grouchy old Max would pay a lot less than

19

the car was really worth but, on the other hand, a lot more than it had cost Stan. A pleasant transaction for all concerned. Almost all.

Tonight's catch was a brand-new four-door Mercedes, a rich dark green in color, with fawn-colored leather upholstery. It took no time at all for Stan to enter the car, luxuriate in the feel of the upholstery, discover which of his keys would ignite the ignition, and drive away from there.

Unfortunately, he was already on the Northern State Parkway heading west toward Max when he realized that this time something was fishy. To switch metaphors, he had picked up a lemon. The Mercedes must have been in an accident or something, then had been made pretty again. The steering pulled *hard* to the left, for instance; not too bad on a divided highway like the Northern State but maybe a little hairy in traffic on a two-way street. Also, at higher speeds, it took too long to switch through the gears, so the engine was half the time racing and straining and making loud, uncomfortable groan noises. Also, it was running hot.

Well, if they give you a lemon, trade it in. Instead of going straight to Max—who would be open till 10:00 P.M. this Friday night to grab that impulse buyer who just had to have that reconditioned eleven-year-old Dodge Dart with the bullet holes in the doors carefully filled and sanded and painted over—Stan drove on into Queens, switched to the Van Wyck Expressway, and sped on down to Kennedy Airport, where he took a ticket at the entrance to the long-term parking lot and went trolling. (We're back to the fish metaphor.)

There were a lot of nice cars here in the long-term parking lot. Stan would come here more often, actually, but there was just something about the *name* of the place—long-term parking—that sounded like what the judge would say at sentence time. It put Stan off his feed.

But there were times when this resource should not be lightly dismissed, and this was one of them. Stan drove, slow and easy, passing a lot of excellent vehicles that Max would really appreciate, but the fact was, Stan had his heart set on dark green Mercedes with fawn upholstery tonight, and *there it was!*

Perfect. The same car. Stan stopped the lemon, got out, incursed the new Mercedes, backed it out of its slot, drove the lemon into that location instead, and briefly considered switching license plates. There was nothing to be gained from that, though, except the long-distance scrambling of a onetime Mercedes owner's brain, so Stan left the lemon intact and drove to the exit, where the toll taker looked at his ticket and said, "You weren't in there long."

"I realized," Stan told him, "I don't want to go anywhere. I'm going home and tell the little woman everything, and see can we work it out."

"Good idea," the tolltaker said. He took Stan's money, and when he gave him his change he also gave him some advice: "Probly," he said, "you don't have to tell her *everything*."

"You may be right," Stan said, and drove the new Mercedes—a cream puff, a delight—to Maximilian's Used Cars, lighted, after dark, by what appeared to be all the night-game lights from the former Wrigley Field. A little discussion with Max provided a dollar figure they could both be happy with, and then Stan took the subway home to Canarsie, where his Mom, eating a pizza before taking her cab out for some of the late-night airport action, said, "Sit down, Stan, have a slice. Pepperoni."

"Thanks, Mom." Stan got a paper plate from the shelf and a beer from the refrigerator and joined his Mom at the kitchen table. "You gonna be late tonight?" he asked.

"Nah," she said. "Just a couple hours. Go over to Kennedy, take a fare to Manhattan, hang around the hotels, the next one brings me out to the airport, I call it a night."

"I was at Kennedy a while ago," Stan said. "Traffic wasn't bad. You could do a Hundred-thirtieth Street, get there like that." He tried to snap his fingers, but they were full of oil from the pizza slice and just slid around together, not making any noise at all.

"Thank you, Stan," his Mom said. Companionably, they ate some pizza, drank some beer, and then she said, "Before I forget. Actually, I already forgot, but now I just remembered."

"Yeah?"

"Tiny Bulcher called. He'd like a meeting tonight at midnight."

Stan glanced at the wall clock; not yet ten. "I guess so," he said. "He say who's gonna be there?"

"John, he said, and Andy, and some other guy."

"At the OJ?"

"No, he said the other guy got drunk after the meeting last time and kind of broke some things at the OJ, so Rollo eighty-sixed him."

"Eighty-sixed *Tiny?*"

"No, the other guy. I didn't get the name."

"Grijk Krugnk."

His Mom gave him a concerned look. "You coming down with something?"

"No, that's the guy's name. Grijk Krugnk. I may not be pronouncing it exactly right."

"Well, you won't get an argument from me," his Mom said. "Anyway, Tiny says, you should meet at his place."

"Yeah?" Stan finished his pizza and smiled. "Tiny's place. Okay. Be nice to see J. C. Taylor again."

4

J.C. Taylor looked at herself in the mirror and saw how the frown lines detracted from her hard beauty. Knowing that anger ruined her looks only made her angrier; with her pale skin and heavy brunette hair and hard eyes and now these deep frown lines all over the place, she was beginning to look like the Queen in "Snow White" when she looks into *her* mirror. However, instead of asking who was the fairest of them all, J.C. glared past her own reflected shoulder at the reflection of Tiny on the other side of the bedroom and said, "A party at midnight. I haven't had so much fun since I was the sweetheart of Iota Kappa Rho."

"Come on, Josie," Tiny said. He looked right now like a baffled bear, disturbed in his hibernation by a census taker, wanting to answer the questions but having trouble getting the situation into focus. (He was also the only person on earth who called J. C. Taylor Josie.) "It ain't a party," he tried to explain, "it's a meeting. And you don't have to be there, you don't want."

"Oh, sure," J.C. said. "You're bringing John and Andy and Stan into the house, the whole crowd from the Avalon caper, and when they say, 'Where's J.C.?' you'll say, 'She didn't want to see you guys, she went to the movies.'"

Tiny shrugged, an impressive movement. "So you come to the meeting."

"Looking like this?"

"You look great," Tiny told her, with such sincerity that she had to accept the compliment as real, if ignorant. She knew what she looked like.

Tiny came around the bed to stand behind her, his head now above hers in the mirror, and grin at her reflection. "You're terrific, Josie," he rumbled, his usual airplane engine of a voice modulating down to a kind of heavy purr, like a well-fed lion. "Any room you walk into," he said, "you own it."

She loved it when he talked like that, but she didn't want entirely to give up her bad mood. "Not dressed like this," she said, and the doorbell sounded at the other end of the apartment. "Go on, Tiny, I've got to change."

"Okay." He patted her head and her back—she braced herself against the mirror—and left the room.

He'd sprung this party/meeting on her at the last minute, of course. She was still dressed for the office, in a demure long-sleeved white blouse and full-cut black slacks and soft leather black boots; which would not do. (She'd been working late, filling orders.)

Oh, well. She crossed to the closet, opened the door, and stood looking disconsolately into its interior like a teenager into a refrigerator. Nothing to wear, not a thing, as anyone on earth except Tiny would realize at a glance.

After some little time, with deep reluctance, J.C. began to reach into the refrig—into the closet, and toss vague possibilities onto the bed. Then she put some back. Then she took some others out.

When, a mere twelve minutes later, J.C. entered the living room—this had been her place originally, which Tiny had moved into, rather than the other way around, so it looked like a normal apartment in a building on Riverside Drive and not like a hollowed-out tree—she was dressed in charcoal silk slacks, chartreuse silk blouse, and black satin slippers. Also, she'd changed to more dangling earrings, the ones with the diamond chips, chosen a slender silver bracelet, and rearranged her hair to more of a Rita Hayworth look. All makeup, naturally, had had to be redone, to go with the new outfit. And all this, she knew in her heart of hearts, for a bunch of slobs who wouldn't notice if she walked in wearing a poncho and shower clogs.

We do it for ourselves, not for them, she reminded herself, as *them* got to their feet, smiling in pleasure, and cried, "J.C.! Hey, J.C.! Long time no see!"

So. John looked as hangdog as ever, Andy as chipper as ever, and Stan as bluntly serviceable as ever. They'd been sitting with beers, and now Tiny offered her one, which she accepted. "In a glass, please." It was provided, she sat in the black slipper chair in the corner—Grijk Krugnk was in her normal morris chair, over by the view of the river and New Jersey—and settled herself to listen.

Normally, J.C. didn't concern herself about Tiny's business, nor did he concern himself with hers, except to wish out loud every once in a while that she'd drop her best-selling line, which she had no intention of doing. From a two-room midtown office, J.C. ran a mail-order business; in fact, three of them. There was Super Star Music, which would—depending on the customer—put music to your lyrics or lyrics to your music, at a really very moderate cost, when you consider the salaries of people like Mick Jagger and Carly Simon. There was the allied Commissioners' Courses, which was a book that taught you how to be a police detective; bonus handcuffs and badge were included with every order. And there was Intertherapeutic Research Service, a profusely illustrated marital sex manual allegedly translated from the Danish but with here and there a somewhat younger J.C. identifiable in the persona of the "wife." (Guess which line Tiny wished she'd drop.)

So, being a one-person operation, she had plenty to think about without worrying about Tiny's business. But, as long as she was here—or *they* were here—she might as well listen. And John was now saying, "So all of a sudden you got money."

He'd said that to Grijk Krugnk, but it was Tiny who answered, saying, "Not all of a sudden, Dortmunder. It was hard for this tiny country."

"Bud ve have American recognition," Grijk said, raising a fat finger. "Wery helpful."

John turned toward him. "You don't mind my asking," he said, "you guys were dirt-poor last time we talked, didn't have any whatchacallit currency—"

"Hard," Grijk said, nodding his big bald head.

"Right. So where'd you get the money?"

"Ve took a loan," Grijk told him, "from Citibank."

That astonished everybody. "From a *bank*?" Andy said. "In *New York*?"

"Wery easy," Grijk assured them all. "Wery simple. Our first tought vas da International Monetary Fund, but dey god too many forms you fill out, inspectors come to your country, dey look at your fi-*nan*-cial records, id's just too much trouble. So da hell vit it, ve vent to da bank."

"Banks won't give loans to *people*," Stan said in the tones of outrage he usually reserved for traffic jams. "My Mom knows some cabdrivers, can't get *any* kind of loan. Working stiffs, good credit. Taxi loan, house mortgage, home improvement, refinancing, you name it, you can forget it."

"Oh, no, no," Grijk said, "not if you're a pipple. Pipples don't ged no money from a bank. Bud if you're a country, no problem."

Tiny said, "I looked into this with Grijk, and it's true. There's countries haven't even paid the vigorish on their loans in nobody remembers how long, never mind the main money, and the banks go ahead and loan them some more, anyway."

J.C., more interested in this conversation than she'd expected to be, said, "How do I get to be a country?"

Grijk took that as a serious question, having recently gone through the experience himself. "First," he answered, "you have a var."

John, ever the pessimist, said, "Uh, Grijk, you got an *okay*, or you got the money?"

"Da money," Grijk announced.

"That's good," John said. "So you can actually pay us for this operation."

"Ten tousand dollars a man," Grijk said, and slapped his palms down onto his thighs, as though he'd just said something really terrific.

The others exchanged glances, and J.C. sensed a little discrepancy here. John said, "Uh, well, Grijk, last time we talked it was fifty thou. Remember?"

"Bud dat," Grijk pointed out, "vas in draffs."

"Still."

"In Tsergovia."

This was apparently an irrefutable argument. J.C. watched the troops silently consult among themselves, with much shrugging and grimacing and eyebrow waggling, and then John turned back to Grijk and said, "How much in front?"

"One tousand dollars," Grijk told him promptly, as though it were a number he was proud of. "Each man."

John looked at Tiny. "Tiny," he said, "are you putting this guy up to this?"

"I told him, Dortmunder," Tiny said, "and he wouldn't listen to me, and I accept no responsibility." To Grijk, he said, "Didn't I tell you? They're gonna want fifty percent, I told you."

Grijk spread his hands, showing bewilderment. "You give a man half da money, he's doing nutting," he said, "den he's supposed to do everyting, and all he gets is anodder half? Why don't he just take da first half and quit right dere?"

"Because, Cousin," Tiny said, sounding like somebody on the brink of relative trouble, "I guarantee them to you, and I guarantee you to them. You got a problem with my guarantee?"

Grijk studied his American cousin. He could be seen to weigh the pros and cons of certain alternatives. He said, "Okay, Diny." With a big smile at the troops, showing more spaces than teeth— That's why he doesn't smile very often, J.C. realized, having previously guessed at other motivations—he said, "Half da money. Okay?"

"Fine," John said.

Grijk sat back, still smiling, pleased, ready to go on, and the troops sat there and looked at him, and the silence grew. J.C. was almost beginning to feel sorry for the guy, as Grijk finally noticed that something was *still* wrong and said, "Okay? Not okay?"

"You're paying us half," John said, "in front."

"Yes, yes, I agree to dat."

"When?"

"Vad?"

"When is 'in front'?"

Grijk looked toward Tiny for guidance: "Now?" he suggested.

"No time like the present," Tiny told him.

It was then J.C. noticed the big old-fashioned brown leather

27

briefcase sagging on the floor beside the morris chair. Grijk brought up this collectible, put it on his lap, undid both leather straps, unhooked the central brass clasp, opened the wide-mouth top, and let his fingers do the walking down inside there for a while. He brought out a thick manila envelope, studied it, put it back, did more vamping inside there, brought out another thick manila envelope (or maybe the same one, doubling in a second role), put *that* on his lap, and returned the still-open briefcase to the floor. He unclasped and opened the manila envelope and shook a lot of wads of bills onto his lap. Tucking the empty envelope into the space between his thigh and the chair arm—the *narrow* space, even when he hunched over a bit—he held up one of these wads, with a Citibank band on it, and said, "Fifty twenty-dollar bills. One tousand dollars. Five each man. Okay?"

"Sounds good, Grijk," John said.

Grijk smiled at John. "You da only one can say my name right," he said.

"Oh, yeah?" John didn't seem to know exactly how to handle this information. "I'm glad," he said.

"So lemme gi-your money."

"Okay," John said.

Grijk struggled and floundered, having trouble getting out of the soft morris chair with all the wads of money in his lap. After he got nowhere for a few seconds, Andy said brightly, "Let me help with that," and bounded out of his chair and across the room to grab up a lot of cash.

"Tanks, Andy."

Andy turned to Tiny, but Tiny waved him away, saying, "I got a different deal. Not a better one, Andy, believe me. Believe me."

"I believe you, Tiny."

Andy distributed wads of money to John and Stan and himself, and it was fascinating to J.C. how all that paper just seemed to disappear. Very soon, the three were sitting there just as they had been before, beers in hand, expectant expressions on faces, money nowhere to be seen.

"Before we start," John said, "I know this doesn't have anything to do with the job itself, the job itself is we just go in and get the bone and come out and hand it over, but before we start I just got to ask you: How can a *bone* get you into the *UN*?"

Grijk would have answered, but Tiny stopped him with a raised hand, saying, "Let me, okay?" To the others, he said, "I had the same question, and I asked Grijk, and he told me, and an hour and a half later I understood. So you could hear his version, or you could hear my version that leaves out all the wonderful details."

"Your version," John said, and Stan and Andy nodded. Grijk looked sad.

"Okay. In twelve hundred and something, this girl got killed and eaten by her family, all except the leg with the gangrene. So when the Catholic Church decided she was a saint, that leg—or the bone, there was just a bone by then—it was a relic."

"A relic with gangrene," John said.

"Not by then," Tiny said. "I'm just giving you the highlights here, Dortmunder."

"Okay, Tiny."

"By that time," Tiny went on, "the bone was in the cathedral at a place called Novi Glad, that was the capital of one of the provinces of the Austro-Hungarian Empire. That province was half Tsergovia and half Votskojek."

Grijk made a weird sound in his throat, almost like a growl. J.C. blinked at the sound, but no one else paid any attention to it.

Tiny continued: "Also by that time, you got two religions involved. You got the regular Roman Catholic Church out of Rome, that said that leg was a saint to begin with. I mean, the *girl* was the saint, the whole girl. And then there was a schism, the Eastern Unorthodox."

Stan said, "Jewish, you mean."

"No, no," Tiny said, waving a big meaty hand. "There's no Jews around there."

"Dere was vun," Grijk said, "bud he vent to Belgrade. Or Lvov, maybe. Somevere. Anyway, now ve godda ged our suits from Hong Kong. It ain'd da same."

"That's the long version, Grijk, do you mind?" Tiny said, and turned back to his audience. "The *Catholic* Church split up," he said, "just like all those countries over there keep splitting up."

"Balkanization," Grijk said with astonishing clarity.

"That's the long form," Tiny warned him. "Anyway, out east you got the Eastern Orthodox Catholic Church, that's a schism from the regular Roman Catholic. And in some little places, you got the Eastern *Un*orthodox, that's a schism from the Orthodox. Okay? We set on that?"

"All set," John agreed. "That's all the religion I'm gonna need for a month."

"Me, too," Tiny agreed. "Anyway, when the Austro-Hungarian Empire broke up, that province that was the two countries got to be *one* country, and the Commies kept it that country, and now the Commies are out, and it's splitting into two countries. So when it was one country, it was a member at the UN, it had a seat, and the question is, which of the halves gets to have *that* seat, because that's the one with the seniority and the financial help already in place and all of that, and the loser has to *apply* to become a member, and there's some countries in the world might want to blackball the loser, whichever one it is, so the important thing for both Tsergovia and Votskojek—"

Grijk made that sound again.

"—is to get the seat that's already there. To be the successor to the previous country."

Andy said, "Tiny, I can't seem to remember the name of the country before it split up. I mean, you mentioned it, didn't you?"

Thunderclouds crossed Grijk's face. It was fascinating to watch, like being in a car, driving across the plains of Nebraska, and seeing the storms far away as they march over the wheat fields. Darkness, lightning, slanting rain, all moved this way and that over the rugged terrain of Grijk Krugnk's face. J.C. was so interested in this visual phenomenon that she almost forgot to listen to Tiny's answer, which was:

"No, I didn't mention it, Andy, and I'm not gonna mention it, and I'll tell you why. You want to think of Tsergovia and Votskojek—"

There went Grijk again, through the storms.

"—as a really bad marriage, so when it came to the end what you got was a really bad divorce, so in *both* countries now it's illegal to mention the name of the old country that used to be."

"Punishable," Grijk said with gloomy appetite, "by det."

"If anybody from those two countries," Tiny went on, "even *hears* the old name, they go berserk. You want Grijk here to go berserk?"

Everybody in the room contemplated Grijk, who was looking

half-berserk as it was. Everybody in the room came to the same conclusion, which Andy voiced for them all: "I don't think so."

"Good," Tiny said. "I can tell you this much. In the list of the hundred and fifty-nine countries that are in the UN—"

"You're kidding," Andy said. "There can't *be* that many countries."

"You're right, there can't," Tiny agreed, "but there are. And on the list, where this old country used to be, there's now a space between Benin and Bhutan."

Stan said, "Between what and who?"

"Benin and Bhutan. Those are countries, both of them."

This time, when Andy said, "You're kidding," Stan said it right along with him.

"I'm not," Tiny assured them. "Hanging out with Grijk here, I been picking up stuff about a lotta places. You won't believe the countries there are. How about the Comoros?"

"Isn't that," Andy asked, "what happens when you get knocked out?"

"No. How about Lesotho and Vanuata?"

"They sound like medicines," John suggested, "meant to keep people calm. People like Grijk over there."

Grijk grinned, flashing a couple of teeth. "Boy," he said to John, "you god id down perfect."

"Thank you," John said.

Andy said, "Tiny? Tell us some more countries. You got any more like that?"

"Tons," Tiny said. "How about Cape Verde?"

"I thought that was in Louisiana."

"It isn't. It's in the Atlantic Ocean off Africa."

"Next to Atlantis," John suggested.

"I don't know that one," Tiny said. "But I do know Bahrain and Qatar—"

"You get that in your throat," Andy said.

"—and Burkina Faso, and Oman—"

"No, man," Stan said.

"Yes, man," Tiny said. "And Djibouti."

John said, "How can you say that without snapping your fingers?"

"Say what?"

"Djibouti," John said, and snapped his fingers. It did something for the name.

"I will from now on," Tiny promised. "And there's the Maldives. And São Tomé and Principe, that's one country."

"What's one country?" Andy wanted to know.

"São Tomé and Principe," Tiny repeated, and shrugged. "Maybe they're gonna break up, like Grijk's crowd. You all had enough?"

While they all agreed they'd had enough, J.C. pondered. What would be a nice name for a country? Jaycenia. Tayloronia. Needs work.

"So here's the situation," Tiny was saying while J.C. mused. "The whole problem of who's gonna be the successor country at the UN is such a political mess that nobody wants to touch it. So they turned it over to a priest. An archbishop."

"I get it," Andy said. "He's gonna be on the side of the religion in the country, right? I mean, the same religion he is."

"Wrong," Tiny said. "What you got in the country—the two countries—is Roman Catholics and Eastern Unorthodoxes. So the UN made up a commission, and at the head of the commission they put this Eastern Orthodox archbishop from Bulgaria or Poland or someplace, that wouldn't automatically agree with either side, in fact he'd automatically *disagree* with the whole crowd, and the commission he's in charge of is gonna decide. Which means, he is. And the word is, the archbishop, being another kind of nut—"

"A religious nut," Andy suggested.

"The world is full of those," John said.

"If they were a money crop," Tiny agreed, "nobody'd ever go hungry again. Anyway, the archbishop decided, this saint's relic is the crucial factor. It's the thing gives the legitimacy to the country, makes the straight line back to the founding, before the Austro-Hungarians and *all* those people, so whoever's got the bone has to be the legitimate heir."

"And he won't mind," John asked, "if Grijk's bunch *steal* it? Are you sure of this?"

"That's not the way it works," Tiny said.

John nodded. "I didn't think it was gonna be."

"The way it works," Tiny said, "the bone was in the cathedral at

Novi Glad, and Novi Glad's now the capital of Votskojek—so those are the—Grijk, I wish you wouldn't keep doing that every time I mention the name of the place; it's getting me all geechy."

"I vill try," Grijk said, "do restrain myselv."

"Thank you. Where was I?"

John said, "Still the capital."

"Right. So they got it, they got the bone right there. So to stall things a little, the Tsergovians told the UN that isn't the real bone, it's a fake, so the bone was brought to New York to authenticate it."

John said, "How you supposed to do that? You can't put an eight-hundred-year-old bone on a lineup, get a positive ID."

"They turn it over to the scientists," Tiny explained. "They can do these tests, tell you is it a human bone, the right bone from the left leg, is it that old, did it have gangrene, all that stuff."

"So Grijk's people are screwed," John said, and Grijk nodded sadly.

"Unless," Tiny said, "we can switch bones before the tests get finished, and they just got started. We would've been ahead of them completely if it hadn't been for this little delay about money, but that's okay, that's nothing for you to worry about."

"You're right," John said.

"Meantime," Tiny went on, "Tsergovia's telling the UN the other guys're fulla shit, that's a fake bone, and when the scientists prove it's a fake bone Tsergovia will come out with the real one. The archbishop will get mad at Votskojek—mmmmm."

"Sorry," said Grijk.

"Keep trying," Tiny urged him, and told the others, "The archbishop'll get mad at Votskojek for blasphemy with the relic, and the commission will recommend that Tsergovia inherits the seat, and the good guys win."

"I'm not sure about that last part," John said, "but never mind, I get the idea. So where's the bone now, in some lab somewhere?"

"Oh, no," Tiny said. "Both countries got these UN missions, only they're what they call observer missions now, until they get a seat, and Votskojek's got tight—very good, Grijk—got tight security on the bone by keeping it in their mission and only letting the scientists study it inside there."

"And where is this mission?" John asked.

"On a boat in the East River," Tiny said.

"A boat," John said, while the others looked troubled. "So we row out to it, is that the idea?"

"Naw, it's tied up to a dock in the East Twenties," Tiny said, "where there used to be a ferry across to Long Island City a long, long time ago. The city owns the dock and the old ferry building there, and the Votskojeks rent it from the city for like nothing a year."

"That sounds like New York," John agreed.

"You got to remember," Tiny said, "both of these countries are poor. Their principal export is rock."

J.C. had promised herself to remain silent, since this wasn't her meeting, it was theirs, but this news was too compelling. "Rock?" she blurted out; as a businesswoman, one whose mail-order businesses could be thought of as a kind of export, she wanted to know how you made money out of exporting rock.

No one seemed to object to her horning in like this. The guys, in fact, seemed just as interested in the answer as she was and paid as close attention when Tiny said, "Countries with more regular land, like dirt-type land, they use Tsergovian and Votskojek rock when they're making new roads."

"Tsergovian rock much better," Grijk announced. "Dests prove."

"No argument," Tiny said. "Anyway," he told the others, "the point is, these countries are poor, so they don't go in for UN missions in fancy town houses in the East Sixties and all this stuff. *You* know, they had to float a loan just to hire you guys."

"Which raises a question, Tiny," John said. "You did explain to Grijk about expenses, didn't you?"

"Absolutely," Tiny said. "Subway fare, stuff like that, you take care of yourself. A real expense, like a bribe or a vehicle or a weapon, Tsergovia pays."

"In front."

"He knows that, Dortmunder," Tiny said.

"No limousines," Grijk said, raising an admonitory finger.

"They know that, Grijk," Tiny said.

Andy said, "If they're so poor, how come they got a yacht?"

"Did I say yacht?" Tiny asked. "I said boat, am I right?"

"So the first thing we better do," John said, "is go look at this boat."

"I'll take you over there and show you," Tiny offered, "whenever you say."

"What about now?"

"Good," said Tiny.

Andy said, "Grijk, you coming with us?"

Grijk said, "Andy, you must led John teach you how pronounce Grijk. And I don'd go, because if dehr guards vould see me, dey vould shood me."

Andy raised an eyebrow at John. "A fun crowd."

And that was the end of the meeting. Everybody stood up and all the men shook hands with Grijk, and Grijk assured them their praises would be sung forever in the schoolrooms of Tsergovia, even if anonymously, and then J.C. said, "Nice to see you fellas again," and the fellas said it was *great* to see her again, and then they all trooped out and away down the hall toward the elevator, and at last J.C. was alone. She went to the kitchen and poured out her one-of-the-guys beer and filled a different glass with a nice Pinot Grigio and went back to the living room to kick off her satin shoes and sit in *her* morris chair, which seemed larger and lower than before, and to think about countries.

A cacophony of countries, a mob, a milling throng, a legion of nations. Who would have guessed there were so many mother and father lands? You could hide in a crowd like that.

And do what?

5

Dortmunder looked at that Votskojek boat over there and was not impressed. On the way across and downtown, in a Honda Accord Stan had borrowed for the occasion, Tiny had told them the boat had originally been a tramp freighter on the Black Sea or the Bosporus or one of those places and had just barely made it across the Atlantic last winter, and Dortmunder could well believe that.

Much smaller than a Caribbean cruise liner, and a lot dirtier, too, the ship was a tall black hulk held by heavy, thick, hairy ropes around metal stanchions on both sides of the old ferry slip. If it weren't for the few lights on inside the vessel, defining circles and rectangles of dim yellow light, it would look mostly like a barge piled with scrap iron.

Their nearest vantage point to view the scene of the crime-to-be was the FDR Drive, the elevated highway running—crawling, really—up the eastern shore of Manhattan Island. This time of night, traffic on the Drive was moderate—if hurtling taxicabs, drunken commuters, and illegal aliens fleeing petty crimes could ever be called moderate—so Stan had merely stopped the borrowed Honda in the farthest right lane (there is no shoulder, no verge, no space to pull over on the FDR Drive) and everybody got out. Stan opened the hood and stood in front of the car and from time to time glowered at the inoffensive little engine in there as though it had failed him in some way. Meantime, not very satisfactorily, they cased the joint.

Hell of a joint. The boat was tucked into that old ferry slip beyond a blocky brick three-story building that had been empty and unsafe and unused for years. On the boat's rounded black stern, seen beyond the building, *Pride of Votskojek* was faintly visible in dirty white letters.

Access. A potholed blacktop road came out from under the FDR, pointing toward the ferry building, but before getting even halfway there it ran into an eight-foot-high chain-link fence with rolls of razor wire across the top. The metal support poles of this fence were sunk into concrete right in the roadway, making it absolutely clear that no more cars or other vehicles were ever going to be invited through there ever again. This side of the fence, to the right of the truncated road, a small parking area was illuminated by one floodlight; it contained five beat-up old cars parked with their noses to the fence, two of them with red-white-blue diplomat plates visible at the rear. Near the cars, a narrow chain-link door was inset in the chain-link fence and was guarded by two short, squat guys in uniforms with side arms.

Beyond the fence, if it were possible to get beyond the fence, hulked the ferry building, as dark and dense as a Mayan temple, its boarded-up top-floor windows at the same height as the FDR Drive, so that from where they were standing they would be able to look right in, if the boards weren't there and the lights were on inside (and there were lights inside to *be* on), and if they cared, which they didn't. It was about twenty yards from where they now stood to the facade of the dead ferry building, not too far to bloop a little forward pass on a trap play, but *far* too far to stretch a plank over in case you had this idea, for instance, to crawl along, one end to the other, above the fence.

The top two stories of the building stood on two fat legs, which were the ground floor and between which used to be access (for cars? horse-drawn wagons? how long ago was this eminently sensible technology abandoned?) to the ferries. Beyond the building—best seen from just north of it on the FDR, where they were stopped, Stan giving the finger to the occasional wise-guy honker—was the slip where ferries used to dock for loading and unloading vehicles and foot passengers (eminently sensible) and where the *Pride of Votskojek* now wallowed, round rusty stern toward the building, blunt prow nodding stupidly at the river.

"The guards," Kelp said, "those *armed* guards down there, can see the parking lot. From the corner there, where they're stationed, they can see the whole fence. Those guards, those *armed* guards right there, could see *us* if they looked up, and they could see all along the FDR here. And those look to me like walkie-talkies they got on their belts there, next to the *guns*. So what I think, I think if we go and put a bunch of sleeping pills in some hamburger meat and throw it over the fence, it won't work."

"I knew they were gonna get me on a boat," Dortmunder said. Not too long ago, he'd been involved in an involved little caper upstate involving a reservoir, which most of the time had been on top of him. His attitude toward boats and large bodies of water remained negative.

"Well, Dortmunder," Tiny said, leaning on the crumbling low wall of the FDR, "it does kinda play like that. A boat. At least to get a better look at the thing. By daylight."

"Nighttime, right now," Dortmunder pointed out, "is the best conditions we can hope for. And right now, our best conditions include armed guards, bright lights, chain-link fence, and razor wire. And that's just to get to the pier. We don't know *what* fun there is when you're trying to get on the *boat*."

"My guess," Kelp said, "is more lights and more armed guards, but probably no more razor wire. Just a guess."

"And thank you for it," Dortmunder said. Turning to Tiny, he said, "So this is an expense for your cousin."

"A boat, you mean," Tiny said.

"We shouldn't hang around here too much longer," Stan mentioned.

"Give me a minute here, Stan," Dortmunder said, and to Tiny he said, "A *safe* boat. No leaks, no running out of gas, no bad stuff."

"Naturally," Tiny said.

"There's nothing naturally about it," Dortmunder said.

Tiny spread his hands. "But he doesn't have to buy this boat, right? Just rent it."

"From a renter," Dortmunder said, "that's never lost a boat."

Kelp said, "Also, it should look like a boat that you'd see out there. One that would fit in."

"Sure," Tiny said.

"That doesn't sink," Dortmunder said. "That doesn't even get wet inside."

"You got it, Dortmunder," Tiny promised him.

"What I want," Dortmunder said, "is a boat you could grow cactus in."

6

"Ve are a wery poor country," Grijk said.

"We know that," Tiny told him. "The guys know it, and I know it." And, he might have added, anybody who walked into the place would know it.

The Tsergovian mission to the United Nations was not on a former tramp steamer in the East River. It hadn't occurred to the Tsergovians, frankly, to come up with the kind of cute and clever way to avoid high New York rents that the Votskojeks had; another reason, if another reason were needed, for the Tsergovian nose to be out of joint.

No, the best the Tsergovians had been able to come up with was a storefront on Second Avenue, *below* Twenty-third Street, where commercially the property values are much lower than up in the Forties, nearer the UN and the live theater and the good restaurants.

They were on the east side of the avenue, and the other side was a whole block of taxpayers,* so the sun beat in through their big plate-glass windows all afternoon of every sunny day, or would if

---

*A temporary structure, commonly one story in height and containing shops of the most ephemeral sort. Constructed by the owners of the land

they didn't have the awning. So, with much reluctance but finally with fatalistic acceptance, they'd kept the awning, which still said, in white block letters on the dark green canvas, HAKIM CLEANERS & LAUNDERERS, all but HAKIM very clean and neat. HAKIM was clumsily painted over IRVING, which in turn had been ineptly sewn over ZEPPI.

Even though the front door clearly said on its long glass window

FREE & DEMOCRATIC NATION OF TSERGOVIA
> *Embassy*
> *Consulate*
> *Commercial Attaché*
> *Tourist Office*
> *Cultural Exchange Office*
> *Military Attaché*
> *United Nations Mission* (pend.)

and even though the two large side windows both featured rather fanciful posters of the purported tourist attractions of Tsergovia, people *still* brought in their tablecloths after dinner parties.

The front room, which was all Tiny'd ever seen, no longer looked anything at all like a dry cleaner's. The functional dropped ceiling with the egg-tray fluorescent lights was all that had been retained (changing it would have been very expensive). On the floor now was some nice pale green broadloom, bought cheaply at a carpet sale out on Long Island, which was actually three remnants cunningly placed so that the seams—and the slight differences in color—were barely noticeable unless you were really looking for them.

On this thick-piled Reinhardt were placed three desks,

-----

when a delay is anticipated, sometimes of several decades' duration, between the razing of the previous unwanted edifice and the erection of the new blight on the landscape. Called a "taxpayer" because that's what it does. +

+ Didn't expect a footnote in a novel, did you? And a real informative one, too. Pays to keep on your toes.

each with two chairs and one wastebasket, all bought from a used office furniture store on West Twenty-third Street. One of these desks was near the door, where a young black American woman named Khodeen, their only non-Tsergovian employee, deflected tablecloth bearers. The other two desks, back toward the rear corners of the deep room, formed a long triangle with the first. The left one of these was home base for a stout older woman named Drava Votskonia, who wore a different dark headkerchief every day, who had warts on her face you could use for cup hooks, and whose portfolios were Commercial Attaché, Director of the Tourist Office, and Mistress of Cultural Exchange. The other desk belonged to Grijk Krugnk, and *his* areas of responsibility were Military Attaché, Passport Control Officer, and Chief of Security (also the entire security staff) for the embassy, the consulate, and the mission (pend.).

It was at this desk that Grijk and Tiny now sat, each with one meaty forearm on the scarred surface as they talked. Across the way, Drava Votskonia was on the phone, continuing her perpetual quest for an American interested in reviving the craze of the pet rock. "*Imported* pet rocks!" (After all, the hula hoop had come back, if briefly, had it not?) And up front, between tablecloths, Khodeen retied her cornrows.

"We're talking about *renting* a boat," Tiny now explained. "Not *buying* one."

"*Dat's* for sure," Grijk agreed. "Vad are ve gonna do vid a boad? Ve're a landlocked country."

"So that's why we'll rent," Tiny explained. Sometimes he had to be very patient with his cousin, a lot more than with somebody whose blood, when spilled, would not be familial.

"How much you rent for, dis boad?" Grijk demanded.

"I don't know yet," Tiny said. "This is just I'm dropping by to keep you informed, let you know, there's gonna be an expense."

"Vad informed? You don't know *how much* expense."

"Let's put it like this," Tiny said, reminding himself that this was, after all, a distant cousin, an extremely distant cousin, and maybe he didn't have to be *that* patient, maybe. "What we'll say is, if the boat rent's less than five hundred dollars, we'll go ahead and do it, and you'll pay us back. And if it's over five hundred dollars, we'll call you and let you make the decision."

Grijk thought this over. "I donno," he finally decided. "I tink I godda talk to my boss. You wait a minute?"

"Even a couple minutes," Tiny offered.

"Tanks." Grijk reassured himself that all the desk drawers were locked, and then he hurried away to the back room, where Tiny'd never been, to confer with his "boss," whom Tiny'd never seen, and who was presumably the ambassador, consul, head of mission (pend.), and chief spokesman for Tsergovia in the United States. And a hard guy to get along with, from Grijk's nervousness every time he thought about the "boss" or actually had to go in and deal with him.

Tiny stretched in his seat, wondering whether this was a good idea in the first place, to be involved with these clowns, old country or no, and to pair up with Dortmunder and that crowd again, or if maybe what he ought to do was make a clean break with the past and...

"Pah!" The smack of Drava Votskonia's telephone into its cradle roused Tiny from his reverie. He glanced over and La Votskonia was looking stormy. She noticed Tiny watching her and turned her glower in his direction. "You're an American," she said accusingly. Her accent was similar to Grijk's but less pronounced, more like an irritating buzz around the words than real distortion of the words themselves.

Tiny thought that over and shrugged. It was an admission he felt he could safely make. "Right."

"So tell me," she said, "what do Americans do with rocks?"

Now, here we have an unexpected question. Tiny's brow puckered with thought. Rocks? What do Americans do with rocks? What, Tiny asked himself, do *I* do with rocks, and the answer was, nothing. "Well," he said, thinking as fast as he could, "they used to make these long low walls out of them, up in the woods, and—"

"*Used* to!" Ms. Votskonia cried. She was clearly at, or very close to, the end of her rope. "Don't tell me about *used* to! They used to make *pets* out of them! But what do they do with them *now*?"

Tiny thought some more. "Heat them and put them in saunas," he suggested.

She considered that, then shook her head. "Too limited a market."

Tiny wracked his brains. "Groins," he said. "I don't mean nothing dirty, I mean like walls out of rocks they put out from the

43

beach, out into the ocean, to keep the sand from going away."

"Ecological unsound," Ms. Votskonia told him. "Already I have pursued this question with many beachfront communities, and they have all turned against it."

Tiny felt a sharp little pain growing between his eyes. What do Americans do with rocks? Cairns? No, not anymore.

The inner door opened and Grijk stuck his head out to say, "Tiny? Could you come in here vun minute?"

"I could," Tiny told him, and rose to his feet. With his biggest and most insincere smile, he told the fuming Ms. Votskonia, "Sorry I couldn't be more help," and lumbered away through the door Grijk was holding open into a small office where he found himself confronting a woman who made Ms. Votskonia look like Mother Teresa.

This woman was about the size and shape of a mailbox, with a black-haired white lunch box on top for a head. She wore a uniform much like Grijk's—the dark olive tunic, the black piping, the dark wide trousers, the black boots—and, in fact, she *looked* much like Grijk, in the same way that Grijk looked much like Tiny. In other words, this was a woman who looked like the paperback version of Tiny, which is not a good way for a woman to look.

Grijk, as nervous as a kid introducing his father to the school principal, said, "Tchotchkus Bulcher, dis is Zara Kotor, Tsergo-vian ambassador to the United States."

When called upon, Tiny could be a social animal. Nodding pleasantly, "How are ya?" he said.

Zara Kotor said, "Extremely unhappy." She sounded tough as nails, and had no accent at all.

Ignoring the content of the words, and referring only to their delivery, Tiny beamed and said, "You talk good."

"I was educated in your country," she said grimly. "Bronx Science."

"Oh, yeah? I hear that's a good school."

"We learned our mathematics there, in Bronx Science," Zara Kotor said, beetling an already beetled brow at Tiny. "And five hundred bucks could *never* be the answer to 'How much does it cost to rent a boat for a little ride on the river?'"

Tiny felt himself getting just the teeniest bit annoyed. To go through all this crap for no gain, and then to have your judgment

44

questioned? He could roll this dame in that cheap broadloom out there and take *her* for a little boat ride. He said, "If all we were doing was a nice day on the water, we could go rent a rowboat in Central Park. The idea is, we gotta spend a bunch of time on the river and not have anybody wonder who we are and what we're up to."

"And for this you need a luxury yacht," Zara Kotor suggested. "Probably with champagne, and girls in bikinis, to make it look more natural."

"For five hundred bucks?" Tiny grinned at her, not in a friendly way. "You got a deal," he said.

She shook her head. "I don't see why all this expense is needed at all. You know where the Votskojek embassy is, you—I've told you before, Grijk, don't do that—have even seen the place. I understand that you and your friends are professionals."

"That's why we do things right," Tiny said. "Or not at all—that's another possibility."

"I don't see," Zara Kotor said, speaking as though used to her word being law, "the necessity for this expenditure. I don't see that it can be approved."

"Okay by me, lady," Tiny said. "Find yourself another descendant; I'm gone."

He was turning away, reaching for the doorknob, when she said in tones of outrage, "You've taken our money!"

"Not me," Tiny told her.

Grijk hurriedly muttered something in some language that sounded like a can opener being used on a rusty can. Zara Kotor raised a cynical eyebrow. "And I suppose your friends won't share with you?"

"They never did before," Tiny said. "I got into this because Grijk here talked me into it. And now you talked me out of it again, and that's fine." And once again, he reached for the knob.

"Now, wait; now, wait," Zara Kotor said, and when Tiny turned back, exasperated, he saw that doubt had somehow penetrated that lunch box she used for a head.

This time, he kept his hand on the knob. In fact, he considered removing the knob from the door, opening the top of the lunch box, and placing the knob inside it. Instead, "What is it?" he demanded. "I gotta hurry. I gotta go tell the guys, don't buy that sunscreen after all."

"What boat," she wanted to know, "costs five hundred dollars a day to rent?"

"I don't know," Tiny said. "See ya."

"Wait!"

"For *what*?"

"All *right*," she shouted, as though he'd been the one brow-beating *her* all this time. "All *right*. You say you're doing this pro bono, is that what you're saying?"

Now Tiny beetled his own beetled brow. Staring *hard* at this woman, as though she were an assistant DA, he said, "You putting words in my mouth?"

"Pro bono," she repeated, as though it would make more sense the second time around. "You're, you're . . . you're not doing it for profit."

"Damn right I'm not," Tiny said, "and beats the hell out of me why, so I'm just as happy to say—"

"No, no, wait," she said, patting the air between them. "We started off on the wrong foot, that's all."

"Oh, yeah?"

"We are a very poor country," she reminded him.

"That's no excuse."

Surprisingly, she nodded. "You're right," she said. "I was too suspicious. Could we begin again, as friends this time? As fellow patriots of Tsergovia?"

Tiny thought it over, and shrugged. They'd started. And the thing had some interesting aspects. "Sure," he said.

"You'll spend what you have to spend on the boat," she said.

"Good," he said. "And we'll keep it down as much as we can."

"I'm sure you will." She stuck out a hand like an order of cold-cuts. "Friends? Partners?" (Grijk stared openmouthed at this development.)

"Sure," Tiny said, and took the hand, which also felt like an order of cold cuts. He shook it.

Suddenly, she was twinkling at him. "I wouldn't want to be enemies," she said, "with a cute guy like you."

Tiny fled.

7

"That's an awfully small boat," Dortmunder said.

"It's plenty big," Stan said. As the vehicle specialist in the group, he was the one who'd made the arrangements for the boat and, as he'd assured Dortmunder several times already, he'd kept Dortmunder's qualms about water transport in the forefront of his mind throughout the decision-making process.

Nor was he even going to drive this boat—"pilot," they liked to say, as though it were an airplane. He would leave that to its owner, the cheerful bearded giant over there in the wheelhouse, looking out all his windows and waiting for them to board, which Tiny and Kelp had already done.

But not Dortmunder, who stood on the pier and frowned and said, "It just looks small. To me, it looks small."

"Dortmunder," Stan said, losing his patience, "it's a *tugboat*. It's the safest thing in New York Harbor. This boat has pushed around *oil tankers*, passenger liners, big cargo ships from all over the world."

But not recently. Labor strife, changes in the shipping industry, competition from other Eastern Seaboard ports; what it all comes down to is, the New York City tugboat is an endangered species.

Most of the sturdy little red and black guys with the hairy noses and the old black automobile tires along the sides are gone now, and the few still struggling along, like the hero of a Disney short, don't have much of a livelihood to keep them going.

So it hadn't been hard for Stan to find a tugboat owner—a good percentage of the surviving boats are still privately owned—happy to swing around the Battery and over to the East River and spend an afternoon dawdling in the offing, no questions asked, no heavy lifting involved, for three hundred bucks. (Tiny had kept his promise to Zara Kotor. He would also keep his distance from her.)

Dortmunder stood on the pier, this tugboat—the *Margaret C. Moran*, it was called—at his feet, and memories of the Vilburgtown Reservoir rose up around and over his head. "It's moving up and down," he complained, watching the side of the boat do just that in relation to the pier.

"Sure it's moving up and down," Stan said. "The *water*'s moving up and down. All New York Harbor is moving up and down."

"I'm sorry you pointed that out," Dortmunder said.

"Look, John," Stan said gently, his manner calm and patient and sympathetic, "I understand how you feel, I do. But we either gotta do this or don't do it, and one way or the other I gotta pay Captain Bob. So you wanna get on the boat, or you wanna go home and get three hundred clams?"

"Not clams," Dortmunder said. "Smackers; bucks; simoleons; even dollars."

"Come on, John, which is it?"

"Forward," Dortmunder said, and stepped onto the top of the tug's rail, which dropped away beneath him, so that he pitched forward into the boat, to be caught like a beach ball by Tiny, who stood him on his feet, brushed him off, and said, "Welcome aboard."

"Right," Dortmunder said.

The cheery madman up in the wheelhouse smiled down upon them and roared, "All set?"

"Ready," Stan yelled back, leaping lightly aboard, and half-saluted, as one wheelman to another.

Dortmunder looked about himself and the tugboat *was* small, dammit. The front half was dominated by the wheelhouse, an oval superstructure built up from the deck, with an octagon of windows around the top, inside which Captain Bob could steer his mighty mite and keep an eye on everything that was happening everywhere all around him. The back half was a small deck area crowded with coils of rope, jerricans of fuel and oil, harpoons, clubs, and general *stuff*. Under Captain Bob's station at the wheel, a door led into the lower part of the superstructure, and when Dortmunder looked in there he saw a tight spiral staircase coiling downward into a constricted area of loud humming. Tugboats are, after all, merely the smallest possible superstructure surrounding the largest and most powerful possible engine.

Kelp reclined at his leisure on a coil of rope, back against the side rail that had so betrayed Dortmunder as he fell aboard. Having caught Dortmunder then like a forward pass, Tiny was now seated on the net-covered rail at the stern, seemingly relaxed even though he was just above the churning, foamy wake. Stan had chosen to scramble up to the wheelhouse with Captain Bob, where he stood swaying in the doorway, exchanging shouted pleasantries with the pilot. Dortmunder looked around at all this, wondering where safely to stash himself, and then Kelp patted the coil of rope beside him. "Grab a seat," he said. "Take a look at the view."

Dortmunder grabbed the seat, grateful to give over the question of balance from his feet to his ass, and took a look at the view, just as Captain Bob *vroomed* the engine and they went angling and roaring away from the pier and out into the greasy, gray, grimy Hudson.

Well, it was a view, no argument about that. You don't get to see a sight like this every day, unless you happen to own one of the few remaining tugboats working New York Harbor. On one side, Manhattan, a narrow, crowded aisle of stalagmites that have lost their cavern and been unaccountably exposed to the open air, making for a scene as outlandish as it is spectacular. Look at all those windows! Are there people inside *all* of those? You see all those buildings, you don't see any people at all, and yet all you're put in mind of is human beings, and just how many of them there must be for the world to contain a view like this.

So much for Manhattan. On the other side, New Jersey, and so much for New Jersey. Up above, far away, the George Washington Bridge, like the hawser holding Manhattan to America (reluctantly, on the part of both), and down below, the jolly green giant's mother, looking for an honest ship.

Or any ship at all. A few garbage barges, the Circle Line boat, an occasional weekend cruise ship, the waddling Staten Island ferry, now and then a small freighter that looks as though it must have made a wrong turn somewhere; the teeming New York Harbor of yesteryear is no more. So how come the water's still so disgusting?

Captain Bob steered the *Margaret C. Moran* southward past the new Imperial Ferry pier with its recently established ferryboat service over to New Jersey (an eminently reasonable technology) and down past Battery Park City, where the World Trade Center (so good they did it twice!) stands as the final failure of architecture; not an idea, not a design, not a whimsy, not a grace note, not a shred of art or passion wrinkles those sharply creased trouser legs.

Then the heliport, where a *very loud* helicopter took off through Dortmunder's head; in the left ear, out the right, scrambling his brains along the way. Then, at the southern tip of Manhattan, the Staten Island ferry terminal, with the fat ferries as a Mother Goose–like reminder of a more possible New York.

Down here at the tip of the island, the seas got a little rougher. Dortmunder held on to his coil of rope with both hands and both knees, and the magnificent view went *up* and *down* and *up* and *sideways* and *down* and *up* and *down* and *sideways* and *up....*

Tiny held on to him while he leaned over the rail.

Later, he felt somewhat better, though kind of hollow. And by now, they were in the East River, between Manhattan and Brooklyn, a much more bustling world, though still eerily unpopulated on the water. But you've got *another* heliport, and then two bridges in a row crawling with traffic—the Brooklyn, and then the Manhattan—and over on the Brooklyn side you've got the Promenade, which looks nice, people standing around, posed as though in the artist's impression of how it will look if the money is raised and the project completed.

Dead ahead was the Williamsburg Bridge. Kelp nudged Dortmunder's arm and pointed at it, grinning. "Remember the fish truck?"

"No," Dortmunder said.

Off Twenty-third Street is a dock for seaplanes, mostly taking people out to the Hamptons or Fire Island, or maybe up to New England. Dortmunder hadn't known about that until he looked up—one of the rare times he looked up—and there was an *airplane* taxiing directly at them! On the water!

"Holy shit!" Dortmunder commented, and stared up at Captain Bob, who was cheerily—a madman, a definite madman—waving in comradely fashion at the oncoming airplane.

Which veered off, roaring, and suddenly ran away northward, and now Dortmunder could see the pontoons and understood it was all right for that airplane to be out here in the river, and particularly all right when, thirty or forty blocks farther uptown, it lifted off the water and banked away over Queens, taking four or five of the nation's trendsetters out east for R and R.

"There it is," Kelp said at the same moment that the low growl of the *Margaret C. Moran*'s engine changed quality, becoming lower and less powerful. Feeling the ship slow beneath him, Dortmunder looked where Kelp was pointing, and, after a minute of not knowing what the hell he was staring at, there it was. The *Pride of Votskojek,* hunkered down in its slip, pointing out, dwarfed by the piled layers of brown and black and gray apartment buildings behind it.

Their vessel was slowing and slowing, almost to a complete stop, or as complete a stop as you can get on a ceaselessly moving surface like a large body of water. Dortmunder looked around, and out toward the middle of the river, some distance away, another tug was pushing a big bargeful of junk downstream, toward the ocean. Other than that, they were now the only vessel in sight—except for the moored hulk of the *Pride of Votskojek,* of course.

Stan came down from the wheelhouse to say, "Cap'n Bob's gonna bring us in a little closer, then just hang around there until we're ready to go."

Dortmunder looked at him. "Cap'n Bob?"

Stan looked back. "So?"

The *Margaret C. Moran* made a long slow loop till it faced downstream, and was now close enough to the Manhattan shore so that individual details on the *Pride of Votskojek,* like the windows up above and the rust streaks down below, were clearly visible. They all sat on the coils of rope or the rail and looked at that ship moored over there, and Tiny said, "I don't get it. The Tsergovia mission's just a storefront, anybody can walk in, no armed guards, no fences, none of this crap."

Stan said, "That's security for the bone."

Tiny said, "Not that fence. Posts sunk into concrete? For a bone's gonna be there just a couple months?"

Kelp said, "All that stuff would have been there anyway, from before, put up by the city because the ferry building isn't safe and they didn't want any junkies to sneak in there and hurt themselves."

Tiny said, "Why not?"

Nobody had an answer to that, so they turned their attention back to the Votskojek mission floating over there.

The wake from the barge finally reached the *Margaret C. Moran* just about then. The wake consisted of very long slow mounds of water, ridges of water like corduroy that rolled in stately inevitable fashion across the surface of the river, like cows coming home at the end of the day, one after the other, each billow rocking the tug first *this* way, then *that* way, then a pause, then *this* way, then *that* way, then a pause. And so on.

"That's it," Dortmunder said.

Kelp raised an inquiring eyebrow. "John?"

"I've had enough," Dortmunder said.

Tiny said, "Dortmunder?"

Dortmunder turned to Stan. "Tell your cap'n," he said, "I want to go ashore."

Sounding surprised, Stan said, "You saw enough? You know how to pull the job?"

"I didn't see anything, and I don't know anything," Dortmunder told him, "except I want off this carnival ride *now*. Tell Admiral Bob to put me ashore." He pointed toward the *Pride of Votskojek*. "There," he said.

8

So far as Hradec Kralowc was concerned, he had the finest apartment in New York City, with the finest views, the best closets and other amenities, and an unbeatable location. His apartment was, in fact, the former captain's quarters aboard the former *Mstslov Enterprise III*, now the *Pride of Votskojek*, and he luxuriated in its lushness, far from the stony splendors of Votskojek, and just as far from the stony splendors of *Mrs.* Kralowc.

Hradec Kralowc was, at forty-seven, his brand-new nation's ambassador to the United States (with a small apartment at the Watergate in Washington where he was almost never in residence) and was soon to be its UN delegate as well, once this nonsense about the authentication of the femur of St. Ferghana was cleared up. In the meantime, he had to live here in a somewhat seigelike fashion (security for the femur), but he did not permit that fact to keep him from enjoying his position in life and in New York and in this glorious apartment.

He was a friendly man, Hradec Kralowc, a diplomat to his toes, and it so happened that one of the people he had befriended a few years ago was a hotel mogul named Harry Hochman, who had grown interested in the idea of constructing some of his world-famous Happy Hour Inns behind the Iron Curtain, once the Iron Curtain had been taken down and packed away in the attic with iron mothballs (just in case it's ever needed again).

Harry Hochman also owned upscale hotels in major cities, and ski resorts, and Caribbean islands, and was generally a good sort of millionaire to know. More specifically, he also had access to an army of carpenters, plumbers, and electricians, and when Hradec had arrived in New York last year on the *Pride of Votskojek* Harry Hochman had been as happy as one of his inns to provide all the services necessary to convert what had been a fairly grim and utilitarian set of rooms aboard the ship into a diplomat playboy's fantasy. (Previously, back in Novi Glad, capital of Votskojek, Hradec had found it possible to be of some small service to Harry Hochman, seeing to it that the bureaucratic snarls in which the representatives of Hilton, Marriott, and Sheraton found themselves enmeshed faded away somehow whenever the Harry Hochman representative appeared. One hand washes the other.)

The apartment that had resulted from all this hand washing, here on the top deck of the *Pride of Votskojek*, was a sheer delight. Its living room was toward the stern, with large wraparound windows through which could be seen, unfortunately, the dead carcass of the former ferry building; but if one ignored that and looked up and beyond, all of Manhattan's skyline was spread out before one, magnificent by day, romantically beautiful by night.

The bedroom was forward of this and rather large and pleasant now that the wall had been removed from between what had been two small and nasty cabins. The views from here were southward, toward the necklaces that were the bridges strung between Manhattan and Brooklyn.

And at the forward end was the former bridge, now a sitting room with views eastward across the river at Brooklyn and Queens. Less of a view than the living room's under normal circumstances, but wonderful in stormy weather; ah, the lightning displays over Long Island City! When the sun shone, Hradec tended to ignore the bridge and the scenery beyond its windows, but today he just happened to be passing through, checking the apartment for general tidiness, since he expected to entertain a

Hungarian ballerina this evening, after her work at Lincoln Center was completed, when he noticed the tugboat out there on the river.

What attracted his attention first was the fact that one so rarely saw tugboats at all, and then they were never alone. Any tugboat one saw would be either pushing or pulling some larger and much more ungainly vessel. A tugboat at rest, or at play, was a diverting thing to see.

Then there was his realization that this particular tugboat wasn't going anywhere. It merely bobbed along in more or less the same place, pointlessly. Was it adrift, lost by its owners? Was it out of fuel, or in some other way in trouble? As a fellow boat person—boat resident, as it were—should he phone someone, take some sort of action?

He was still considering exactly what sort of action he might take, should he decide to take some sort of action, when the tugboat abruptly began to move. What a relief; no action would be needed.

But then it became clear the tugboat was moving in this direction. It was coming *here*, to the old ferry slip, to the Votskojek mission, to Hradec Kralowc's happy home.

For one mad instant, Hradec thought of the femur of St. Ferghana, locked away in the makeshift laboratory below. Could this be a nautical attack by the depraved Tsergovians, hoping to steal the relic to further their own miserable United Nations aspirations? But that was absurd. Wasn't it?

Still, the tugboat was definitely steaming this way. There was at least one person up in the wheelhouse, and four more in back, on deck. Did they look Tsergovian? As a matter of fact, one of them did; huge and heavy, like a full oil drum.

Should he call the guards, out at the gate? The walkie-talkie they'd given him, in case instant communication were ever required, was around here somewhere. True, he'd never used it, but how difficult could it be if the rather simple thugs employed by the security agency could routinely use the things?

Hadn't he put the walkie-talkie somewhere in this very room, the former bridge, as being somehow a more philosophically correct location than any of the nonprofessional precincts farther back? Yes, he had; but the former bridge had retained more of its former decor than the rest of the suite, including the wheel itself and all the equipment for captaining the ship. (It was still a ship, and could theoretically still be moved about on the open sea if desired, though *not*, DV, with Hradec Kralowc aboard. That transatlantic crossing on this fat and awful old scow had been more than enough, more than enough.)

Drawers, too; beneath the former bridge's many windows were many drawers, containing God knows what. And somewhere, somewhere in all this nauticalness and officialese and professionalismo there reposed, Hradec was almost sure, the walkie-talkie.

But wait. What if he *did* find the walkie-talkie, and did figure out how to operate it, and did call the current two guards in from the gate, and it turned out this tug was a *Tsergovian feint?* That the real attack would be coming from the land, not the sea?

What to do? What to do?

While Hradec dithered and did nothing—the primary and most necessary character trait of the professional diplomat—the mysterious tugboat hove to at the end of the ferry slip, just barely within Hradec's sight. He pressed his forehead to the—cool!— glass of one of the former bridge's windows and gazed downward past his cheekbones. What was going on down there?

An argument, apparently. The huge man who looked very much like a Tsergovian had clamped one meaty fist around a metal pole at the end of the slip, thus holding the tug in place while the other three on deck argued and the one up in the wheelhouse occasionally shouted down some valuable addition of his own.

At last, one of the men in back, not the possible Tsergovian but a slope-shouldered, furrow-browed individual whose lifeless brown hair flopped around on top of his head in the breeze like dead beach grass, clambered up over the side and off the boat. He stood on the rotting planks of the slip and continued to argue with the men still in the boat, until at last he gave what appeared to be a disgusted wave of dismissal and turned away. At the same time, the perhaps-not-Tsergovian giant released the pole and the tugboat angled off, heading back out into the river.

There were doors on both sides of the former bridge, leading out on deck. Hradec took one of these, saw the stranger clumping along shoreward two decks below, and called out, "You, there!"

The man stopped. He looked around. He started forward again.

"You, there! Up here!"

The man stopped again. He angled his head back horribly and stared straight up to meet Hradec's eye.

It was a strange moment, the two staring at one another through the vertical air. Hradec, a cultivated and civilized man, was horrified to find that he wanted to spit. Quelling that unworthy notion, he called instead, "This is private property!" (That was usually the best magic rune to pronounce in America.)

"I'm just goin through," the man called, pointing landward. "Catch a cab."

"Why didn't you stay on your boat?" Hradec called, more out of simple curiosity than anything else.

"Not me," the man said with gloomy fervency. "Not on that thing. No more."

A fellow sufferer, Hradec thought, remembering again, more vividly than before, his own trip to the New World aboard this very tub, and an unexpected sense of camaraderie came over him, a rare feeling in this faraway posting among aliens, with only a few serfs around who spoke his native tongue (Magyar-Croat). "Wait there," he called. "I'll be right down. Wait there; the guards won't let you out without me."

There was an elevator amidships, across from his bedroom. It was small, noisy, dark gray in color, and smelled of crankcase oil, but it was better than the stairs. Hradec unreeled downward through the ship's innards and stepped out to what had once been the upper center hold, the ship's lowest two decks having been devoted to storage, with large, wet, smelly rooms called holds, three on each deck, all with oval doors through the ship's side for access.

Nowadays, however, five of these six holds were simply ignored, the Votskojeks having no use for damp, cavernous storage spaces, but Harry Hochman's carpenters, with the aid of inexpensive paneling and carpet, had made of the sixth a suitably ambassadorial entrance to the ship and its elevator. Beyond these smooth walls and this dropped ceiling, the rest of the upper center hold continued, no doubt, to echo and to reek, but Hradec had no need to concern himself with that.

The oval door to the outside world stood open, as it always did in good weather. Hradec went up the one gradual ramp and down the other and there he was on the dock, with the stranger a bit to his left, looking sullen. Hradec approached him and, with one of his stock, amiable opening gambits, said, "You will probably be surprised to hear that you are no longer in the United States of America."

The fellow, naturally, looked at him as though he were a lunatic, possibly dangerous. "Is that right," he said.

"That is very right," Hradec told him, with his faint but friendly smile. "Embassies and missions of foreign nations on American soil legally exist in their own countries. Our law and our flag, not yours. Therefore, this is not America." With a sweeping gesture, he concluded, "Welcome to Votskojek!"

"Oh, yeah?" The man looked up at the ship, seeming not that impressed. "That's what it says on the back of this thing," he commented, and jabbed a thumb in the ship's direction. "That's the whole country?"

"No, no," Hradec said, delighted at the response, thinking of fellow diplomats over at the UN he could share this anecdote with. "We are the United Nations mission, or soon shall be, and the embassy." He drew himself to attention. "I am Hradec Kralowc, the ambassador." Extending a hand, he said, "And you—?"

The man seemed to have to think a minute before remembering his name; he must have *really* disliked that boat ride. Then he grabbed Hradec's hand, pumped it, and said, "Diddums."

Hradec blinked. "Diddums?"

Diddums blanched, then recovered. "It's Welsh," he said.

"Ah," Hradec said. "And the first—"

"John. John Diddums."

"Well, uh . . . John. May I call you John?"

"I was just gonna get a cab."

"I take it, John," Hradec went on, "you didn't much care for the motion on that small boat."

"Don't remind me," John Diddums said, and pressed a hand to his stomach.

"I feel the same way," Hradec said. "Believe it or not, I came here all the way from Odessa on *that* thing"—jabbing his own thumb at the ship—"and it was horrendous."

"Boy, I don't doubt it," John Diddums said.

"Along the way," Hradec said, "I learned a wonderful cure, just the thing to make that discomfort go away. Have you a few moments?"

John Diddums seemed surprised. "You want me to go on that thing?"

"It doesn't move," Hradec assured him. "Not like a small tug-boat, at any rate. Frankly, I have nothing to do till the ballet this evening. Come aboard and I'll fix you the restorative and you can tell me about yourself."

"Ballet?"

Never had Hradec heard so much blunt suspicion packed into one small word. To deal with *that* problem once and for all, "I'll be having supper with one of the featured ballerinas after the performance," he explained. And then, just in case that explanations wasn't enough, he explained further: "Ballerinas are girls."

"Everybody knows that," John Diddums said.

Feeling vaguely irritated, and not entirely sure why, "In any case," Hradec said, "come aboard."

9

It wasn't supposed to be this easy. Dortmunder walked around the ship, the very sweet drink in his hand that Hradec had given him to settle his stomach, and Hradec showed him everything. *Everything.* He even saw the bone.

Has anybody before ever had the householder help case the joint?

The tour started in the kitchen, where Hradec concocted—Well, no. The tour *started* in a small, loud, evil-smelling elevator that took them up from the motel lobby-looking entrance to where the kitchen was off to the right down a narrow, long hall. That was where Hradec got out a big glass and a lot of *stuff* and a Cuisinart and made this magic elixir of his that was supposed to settle Dortmunder's stomach. Dortmunder carefully looked the other way— *all* the other ways—while this alchemy was going on, because he had the feeling it would be considered proper manners for the guest to drink the thing, whatever it turned out to be, and so he didn't want to know what was in it.

After the kitchen and the glass of medicine—which turned out to be amazingly sweet, with some kind of like Chinese tartness in behind it, but not bad at all, and might even be working to settle his stomach—Hradec led the way up a flight of stairs to his own apartment, of which he seemed to be very proud.

Well, it was okay. Nice views. Dortmunder didn't want to say anything, but up top here like this you could feel the *Pride of Votskojek* moving, just a little, swaying back and forth, constantly adjusting itself to the water and the ropes and the little heave and tow going on between the river and the slip. But Dortmunder didn't mention this, nor did Hradec, and the glass of restorativeness actually was making a difference, and they didn't stay up top in the apartment too long, anyway.

No. Next they called for the elevator again and went down two levels, one lower than where the kitchen was, and this is where you found the embassy offices. And the bone.

But first, the embassy. There was a big office, which was Hradec's, full of flags and photos and statues and mementos, and with a few round windows showing the Manhattan shoreline northward, with the UN building itself pretty prominent up there, glinting like Paul Bunyan's bathroom mirror in the afternoon sun.

And then there was a smaller office, with no windows at all, but with two people in it, a man and a woman, the ones who actually did all the work around here, and who spoke English with thick accents, like Grijk.

Hradec introduced him and, "Diddums?" said the man, frowning.

"It's Welsh."

"Oh."

"If you ever decide to visit our beautiful country, John," Hradec said, "one of these very efficient clerks will arrange your visa, your hotels, transportation within the country, exit tax, everything."

"I thought you said you had guards out front," Dortmunder said, being clever.

"Oh, you just tell them you're here for a tourist visa," Hradec said. "During normal business hours, of course."

Dortmunder knew when people talked about normal business hours they meant theirs, not his, so he just nodded and told Hradec's workers he'd see them around. The man smiled grimly, the woman smiled shyly, and they got back to work.

Next was the bone.

"Now, here's the most amazing thing," Hradec said as they walked down the long central hall away from the embassy offices. "This relic, a saint's bone, is normally kept at the Rivers of Blood Cathedral in our capital city at Novi Glad—a beautiful city, you must see it some time—but through a fantastic sequence of events it has become crucial to our application for membership in the United Nations; too complex a story to go into."

Dortmunder wondered, Should I ask? Should I be interested? On the other hand, could I bear to hear that story again? "Uh-huh," he said.

Hradec seemed slightly surprised at this lack of curiosity, but on the other hand he also seemed as pleased not to have to tell the story as Dortmunder was not to have to hear it. Thus companionably, they made their way down the hall, and Hradec opened a door, and they entered the laboratory out of the Frankenstein movies.

No, wrong. The Frankenstein movies were in a castle, and the laboratory there was *huge*, with a very high stone ceiling like a church, maybe like the Rivers of Blood Cathedral. But this was a low-ceilinged room, an inside cabin—or three cabins, with their partitions removed—filled with metal tables on which all kinds of jars and retorts and metal boxes and Bunsen burners and stacks of instruction booklets and piles of photographs and general junk were spread and jumbled. In front of the tables were high stools. On the windowless walls were blown-up photos of the bone, X rays of the bone, a lighted-up X-ray viewing box, a calendar that showed two grazing deer in a forest glade—whatever happened to the calendars of smiling girls holding pipe wrenches?—a fire extinguisher, and a pennant from MIT.

No guards. Door unlocked.

Inside this room were two men, both wearing white lab coats. (On a portable metal coatrack near the door hung half a dozen more lab coats.) One of the men stared morosely into a microscope while the other gazed intently at a computer screen, but both raised their heads, much like grazing deer, when Hradec and Dortmunder entered.

Hradec smiled at the microscope one, who was nearer. "Hello, John, here's another John. John McIntire of Johns Hopkins, may I present John Diddums."

62

McIntire, a distracted-looking guy with an orange walrus mustache, two orange walrus eyebrows, and an unchecked growth of orange hair all over his head, offered his hand but then frowned and said, "Diddums?"

"It's Welsh."

"Oh."

Meantime, Hradec had turned to the second man, who had risen from his computer and walked around several metal tables toward them. "I don't think I know you," Hradec said, not suspiciously but like the host at a large party. That's how tight security was around here.

"Another John, I'm afraid." This one had an English accent. Extending his hand to Hradec, he said, "John Mickelmuss, Cambridge. John Fairweather asked me to come over and help out for a few days."

"Oh, yes, of course," Hradec said, unable to hide the vagueness.

"I take it you are Ambassador Kralowc."

"Oh, we're much less formal here. Call me Hradec."

You sure are less formal, Dortmunder thought, looking across the room at what had to be it itself, the thing, the very thing. It rested on a piece of black velvet, under blue light for some reason, and it was smaller than Dortmunder had expected, less than a foot long. But a young girl, in the Middle Ages, she probably wouldn't have been so very tall. The blue light made the bone gleam in an unearthly fashion, as though it were polished ivory, an elephant's tusk rather than some dead saint's leg, amazingly white, with a hint of pale blue behind the whiteness, like some very pale skin.

Dortmunder was recalled from his reverie on the bone by being introduced to John Mickelmuss, who frowned and said, "Diddums?"

"It's Welsh."

That usually ended the conversation, but this one said, "I knew some Diddums from Cardiff, I believe."

"Could be," Dortmunder said.

"Come look at the relic," Hradec said.

10

It is absolutely the easiest thing I have ever seen in my life," Dortmunder said. "It's almost a shame to do it. We could phone for it. We could send a kid to pick it up. It's so easy, I can't believe it."

They were meeting at Tiny's place again, this time without J.C., who, Tiny said, had decided she was overdue for a vacation. "She got on a plane, and she said, 'I'll be back when I'm back,'" he told them. "No, it was the other way around."

"We understood that," Dortmunder said.

So the five sat in Tiny's living room with cans of beer in their hands, and after the discussion about Dortmunder's unauthorized departure from the *Margaret C. Moran* was run into the ground, with Dortmunder pointing out how *all* their predictions when he'd abandoned that alleged tugboat—more like a bouncing rubber ball, if you asked him, and increasingly so in memory—had turned out to be false. He had not been arrested, their plans had not been revealed, his connection with Tsergovia had not been exposed. No, and he hadn't had the pleasure of the return trip with them, either, including the unexpected squall down around the Battery about which the others were very reluctant to speak.

No, the only thing that happened was, the Votskojek ambassador, a nice fella, really, had shown Dortmunder the ship, the entire ship. Including the bone.

"He is well known," Grijk said grimly, "dis Hradec Kralowc, do murder babies and ead dem."

"Well, he didn't do any of that while I was there," Dortmunder said. "All he did was show me the place, and we can walk in there and walk out again playing *catch* with that bone, and no problem."

Kelp, Stan, Tiny, and Grijk all looked interested. "Tell us how," Kelp said.

Dortmunder told them.

11

"The *Pen*-ta-*gon* to-*day* in-*formed* the *Con*-gress," Linda the newsreader gasped, punning, beads of sweat running down her throat and between her unnaturally firm breasts, "*that* I *can't* go *on* much *lon*-ger, *oh!*"

Supine beneath the sometime-substitute anchor, Hradec Kralowc smiled up in delight at her fevered face as she paused in her recital, but not her aerobics, to pant a bit. "I love it when you talk politics," he encouraged her. For years, he'd wondered why the female reporters on the television news all spoke in that same rhythmic, pulsing way, regardless of the sense of what they were saying; now he knew. "More," he urged her, urging as well with his own rhythmic hip pulsations. "More. More."

"The *Pre*-si-*dent* has *joined* the *sum*-mit *at* Ge-*neeeeeve! Oh! Oh! Oh!*"

Join her? Hradec was just coming to the conclusion that a nice shower *à deux* at this time would be preferable to further extended activity here on the bed when *the phone rang!* Damn and blast; throwing him off.

But not Linda. Her red light was well and truly lighted, and

Linda was flying. Forget the phone; insert its own rhythm into the insertion. Fly with me.

Daredevils of the air, wingtip to wingtip, banking through the clouds, coming in side by side for the smoothest of landings, touching down together; sigh. Engines off.

Blond hair lank around her anonymously beautiful face, Linda smiled down upon this ambassador—from a minor Eastern European nation, granted, but she was herself only a local feed, so they could both feel pleased with the accomplishment—and murmured, "We'll be back, after this."

As she climbed off and went tripping away toward the bathroom, lovely behind gleaming like a beacon of hope in a dark and dangerous world, the ambassador rolled over, grasped the bedside telephone a bit more savagely than necessary, and said, "Yes?" (Being a professional diplomat, he kept all his snarls and savageries inside, beneath a calm, polite exterior.)

It was Lusk, from the office, of course. "Diddums, Ambassador, on one."

What? Baby talk? Hradec said, "Lusk? *What* did you say?"

"John Diddums, Ambassador. The man you introduced us to the other day."

John Diddums! The unexpected visitor from the sea. Or from the river, actually. "Call me anytime," Hradec had said to the fellow, in his diplomatic way, and now, be damned if the man hasn't done it. "Right," Hradec said, sitting up, listening to the toilet flush—maybe he should ask Harry Hochman if one of his hotel maintenance people could put in a quieter fixture there—and punched the button for line one. "Mr. Diddums! What a pleasant surprise!"

"You said I oughta call."

"Yes, I did, and I'm glad you took me at my word." Sound of the shower running; vision in mind of Linda soaping herself. Here, let me help with that, but not yet.

Diddums was saying, "The way you talked about, uh, Votskojek, you sure made it sound interesting. I got some vacation time coming up—"

"Really?"

"—and I thought maybe, well, maybe I could come around, talk to you and the other people there, work out a whatchacallit."

"A whatchacallit?"

"Itinerary," Diddums said. "That's what it is, itinerary."

"Yes, of course," Hradec said, keeping calm, keeping the excitement out of his voice as he had earlier kept out the irritation. A tourist, in Votskojek! An actual tourist, a vacationing traveler, in Novi Glad, in the Schtumveldt Mountains, in the Varja River—

Well, no, *on* the Varja River, let us hope, it not being a river for a human body to enter. No need to go into that now, though, with this sudden prospect of an actual deliberate visitor to the ambassador's native land.

Deliberate. Not an escaped homicidal lunatic from Transylvania; not a bewildered Ukrainian in a four-door Lada who'd made the mistake of trusting his Soviet maps; not a French balloonist blown off course, nor a Berliner full of berliners who'd fallen asleep on the through train, nor a Zemblan lepidopterist insensibly crossing the border net in hand in pursuit of some rare butterfly, nor a Tsergovian with a bomb to plant in the Chamber of Deputies, but an actual tourist, on purpose, *intending* to visit Votskojek. And an American at that, with dollars!

"I'd be delighted," Hradec said with simple honesty, "to see you, Mr. Diddums, and work out an itinerary for your visit to Votskojek. At your convenience. When would you like to come by?"

"Uh, this afternoon?"

"Couldn't be better," Hradec assured him. "What time?"

"Uh, four o'clock?"

Hradec was slightly disturbed by Diddums's apparent inability to answer any simple question without first studying it for snares and pitfalls, but he was so dazzled by the prospect of this first swallow of the Votskojek tourist trade that he was blind to whatever warning signals Diddums might be tossing out ahead of himself. "Four o'clock is the *perfect* hour," the ambassador was pleased to tell his country's guest. "I'll alert my staff to be ready for you, and I look forward to greeting you myself."

"Me, too," Diddums said. "That's what I want, all of us together, working on my trip."

"And that," Hradec said, hearing the shower stop—ah, well, too bad—"is what I want, too, Mr. Diddums."

12

Three-fifty P.M. In the offices of the Votskojek embassy aboard the *Pride of Votskojek*, Ambassador Hradec Kralowc and his office staff—Lusk and Terment—searched in vain for more pamphlets, photos, press releases, and other bumpf to fill out the truly anemic travelers' information packet they were assembling for John Diddums. (Down the hall, in the room with the relic, John Mickelmuss completed inputting into the computer his latest test data and turned to the rather more complicated matter of making a cup of coffee.) If he'd had more time, Hradec would have asked his hotelier friend, Harry Hochman, for help. Oh, well.

Still 3:50. Andy Kelp and four men wearing eye shadow and carrying canvas purses that were supposed to look like ammunition carriers but looked like purses were standing on the raft moored in the East River at the end of East Twenty-third Street, where the seaplanes ingest and egest their passengers. And here came the plane now, plowing heavily shoreward like an Indian elephant wading through the monsoon. The other four men adjusted their crotches and shoulder pads while Kelp looked away downriver, frowning slightly.

Still 3:50. Murch's Mom steered her cab past four perfectly legitimate customers on Third Avenue between Nineteenth and Twentieth streets, all four of them frantically waving—hand, cane, attaché case, dollar bills (that was the hard one to pass)—in order to yank it to a halt in front of Dortmunder, who hadn't been waving at all. Dortmunder got into the backseat, saying, "Hi," and Murch's Mom reached for the meter, explaining, "I gotta throw the flag on you, John. Otherwise, some candyass inspector's gonna write me up."

"That's okay," Dortmunder said. "I'm feeling rich. Besides, it's only a few blocks."

Three fifty-*one*. Tiny Bulcher strode eastward across Twenty-eighth Street like the scythe of fate, leaving a broad, empty swath in his wake. He merely walked, arms swinging at his sides, face with no particular expression, but nevertheless: Not just ordinary citizens but junkies, released maniacs, unsupervised retards, even mothers pushing babies in strollers, all moved out of the way when they saw Tiny coming. And he paid no attention at all.

Three fifty-two. "Well, this is all we have," Hradec said, "and therefore this is all we have." (It sounded better in Magyar-Croat, which he happened to be speaking.) "So," he said, "we'll simply fill in verbally with our own comments and descriptions of our native land. Of a *positive* nature, please."

Lusk and Terment nodded and looked subservient.

Three fifty-three. The seaplane lumbered to a halt at the raft, immediately ejecting its pilot, a short, chunky, barefoot man in silvered aviator glasses (what else?), string T-shirt, and khaki British army shorts, who held his mount fairly steady by a strut while two slightly sick ladies in Day-Glo spandex disembogued. Kelp continued to peer downstream.

Three fifty-four. Murch's Mom's cab, with Dortmunder in back and the meter running, remained stuck in the right lane on Third Avenue just below Twenty-third Street, where Murch's Mom wanted to make a right turn but where some sort of construction or destruction was going on and a backhoe kept lumbering around in the way of the traffic flow, backing up (beep beep beep beep) and going forward (   ) and backing up (beep beep beep beep) and going forward (   ).

"How we doing?" Dortmunder asked, as though innocently.

"Just fine," Murch's Mom snarled.

Three fifty-five. Five blocks due north, Tiny, unencumbered by an automobile, crossed Third Avenue against the light and was not honked at.

Three fifty-six. John Mickelmuss tasted his coffee and found it not particularly good but somehow acceptable. That accomplishment behind him, he returned his attention to the sacred relic, the left femur of St. Ferghana, lying now like the nakedest of majas on a black cloth on a chest-high metal examining table beneath an X-ray camera.

The problem with testing this bone was that the parameters of the investigation included the instruction that the physical integrity of the artifact must not be invaded. In other words, it's no fair chipping off little chunks of the thing and dunking them in vials of acid. So testing had to be done from a distance, by light and temperature and weight and so on, which took longer than chipping and dunking, but there you are.

Three fifty-seven (beep beep beep beep beep beep beep beep). "Maybe," Dortmunder said, "we should take some other way."

"You're sounding," Murch's Mom informed him in a not friendly fashion, "like my boy Stanley."

Still three fifty-seven. The four purse-toting guys completed their boarding process into the wallowing seaplane, and the pilot raised an eyebrow at Kelp. "You coming or not?"

"Not," Kelp replied, and looked downstream.

The pilot didn't get it: "Listen, pal, I'm leaving."

"Good-bye," Kelp said.

The pilot shook his head, exasperated. "This is the seaplane dock, you know. If you don't want a seaplane, what are you doing here?"

"Waiting for the crosstown," Kelp said. Then, seeing that the pilot was *still* not satisfied, and so to forestall more verbiage, Kelp added, "Your people are gonna throw up in there, pretty soon."

Which was true. A seaplane idling at a dock is a restless thing indeed, and a couple of the passengers inside this one had already turned all over the color of their eye shadow. The pilot, seeing this, expelled an expletive, jumped aboard his trusty steed, and hi-hoed out of there.

Three fifty-eight. Hradec consulted his watch, which read 3:56. "He'll be here soon," he told Lusk and Terment, who looked passive.

Three fifty-eight again. "Enough!" cried Murch's Mom, as she yanked the wheel hard left, gunned through the intersection, and caused a seven-car collision behind her, of which hers was none of the seven cars.

"About time," Dortmunder muttered, with one eye on his watch and the other on the meter.

Three fifty-nine. Tiny marched across First Avenue; traffic waited for him.

Four o'clock, on the button. As the seaplane trundled away from the raft upon which Kelp remained the only survivor, a small, sleek outboard motorboat of the sort James Bond used to leap into from passing seaplanes came slicing northward along the shore. Stan Murch stood at the wheel, in wet yellow slicker and hat, and with brisk, tricky adjustments of speed and rudder he brought his little boat to a perfect stop at Kelp's feet. "So what I did," he began, leaning over to press his palm on the rough planks of the raft to hold the boat steady while Kelp boarded, "I came around the *Brooklyn* side of Governor's Island, because that way you don't have the Statue of Liberty ferry to contend with, but then I came over to the Manhattan side before the turn for the Williamsburg Bridge, because you've got less commercial stuff over here."

"Good," Kelp said. "I thought that plane would never get the hell away from here."

"We've got time," Murch said, not bothering to look at his watch.

Four oh-one. "I don't like to say anything—" Dortmunder began.

"Then don't," Murch's Mom advised him as she careened eastbound through the intersection at Twenty-sixth Street and Second Avenue not very long after the light had turned red against her, horn screaming defiance at those on Second Avenue who had it in mind to continue their own journeys downtown.

Four oh-two. Tiny strode through drifts of litter into the shade beneath the FDR Drive; no muggers followed. Ahead stretched the chain-link fence, the rotted old ferry building beyond it. To

72

left and right, beneath the elevated highway, sagged the carapaces of former cars. But where, Tiny wondered, where were Dortmunder and Murch's Mom and the taxicab?

Coming, coming. (Still 4:02.) *Screaming* left turn onto First Avenue, another shaving of a red light at Twenty-seventh Street, cab wheels *smoking*. Murch's Mom clung grimly to the wheel, sharp chin just above it, jutting out at the windshield. In back, Dortmunder clung to the ashtray, it being the only thing he could find to hold on to.

Four oh-two. (Yes; still 4:02.) Kelp took the white lab coat out of the D'Ag Bag as Murch steered the little motorboat slowly north along the tumbled shore. Shaking out the lab coat, borrowed earlier today from a clinic farther downtown, Kelp said, "We don't want to be late."

"You don't want to be all over wet, either," Murch pointed out, "which is why I'm easing along here. Don't worry, we're doing fine."

Still 4:02. "It's four o'clock," Hradec said, looking at his watch. "I'll go down and meet him."

Four oh-three, at last. Tiny emerged from under the FDR Drive, the fence closer now. The parked cars, a couple of them with diplomat plates, were just ahead and to his right. The guarded gate was beyond the cars over there, the sentries not yet aware of Tiny's existence. But they would be.

And here came the cab, a yellow comet streaking beneath the FDR Drive, slashing by Tiny's left elbow like a surface-to-surface missile, and slamming to a stop *just* short of the fence. The two guards looked over in mild amaze as the dust of decades gently rose and slowly settled on the cab and its surround. "Why don't we just crash on through?" Dortmunder suggested from the floor.

"That's three bucks eighty," Murch's Mom said, belting the meter with a solid right hand.

"About time," Tiny muttered to himself, and slowed his pace as he approached the cab from the rear.

"Not here yet," Kelp said, peeking around the wall just south of the ferry slip, as Murch held the little boat steady on the unsteady water.

"Told you we had time," Murch said.

Dortmunder, grousing, paid the meter and a fifty-cent tip.

"Big spender," Murch's Mom commented. Dortmunder, maintaining his dignity, got out of the cab and approached the gate, while behind him Murch's Mom switched on her OFF DUTY sign; part of the plan.

"Diddums," said Dortmunder. When the guards looked at him funny, he said, "The ambassador's expecting me."

One of the guards spent a long time consulting the top sheet of paper on his clipboard, a sheet of paper that contained only one entry: "Diddums—4:00 P.M." "Right," he allowed at last, and pulled open the unlocked gate.

Tiny pulled open the cab's left rear door. "Take me," he bellowed, loudly enough to be heard by the guards over at the gate, "up to a Hunnerd and forty-seventh Street."

Murch's Mom came boiling out from her cab as Tiny started to squeeze himself in. "Get outta there!" she screamed, *plenty* loudly enough to be heard by the guards, the sea gulls, and the traffic up above on the FDR Drive. "Don'tcha see the off-duty light?"

Dortmunder, pretending not to hear all that yelling in his background, walked on through the ferry building's open middle. Ahead lay the old thick planks of the ferry slip, with the ship alongside and, at the far end, Kelp's head peering into view in the lower right, like the artist's self-portrait in a heroic mural. And coming out of the *Pride of Votskojek*, as the self-portrait modestly erased itself, was Hradec Kralowc, right on time.

The guards, with growing interest, watched the big mean mountain of a man and the feisty little lady cabdriver yell uncomplimentary things at one another. But then the feisty little lady cabdriver slapped the big mean mountain of a man across the chops, and the mountain responded with a straight right jab that drove the little lady back into the fence with a *clang*.

"Say," one of the guards said. And the mountain was advancing on the little lady, shoulders bunched.

Tiny had pulled his punch; Murch's Mom had not. "You shouldn't hit," Tiny announced. He reared back.

"Hey, stop that! Cut that out!" The two guards deserted their post, rushing to the defense of the little lady.

Dortmunder and Hradec shook hands. Hradec said he was happy Dortmunder could make it; Dortmunder thanked him and said it was his pleasure. Hradec looked upward and declared the weather fine; Dortmunder agreed. Hradec confessed his liking for New York City, after all; Dortmunder allowed as how the old place still had a couple things going for it, if you didn't count its population and government. In the lower-right periphery of Dortmunder's vision, the self-portrait reappeared. "Why don't we go aboard?" Dortmunder said.

"Fine idea," Hradec agreed, and led the way, saying, "We've prepared some literature for you. Not too much; we didn't want to overburden you."

Tiny held guard A and hit him with guard B.

Kelp clambered up onto the slip, paused to brush off his lab coat—white shows *all* the dirt—and scampered forward as Murch steered the little boat away upriver, planning to circle Roosevelt Island just for the hell of it.

Hradec and Dortmunder crowded together into the little elevator and rode up.

Kelp slipped through the open door into the ship, found the stairs where Dortmunder had said they would be, and walked up.

"That's enough foolin around," Tiny decided. Dropping the guards, he turned to Murch's Mom and said, "Take me to Kennedy Airport."

"The airport!" Murch's Mom cried in manic pleasure. "Why didn't you say so? Get aboard!"

Tiny did so, with difficulty—even normal-size people have difficulty getting into the space allotted to the paying guest in New York City taxicabs—and Murch's Mom got behind the wheel, flicking off the OFF DUTY sign. While the dazed guards sat up and watched openmouthed, the cab backed around in a half circle and drove away.

"I'm gonna have to throw the flag on you, Tiny," Murch's Mom said. "Otherwise, I'll get a citation for sure."

"That's okay," Tiny said. "You can just deduct for the smack in the puss you give me."

"Oh, did you feel that?" Murch's Mom asked, sounding surprised.

"I *heard* it," Tiny told her. "That was bad enough."

Once again, Hradec introduced Dortmunder to Lusk and Terment. He nodded to the woman and shook the man's hand, then had an afterthought and shook the woman's hand, then decided to go the whole hog and nodded at the man.

Kelp, following Dortmunder's really excellent maps and directions, moved casually but swiftly down the hall away from the offices where Dortmunder and Hradec's staff were inventing a new folk dance, and opened the correct door for the makeshift lab where the left femur of the martyred St. Ferghana would be found. The real one.

And where, unfortunately for Kelp's devices, the femur was currently undergoing investigation. John Mickelmuss looked up at the interruption, saw someone in a white lab coat, made the natural assumptions, and nodded. Kelp nodded back.

"Mickelmuss," Mickelmuss said, extending his hand. "John Mickelmuss, Cambridge."

"Kelly," Kelp said. "John Kelly, Park Slope."

"Sorry, don't know that school," Mickelmuss said.

Kelp hadn't known they were talking about schools. "It's just a little one," he explained. "Very specialized."

"I know so few of the American schools," Mickelmuss said, politely putting the blame on himself. "Just taking a few X rays here," he added, gesturing at the bone and the equipment. "Turn it over to you in a jiff."

"Take your time," Kelp assured him, smiling to show he meant it, and not meaning it in the slightest.

"Won't be long," Mickelmuss said, smiled, and went back to his adjustments. Kelp began to lurk.

Dortmunder, Hradec, Lusk, and Terment discussed visas, accommodations, sight-seeing, climate, exchange rates, and cuisine. The airport exit tax was touched on but not emphasized.

Stan Murch sat at the wheel of his idling motorboat and idly watched the high cable cars swing back and forth between Manhattan and Roosevelt islands; red cars dangling from black cables way the hell up in the air there. *Way* up in the air. Look like something in Switzerland. Nice view of the city from out here. Bring Mom sometime, get her out of that cab for once.

Since Tiny and Murch's Mom were done for today, she delivered him to his empty home on Riverside Drive, J.C. being still away on vacation. At that point, there was a brief dispute about the fare, but Murch's Mom *never* lost a dispute about the fare.

John Mickelmuss adjusted the light, the table, and the angle of the camera. The other fellow, Kelly, was over at the service table, among the flasks and burners, moving them about this way and that. If Mickelmuss didn't know the idea absurd, he'd think this chap Kelly was playing tictacktoe with lab equipment, left hand against right. He lifted his head and smiled warmly at Kelly, saying, "Won't be a minute."

"Hey, no problem," Kelly said; odd chap. "You know," he said, "this stuff over here almost smells like coffee."

"It is coffee," Mickelmuss assured him. "Not very good, I'm afraid, but do have some. Won't be long now."

Dortmunder asked more questions about tour guides, translators, bus transport from the capital, and cruises on the Varja River. The idea was, he should give Kelp all the time he needed to switch bones, because the idea behind *that* was, the Votskojeks shouldn't know the bone had been switched until well after the event. That's why Tiny and Murch's Mom had done the diversion when Kelp slipped aboard, and why Dortmunder himself would do a diversion on his way out, to let Kelp depart unnoticed with the real femur concealed on his person.

But Kelp himself had to be concealed in the stairway, just off the big entrance foyer, when Dortmunder did finally come down, presumably with Hradec Kralowc and certainly by elevator. Then Hradec would wish Dortmunder godspeed and would elevate himself away again, Dortmunder would make the diversion out at the gate to distract the guards, and Kelp would scoot off the ship and down to the far end of the slip, where Murch would be waiting with the getaway motorboat. Precision. Perfection. Easy as falling off a house.

"Won't be but half a tick now," Mickelmuss said, frowning and frowning and adjusting the tray that he'd now decided should hold the femur beneath the X-ray machine.

Kelp sipped at the really foul coffee and considered the possibility of merely belting this foreigner over the head with one of these heavy objects available around here. That would be the end of the surprise aspect of the caper, of course, but, on the other hand, if this guy didn't finish setting up and take his goddam X-ray picture pretty soon, that would be the end of the entire heist. Kelp had to be in position, ready to scoot, when Dortmunder did his diversion.

Murch stretched and yawned. Time to go back, get in position, be ready to go full throttle the instant Kelp's foot hit the deck, ready to scoot straight across to Long Island City where the getaway car was stashed.

"Closing with it now," Mickelmuss said.

"Of course, if I went in the *winter*," Dortmunder said, beginning to feel as desperate as Hradec and Lusk and Terment, "I suppose there'd be places to go skiing."

The idea of John Dortmunder on skis was on the face of it too ludicrous to be entertained, but that's the task Hradec and Lusk and Terment had set themselves, and they stood up to it as best they could, Hradec gaining confidence in his answer as he climbed through it, saying, "Well, yes, of course, we have mountains, many many mountains, and the winter, you say the winter, certainly we have snow in the winter, a great deal of snow on the mountains, yes, of course, certainly, opportunities for skiing, absolutely, I don't see why not."

"Of course," said Lusk. But the best Terment could do was nod.

This time, Stan Murch was the self-portrait in the mural's corner. All clear on the slip, rumpled guards down at the far end by the gate, strutting back and forth, trying to act as though nothing at all had recently occurred.

"*There!*" Mickelmuss said. Then: "Oh, blast, I think I moved it. Best give it one more."

Dortmunder clutched the manila folder of Votskojek information to his chest with his left hand while shaking hands generally with his right. "I appreciate this," he assured them all. "Appreciate the time, hope I didn't take you from, from, from . . ."

"Not at all, not at all."

"Our pleasure."

"*Do* enjoy Votskojek."

"I'm sure I will," Dortmunder said. And I'm sure Kelp's out of there by now, he thought. He has to be.

"I'll see you down," Hradec said with more obvious relief than diplomats usually show.

Has to be out of there by now; *has* to be.

But, no. "Hm hm hm hm hm," said Mickelmuss, bending over the equipment, while Kelp's hand reached out to a knobby fist-

78

sized machine on a nearby table. Enough, one way and another, was enough. Kelp lifted the machine.

"Got it! At last," Mickelmuss announced, and turned his smiling face to observe the machine in Kelp's hand. "Ah!" he said in delight. "Spectropolaric analysis! *That* ought to clear up a few matters."

"Yeah, it ought to," Kelp said.

"Well, she's all yours," Mickelmuss told him, with a careless wave at the bone, while with his other hand he patted his tummy and said, "Frankly, that coffee seems to go right through one. Perhaps I should have alerted you. Pardon." And he left.

Dortmunder and Hradec zoomed down the ship's innards. Hradec wouldn't even leave the elevator. "You'll know your way," he said, smiling blankly, and waited for Dortmunder to exit. Which Dortmunder did, and the elevator door slid shut. Dortmunder crossed to the open door leading outside the ship, looking all around as he went, hoping to see Kelp lurking, but not.

From beneath his lab coat, Kelp took the shoe box containing the fake femur, provided by Grijk Krugnk. "It's a real bone, from a real zevendeen-year-old girl," Krugnk had assured him. "Dat's all I know."

"Dat's all I want to know," Kelp had assured him right back.

The shoe box, with a rubber band around it to keep the top on and the bone in, had been suspended all this time from a hook stuck through one end of the box and then attached to a preexisting loop in the middle of the lab coat's back, at waist level. Wearing the loose garment with the shoe box in position had made Kelp look rather lard-assed for such an otherwise-slender guy, but science is a pretty sedentary occupation, so it was okay.

Kelp put the shoe box on the table near the real bone. He slid off the rubber band, opened it, and removed the copy. The two bones looked remarkably similar to the naked eye, except that the real one was slightly less shiny and had somewhat deeper shadows at its knuckly ends. Being very careful to keep it clear in his mind which bone was which, Kelp made the switch, closed the shoe box, put the rubber band on it, and had a hell of a time trying to hook it back onto that goddam loop. (Murch had done it for him in the motorboat.) Finally, he decided the hell with it, he'd just carry the goddam thing, so he tucked the shoe box under his arm and crossed to the hall door.

Two doors in that hall simultaneously opened; that to the lab and that to the elevator. Kelp and Hradec stepped out; Kelp stepped smartly back. Hradec turned the other way, and a third door opened, beyond the elevator; that to the office. Lusk and Terment hurried out, complaining in Magyar-Croat, a language in which even a declaration of love sounds like a declaration of war; complaints can really bend the molecules of the surrounding air.

Kelp waited. The three in the hall stood jawing. Would they still be at it when Mickelmuss returned? What would Kelp do with the shoe box? What if he was to take the lab coat *off*, hang the shoe box, and then somehow put the coat back on again without dislodging the—

No. Slam; the complainers had gone. Kelp left the lab and hightailed for the stairs, hoping against hope that Dortmunder hadn't started the diversion yet.

Ah, but he had. While Kelp was still failing to rehook the shoe box inside his coat, Dortmunder had already reached the gate, where he took from his jacket pocket the small black collapsible umbrella that was his prop for the occasion. One guard opened the gate, and Dortmunder looked up into an almost perfectly blue sky to say, "Well, it looks like rain."

The guards frowned at him. They frowned at the sky. One of them said, "It does not."

Dortmunder kept looking up. His free hand pointed up and he said, "What about that cloud there? That dark one." Meanwhile, his other hand was pushing the still-closed umbrella, ten inches long in its collapsed state, through one of the diamond-shaped spaces in the fence right next to the opening for the gate.

"*What* dark cloud?" demanded a guard.

"That one, by the tall building," Dortmunder said, pointing generally upward.

"Well, I don't see it," said the guard.

"Neither do I," said the other one.

"I don't care what anybody says," Dortmunder announced, still looking up, "I'm opening my umbrella." And he pushed the button in the handle that did so.

Pop. Dortmunder looked down. "Whoops," he said.

The guards also looked down. "Now what?" one of them demanded.

The answer was, the umbrella was in the fence. That is, the open black fabric foliage of the umbrella was on one side of the fence and the handle was on the other side of the fence, with the shaft that connected the two now passing through that diamond-shaped hole. The business end of the umbrella was *far* too wide to fit back through the diamond, and the J-shaped handle was just a little bit too wide to go through it.

And not only that, but with the umbrella in this position it would not be possible to close the chain-link gate. "Well, for Christ's sake," said the second guard. "How did you *do* that?"

"I don't know," Dortmunder said, looking chagrined.

In fact, he knew exactly how he'd done it, having practiced with half a dozen other umbrellas on a different chain-link fence for a couple of hours earlier today. Having practiced so many times, and having had to retrieve the umbrella after each successful trial, Dortmunder knew also the fairly tricky but rather simple way to reclose the umbrella and slide it back through the hole in the fence to free it, but before becoming proficient at such umbrella retrieval he had wrecked several of the harmless little things and had come close once or twice to losing his temper. He had also on one occasion jabbed an umbrella rib rather painfully into the palm of his hand. All in all, he expected this situation to keep the guards distracted for some little time to come.

Plenty of time for Kelp to make his escape. Surreptitiously peering backward under his own armpit, Dortmunder scanned the ferry slip and was disheartened to see no Andy Kelp at all back there, dogging it for the river. Where the hell was he?

On the stairs, at that instant, having gone through the stairway door just an instant before Hradec Kralowc hurried back out of the office, an extremely important color photograph of the Rivers of Blood Cathedral in Novi Glad, which John Diddums had inadvertently left behind, clutched in his hand. Hradec zoomed downward in the elevator and reached the entrance level long before Kelp.

"I think we need a hacksaw," said one of the guards.

"No, I can do it," said the other guard. "I'll just close the damn thing again and pull it back through."

"I feel really stupid about this," Dortmunder admitted, bending down to peer very closely at the trouble he'd caused, hoping by his bumbled eagerness to appear to try to help but actually to make things even more difficult than they already were.

But not as difficult as they got. The guard who felt he knew how to handle the problem reached out and compressed the umbrella, Dortmunder crowding too close in his palpable desire to make up for his clumsiness. A rib jabbed the guard in the palm; the guard's hand jerked back; his elbow caught Dortmunder square in the eye; Dortmunder fell all of a heap, unconscious.

Hradec stepped from the *Pride of Votskojek*, to find his nation's first volunteer tourist being beaten up by the hired guards. "Here!" he cried. "Stop that!"

The guards, not particularly having wanted a victim, now found themselves standing over their victim, looking and feeling both sullen and sheepish, as Hradec ran forward.

Kelp thudded down the stairs.

Murch sneaked one more peek over the edge of the ferry slip and could *not* figure out what he was looking at. Some sort of procession?

The sheepish, sullen guards, under Hradec's incensed instructions, carried the unconscious Dortmunder back toward the entrance to the *Pride of Votskojek*. The bumpiness of the journey revived Dortmunder, who opened his remaining good eye just in time to see Kelp hurtle out of the broad doorway in the side of the ship and crash head-on into Hradec. Both went flying, and so did the shoe box, which opened, spilling its femur onto the rough planks of the slip.

Kelp rolled around on the planks, found his footing, found the bone and grabbed it, struggled to his feet, and saw Dortmunder in the grip of the two gate guards. They'd caught him! "Run, John!" Kelp yelled, and belted one of the guards across the head with the bone.

"Not with the relic!" screamed Hradec, still all asprawl on the entrance ramp.

The guards, bewildered about most things but quickly understanding violence, dropped Dortmunder (thud!) and turned to confront this new and less ambiguous threat. Dortmunder, one-eyed John, scrambled up the back of one of the guards to his feet

82

as Kelp slashed and parried with the bone, using it as a saber as he yelled again, "John! Run!"

Oh, it was hopeless, and Dortmunder knew it, but he couldn't help trying just one last dodge: Squinting his good eye at Kelp, he said, "I don't know you?" Except it came out a question, rather than the ringing declaration he'd been hoping to hear.

Everybody stopped. Everybody looked at Dortmunder. Stricken, Kelp whispered, "You weren't blown?"

"Not till now."

"Grab him!" Hradec cried, and pointed at Dortmunder.

"*Run*, John!" Kelp yelled, and showed how by showing his heels to the group, scampering hell-for-leather toward the end of the slip.

Dortmunder, with no time to think and with guards already reaching for him, also ran. But as he ran, arms pumping, legs quaking, face muscles distorted in a grimace as though he were in a rocket ship undergoing pressure of three gravities or more, he squinted like Popeye at the world out ahead of himself, saw what he was running toward, and couldn't believe it. That's the river out there!

Murch, seeing his passenger in view at last, eased the motor-boat forward, and Kelp leaped from the end of the slip, landing in the boat on his feet, then knees, then elbow, then bone, then face.

Dortmunder gasped like a cappuccino machine as he reached the end of the slip and juddered to a stop. He looked down at that teeny target, miles below him on top of the deep river.

Kelp and Murch stared up at him, both making many urgent gestures. "Jump, John!" Kelp cried.

"Come on, come on!" Murch shouted.

Dortmunder panted. He stared downward, managing to see double with only one working eye. He tried to jump; he tried to come on, come on; he really did; but he just couldn't do it. And then hands closed on his elbows, shoulder, and head.

Kelp knelt up in the bottom of the boat, bone in one hand, gunwale clutched in the other, and Murch steered them briskly away from there, aimed at Long Island City. Kelp stared back at the receding Dortmunder, in the firm grip of the private law. "He's going to blame *me* for this," Kelp said, "I just know he is."

Dortmunder closed his remaining eye.

13

Hradec sat at his desk and considered the situation. John Diddums, or whoever he really was, sat in a slatback chair facing him, handcuffed behind his back, with the cuffs looped through a slat. The guards had returned to their useless post at the gate, carrying a hacksaw for the umbrella, and with orders to let in no one, including the scientists previously authorized to be aboard the embassy. John Mickelmuss of Cambridge had been requested, gently but firmly, to abandon ship; some political problem at home in Novi Glad was hinted at. Lusk and Terment stood around looking worried but willing. And some anonymous bone lay shamelessly upon Hradec's desk.

He prodded the pale thing with the business end of a ballpoint pen. It did nothing. He frowned at Diddums: "Where did they go with the real relic?"

Diddums's open eye looked introspective, almost meditative. The other was blackening up pretty well; he was going to have some shiner there. Good.

But he wasn't answering the question. Hradec said, "Don't make me call the police."

Diddums sighed, but that was all. He didn't answer, didn't even focus his one good eye on his interrogator. He was as forthcoming as this phony femur.

Of *course* Hradec couldn't call the police, which Diddums must understand as completely as Hradec. The Tsergovians' strategy from the beginning was now clear; to claim the real relic was false, to force a period of scientific testing of the sacred object, to await their opportunity, and then to steal the honest leg bone of the saint and replace it with this shoddy imitation. Not imitation bone, real bone, but imitation saint.

And what would the Tsergovians do at this point, now that their fell plan had come to fruition? Would they announce they'd had the relic all along? Present it, say, at a press conference, so Archbishop Minkokus, that senile dodderer who held all their futures in the palm of his palsied hand, would turn his toothless, drooling smile on *their* application for the disputed United Nations seat?

No. Hradec Kralowc knew something of political strategy, and so he knew the best thing for the Tsergovians to do at this point was nothing, particularly since they'd already been claiming to have the true relic in their possession but would not produce it until the pretender had been exposed.

So the bone was with Tsergovia, but the ball was in Hradec's court. If he were to suddenly claim the actual relic had been stolen by unknown raiders, with no unbiased outside eyewitnesses, the Tsergovians would plausibly suggest that the report of the theft was itself false, to cover the falsity of their imitation. If, on the other hand, the Votskojeks—meaning Hradec, at this moment—did nothing, it wouldn't take long for the scientists to see through the pathetic claims of *this* gnawed chicken leg.

Their only hope was to find out where the raiders were taking the relic, where the Tsergovians planned to keep it hidden until the Votskojek humiliation was complete. Which meant their only hope was Diddums.

Hradec gazed on the man and saw that he was a brick wall, a mystery clothed in an enigma surrounded by a conundrum. There was something about Diddums's very fatalism that would make him a hard nut to crack.

But cracked Diddums must be, and soon. Watching, thinking, considering his options, Hradec began to hatch a plan. It was a crazy idea, but it just might work. Turning to Lusk, he said, "I'm afraid it's time to telephone—"

"The police?"

Lusk would never make a diplomat. "No, not the police," Hradek said. "This is the time for desperate measures. I'm afraid it's time to telephone... Dr. Zorn."

Under his furrowed brow, Diddums's good eye widened.

14

It didn't seem to take any time at all. Stan Murch stood at the wheel, steering straight and true across the choppy river, and the last thing Andy Kelp saw was his comrade and partner John Dortmunder being led away down the ferry slip like a blind man by people whose body language suggested they were not his friends. And the next thing he saw was a shiny badge being held out by a guy whose fashion statement was thick black shoes and sharp-creased navy blue trousers and a nerdy dark blue plastic zip-up jacket, and whose verbal statement was, "Okay, hold it right there. That's good. Now get outta the boat."

The Queens-Brooklyn side of the East River is very different from the Manhattan side, Manhattan being almost completely residential along that shore, tumbled blocks of apartment buildings that advertise river views but actually offer industrial views of Brooklyn and Queens: factories, warehouses, storage yards, junkyards, piers for barges and tugs and small cargo vessels, all the vast nethers of a busy metropolis laid out like a picture in a pop-up book for the aesthetic viewing pleasure of rich Manhattanites. Of course, these days rich Manhattanites tend to be people for whom such a view is a step up from the oil refineries and sand of home, so it's okay. And it was into this Dickensian warren of riverside grunge that Stan Murch steered their trusty little motorboat, near to where he'd stashed the getaway car, just north of Newtown Creek, that industrially useful channel of near-water that forms the Brooklyn-Queens line. Here they could be alone and unnoticed, as quietly they and the bone slipped away.

So why was their landing spot—thick, splintery planks and rusty old iron mooring posts that used to front a rural mailbox factory until its owners gave up on the city and moved to pleasant, safe, cheap, boring quarters in deepest Pennsylvania—full up with prissy guys in blue with shiny badges? Guys who wanted Kelp and Murch outta the boat *now*.

Could the Votskojeks be that fast? Impossible; it was a bare five minutes since they'd zoomed away from the ferry slip. Nevertheless, feeling he'd rather not work out an answer to the question "What are you doing with that bone?" Kelp kicked the sacred object under a corner of tarpaulin in the puddly bottom of the motorboat while climbing out. "Here I come, here I come."

And here came another surprise; like the first, not a happy one. A couple of the many guys—many guys—in blue hanging around on this pier happened to turn their backs while moving briskly about their brisk business, and in big block white letters on the back of their dark blue zip-up jackets—they were all making essentially the same fashion statement—were the letters *D* and *E* and *A*.

Oh, boy. The feds. The Drug Enforcement Administration. Murch and Kelp looked at one another knowing they were in deep shit but not whose, and one of the boys in blue came over to say, "Which of you is Walter 'Pepper' LaFontaine?"

"Neither of us," Kelp said.

"He's the guy we borrowed the boat from," Murch said, which was probably true when you stopped to think about it, and pretty quick-witted of Murch, all in all.

"You borrow it from him often?" asked the guy.

"First time," Murch said. "And if it's gonna be like this, last time, too."

"Let's see some ID."

Easiest thing in the world. Kelp and Murch showed impeccable identification, in the form of actual driver's licenses with their actual photos and names and addresses on them, ID reserved for only the most special circumstances. The guy glowered over these licenses as though he mistrusted the State of New York, which had issued them, and then turned everything over to somebody else. That is, he turned the licenses over to one guy to "check" and Kelp and Murch over to a number of other guys to "hold on to."

Which meant being placed in the backseats of two vehicles laughably known to the trade as "unmarked" cars. (Tip: If you see an American car, a few years old, pale gray or pale blue or medium tan, kind of beat-up-looking, with no whitewall stripe on the tires and no styling package on the body, containing two beefy guys in the front seat who keep looking left and right as they travel, that is an *unmarked car*, and those are police—federal, state, or local. A CrimeStarter.®)

Being placed in separate cars meant that Kelp and Murch couldn't get together and plan their strategy or their testimony or any of that, but it didn't matter. They were both professionals and they both knew the code of the underworld, which is: Never sell out your partner until you get your price.

After a while, both Kelp and Murch individually got chummy young cops in the front seats of their cars, to chat with them about the weather and sports, offer cigarettes, and kind of lead the conversation this way and that. Both Kelp and Murch knew how to be friendly and easygoing and give them not a damn thing they could use, and after a while both chummy cops gave up, and law enforcement went into Phase Two of the overall strategy, known as "let em think it over for a while."

About an hour, actually. During that time, the detainees in the backseats of the unmarked cars got to watch many conferences among the troops in dark blue plastic; got to watch a big truck back (beep beep beep beep) onto the pier and hoist the little motorboat out of the water and drive it away; got to watch the city police cars arrive and the city police walk around being sure they were a part of the joint operation; got to watch an older guy in a suit (he would have been cast black in the movie) come around and glare through their side windows at them but not speak to them; and then got their own interrogators.

These were older men, but in the blue plastic zip-up jackets, as though they were coaches of Little Police League teams. They got into the front seats of the cars, grunting because they were just a tiny bit overweight. They rested one arm on the seat-back, leaned against the passenger door, nodded at Kelp and Murch, and said, "This shouldn't take long, and you'll be on your way. How long you known Pepper?"

"I don't know him," Kelp said, "my pal Stan knows him."

"He's my wife's cousin," Murch said. "I hardly know him at all."

"But you're in his boat," the interrogators said.

"It was a nice day," Kelp and Murch both responded, but then their answers veered. Murch explained he knew his wife's cousin had a little boat, and he'd asked could he make a borrow and Pepper said sure. And Kelp said his pal Stan had told him he was borrowing for the first time this other guy Pepper's boat and would Kelp like to go along and Kelp said sure.

It went on like that. They didn't know anything, they hadn't done anything, and they were more than happy to be of any assistance they could, which was none. And would they object to a frisk? Certainly not.

All of this was so neatly choreographed that Kelp and Murch emerged from their unmarked cars within a minute of one another, assumed the lean-forward, legs-spread position against the unmarked cars, got frisked, and were found clean. Just like that. Simple.

At that point, the two watermen were permitted back in each other's presence, while one of the interrogators—Murch's—joined them to say, "It could be we'll want to talk to you fellas again, but at this point you're free to go."

And he himself at that point would have gone, except Murch said, "Excuse me. If you don't mind, my wife's gonna want to know what this is all about, that it's her cousin and all. Is there anything I can tell her?"

"Well," the interrogator said, "we're DEA, and your wife's cousin is now in custody, and the boat has been impounded. What do *you* think is going on?"

"It's beginning to look," Murch said, "as though Pepper was using that boat to move illegal drugs from one place to another."

"Very good," the interrogator said. Then he thawed a little and leaned close to speak a bit more confidentially. "Just between us, Pepper's claiming he doesn't even know you guys. He's claiming you stole his boat."

"Why, that nasty person," Murch said. "Wait'll I tell my wife."

"What he's claiming," the interrogator said, "is that he never did any dope smuggling or dope dealing at all, it was always you two guys stealing his boat."

Kelp looked astounded. "Can you believe there are people like that?" he demanded.

"Yes, I can," the interrogator answered. "Fortunately, we've got the goods on Pepper; we've got videotape; we've got witnesses; we've got him cold. Otherwise, I'll be honest with you, you two guys could maybe of had a couple bad weeks."

Murch and Kelp looked at one another. "Just for a boat ride," Murch said.

"Go know," Kelp said. "Go figure."

"Here's a tip for you," the interrogator said. "Your wife's cousin isn't necessarily your friend."

"I'll remember that," Murch said.

"He isn't even my wife's cousin," Kelp said.

"You're free to go," the interrogator said, and turned away.

Kelp said, "Uh."

The interrogator turned back. "You want to be driven someplace?"

"No, no, that's okay. It's only—I left some personal property in that boat."

The interrogator looked troubled. "I'm sorry to hear that," he said. "You should have taken your property with you when you debarked."

"Well, it was all kind of nervous and exciting," Kelp explained.

"I suppose so." The interrogator thought it over. "What you'll have to do," he said, "you'll have to come down to our offices in the Federal Building, fill out a form, describe the articles that are yours. Because that boat and everything in it has been impounded."

"Well, if I could just go get the stuff," Kelp said, imagining himself writing the word *bone* on a form down at the Federal Building.

"Sorry," the interrogator said. "It's impounded."

"Where?"

"Impounded."

"No, I mean *where* is it impounded?"

The interrogator gave Kelp a less friendly look. "You just go on down to the Federal Building," he said coolly. "They'll fix you up."

I'll just bet they will, Kelp thought. "Thanks," he said, with a nice smile, and the interrogator stalked off, and Kelp and Murch slunk on around the onetime mailbox factory and down the block and into the stolen car and drove away from there.

15

When Dortmunder woke up, he was in a dungeon. His bruised eye hurt, his head hurt, his stomach hurt, his shoulderblades hurt, his . . . Well. He hurt.

Recent history passed before his eyes like an atrocity reenactment on television. Diversion, delay, capture. Interrogation by Hradec Kralowc. "Time for Dr. Zorn."

When Kralowc had said that, Dortmunder had really started to worry. Thoughts of truth serum flashed through his mind. How would his system react to truth serum? Wouldn't it be like an antibody inside him? Would his vital parts survive such an invasion?

Was there a story he could tell? Was there any gloss on events, any spin-doctoring he could do before the real doctor got here? He cast his aching mind back over recent events, and was appalled at the sight.

Something had delayed Kelp—that much was clear—so that he hadn't been in position when he should have been in position. If ever Dortmunder managed to get his hands on Kelp—that is, if he ever in the future found himself in a position to have an opportunity for a quiet chat with Kelp, it would turn out not to be

93

Kelp's fault, and yet, as Dortmunder already knew without a doubt, at some deeper level, at some more totally true level (far below the level truth serum could possibly reach), *it was Kelp's fault!*

Why do I do it? Dortmunder asked himself, not for the first time. Why do I associate with bad companions, by which I do mean Andrew Octavian Kelp? But answer came there none.

It was too late to claim mistaken identity. Seated there in Kralowc's office on the *Pride of Votskojek*, handcuffed to a chair, Dortmunder studied again that moment when he'd been lying supine on the ferry slip as the bone-wielding Kelp shouted, "*Run*, John!" Followed—*click-click*, the slide show—by that moment when he'd been somehow on his feet, everyone intensely aware of his existence, and Kelp whispering, "You weren't blown?"

Oh, is there no story to cover this? Let's see:

"I'm an undercover CIA agent, infiltrating the Tsergovian secret police, and . . ."

"I had amnesia! Wait a minute, my past life is coming back to me! The year is 1977, and I live in Roslyn, Long Island, with my dear wife, Andreotta, and our two charming children, uh . . ."

"FBI! You're all under arrest!"

"Thank God you understood those signals I was sending. Those bloodthirsty fiends kidnapped my mother and forced me to help them in their evil . . ."

"My left leg is artificial, and filled with dynamite. If you don't release me at the count . . ."

"Whu— Where am I? Who are all you people?"

That last one was almost worth a try. Dortmunder was still trying to work out exactly the facial expression that went with it— and where this particular ploy might likely lead—when Dr. Zorn entered the office.

No question. You could see this person anywhere, the supermarket even, and you'd say, "That's Dr. Zorn." And not just because of the floppy black leather doctor's bag with stainless-steel locks that he carried in his big white thick-knuckled, hairy-backed, scrubbed fist, either.

The strangest thing about him was, he didn't look old. Or parts of him didn't. He was tall and slender, with a lithe and youthful body like a long-distance runner, but on top of that body was the absolute Dr. Zorn head: round, bald, without eyebrows, gleaming, with jug-handle ears, like an old chamber pot. The manically glittering eyes shone from the bottoms of deep crystal-cave eyeglasses, eyeglasses with hypnotic spirals etched in the lenses, eyeglasses with clear plastic frames hooked over the big pale ears, so there was no color at all above Dr. Zorn's neck except for those eyes deep inside the eyeglass lenses, which were: red.

Was Dr. Zorn twenty-five, or sixty-five? Was he really an old guy, a successful mad scientist who'd managed to graft his own head onto a young and virile body? *That* would have been some operation to watch.

Dr. Zorn and Hradec Kralowc proceeded to engage in a conversation together in some language that sounded mostly like crickets in armor jousting, in which Kralowc made detailed explanations of something or other while pointing at Dortmunder, and Dr. Zorn cackled maniacally a lot while looking at Dortmunder. None of this was reassuring.

Nor was the lethal-looking hypodermic syringe when it made its inevitable appearance from Dr. Zorn's black bag. "I'm allergic!" Dortmunder cried out at the sight of the thing.

Kralowc and Dr. Zorn stared at him. Even Lusk and Terment gazed in his direction. Dr. Zorn spoke in English for the first time, a rubbery, feltish kind of English, best suited to obscene phone calls: "You are allergic? To what?"

"Truth serum!"

Dr. Zorn gave him the simpering, condescending chuckle of the scientist for the layman. "This is not truth serum, you pathetic creature," he said. "Truth serum does not work." His smile turned toward Kralowc, becoming conspiratorial. "We have learned that, have we not?"

Kralowc shrugged, uncomfortable and nervous. "Let's just get on with it."

"But of course." Turning back to Dortmunder, Dr. Zorn said, "Someone roll up his sleeve."

Lusk and Terment both dashed forward to do it, the four hands like spiders on Dortmunder's arm, getting in each other's way, delaying the process, but not, unfortunately, forever.

And while it was going on, Dr. Zorn smiled his smile again at

Dortmunder and said, "Some powerful personalities can override the impetus of either amobarbital or thiopental, the so-called truth serums. While you probably do not have a powerful personality—just a first impression, of course—the results of such things are too likely to be unreliable."

"And we don't have a lot of time," Kralowc said, cracking his knuckles.

Dr. Zorn pointed the needle upward and did that little pumping thing that gets out the deadly air bubbles and puts a tiny, beautiful, brief spray of serum into the light. Then he cupped one hand around Dortmunder's arm and approached it with the needle. "Hold still."

"Then what is it?" Dortmunder asked, trying and failing to hold still.

"It will render you unconscious," Dr. Zorn told him, "and therefore malleable for the flight."

"Flight? Where am I going?"

"Why, to Votskojek, of course," said Dr. Zorn. "Isn't that where you wanted to go?" And he smiled and jabbed with the needle.

"But—" Dortmunder said, and woke up in a dungeon. On a rough wool blanket on the cold concrete floor of a low, nasty, dim room with stone walls and the combined smells of hay and mildew. One small window, a rectangular opening in the deep stone wall, was covered on the outside by a thick metal mesh screen; that was the only source of light. Peering through that window, Dortmunder could see a bit of dirt ground under what was apparently a cloudy sky, and across the way another stone wall. Nothing else.

A dungeon. In Votskojek.

How do I get out of this? Dortmunder asked himself, and as he did so a soldier went by out there, a sentinel on duty, wearing a bulky uniform of a particularly decayed-looking grayish blue, plus mean-looking black boots. And a submachine gun on a leather strap over his shoulder.

Dortmunder flinched away from the window at the sight of that guy, and when he dared to look again the soldier was gone. But wafting in the window, on the coolish air (colder than New York, he noticed), from far away, thin, attenuated, barely audible but unmistakable, came the sound of a human scream.

DON'T ASK

Oh, boy, Dortmunder thought. He looked around his dungeon and there was no furniture at all except that insultingly thin rough brown blanket on the floor on which he'd awakened. So he slid down the wall beneath the window, sat on the cold floor, rested his back against the hard stone wall, and thought it again: Oh, boy.

There's no way out of here, out of this dungeon in this prison or whatever it is. And if there was a way out, what then? I'd be in Votskojek, *that's* what then, without a draff to my name. No useful ID, no sensible story to tell, and no language to tell it in.

Maybe I could trade them the bone for letting me go, he thought, and even as he thought it he also thought, That's what they want me to think. Okay, fine, that's what they want me to think, and I'm thinking it. Maybe I could trade them the bone for letting me go. Because what else do I do?

But wait a second. If that's what they *want* me to think, what is it they *don't* want me to think?

Well, they don't want me to think there's any way out of here. So that's one for their side, then. I *don't* think there's any way out of here.

I hope the guys are taking good care of that bone.

16

Tiny said, "You lost it?"

"And Dortmunder, too," Kelp pointed out. "We also lost Dortmunder."

"I don't give a fat rat's ass about Dortmunder," Tiny explained. "Dortmunder ain't gonna get nobody into the UN."

"Unless he breaks in," Murch commented.

"So let him break out," Tiny suggested, "from wherever he is. The question is, What about the fucking femur of Saint Ferghana?"

"The feds filched it," Kelp said, and Grijk Krugnk, seated over there in what was normally J.C.'s chair but she was still out of town, moaned low.

This was supposed to have been the triumphant meeting, the celebration, the victory party. There were Tiny and Grijk at Tiny's place, waiting, expectant, eager for the whole experience to be over and done with and accomplished and *successful*, and here came Kelp and Murch with bad news.

Which neither Tiny nor Grijk was taking at all well. Tiny was becoming more aggressive and hostile and generally dangerous by the minute, but Grijk had undergone some sort of collapse;

perhaps the crash from his high hopes had given him the bends. Anyway, he merely slumped over there in that morris chair like melting ice cream, and from time to time he moaned, and from time to time he muttered what might very well have been imprecations, in Magyar-Croat. They sure sounded like imprecations.

Tiny said, "We gotta get it back."

"I thought you'd feel that way," Kelp admitted.

Murch said, "They impounded it, Tiny. The DEA. You don't get a thing back when the DEA impounds it. Everything they impound, they use later on in their task forces."

Tiny gave him a look. "How are the narcs gonna use a *bone* in a task force?"

"Maybe they feed it to their drug-sniffer dogs," Murch suggested, which wasn't a very tactful thing to say in the presence of Grijk Krugnk, who made that clear by leaping to his feet and bellowing out several short sharp statements in Magyar-Croat.

Tiny nodded. He didn't speak Magyar-Croat, but he understood the general idea behind Grijk's distress. "We can't lose that bone," he said. "It's a relic; it's a sacred Catholic relic and a important historical whatchathing."

"Artifact?" Kelp suggested.

"That's it," Tiny agreed. "One side or the other, they got it, they fight over it, that's one thing, but at least they know it's still somewhere on display, it *exists*. But if it disappears—"

Grijk groaned.

"If it's destroyed—"

Grijk groaned louder.

"If it isn't around anymore," Tiny shouted over Grijk's whale music, "if *nobody's* got it, there's gonna be blood in the streets. These people will kill each other to the last baby, believe me they will. There's things that these people got no sense of humor. I mean, look at Grijk for yourself."

They did. They nodded. They saw what Tiny meant.

Tiny spread big hands. "I'm telling you two guys," he said, "and I'm telling you now. You went out to get that bone. You're gonna come back with it. Or you're gonna answer to me."

"I thought you'd feel that way," Kelp said again.

Tiny glowered. "So you thought I'd feel that way, did you? So what are you doing *here*?"

"Well, these things take time," Kelp said.

Tiny lowered an eyebrow at him. "What things take time?"

"Well," Kelp explained, "the first question is, When the DEA impounds something, what do they do with it? Where do they put it? The guy at the place wouldn't tell me, so I gotta ask another guy, so I called him, and we're gonna do lunch."

Tiny lowered the other eyebrow. Now he looked like an angry shag rug. "You're gonna *do* lunch? What is this guy, in the movie business?"

"No," Kelp said. "As a matter of fact, he's a cop."

17

When May got back to the apartment early that evening from her cashier job at the Safeway, carrying the bag of groceries that she thought of as a fringe benefit the company just hadn't happened to think of offering on their own, John wasn't yet home. She knew he and Andy Kelp and Tiny Bulcher and Stan Murch had gone off to retrieve something or other for a friend of Tiny's today, and such retrievals sometimes took a little longer than expected, so she didn't worry overly but merely planned a dinner menu that would make maximum use of the new microwave once John did walk in. A tall, thin woman with slightly graying black hair, who still had many of the twitchy mannerisms of smoking even though she'd given up the filthy habit some time ago, she carried her fringe benefits to the kitchen, put them away, opened a beer for herself, put on her after-work gray cardigan, and went to the living room to relax and watch TV until John got home.

Also to look at the mail, which was mostly magazines—May subscribed to *everything*—but which today also included a long, chatty letter from her sister, that she couldn't stand, in Cleveland. Thank God she was in Cleveland.

May was just finishing this letter—tonsillectomy, pregnancy, and second-prize essay award were prominently featured—when the phone at her elbow rang and she picked it up. "Hello?"

"Hi, May." It was Andy Kelp, sounding as chipper as ever, but with maybe a bit of an unfamiliar edge in his voice. "John there?"

May knew. Don't ask how she knew, she just knew, that's all. The literature is full of such instances, anybody can tell you. She knew. She didn't know exactly *what* she knew, but she knew. Something in Andy's voice maybe. "No, he isn't," she said. "Why? Should he be?"

"Well, May," Andy said, "maybe I better come over," and before May could point out that that was no way to leave the conversation, he'd hung up.

Twenty minutes later, the doorbell rang. Not the outside bell by the street door, the upstairs bell by the apartment door. Could this be Andy? Usually, Andy just picked the lock and walked on in. If this was Andy, and he was standing on ceremony enough to ring the doorbell, having only picked his way in through the street door downstairs, this was anything but a good sign.

May left the living room and went down the hall to open the door, and indeed it was Andy, with a worried smile on his face. Even worried, he was smiling, but nevertheless he was worried. "Come on in, Andy," she said. "What are you worried about?"

"Well, I wouldn't say I was *worried*," Andy said, brow furrowing. "You been watching the news at all?"

May shut the apartment door and they walked together to the living room as she said, "Why? What's on it?"

"Nothing, I think." They entered the living room and he gestured at the set, saying, "Okay?"

"Sure."

Switching it on, looking for the evening news, he said, "There was nothing on the radio news, anyway, in the cab, but radio news is all sports, so who knows?"

Here was the local evening news, well under way. They both studied the newsreader, a blond lady who seemed delighted to report the deaths of four infants in a tenement fire, then switched them over to a blackhaired, stocky, blunt-featured guy who gripped actual paper notes in his fist and told you the news like he'd much

102

rather punch you in the mouth. "That's Tony Costello," Andy announced, "their police and crime reporter. Let's see."

Tony Costello announced that again today federal and state law-enforcement officers in a joint operation had impounded the largest haul of illegal drugs in history, umpteen zillion dollars' worth of this and that, all found in an apparently undistinguished house in the middle of Long Island. Some fat people who lived down the block were asked what they thought of this; most thought they didn't know what they thought, is what it came down to. And back to the blond lady, this time brimming with the happy news of a midair collision.

Andy said, "Is this one of the ones that does the recaps?"

"I think," May said uncertainly, "this is one of the ones that does coming-next."

Andy shook his head. "I went by the mission," he said, "and there wasn't nothing, no police cars, nothing. In fact, it looked kind of closed up. I phoned their number, and they got their answering machine on, in some foreign language. Can you imagine? A whole country's mission, and not only they got their answering machine on, it's a foreign language."

"Andy," May said, switching off the TV right in the middle of ethnic violence, "if you don't settle down and tell me what's going on, you're going to drive me back to cigarettes."

"Oh. Sorry. Sit down, I— Listen, could I have a beer first?"

"Yes," May said, long-suffering. "And get me another. You know where it is."

He knew. He went and came back, and they sat in the living room together and he said, "Tiny's got this foreign cousin, and to help him out we lifted this special thing from another country's mission, that's got offices on this boat on the East Side. We got the thing, at least for a while, but John got stuck getting away from the boat. I figured, we'll find out where the cops have him, maybe bust him out, something, I don't know. But there's no cops around, the mission all shut down, nothing on the news; it's like they didn't even report the theft. So, I'm sorry, May, I hate to be the one that brings the bad news, but the thing is, we don't know where John is, right now, this minute."

May's left hand clawed in her cardigan pocket for nonexistent cigarettes. She said, "You don't know if he's dead or alive?"

"May," Andy said, "when I last saw him, these private guards had their hands on him. He was alive and standing up, and he wasn't resisting or being hit or anything like that, and for *sure* they'd want him to tell where we were going with the special thing. So he's alive, we know that much. We just don't know *where* he's alive."

Where there's life, in fact, there is hope. May nodded, feeling somewhat reassured. Her hand stopped stretching the cardigan pocket all out of shape. She said, "This special thing you took. What is it?"

Andy drank beer. He sighed. "To tell you the truth, May," he said, "I was hoping you wouldn't ask that question."

18

Diary of a Prisoner—Day One

No food, no contact with anyone. Just as darkness was falling, there was suddenly and startlingly switched on a bright fluorescent light inset in the plank ceiling and protected by a heavy iron grating. It shone whitely on the floor in the center of the room, leaving a periphery in the semidarkness, full of shadows, all of which looked like rats.

Then nothing else happened for a fairly long period of time—the prisoner had no watch—until all at once a great clanking of chains and rattling of giant keys roused him from a groggy half doze and the big old wooden dungeon door creaked open, and four men entered. Two were skinny, unshaven, scared-looking people in dirty white shirts, barefoot; they carried a heavy square wooden table with a bowl and a mug on it. The other two were soldiers in bile-blue uniforms, submachine guns in their hands.

The soldiers shouted barkinglike orders at the men in white, who put the table down near the door and backed away to the stone wall, keeping their eyes downcast all the time. Then the soldiers shouted a lot of stuff at the prisoner, who'd through all

105

this remained seated on the floor against the wall under the lone window, thinking thoughts as dark as the view outside. The shouting, helped quite a bit by a lot of mean, threatening gestures with the submachine guns, communicated even without a common language the idea that the prisoner was to stand, which he did; was to come over to the table and be quick about it, which he did; and was to eat. "No chair?" asked the prisoner.

They either didn't understand or considered the question too effete to be worthy of an answer. In any event, they simply kept pointing their gun barrels at the bowl—better than at the prisoner—and kept shouting the same short, sharp sentences over and over.

The prisoner looked at his dinner. The bowl contained a thick green sludge, the mug a clear liquid. To the left of the bowl was a torn-off chunk of dark bread, and to its right a large metal spoon. The prisoner considered his options—considered his option. He picked up the spoon, dipped out some of the green sludge, lifted it, lowered it, poured some back in the bowl, lifted it again, scrunched up his face like a little kid taking medicine, and inserted the spoon into mouth.

And smiled. Smiled around the spoon. Removed spoon from mouth, and went on smiling. "Tastes like curry," he told the soldiers.

The soldiers laughed coarsely and jabbed one another in the sides with their elbows and made raucous comments.

Better to go on thinking of it as curry. The prisoner ate some more, tried the bread and found it fresh and tasty, tried the contents of the mug and found it water; not very cold and also kind of metallic-tasting, like it had been in a pipe somewhere too long, but water.

The prisoner was really very hungry. He had no idea how long he'd been a prisoner, how long he'd been unconscious—plenty long, to permit a plane trip all the way from New York City to this terrible place—but this was the first food he'd tasted since lunch at home before boarding the *Pride of Votskojek,* an embarkation he had come to regret, and he was hungry. He ate it all. He even licked the back of the spoon, then put it down and used his finger to scrape the rest of the curry-tasting sludge off the inner sides of the bowl. Then, quite naturally, he said to the soldiers, "I have to go to the bathroom."

106

DON'T ASK

They didn't understand. They had apparently not one word of English, nor had the men in white—fellow prisoners, they must be—so the prisoner was forced to resort to uncouth gestures, the most universal of universal languages. The soldiers laughed in that heartily nasty way of theirs, then prodded the prisoner back to the center of the room and pointed to a small round hole in the floor there.

"That?" said the prisoner. "You gotta be kidding."

These people didn't kid. These people didn't know anything about kid. They just did a little more of their hearty obscene laughter, then suddenly turned mean and impatient as they barked a whole lot of fresh orders at the men in white, who scuttled forward, still keeping their eyes down, picked up the table, and lugged it back out of there. The two soldiers swaggered after them, both pausing deliberately to fart into the prisoner's airspace, then exited, slamming the door and creating another great hubbub with chains and locks.

Silence. The prisoner gloomily hunched over the little hole in the floor. He thought, How do I get outta here? He looked up at the light and thought, I bet they don't turn that off. He rolled himself in the thin, rough wool blanket on the floor and thought, I'd tell them everything I know, if there was anybody around who talked English.

And thus ended day one.

19

Andy Kelp was a gregarious fellow. He got along with all kinds, even people in the NYPD. Not *all* the people in the NYPD, of course. Not even a *lot* of people in the NYPD. Well, one guy in the NYPD, actually; but that was plenty.

The first time Kelp called the precinct and asked for Bernard Klematsky, the voice said, "Not on duty," but the second time the voice said, "Hold on," and then the voice was Bernard himself, saying very officially, "Klematsky."

"Hi, Bernard," Kelp said. "It's me, Andy Kelp."

"Well, hello, Andy. I was just thinking about you."

"That wasn't me," Kelp said promptly. "I've been clean."

"Want to come on down? I got something you could sign."

"Maybe not right now," Kelp said. "I thought, though, maybe I could buy you a drink when you get off."

"You want something," Bernard guessed.

"Of course I want something," Kelp said. "Everybody *wants* something."

"And I want dinner," Bernard said. "When I get off the job, I always want dinner."

"Italian, right? Spaghettini with clam sauce."

"Very tempting," Bernard said, "but I discovered a new cuisine recently that I like a lot."

"Expensive cuisine, Bernard?"

"Nah," Bernard said. "Nothing Asian is expensive, am I right?"

"Oh, you mean Chinese."

"No," Bernard said. "Tie."

"We're keeping score?"

"Thailand," Bernard explained. "Food from Thailand. You know what's great about food from Thailand?"

"No."

"They put peanut butter on everything."

"That's what's great about it?"

"You just wait. Toon's, on Bleecker Street. Ten-thirty?"

"I'll be there," Kelp said, and was, in a smallish dark restaurant that smelled better than a place that would put peanut butter on everything. Bernard, of course, was late.

But here he came, at last, at 10:45, grinning and rubbing hands together and saying, "Always nice to see you, Andy."

"You, too, Bernard."

Bernard Klematsky was an absolute average guy, mid-thirties, with bushy black hair, a long and fleshy nose, a rumpled gray suit and rumpled blue necktie, and no cop look to him at all. In fact, your first guess would be: math teacher, high school. Easy marker.

Sitting across the little table from Kelp, not seeming to mind his back to the window, Bernard said, "Drinking beer, I see."

"You want?"

"I'm strictly a white wine man now," Bernard said, and whupped his own stomach with his palm, making a hollow *gong* sound like a temple bell; appropriate to the surroundings. "Gotta watch my weight. Too much time on the desk."

"So you want a glass of white wine," Kelp hoped.

"I thought a bottle," Bernard said. "We could share it. Or you don't have to drink any if you don't want."

"Thank you, Bernard," Kelp said.

The waiter came by then, looking alert. He was so thoroughly Asian that he was as tall standing up as they were sitting down, which made it easy to converse with him. Bernard said, "Well, Andy, you had time to look at the menu?"

"Plenty of time," Kelp said, which Bernard ignored. "Not everything has peanut butter on it," he said, "that I can see."

"So you pick the stuff that does," Bernard said, and did just that, ordering his dinner without even glancing at the menu.

Kelp ordered things that didn't mention peanut butter, and Bernard said, "You don't know what's good."

"That's okay."

"Oh, and a bottle of the Pinot Grigio," Bernard said before the waiter could get away.

Kelp said, "You own a piece of this place?"

"Maybe I should, huh?"

Kelp sipped beer, gathering his thoughts. Bernard smiled on him and said, "Well, Andy, you're looking pretty good. Clean living, huh?"

"You know it."

"The last time we talked like this," Bernard said, "you wanted some information about a guy. Remember that?"

"Leo Zane," Kelp said, nodding.

"A very bad customer," Bernard said. "Not your kind of guy at all. A hit man, wasn't he? And some cousin of yours got on his wrong side."

"That's right," Kelp said, and blinked.

Bernard grinned at him. "You still do that thing, Andy," he said. "You blink when you're lying."

"Everybody blinks," Kelp said, not blinking.

"Sure. Anyway, you promised me nothing violent would happen to Zane if I could find him for you, and a few months later, you know what?"

"No, what?"

"Zane was arrested," Bernard said, "in Scotland of all places."

"Oh, was he?" Kelp said, blinking.

"You wouldn't know anything about that."

"Of course not." Blink-blink-blink-blink.

"But the funny part," Bernard said, "he was arrested for burglary, resisting arrest, leaving the scene of an accident, and a few other things, *none* of them crimes that fit his MO."

"Huh," said Kelp, holding his eyelids up by an effort of will.

"He's still doing time over there," Bernard said, and grinned again, shaking his head. "That cousin of yours must be something."

"Oh, he is, he is," Kelp said, and rubbed his forehead with a band that partially screened his eyes.

The waiter came back with the wine then, giving Kelp's eyes a rest. Bernard went through the tasting ritual, found the wine acceptable, and said, "Andy? You want some?"

"Oh, I might as well," Kelp said, since after all he was paying for it. He finished his beer and the waiter filled his wineglass and went away.

"So," Bernard said. "Is this another problem with your cousin?"

"As a matter of fact," Kelp said, hiding his blinking by holding the wineglass up to the light, "that's just what it is. What he did this time, he went for a ride in a guy's boat. A little outboard motorboat. And he left his reading glasses in the boat."

"Relax, Andy," Bernard said. "You're right, everybody blinks."

Grateful, Kelp put the glass down, blinked fiercely at Bernard, and said, "After he was in it, the DEA impounded the boat. Now, my cousin has nothing to do with drugs, okay?" Not blinking at all, he said, "What I'm asking you about has nothing to do with drugs."

"Good," Bernard said.

"Only what it is," Kelp said, "my cousin's afraid to go to the DEA and ask for his reading glasses back, because maybe they'll think he *does* have something to do with drugs, being he was in that boat that one time. So he just wants to go over and get his glasses back, so he can read the *Racing Form* again, and that's the end of it."

"Okay," said Bernard.

"The problem is," Kelp explained as a smell of peanut butter wafted over him, "he doesn't know where the DEA keeps impounded boats." And the waiter put down a lot of plates in front of them, all covered with mysterious foods. Delicious aromas came from the plates in front of Kelp. So much peanut butter smell drifted over from Bernard's side of the table that you automatically looked around for the jelly.

"Let's eat for a while," Bernard said, "then we can talk."

"Sure, Bernard."

So they ate for a while. Kelp recognized chicken and shrimp and some vegetables and a couple other things, but he didn't recognize anything that had been done to them. It was good stuff, and it was absolutely free of peanut butter.

"Ah," Bernard said, smacking his stomach again, which now made a padded *whum* kind of sound. "A little brandy on top, and it's good to be alive." And he waggled his hand over his head, looking past Kelp's shoulder. Which is why he hadn't minded sitting with his back to the window; it put his front to the waiter.

Who was here again, at Kelp's elbow, looking as content as Bernard, "After-dinner drink?"

"Some of that nice Hennessy you have back there," Bernard suggested, and raised an eyebrow at Kelp, "Andy?"

"No, thanks," Kelp said. "I'm watching my weight."

"More clean living," Bernard said, and grinned as the waiter went away, carrying their emptied plates. Bernard then rested his forearms on the glass tabletop where his food used to be, nodded thoughtfully at Kelp, and said, "Your cousin—let's say your cousin—your cousin left something in a boat the DEA impounded."

"His reading glasses."

"Let's not worry about details," Bernard said. "It's something, and it's in a boat, and the DEA impounded the boat, which means the boat was involved in the drug trade, but your cousin is *not* involved in the drug trade. Oh, don't worry, I believe that part. We're just doing the parts I believe."

"You're a hard man, Bernard," Kelp said.

"Oh, not really," Bernard said, comfortable in his persona. "Anyway, this something in the boat is not something that would let your cousin just go over to the DEA and say, 'Excuse me, I left my reading glasses in that boat over there, can I have them back, please.' So—"

"Because my cousin," Kelp said patiently, "doesn't want the DEA to think he's connected with that boat."

"Sure. Fine. So your cousin wants to know where the DEA's got the boat right now. This happened—what? Yesterday sometime, that's when you first called."

"Uh-huh."

"So your cousin," Bernard said, "plans to go over a fence or through a locked door or under a wall or whatever it takes to get those special reading glasses of his. In other words, Andy, you are asking me to point my finger at where the burglary should take place. Is that nice?"

"Oh, no," Kelp said, blinking hard enough to blow out candles, "nobody's gonna commit any burglary."

"You've been known to do some of that sort of thing yourself," Bernard pointed out.

"That's before I got on to clean living," Kelp said. "What my cousin figures, there'll be like some sort of property clerk or something, he could maybe slip him a bribe, I don't know, maybe give him dinner, a bottle of wine—"

The waiter brought the brandy, set it before Bernard, went away again.

"—a glass of brandy," Kelp went on, "something like that, just to go get those reading glasses and see for himself they don't have anything to do with drugs or crimes like that at all, and hand them to him. See what I mean?"

Bernard nodded, thinking things over. "I couldn't help watching your eyes, Andy," he said. "I apologize. I know it's unfair, but I couldn't help it, and that there you just told me was such a crazy mix-up of lies and truth, I don't know *where* the heck I am."

"Oh, Bernard. Come on, will ya?"

"Andy," Bernard said, "there's a fine line we walk, you and me, and you know it."

"I do."

"I will not aid or abet a felony, Andy, and you know better than to ask me. I *hope* you know better."

"Okay, Bernard," Kelp said, and his eyes stopped blinking. He said, "What my cousin wants to get is property that he feels he's got a claim to, that the DEA doesn't even know it has, that has nothing to do with their case or anything like it, but that could maybe cause complications in my cousin's life if he doesn't get it back quickly. It was a dumb slipup that the reading glasses got in that boat in the first place. Now if it does turn out, and I'm not saying it will or it won't, but if it does turn out that my cousin has to maybe sneak in somewhere and take something on the sly and sneak back out again, he is *not* going to be taking anything except what he left in the boat, that's his anyway. Is that a crime? I know, I know, technically it is a crime, because technically everything is a crime, but is it a *crime*?"

Bernard thought that one over for a *long* time, and finally he said, "I'll see what I can do to help you on this one, Andy."

"Thank you."

"I'll do it because I more or less believe whatever it was you said the last time, but I'll do it only on one provision."

"If I can, I will," Kelp promised.

"Someday," Bernard said, "when the statute of limitations runs out, you'll tell me the whole story on this thing."

"Done," said Kelp.

"Okay. The DEA impounded this boat in the five boroughs?"

"Well, on water."

"But the water's in the five boroughs. It's New York City water."

"Oh, sure."

"Okay. I'll make a phone call." Bernard got to his feet.

"You want anything else?"

"That's very thoughtful of you, Andy," Bernard said, "but I think maybe not. I don't want to break you, and drive you back off that clean living."

Bernard went away to make his phone call, and Kelp signaled for and paid the check, which wasn't as bad as he'd feared nor as good as he'd hoped. Then Bernard came back and sat down and said, "Governor's Island."

"That's out in the harbor someplace," Kelp guessed.

"There's a Coast Guard station out there," Bernard told him. "That's where the federals have their marina, and that's where the impounded boat would go, until it's sold or some federal agency takes it over for their own use."

"Uh-huh," Kelp said, deadpan.

Bernard grinned at him, but not without sympathy. "I know what you're thinking, Andy," he said. "The Coast Guard, an armed force of the United States. A fortified island in the middle of New York Bay. You're thinking maybe your cousin oughta go buy another pair of reading glasses."

20

When Tiny walked into the storefront Tsergovian embassy the next morning at 10:30, Khodeen, the receptionist, was listening to a Walkman, turning the pages of a comic book about a black woman astronaut saving a rain forest, and sipping through a straw something white, sweet, dead, and wet from a nearby junk-food store. All of this activity left her no opportunity to acknowledge Tiny's presence, so he just walked on by, back to where Grijk Krugnk slumped pathetically at his desk, as mournful as an unfed basset hound.

This air of gloom was pervasive, in fact, except for the infidel Khodeen. Drava Votskonia, the commercial attaché at the other desk, sat in a cloud of misery, dabbing at her eyes, not even trying to sell anybody Tsergovian rocks.

Grijk Krugnk, too, still suffered from the recent unhappy turn taken by events, but at least he was no longer doing foghorn imitations. He roused himself when he saw Tiny approach, and with a hopeless look in his eye he said, "You god id back?"

"We know where it is," Tiny said. "We *think* we know where it is. If they didn't toss it and toss it, we know where it is."

Grijk's despair became mixed with perplexity: "If dey didn'd vad and vad?"

"Toss it and toss it," Tiny repeated. "Toss the boat, see."

"Toss da boad?"

"That means to search it."

"Id does?"

"Sure. And if they did, and they found the femur, maybe they didn't know what it is, so they tossed it."

"Search da femur? How do you search a femur?"

"No, no," Tiny said. Funny how foreigners couldn't dope out the simplest thing in English. "Toss it like throw it away."

Grijk groaned. "Id vas bedder," he said, "ven I didn'd unnerstand." With a sigh like a paddle wheeler venting, he rose to his feet. "Zara Kotor vands do dalk do you."

"I guess I owe her that," Tiny acknowledged. "But don't leave me alone with her." Then, at Grijk's look of incomprehension—a favorite look of his—Tiny said, "Never mind, just do it."

"Okay, Diny."

Grijk led the way through the door at the rear of the shop area to the office in back, which today was empty. He then crossed to a door in the side wall and opened that, saying, "Vad ve also god is d'apartmend upstairs."

"That's handy," Tiny said.

"And a nize prize, doo."

This door led to a narrow, steep staircase. They went up it, and at the top was a long, narrow hall. Tiny followed Grijk toward the front of the building, where he knocked on a door, and at a bark from within opened it. He and Tiny went inside.

This was a Tsergovian living room of the upper-middle class, transported intact to this heathen land. Heavy dark wood predominated, slathered with mohair. A narrow shelf at waist height all around the room displayed commemorative plates, many of them cracked or broken, repaired with glue that had yellowed over time. All lamps had pink or amber shades, dripping with balls and tassels. The windows were covered with dark brocade drapes. On the floor were carpets on carpets. Huge, ornate gilded frames on the walls presented small, dark night scenes behind dirty glass, but at least hid some of the flocked maroon wallpaper. If bears had a designer cave for hibernation, it would look like this.

Standing in the middle of all this ursine splendor was Zara Kotor, in the same uniform as the first time they'd met, but with some sort of ineffable difference about her, which at first Tiny couldn't figure out. Then he got it; a halo of perfume surrounded Zara Kotor, like a sprinkling of rose dust in the air. Uh-oh.

On the other hand, her facial expression was in the form of a rebuttal to that hint of scent. She was looking as stern as that hibernating bear itself, disturbed in January. "I have a lot of trouble believing, Tchotchkus," she said, "what Grijk tells me."

"Everybody calls me Tiny," Tiny told her.

"Not everybody, Tchotchkus. So you've lost the relic, have you?"

"Not exactly," Tiny said.

She nodded, emphatic, her darkest suspicions confirmed. "No, I see, not exactly, of course, as I suspected, there was always the possibility, I'd hoped against hope, but you can't change a cat with a cabbage leaf, character will out—"

She might have gone on talking like a person in a Russian novel indefinitely, except that Tiny cut through the crap, saying, "What's this all about? We dropped it; we'll go back and pick it up."

"Yes, of course you will," she said, and would have narrowed her eyes if the roundness of her face had permitted. "And how much more will it cost us?"

"Oh, is that your beef," Tiny said. (Grijk looked around for a steer.)

"It is," Zara Kotor said. "I wasn't born yesterday."

"It was our screwup," Tiny told her. "The guys agree to that. It was our screwup, so we'll throw in the repair for free. It's on us."

The sun abruptly broke through on that stormy face; now Zara looked like a gold-leaf icon in a Russian church. "It is? Tiny? You aren't holding us up for more money?"

"Nah."

"Well, that's wonderful news," she said, and then just as abruptly the sun went back behind the clouds. "But that means," she said slowly, "the relic really is lost. If it isn't a ploy, then you really and truly did fuck up."

"Screw up," Tiny corrected her. "It was just one of those things. We also lost a guy from the crew, we got *no* idea where *he* is. At least

117

with the femur, we think we know where we can lay hands on it."

"Reverent hands, of course," Zara suggested.

"Oh, sure," Tiny said.

The sun peeped through drifting clouds, and she said, "You really think you can get it back?"

"We'll give it a try," Tiny promised. "It's a kind of a tricky place, where we think it is, but the guys are casing it right now, and we'll give it the old try." And he noticed she didn't even ask about the missing member of the crew; *sic transit gloria* Dortmunder.

She smiled; it was damn near girlish. "You'll stay for lunch," she said. "You'll tell me all about it."

21

I'm sorry, May," Murch's Mom said, "but I'll have to throw the meter on you. Otherwise, I'll get a ticket, for sure I'll get another goddam suspension."

"Oh, you can throw the meter if you want," May said, "but that doesn't mean I really pay you any money, does it?"

Murch's Mom's hand froze in the act of flipping down the flag. She gazed into the rearview mirror at May. She said, "Why? What else?"

"It isn't that far," May said. "We could walk it."

Reluctantly, but acknowledging defeat, Murch's Mom dropped her hand instead of the meter. "Okay," she said, being heroic, "I'll chance it," and she drove May up and over to the Votskojek embassy, all on the arm.

There was only one car in the parking area in front of the chain-link fence, and it didn't have the red-white-blue diplomat plates, so it probably belonged to the two uniformed private guards standing around behind the gate like Immigration detainees. Murch's Mom parked beside it, and May got out of the cab, while Murch's Mom stayed in it with the engine running, ready to make whatever move the situation might demand.

119

May walked over to the gate. The guards looked through it at her like cows. She said, "Is this the Votskojek embassy?"

They looked at each other. Either they weren't sure or they weren't sure they should admit it, but finally one of them did look back at May and nod and say, "It's closed."

"I'm here to get a visa," May said.

"It's closed."

"Well, where do I get my visa?"

"It's closed."

"I have to see *somebody* to get my visa."

"It's closed."

May looked at the other one. She said, "Do you think you should take your friend here to a doctor? He's stuck or something."

"Lady," said guard number two, whose tape loop was already more complex, "he told you the story. The place is closed."

"How can an *embassy* be closed?"

"Like this," the guard said, waving around.

"Isn't there *anybody* here?"

"No," said the guard, the functioning guard, "they all left. Got into their diplomat cars, used to be parked right there, the whole bunch of them, said don't let anybody in, and left."

"For how long?"

"Didn't say."

The first guard reactivated himself: "It's closed."

"That's okay," May told him. "You already did your part. Just stand there." To the sentient guard, she said, "Did they take anybody with them."

"Like who?"

"I don't know. Anybody who wasn't like one of them. Like not a Votskojekareeny, or whatever they call themselves."

"Votskojeks," said the sentient guard. "That's what they call themselves, and to tell you the truth, lady, they all look alike to me. All I know is, they come out here with their uniforms on and their suitcases in their hands and said keep it locked, and they drove away. My partner and me just come on duty then, and I guess there was some kind of hassle just before that, only the guys what was on duty then wouldn't say. Maybe they took a couple bucks to keep quiet, the lucky stiffs, I don't know."

"Unconscious," said the unconscious guard.

"That's *right*," said his livelier pal. "So maybe it's a communicable disease or something. They had a doctor with them, too, or anyway he looked like a doctor in *old* movies, or anyway—"

"You said unconscious," May broke in. This, she knew, was a John sighting.

"Yeah. He was in the uniform like the others, with the hat pulled down, but he was out like a light. Two of them carried him out, you know, holding him up on each side like he was walking, but he wasn't walking. They carried him right by me, and he wasn't walking. He was snoring."

Still alive, May thought. "But where did they *go?*" she asked.

"Beats me," said the guard. "All I know is, we stay here until the money they paid for the service runs out. I don't worry about these UN people. I mean, that's the problem with the UN, you know, it brings in all these foreigners, all this element, it runs down like the neighborhood. You *never* know what they're up to. There was one bunch, one embassy I was on guard at, maybe five years ago, *they* all packed up and left, turns out there was an overthrow at home in their country, they all flew straight to Switzerland, took the country's assets out of the bank there, and disappeared. That's the kind of element you got with your UN here. You ask me, they oughta take this whole UN, and this chickenshit glass building up there and the whole thing and move em down to Washington, D.C. I mean, they're *used* to these kinds of creeps down there; that's what Washington's all about. *Soccer* players."

In the face of such scorn, there was little left to say. May had just learned both much more and much less than she wanted to know. Before this cornucopia of a guard could give her his opinion of UFOs or asbestos or the presidential-primary system or whatever was scheduled to hit the surface next, it was time to get out of here. "Thank you," May said. "Thank you both. I'll try again another time."

"Like I told you," said the first guard, "it's closed."

"You did," May said. "I remember that." And she went over to the cab and got into the backseat and said, "They took him away. Alive but unconscious."

Murch's Mom's hand itched, but she did not scratch it on the meter. She said, "Unconscious?"

"Snoring," May said. "And where there's snoring, there's hope."

22

Diary of a Prisoner—Day Two

The prisoner spent a restless night, punctuated by far-off screams. The prisoner tried to convince himself that a church merely happened to be nearby, whose bells sounded like human screams. He had little success making that theory fly.

The fluorescent light in the ceiling was not turned off. Being a fluorescent, it was also unlikely to burn out, and did not.

Just before dawn, the prisoner fell at last into a deep, exhausted sleep, from which he was harried almost immediately by a great clattering and clashing of locks and chains, followed by the entrance of the four Beckett characters from the night before. While the two eyes-down prisoners in dirty white placed the table where they'd put it last night, the soldiers strode over to kick the awake prisoner awake. He clumsily rolled away from them, entangled in the miserable blanket that had during the night neither warmed him—it had been *cold* in here—nor protected him from the hardness of the floor. And *now*, it was tripping him up, on purpose.

Still, he got to his feet at last, looked around, and said, "I really gotta brush my teeth. I mean, *major*."

Linguistic improvement had not occurred with this crowd overnight. The same dumb, hostile, gape-mouthed stares greeted his attempts at communication. Shaking his tousled head, the prisoner stumbled over to the table and found on it the identical same provisions as last night: green slime, clear liquid. He picked up the cup of clear liquid, trusting it to be the same as last night's water, and carried it over to that small hole in the middle of the floor. First, he dipped his right forefinger into the liquid, then he rubbed his mossy teeth with that finger as best he could. Of course, fingers don't have bristles, so it wasn't as effective a cleaning method as it might have been, but still.

Next, the prisoner took a mouthful of water, swirled and swirled and swirled and swirled and swirled and swirled and swirled and swirled—

One of the soldiers came over, glowering, and touched the end of his machine gun to the prisoner's stomach.

—and *swirled* it around his mouth, then spit it out into the small hole and (deliberately) on the soldier's shiny boot. Then he went back to the table, stood there, and had a hearty meal. The instant he was finished—and it didn't take long—the soldiers began to yell at the other two prisoners, who scurried forward, picked up the table, and trotted out with it like a badly confused pair of ricksha men, the soldiers following.

The prisoner was left alone then, for a little while, as the prison yard outside his window paled through varying shades of gray. There was no more screaming, which was nice.

But then here came the clanking and the crashing again. Lunchtime already? It's brainwashing techniques, the prisoner told himself, they're trying to louse up my sense of time. (Why anybody might want to louse up his sense of time was another question.)

But, no. When the soldiers came rousting and roistering into the dungeon this time, they were alone, and what they wanted, making it inescapably clear with boot and fist and gun barrel, was for the prisoner to come away with them. Okay, okay.

The prisoner felt rotten. Unshaved, unwashed, in the same miserable clothing he'd worn on the *Pride of Votskojek,* his lank hair matted on his head, a feeling of cruddiness caked around his eyes, itches everywhere. This was not at all the first time the prisoner had been a prisoner, but it was certainly the first time he'd been a prisoner of people who took so cavalierly their responsibilities in the situation.

Outside the dungeon was a low-ceilinged corridor, stone on one side, old planks of wood on the other, that smelled of animals—horses, maybe, or cows. The prisoner was run through this at a lope, constantly prodded from behind, and shoved through a doorway at the end into a windowless, furnitureless room where a short, fat man in a heavy black beard and a tight uniform slapped him across the face and said, "Where did they take the relic?"

Funny thing. Last night, the prisoner would have told anybody anything about anything. But somewhere in the course of the recent several hours, as his clothing had stiffened with old perspiration and his flesh had tightened up from new bruises and the stubble had started to get really itchy under his chin, a transformation had occurred inside the prisoner, and now he knew, he *knew,* he wouldn't tell these operetta assholes diddley. Fuck em. *And* the horse they rode in on. Therefore, "No speak English," the prisoner said.

The fat man reared back as though it was the prisoner who'd slapped *him;* not a bad idea, come to think of it. "What are you playing at?" the fat man cried. "Of course you speak English! You're an American!"

"Frangipani accalac," the prisoner said.

The fat man looked stern. "We have ways to make you talk," he said.

"Afghanistan bananastand," the prisoner told him.

The fat man looked at the soldiers and pointed at the prisoner. "Club him!" he snarled.

The soldiers raised their machine guns, butt-first. The prisoner looked at the fat man and smiled a small and wintry smile. "*They* don't speak English," he said.

The fat man looked flustered. The soldiers paused uncertainly, looking at the fat man, their guns still raised to club. Nothing at all happened for a long moment, and then the door behind the prisoner opened and Hradec Kralowc entered, in a snazzy suit and white shirt and old school tie (black, purple, and dark blue: Osigreb Polytech). Smiling in a self-deprecatory way, he said, "Well, Diddums, so you've seen through our little charade. Yes, of *course* we've assigned English-speaking guards to your case, in hopes you would let something slip, thinking you weren't understood. Ah, well, such little tricks rarely work, in truth."

The small room was already overcrowded, but now Dr. Zorn entered, too, his spirally eyeglasses spinning reflections of the light, his nasty mouth smiling. The prisoner immediately crossed his arms over his chest, covering his upper arms with his hands.

Kralowc chuckled, "No, no, Mr. Diddums, you won't be getting any more injections. At least not at this moment."

"A fine subject," Dr. Zorn said covetously, "for aversion training."

"Not now, Doctor," Kralowc said, and turned to the fat man. He spoke pleasantly enough to the fat man, or as pleasantly as that language of theirs permitted, but the fat man blinked and looked abashed and fidgeted his feet and answered in frightened monosyllables. The prisoner, having seen good cop/bad cop done a lot better than *this,* spent that interval looking at the doorway and deciding it wouldn't accomplish anything to suddenly run through it.

Finishing with his apparent chastisement of the fat man, Kralowc then spoke pleasantly enough to one of the soldiers, who obediently leaned his machine gun against the wall and reached into his jacket for a none-too-clean handkerchief as Kralowc said to the prisoner, pleasantly enough, "I'm afraid we must blindfold you now as we take you to a new location. There are certain military installations you must not see, particularly as you are known to be a Tsergovian sympathizer. If you *did* see these things, I'm afraid our military command would insist that you be disposed of. You understand."

"Oh, sure," the prisoner said, and the handkerchief was tied around his head, blocking his eyes except for a teeny little strip at the bottom, which made it possible for him to see the front of his own body but nothing else.

Hands took his arms and propelled him forward. The front of his body, and presumably the rest of him as well, went back through that doorway, turned left (away from the dungeon! hurrah!), and walked along a concrete floor, then stumbled over some kind of sill, then walked on crunchy gravel for a while.

"We'll be getting into our car now," Kralowc's voice said from nearby. Hands bent the prisoner this way and that, poked at him, adjusted him, and pretty soon he was, as advertised, in a car. The backseat, from the feel of the flat, soft surface his knees were now pressed against.

Other people got into the car, too, on both sides of the prisoner, pressing him pretty tight. He folded his arms, because there wasn't any room for them at his sides, and sat there peeking down at his arms and his lap for a while.

The car's trunk slammed. Pause. Car doors slammed, four of them. A car engine started; sounded like it needed a tune-up. The vehicle lurched forward, and there was the sound of tires on gravel: crunch-crunch-crunch. Then they reached pavement, a smoother surface, and gained speed, and the car sounded less like an out-of-whack washing machine.

Somebody in the car smelled *bad*. This offended the prisoner, until he realized he was the one stinking up the place, and then he was pleased. The foulest revenges are the most sweet.

After five or ten minutes of driving on a surprisingly smooth road, Kralowc began to speak, apparently from the front seat, saying, "Frankly, Diddums, I'm sorry to see you in this situation. In our two meetings, I'd come to think of you as a sympathetic person, one I enjoyed discussing things with. And now to find you've thrown in your lot with the Tsergovians, it's really too bad. I can only assume you don't know them well, that you took the job for pay or believed some massive pattern of disinformation."

The silence following that statement encouraged a reply, but the prisoner could think of nothing in particular he wanted to say, so the silence stretched and stretched and then broke, and Kralowc said, "Let me try to put the situation in perspective, Mr. Diddums. As caretakers of the femur of Saint Ferghana, as, if I may say so, reverent and awe-inspired caretakers of the sacred relic, we not only deserve whatever rewards such selfless concern might bring but our continued hegemony itself hangs in the balance. And not only ours. I'll tell you, Mr. Diddums, without hyperbole, that the health and well-being of every man, woman, and child in this entire trans-Carpathian region depends on the continued independence and internal security of Votskojek."

A mutter of "hear hears" surrounded the prisoner at the end of this speech, none of which had done more than graze his mind on its way out the windows that had been opened for some reason.

DONALD E. WESTLAKE

Another little silence. An audible sigh from Kralowc, and then his voice again. "I'm sorry you won't meet me halfway, Diddums," he said. (Be interesting to know by what thought processes he chose when to say "Diddums" and when to say "Mr. Diddums." Or maybe not.)

When this sally also produced no response, Kralowc made some sort of guttural remark, apparently to the driver, because at once they speeded up and shortly made a sharp right, and then began to climb.

And Kralowc spoke again, "I want to show you something, Diddums," he said. "So we're taking a little detour. I can't believe you're a man who won't be reached by honesty and sincerity. You *must* want, as we all do, what's best for all mankind. We've met, you and I, we've talked; I can't be that wrong about human nature."

Well, maybe.

They climbed for quite a while. Votskojek was supposed to be a mountainous country, so here was the proof. Then at last, the car slowed, more gravel was crunched, and the car came to a stop. Doors opened. "Here we are," Kralowc said, as though there'd been some doubt.

Many hands worked to get the prisoner out of the car and then to get him back on his feet and brush him off. Then, at last, the blindfold was removed, and what a view! Boy, if only he had a camera!

They stood on a parking area beside a curve in a two-lane road high up on a mountainside, with the land dropping sharply down just past the end of the gravel. But this was not the craggy, rocky mountainside he'd expected; this mountain was as green as a bankroll, pine trees and grasses, wildflowers along the verge of the road, and not a human structure in sight.

Except, far away to the south—no, east—no, uh . . .

It's still morning, and the warm spring sun is *there,* so that's east, so that's kind of southwest. Okay. Except, far away to the southwest, there were two huge gray salt and pepper shakers, round concrete towers, fat at the bottom then tapering in near the top, then curving out again at the upper lip. White smoke or steam came from the one on the left, so that would be the salt. The pepper wasn't in use.

But other than those things, the automobile they'd come here in was the only visible manufactured artifact. This automobile was medium-size, as the prisoner had already known, and black and foreign—Lada, it said on the side, in small, discreet chrome letters—and its license plate was black, with a silver V 27 on it.

Also, the group around this car were the only visible human beings. The group consisted of the prisoner and Hradec Kralowc and the two soldiers from the dungeon, plus Terment from the *Pride of Votskojek* office, who was being the driver, and who was, in fact, staying in the car while the others got out and stretched their legs.

Never mind the people; look at the view. The mountain fell away steeply in front of them, all fir trees and underbrush and flowers. Across the way were other mountains, and the prisoner noticed that two of those mountains out there had green bands down their sides where the trees had been cut away to make meadows. Long strips of meadow stretching down the mountains.

Hradec Kralowc took the prisoner's arm and pointed out toward the salt and pepper shakers. "Do you see that? That's Tsergovia."

The prisoner perked up. That's Tsergovia? Not that far away, really. If he could get over there, if he could get to Tsergovia, he could bounce some names off the people he met—good thing he was so accomplished at pronouncing Grijk Krugnk, gonna come in handier than he'd expected—and eventually find the authorities, and then find rescue. If he could get there.

Well, at least he now knew where it was. Southwest of here.

"And this," Kralowc was saying, as though the prisoner might care about anything except the location of Tsergovia, "is Votskojek." And he waved his hand at the mountains, the greenery all around them. "Do you understand now, Diddums?" he asked.

No. The prisoner said it aloud: "No."

"You don't know what those towers are? I'm sorry, I thought everyone did. Those are cooling towers for a nuclear plant. All of Tsergovia has been given over to the military-industrial complex."

They do pay well, the prisoner thought.

"Disease is rampant in Tsergovia," Kralowc went on. "Cancers, leukemia, birth defects, all the terrible legacy of nuclear plants run by lax, uncaring, unskilled bureaucrats. Air pollution, dead lakes and streams, stunted crops, disappearing wildlife. That's what Tsergovia has chosen, and it's what they want for *us*. Make no mistake, Diddums, if their underhanded methods in this UN matter are allowed to win, we will be helpless. Poverty-stricken, friendless, at the mercy of our historic enemies. Everything you see here, everything we of Votskojek hold dear, will be trampled beneath the Tsergovians' hobnailed boot. That's what we're fighting for, Diddums. Truth, justice, and the Votskojek way!"

"Huh," said the prisoner, impressed not by the argument but by its impassioned delivery.

Kralowc studied him. "You're an honorable man," he said, getting it wrong again. "I know you won't change your allegiance easily. But I want to break through Tsergovian lies and propaganda, I want you to see what *you* will destroy if you refuse to help us in our hour of need. I'm going to show you a Votskojek village. I'm going to show you the life the Tsergovians mean to crush."

Good. The longer the tour went on, the better the prisoner liked it, since he suspected that, at the end of the road, lay Dr. Zorn. "Sure," he said. "Like to see it."

"We discussed," Kralowc said, "when we innocently believed you were a true tourist, we discussed the charming village of Schtum, in the Schtumveldt Mountains."

"Yeah, I remember that."

"Well, these," Kralowc said, waving his arm, "are the Schtumveldt Mountains, and you are going to see Schtum!"

"Sounds good," the prisoner said.

Kralowc rested a commiserating hand on the prisoner's forearm. Sympathetically, he said, "I'm sorry, but we'll have to blindfold you again for part of the way. Our military defenses, you know."

"Oh, sure."

So they did, and stuffed him back into the car like an overripe pimento into an olive, and crowded in on both sides of him, and soon they all drove on.

Uphill, downhill, twisty roads; fast driving, slow driving, imprecations at the driver—they sounded like imprecations—from Kralowc, and then an order barked by Kralowc at the backseat, and the blindfold was removed once again, and the prisoner blinked and looked out the car windows.

This time, they didn't stop, but just drove slowly through the town. Pretty little place, kind of an alpine village effect with the steep roofs and the gingerbread eaves and the cute shutters flanking the windows. It was the shopping street of the village, lined with small stores showing meat or bread or flowers in their front windows, with the tall green mountain as a backdrop.

The narrow street was crowded with pedestrians. They were all in their native costume, wide skirts and full blouses with scoop necks for the women, bright, full shirts and dark pants with elastic bottoms below the knee for the men. Almost all wore buckled shoes, and many of the women had on old-fashioned sunbonnets. Many of these women were young and damn good-looking. Most of the people smiled sunny smiles and waved at the car as it went by.

"Only official vehicles are permitted in the town center," Kralowc explained. "Residents and visitors must leave their automobiles at the parking lots outside town and come in by pony cart."

And, as he said it, a pony cart went by, half full of cheerful people, all of whom waved at the car as they went past. The pony, too diligent to wave, nodded at the car.

"That's our policy throughout the country," Kralowc went on. "Livable spaces for human beings. We refuse to be slaves to the machine. Not like your friends the Tsergovians. Oh, I *wish* I could show you one of their cities. The bloodred sky, the greenish sewage running in the gutters, the grit and grime on every face that has been outdoors for more than five minutes, the public statues eaten away by acid rain to mere lumps, the hopeless look on the faces, the hunched bodies of the children..." Kralowc paused, overcome by his own eloquence. "To think," he managed to say, "that they plan such a future for *these* people."

Terment, at the wheel, said something fast and low, and Kralowc reacted, saying, "Yes, yes, you're absolutely right." To the prisoner, he said, "Now we must blindfold you again. I apologize—"

Everything became dark for the prisoner.

"—for the necessity."

"That's okay."

"Thank you, Diddums."

Soon the car sped up, and now it ran along for a good half-hour or so. From time to time, Kralowc had more bushwah he wished to impart, but the prisoner paid no attention. (It's easy to ignore people when you're blindfolded, without them knowing you're doing it.) While Kralowc pointed with pride and viewed with alarm, the prisoner devoted his thoughts to the question of which direction they were now traveling. Southwest? When they got wherever they were going, when he got his opportunity to escape—would he be able to see those salt and pepper shakers? Those were his beacons to steer by; they would lead him out of Votskojek and into Tsergovia and safety.

After a while, it grew silent inside the speeding car; apparently, even Kralowc was tired of all that political Muzak. The big lumpy soldier bodies to both sides of the prisoner were warm, supporting; the hum of the tires on the road was sedative; he hadn't had much sleep last night...

The prisoner was jolted awake by the sudden jolting of the car, like a bucking bronco, followed by a whole series of imprecations—these were *definite* imprecations—from Kralowc, interspersed with querulous whines from Terment. The car kept bucking, then it coughed, then became silent. Still rolling, but silent.

They ran out of gas! The prisoner couldn't believe it. How did they *do* that? And what was in it for him?

A long walk, blindfolded, probably.

The car rolled along. The prisoner could feel it slowing, could feel the *ba-dump* when it left the pavement, could hear the *squnchy-creenk* as the tires crushed weeds, could feel the little stutter in their progress as Terment tentatively tapped the brakes, and finally he felt them roll to a stop. The sound of Terment applying the hand brake was like a joke in bad taste.

But, then, all jokes are in bad taste, aren't they? Isn't that what they're for?

"Unfortunately, Diddums," Kralowc said into the new silence, "this idiot seems to have permitted us to run out of fuel."

Whining from Terment. Ignoring it, Kralowc said, "Fortunately, we are very near our destination. We'll be able to walk from here."

Oh, will we? "You're the boss," the prisoner said.

"Yes, I am. I think, therefore," Kralowc added, with barely suppressed rage, "we should begin by *getting out of the car.*"

This last wasn't directed at the prisoner. Kralowc spoke to the prisoner only in honeyed tones. The sound of car doors snapping open was followed by the removal of those warm, comforting, supportive bodies from the prisoner's flanks, followed by the removal of the prisoner himself from the car, in the usual fashion; hands clutched various parts of him and yanked. This time, the process was a little worse, since the soldiers were taking out their sense of injustice on the prisoner, as soldiers do.

At last, he was set on his feet. And briefly left alone. Lifting his head to peer down past his own front, he saw grass around his feet, grass and weeds. Putting out his hand, he touched the side of the car and took one step in that direction to lean against it.

Meantime, his captors were hurriedly plotting together in their native tongue; at the end of which Kralowc reverted to English, saying, "You won't be needing that blindfold anymore, Diddums. There's a path we can take that goes near no secret installations. And we wouldn't want you to fall and hurt yourself."

"Good thinking," the prisoner said, and the blindfold came off yet again, was converted back to a dirty handkerchief, and was replaced in its owner-soldier's jacket.

The prisoner looked around. They were parked near a broad, leafy tree. Tire tracks crushing weeds led back around the tree and out at a long angle to the two-lane road. Beyond the road was another view of the Schtumveldt Mountains, with another of those long meadows cut into it. Maybe it was logging. Unfortunately, the salt and pepper shakers couldn't be seen. Still, up there was the sun, so over there—no, over *there*—was southwest. Tsergovia.

On this side, a simple dirt track up from the road skirted around to the other side of the tree and headed upward into the pine forest. That must be where they were going.

But not yet. First, Kralowc had to point at the path and give a lot of quick orders to Terment, who nodded and nodded and nodded and turned to trot away up the path, soon disappearing.

One of the soldiers made a comment, apparently a warning of

some kind, with a gesture at the road, and Kralowc said, "Yes, of course. Come along, Diddums."

The prisoner went along. For a while, they just slogged up the path, through the pines, listening to the bird song and batting at the blackflies. Nasty blackflies, bite chunks out of you. Kralowc went first, then one of the soldiers, then the prisoner, then the other soldier. Up they went, feet thudding on the packed-down path, and the prisoner was pleased to hear, from the panting of the soldiers, that they were in worse shape than he was.

After about five minutes of this, they emerged from the forest into a large, sloping meadow, with Terment way out there on its far side, bobbing right along. Beyond the meadow, more trees clothed a further upward slope, and at the top of that slope was . . . the castle.

Oh, boy. Black against the blue sky, stone, turreted, there it stood, on top of the mountain. The prisoner automatically jerked to a stop at the sight of it, and the soldier behind him went "Oof!" when he blundered into the prisoner's flinched-back elbows.

Kralowc turned, saw the effect the castle was having, and came back a pace to say, "Yes, Diddums, that's where we're going."

"I figured," the prisoner said, trying to act cool.

Kralowc stood beside him, and they gazed up at the castle together. "Few men who go in there," Kralowc said, "ever come out."

"Uh-huh." The prisoner swallowed and cleared his throat. "I guess Dr. Zorn'll be there."

"Waiting for you. *And* General Kliebkrecht."

"Uh-huh."

"Diddums, they have ways to make men talk."

"Uh-huh."

"I don't want this to happen to you, Diddums. You and I understand each other; we're both gentlemen; we don't want to have to deal with thugs."

"Uh-huh."

"I hoped, when I showed you the peaceful village of Schtum, you would understand. Tell *me* where the relic is; don't force me to have Dr. Zorn ask you."

The prisoner licked his lips. He gazed at the castle. He said, "I gotta pee."

"Of course," Kralowc said, as one gentleman to another. "And do take the opportunity of that time to think things over."

"Uh-huh."

The prisoner moved back down the path into the forest, one of the soldiers following. In tandem, they veered away from the trees, until the prisoner stopped and said, "Gimmie a little privacy, okay? You wait on this side; I'll go around that side."

For answer, the soldier—who was still more or less pretending not to speak English—stood where he was but aimed his machine gun at the prisoner, who said, "Fine. Just like that," and walked around the big pine tree.

He really did have to pee, and, as he'd promised Kralowc, while he was doing so he thought things over. And here, even before he was finished, came the soldier, just making sure. "Come on, will ya?" the prisoner said, and then looked down and became wide-eyed as he cried, "A snake! Jesus, shoot it!"

The soldier came closer, peering. The prisoner's free hand pointed shakily at something under the lowest branches of the tree. The soldier extended the gun barrel down ahead of himself into the mass of old needles and general mulch, and the prisoner, all his weight behind it, coldcocked him with a beautiful right across that big jaw.

The soldier fell into the pine tree like a bale of cotton thrown off the *River Queen*, and the prisoner ran pell-mell into the depths of the forest.

Ten extremely painful minutes later, no longer hearing the sounds of pursuit, the ex-prisoner stopped long enough to zip up. Then he looked for the sun, figured out which way was southwest, and made tracks. Next stop, Tsergovia.

22A*

Just five hundred yards south of the island of MANHATTAN (qv) and even closer to the onetime proud city of BROOKLYN (qv) across Buttermilk Channel, but nevertheless governmentally considered a part of the borough of MANHATTAN (qv), lies a darling button of an island that the Indians called Pagganck, which seems unkind, but there you are.

In 1637, some enterprising Dutchmen bought the island from the Manhatas Indians (so *that*'s why!) for two ax heads and a handful of nails and beads, and changed its name to Nutten, which wasn't much of an improvement. But they were still a lot sharper than those other Dutchmen who bought Manhattan Island itself from the Canarsie Indians, who didn't own it, but were just passing through and knew a live one when they saw a live one.

The Dutch held on to Nutten only twenty-seven years before the British adopted it, not payin nobody nuttin for Nutten, and changed its name to Governor's Island, because the governor of the colony of New York was going to live there. And so he did.

---

*Optional—historical aside—not for credit

The first one, Lord Cornbury, was asked to leave when he insisted on wandering around in lady's clothing and instituted a bachelor's tax, but some of the others kept a lower profile and would surely be proud to learn they are utterly forgotten.

Soon the colonists of eastern America declared themselves ready for self-government, and in 1797 built Fort Jay on Governor's Island to deter anybody who might wish to argue the point. The British did argue the point, as it turned out, but John Jay's one hundred big guns deterred them from shelling the bejesus out of New York, so they went and shelled the bejesus out of Washington, D.C., instead, and God bless them for it.

During the Civil War, one of those awful Civil War prisons was set up on Governor's Island, from which only one Confederate prisoner ever managed to escape. He was Capt. William Webb, and he didn't escape to either Manhattan or Brooklyn, though both were quite handy. A true Southerner, he escaped by swimming south. Twelve miles later, he found New Jersey, which was enough to keep him heading south, and after the war he became a United States senator from TENNESSEE (qv).

Around the turn of the century, two transportation developments elsewhere impinged on Governor's Island. One was the Lexington Avenue subway line; earth excavated from that tunnel was used to expand the landmass of Governor's Island from 100 acres to 175 acres, all of them charming. And the Brooklyn-Battery Tunnel, four lanes of automobile traffic between Manhattan and Brooklyn, ran directly beneath the island without stopping.

During World War I, Gen. John J. Pershing (qv), commander of the American Expeditionary Force (AEF) in FRANCE (qv), lived in one of the nice old colonial houses on Governor's Island, which seems pretty darn far from the front, but never mind. In World War II, the island was headquarters of the First Army, but it was a hard place to march to, so in 1966 the army turned it over to the Coast Guard, who intend to keep it. They like it.

Well, why not? It contains Manhattan's only golf course, the only Burger King in the world that serves beer (it's in the bowling alley, and as one Cmdr. Richard R. Bock explained to the NEW YORK TIMES (qv), "You can't have a bowling alley without beer. That's un-American"), and, best of all, nobody else can go there unless the Coast Guard says okay.

The five thousand residents—four thousand mostly deskbound Coastguardsmen and Coastguardswomen, plus their families— have their own frequent ferry service over to a slip at Battery Park on Manhattan right next to the Staten Island ferry, but they rarely use it unless they have to. After all, these are real Americans, which means they're afraid of New York. They'd much rather stay on their neat little island, golf by day, bowl or watch television in the evening, and tuck in nice and early; the morning bugle sounds at 7:55 A.M. and everyone on the island is expected to be up and saluting, clear-eyed, pink-cheeked, as mentally and physically alert by 8:00 A.M. as that Burger King beer allows, when the loud-speakers that are spread across the island like something from *1984* all start chugging out "THE STAR-SPANGLED BANNER" (qv).

The shore of Governor's Island is ringed by nautical installa-tions. The Coast Guard cutter *Gallatin* lies up here when it isn't rousting undesirables in the Caribbean and other eastern waters, and there's a marina where other Federal services—including the DEA—sometimes keep boats, and of course the ferry dock for scary old New York City.

There is also one small structure just off the right shoulder of the island, like an epaulet, that is under the control of the Coast Guard but not directly concerned with its mission. This structure is round and brick-clad and it sticks up out of the water like an extra bit of Vulcan's smokestack. It is connected to the island by a narrow pier, and it is a ventilation tower from the Brooklyn-Battery Tunnel, down below.

23

Andy Kelp's head appeared over the top edge of the ventilation tower. Fox eyes in a fox face scanned the darkness. It was two in the morning, and while the dishonest burglar in the ventilation tower conned the scene the honest burghers of Governor's Island lay peacefully asleep in their beds, dreaming of strikes and spares. (Some were having nightmares about splits.)

The fox face withdrew. The *snipping* of wire cutters vibrated faintly in the air, like the chirps of an android cricket. Then, folding up and away, came the thick mesh screen that kept Coastguardschildren from falling into the ventilator and plummeting like Alice down the rectangular sheet-metal opening with the repair-access metal ladder rungs fixed into its side and through the other mesh screen at the bottom; don't strain yourself.

Kelp climbed out, a lithe, narrow figure all in black except for the gray elks on the ski mask he'd just donned and the amber coil of rope slung over his shoulder. A large four-clawed metal hook was attached to one end of this rope; Kelp fixed it to the edge of the tower opening, dropped the rope over the side, and shimmied down to the narrow wooden doughnut circling the tower not far above the waterline.

Once down, and before crossing the open pier to the main island, Kelp briefly removed the ski mask, leaned back, and just breathed for a while. The air in the ventilation tower, even with the low volume of traffic in the Brooklyn-Battery Tunnel at this hour, had been less than ideal. Gratefully inhaling air that had not been treated by the automakers of America and Japan, Kelp fingered the ski mask with its cheerful prancing elks and remembered buying it some time ago in a sport shop on Madison Avenue. Him and Dortmunder, they'd happened to need ski masks for a certain thing they planned to do, which didn't include skiing. His had these nice chipper elks loping around it, and Dortmunder had wound up with a purple mask splotched with big green snowflakes; not really attractive. Kelp had never told his friend this, but, with the ski mask on, Dortmunder's head looked mostly like a diseased eggplant. With eyes.

And where was John Dortmunder now? Not here on Governor's Island, or his pal Andy Kelp would certainly take the extra few minutes to rescue him—if it seemed safe. Where *was* the poor guy?

Ah, well. There is, first of all, the task at hand. Pulling the ski mask over his head once again, Kelp moved away from the tower's brick wall. Bent low, he hurried across the open pier, with New York Harbor lapping away below him on all sides, and in a few minutes he stood on a smooth, uncracked sidewalk containing not even one cigarette butt.

No one around. So far, so good. Kelp strode along silently on his crepe soles, almost invisible in his dark garb, absolutely alone. What theoretical security measures there might be on this military base were lax to the point of inexistence, since the *real* security was at the frontier of the island's only (normal) access; that is, the ferry dock over on Manhattan.

Kelp continued to stroll, past neat houses in neat settings, with unlocked bicycles neatly placed at their sides, and he could understand why the residents here preferred to see Manhattan—that big thing over there, with all the lights—exclusively on their television screens. After all, it is well known that if you keep a creature for a long time in an antiseptic environment and then put it out in the normal world, it will immediately get sick and die.

The casing of the island, prior to the actual commission of the crime itself, had been a mostly unsatisfactory matter, consisting in its entirety of passing its western shoreline twice on the Staten Island ferry, and both times seeing neither Pepper LaFontaine's boat nor a location that looked as though it might contain it.

So Kelp could leave the westward alluvium for last. Instead, he could walk northward—toward that big thing over there with all the lights—and then skirt the water's edge to east and then south. Which he did, and found many items of interest, and passed them all by, until, well down the eastern side of the island, near the southern end of Buttermilk Channel, there it was. There, by golly, it was, Pepper's little runabout, bobbing in the ceaseless motion of the sea, tied fore and aft to metal stanchions sticking up like iron crabgrass from a concrete dock the other side of a chain-link fence.

You know what a chain-link fence is? A ladder.

Inside the fenced area, Kelp crossed to the motorboat, one of five vessels of varying sizes penned in here, and as he hurried forward he could only hope the bone was still there. He'd watched a quick tossing of the boat—what's known as a "cursory inspection," whatever that might be—from the unmarked car in which he'd been at that moment a resident, back at the mailbox manufacturer's dock, where the DEA had made its unwelcome surprise visit (like that old bit about the Spanish Inquisition, come to think of it, except in blue instead of red), after the boat had been dragged from the water but before it had been trucked away, and he hadn't seen anything taken from it. With any luck, the old cursory i. had been it, and the bone would still be aboard, tucked away under that crumpled tarpaulin where Kelp had kicked it in the excitement of the moment.

A bright floodlight on a high pole lighted Kelp on his way, and when he got to Pepper's boat that illumination showed him an interior as clean as Governor's Island itself. Even the tarpaulin was gone.

Kelp got down into the boat—rockingrockingrocking—to be absolutely certain, even though he *was* absolutely certain, and the damn thing looked as though the cleaning lady had been. Empty, stripped, bare. You could eat off that boat, if you were really hungry.

This was a blow. To return to Tiny, and to Tiny's cousin, and to Tiny's cousin's entire nation, boneless, was an uncomfortable prospect. But what else was there to do?

Nothing.

Reluctant, still hanging back, still studying this spick-and-span bathtub as though a foot-long bone might yet somehow be concealed within it, Kelp abandoned ship. He stood on the dock, loath to depart. Above, the bright light gleamed down, creating of him a shadowed shadow in the pool of white. On one side chuckled the restless water contained in the concrete U of the dock. On the other side stood the clean white clapboard wall of some sort of storage building that looked as though it had been painted no more than twelve hours ago. Behind, the dubious waters of Buttermilk Channel. Ahead, the chain-link fence, departure, and defeat.

Even so. Kelp trudged fenceward.

All this planning, for nothing. Finding just the right truck, a big boxy thing with a door in its side. Giving it new license plates and a quick spray-paint job. Paying just the right city employee a small honorarium for a Xerox of the appropriate architectural drawings of that section of the Brooklyn-Battery Tunnel containing the ventilation tower. Studying the actual physical tunnel and locating the door beside the catwalk that led to the service area beneath that tower. Riding in the back of the truck while Stan Murch drove it into the tunnel at a late enough nighttime hour that there would be moments when no other vehicle was in sight and the duty cop dozed in his glass cage, so he could stop it right next to the access door and Kelp could step briskly from truck to catwalk over the railing and through the door while Murch drove on. Coming here like a mouse in the walls while Murch circled the boroughs in the truck, commissioned to return to that spot in the tunnel every half hour until Kelp should emerge from the access door and slip back into the body of the truck. And all for what?

Bitter disappointment.

Kelp moved away from the denuded boat toward the chain-link fence. Something to his left caught his eye. When he veered toward it, he saw a something or other neatly folded and placed on the concrete ground next to the white building. He bent and lifted a corner of it. A tarpaulin, folded as neatly and compactly as an American flag. *The* tarpaulin?

Next to the possible tarpaulin was a round trash barrel, bright white plastic body and dark blue domed top with a little swing-door inset in it. An exhortation of some sort was printed on the body of the barrel, as though such exhortations were needed around this place.

Kelp would never make a Coastguardsperson; he just didn't have that innate natural neatness. For instance, when he ripped the blue dome off the trash barrel, he just flipped it away any which how. And the Burger King wrappers and chewing-gum wrappers and *Reader's Digest*s he pulled from the barrel, he flung behind him to left and right without *any* regard for symmetry or order. Just a mess.

It was at the bottom of the barrel. Kelp had this much neatness in his character; he wiped the stray flecks of ketchup off the bone with a couple of used Kleenexes before kissing it.

24

Diary of an Escapee

He kept to the woods, which made the going pretty slow. Also, he was not very much by way of being a woodsman, but was more of a city person by habit, experience, and inclination, so that made the going kind of difficult. On the other hand, when the going gets slow and difficult, even a city person knows to keep going.

Downhill wasn't so bad; you could always fall. Roll into a doughnut, breathe slowly and evenly, and hope you don't meet any rocks. But then there was uphill; inevitably, after every downhill, there was another uphill.

From time to time, roads crossed the escapee's path, blacktop or dirt roads of a sort a city person could identify with, employ, travel on; but not this time. This time, whenever he met a road, he paused a while in the deep forest, listened to be sure there was no traffic coming, and then did his awkward, panting lope across the open width to the protective cover on the other side, where he usually leaned for a while against a handy tree before proceeding.

And so he wended roughly southwestward. Very roughly. It

144

was a warm afternoon, filled with bird song and insect buzz. His progress was a slow and dreamy movement through meadows nodding with wildflowers, pine woods rich with sweet aromas, and now and again from afar the tinkling of a brook. Once, the escapee even paused to drink the water from one such brook, clear icy water, delicious; nectar of the gods.

Another time, a little shaky on his pins after jogging over yet another road and then climbing up yet another long, steep hill, he came to a small mountaintop clearing with a spring. Dappled sunlight through the trees made a soft light. The bubbling spring produced a clear music blending with the chatter of the birds. I'll just sit here a few minutes and catch my breath, the escapee thought, and when he opened his eyes it was night.

Dark. You don't get dark like this in the city. Teeny stars way up there in the sky, farther away than you could even think about, and that was it for the light. No bird song. The birds had all gone to sleep, high up on the tree branches, away from the predators of the night.

Uh. The escapee struggled to his feet, wincing and moaning as he discovered himself to be as stiff as if Dr. Zorn had injected starch into his veins. He was rested at last—he'd needed a nap, actually, after last night's disturbed sleep—but *stiff.*

And alone in the woods. Just him, and those predators of the night.

What would they be? Bears, maybe? Wolves? What do they have in the Schtumveldt Mountains? Mountain lions; why not? Mooses and elks; are they predators? Who cares? That big, what difference does it make if they're knocking you down for dinner or for fun?

I wonder if I'm in Tsergovia yet? he thought, and then he thought, I better keep going just to be on the safe side, and then he thought, Whoops. No sun. Which way is southwest, at night?

Well, he couldn't stay here, that was for sure. Aside from stiffness, and predators of the night, and the likeliness of pursuit—hunting dogs, there's something else to think about—there was the fact that it was no longer warm and cozy up here in the mountaintops. It was *cold.* Time to move on.

He had paused here for his nap, as best he could remember,

just as he'd entered the clearing, with the spring still out ahead of him. The only sound at the moment in all this mountain darkness was the bubbling of that spring—covering the approach of predators of the night, no doubt—and the sound came from over *that* way. Theoretically, then, if he walked *that* way, and managed to keep on in a straight line, he would still be traveling southwest. It was a pretty shaky theory, but it was all he had, so he did it, and immediately got a shoeful of water.

Well, *hell*. Left foot squooshing and squeeging, hands out ahead of him in search of trees, he moved on, the sound of the spring now receding behind him, and now gone. The land in front sloped downward. The escapee slogged on, and his thoughts were blacker than the night.

The next fifteen or twenty minutes were all sound effects— thuds, groans, grunts, gasps, the cracking of branches, and the occasional great flurry of whooshes and wheezes and yelps whenever he found himself jammed once again into a mass of bony-fingered shrubbery.

Then he found the road. He was already on it when he realized the hard smoothness underfoot was not a natural forest ground cover. It was a road. Being a road, it was very unlikely to have trees or shrubs or bushes or briar patches growing on it. It was also unlikely to have knee-high boulders concealed on its surface. In human terms, particularly city human terms, it was user-friendly.

Please, let's take it, he begged himself, and told himself that if he followed the road to the left, that was probably southwest-ward, anyway. And besides, he was surely in Tsergovia by now, so this would be a Tsergovian road, and nothing to worry about. And besides all *that*, he'd had enough midnight forest for one day. Please?

And so it was agreed, and the escapee turned left, and limped down the middle of the road, a slightly paler gray surface in the general gloom of night. He never could refuse himself anything.

Headlights. Behind him, coming along. Wheezy old engine, rattletrap vehicle.

The escapee shuffled to the side of the road, automatically thinking to hide himself, then abruptly changed his mind. Enough already. Turning back, standing in the fitful glare of the headlights, waving his arms over his head, trying to look both honest and Tsergovian—neither was possible—the escapee threw his fate into the hands of the gods. Or whoever was driving that truck.

Pickup truck. It rolled to a stop beside him. A heavyset, old, gnarly guy, a farmer from the look and smell of him, gazed out at the escapee and said, "Yar?"

The escapee panted. He said, "Tsergovia?"

"Hah?"

Ready to turn and run into the nearest tree at the first sign of trouble, the escapee said, "Is this Tsergovia, or Votskojek?"

"I don't know them towns," the farmer said.

The escapee gaped. "What?"

The farmer pointed a thick finger at his windshield. "Fair Haven's down thataway," he said.

The escapee clutched the pickup's door for support as all his world whirled about him. "Where am I?"

The farmer stared at him as though he were an escaped lunatic, which by now he almost was. "Where are you?"

Dortmunder said, "This isn't . . . Votskojek?"

"Brother, you *are* lost," the farmer said. "You're right here in Vermont."

25

What do you do with a ski resort in the summer? What Hradec Kralowc's good friend, hotelier Harry Hochman, tried to do was make the damn place—scenery, employees, rooms to rent, entertainment facilities, bars, infrastructure—double as something else. Mount Kinohaha (Ogunquit for *Broken Ankle*), Happy Hour Inns ski center in Vermont, for instance, housed in the snowless months a summer theater, an arts fair, and a variety of conferences and group meetings. Still, the volume of business at the end of ski season dropped off so drastically that most of the shops in the Alpine Village compound attached to the resort simply shut down, their operators living other warm-weather lives somewhere else. Since Kinohaha was one of the seven Happy Hour Inns around the world where Harry Hochman maintained a nearby residence—a château, in this case, based on Swiss models but rather more grandiose when the adaptations to Harry and Adele's tastes were completed—this failure of the ski center to be a year-round money churner griped his ass more than it might have. But what was he to do? Take the bitter with the sweet.

From the instant Hradec, in his office on the *Pride of Votsko-jek,* staring hopelessly at the mulish Diddums, thought to himself, It's a crazy idea, but it just might work, he had become a kind of necromancer, a magus, the Wizard of Vermont: "Pay no attention to the man behind that curtain."

Hradec had been able to do some kindness for Harry Hochman in the past, as Harry had been able to provide skilled craftsmen for the refurbishment of Hradec's quarters aboard the embassy. Harry was very actively interested in Votskojek getting the UN seat it deserved. When, once Diddums had been knocked out by Dr. Zorn's magic elixir, Hradec had phoned Harry and reminded Harry of his, Hradec's, onetime visit to the Vermont château, and then went on to explain the situation—"We have him; we must make him talk; we can't permit this to become public; I dare not let my superiors in Novi Glad know I've lost the relic"—Harry fell in with the idea at once. "We'll gaslight that fella to a fare-thee-well!" he yelled down the phone, with that raspy roar of his.

Hradec didn't get the reference, but he got the idea. "Good," he said.

It had taken a little while to prepare Mount Kinohaha to impersonate an idealized Votskojek, during which time the first part of the charade had taken place in a barn on a nearby former farm, land that Happy Hour Inns had purchased some time ago but not yet turned into anything useful. For this part of the work, two Votskojek college students, currently enrolled at Yale, had agreed to play soldier (one of them was a drama major, anyway, not the one Diddums eventually slugged, that one was an economics major), while two of Harry Hochman's household staff from the château played prisoner/serfs with a conviction born of years of rehearsal. (The fat, uniformed interlocutor who'd mistakenly spoken English to the "soldiers" in Diddums's presence was the only actual military man involved, being Maj. Jhalmek Kuur, Votskojek's military attaché down at the embassy, dragged away for the purpose from Washington, D.C. , and his endless quest for more assault vehicles and medium-range missiles.)

The summer theater proved useful in phase two. As everyone in the whole world knows, if you want your summer theater to be a financial success, you have to give the public three things: musicals, musicals, and musicals. The Mount Kinohaha Music Theater's repertory troupe, augmented by local talent, were happy to accept an unexpected bonus in the form of modest amounts of cash to play extras in an industrial film for the Happy Hours corporation, to be shot at the ski center; hidden cameras, they were told, would record the scene in the manner of cinema verité. (The semipros among the actors rolled their eyes at one another that so old hat an idea as cinema verité was still in use anywhere in the world, even at so talentless a level as industrial films.) The wardrobes for *Seven Brides for Seven Brothers, Brigadoon, Annie Get Your Gun, Finian's Rainbow,* and *Barnum* filled in nicely as generic native costume.

The Lada in which Diddums was driven through the re-dressed Alpine village was an actual embassy vehicle, a Russian-built car from a factory built in the then–Soviet Union by the Italian company Fiat. It had been given to an earlier ambas-sador by an earlier Soviet ambassador, when the Soviets were still trying to win friends and gain influence in the world's various muddy waters. (European joke: How do you double the value of a Lada? Fill the gas tank.) The Lada's license plates were spray-painted cardboard. Unfortunately, Hradec's talent pool of available speakers of Magyar-Croat who could be entrusted with knowledge of the plot was so limited, he'd been reduced to having Terment, clearly an office clerk, double as chauffeur; fortunately, Diddums didn't seem to notice.

But then, Diddums didn't seem to notice much at all, did he? All this elaborate preparation—and the mad scientist's laboratory that had been cobbled together in the basement of the château was a *wonder;* a real pity they didn't get to use it—and it all seemed to wash over Diddums like so much rainwater over a particularly retarded duck.

The problem was, Hradec never did understand Diddums. He neither knew nor understood that Diddums *was* a prisoner and knew exactly how to be a prisoner. Hradec acted throughout as though he were dealing with an amateur, but Diddums was a pro, from his expressionless face to his barely moving feet, and would not be impressed.

All that talk, all those displays of cooling towers and happy peasants. The man Hradec called Diddums cared nothing about any of that. A prisoner does one of two things: (1) he goes along, or (2) he escapes. That's all there is. His keepers give orders and he obeys them. He doesn't think; he doesn't argue; he doesn't engage in philosophical discussion. He does exactly what he's told, and all of his concentration remains exclusively on watching for a chance to move onto (2). Then he sees an opening, and he coldcocks the economist from Yale, and he's gone.

Fortunately, Hradec Kralowc is a resourceful man. He had more than one string to that bow.

26

The only thing that put any kind of damper on the occasion was that Grijk just didn't seem too excited about it. Maybe he wasn't used to getting up early in the morning. Or maybe he was one of those people who enjoys the pursuit more than the capture, like guys who chase women all the time, or dogs that chase cars. Anyway, when they got to the shop, Grijk was a lot less enthusiastic than he'd been over the phone.

Well, the first moment was the one that counted. And the first moment had come at 3:22 A.M., when Andy Kelp and Stan Murch had tumbled into Tiny's apartment waving the bone, big grins on both their faces. Tiny didn't mind it at all that they interrupted his beauty rest. He held the bone flat on his two big palms and smiled on it like it was a baby and said, "So this is the goddam thing, is it?"

"If only John was here," Kelp said.

"He isn't," Tiny said, and so much for sentiment.

Then they called the Tsergovian embassy and, Grijk being head of security over there, it was Grijk they woke up, Tiny telling him, in simple modesty, "We got it."

The initial Grijk reaction was all anybody could ask: "You god id? You *god* id?" All three of them in Tiny's living room could hear Grijk's voice squawking out of the telephone. Tiny flinched and held the receiver away from his head and said, "Yeah. Okay, Grijk? Yeah. Quit hollering like that. We got it. We'll be right over."

And they were, and all of a sudden Grijk wasn't that enthusiastic anymore. He seemed more fatalistic than anything else when he unlocked the front door and let them in. Maybe he'd just remembered that now he was going to have to fork over the other fifteen large; Dortmunder's five would go to May, of course, since nobody could be sure he wouldn't someday come back.

So anyway, here they were in the Tsergovian storefront on Second Avenue, one small fluorescent lamp on Drava Votskonia's rock-obsessed desk the only supplement to the pale gleam angling in through the front windows from the streetlights and an occasional taxicab, and Grijk Krugnk somehow just wasn't with the program. In the pale light, his smile was sickly as Tiny put on Drava's desk under the fluorescent glare the violin case he'd once taken away from a fella he'd suspected of not being a musician—he was right, too—and opened it to show the sacred ossicle nested in the blue felt within. "Is that sumpin?" Tiny asked.

"Dod's vunderful," Grijk agreed, but somehow he didn't sound convinced.

Fortunately, his deputy was there to make up for Grijk's lack of enthusiasm. "Holy bone," this guy said in awe, gazing into the violin case.

The guy's name was Haknal Vrakek; maybe. Something like that, anyway. Who knew? with Grijk's accent. "Dis is my depudy chief a securidy, Haknal Vrakek," Grijk had said when they'd first come in, gloomily pointing to this tall, wolfish, skinny, grinning guy with big teeth, who nodded and nodded, grinning away, until Tiny opened the violin case, and then he said, "Holy bone." Not like Robin the Boy Wonder being a smart aleck, but like anybody having a religious experience.

"So now you're set," Tiny said.

"We sure are," Haknal Vrakek said, rubbing his hands together. He didn't so much have an accent as an internal echo chamber, as though his voice had been prerecorded, as though he were about to tell you the time and temperature, or suggest if you need assistance, push One now.

Everybody looked at Grijk, who was not what you would call forthcoming. Not in any sense. Not in the sense of being as up and excited as he ought to be, given that his fondest dream had just come true, and not in the sense, either, of forking over the fifteen grand. In fact, Tiny—who wasn't even in on the profit this time—had to remind him, "You gotta pay the guys now, Grijk."

"Oh!" Could he really have forgotten? Maybe so. He stared at his deputy, who gazed mildly back at him, then stared at Tiny, then stared at Kelp and Murch, then finally got himself caught up with events. "I'll get you da money," he said.

Grijk took a step forward, hands out, as though he expected to do something with the violin case or its contents, but Tiny closed the lid and rested his paw on the case and said, "We'll watch the bone for you while you're gone."

"Oh," Grijk said. He looked again at his deputy, then nodded at Tiny. "Dod's good," he said, and went away through the door in back, the deputy following after him, leaving the three to look at each other and say, "What's with him?" and "Beats me."

The wait was a little longer than it should have been, but then at last Grijk returned with two white legal-size envelopes, one of which he gave to Kelp and the other to Murch, saying, "Da nation of Tsergovia tanks you a tousand dimes. You have saved us." Only he said it like it was something he had memorized, like he was just being polite.

It was the deputy who showed the real spirit of the occasion. "It's wonderful to see the sacred relic," he assured them with his echo-chamber voice. "Awe-inspiring to touch it with this hand. What magnificent work you have done!"

"Thanks," Tiny told him, pleased; but he would have preferred to hear it from Grijk.

Kelp smiled again at Grijk. He held up his envelope and said, "This is five thousand."

"Dod's right."

Kelp pointed at Murch's envelope. "And that's five thousand."

Before Grijk could answer, Tiny said, "Grijk, are you gonna embarrass me again? Come up with the other five. Don't fool around."

154

Grijk didn't even look ashamed of himself, just gloomier than before. Talk about cheap. "I vasn't sure," he said, pulling a third envelope out from his inside jacket pocket, "vad I should do vid—"

"We're sure," Tiny said, plucking the envelope out of his hand. "And I'll tell ya, Grijk, don't ask for no more favors."

"You fellas did vunderful," Grijk said, sounding tragic but smiling through. "I mean id, and I'm gradeful. You vas really vunderful."

"Thank you," Tiny said. "And now we're going home."

"Okay, Diny."

The deputy unlocked the door to let them out. "Good-bye, Diny," Grijk said.

"Sure," Tiny said, and led the way up Second Avenue.

Very few empty cabs this time of night; maybe up at Thirty-fourth Street. They sloped along, hands in their pockets, feeling dissatisfied, incomplete somehow, and Kelp said, "I'm really surprised at that cousin of yours, Tiny."

"I'm embarrassed by him," Tiny said. "I don't even want to talk about it."

Stan Murch had been walking along, silent, frowning, and now he said, "Tiny, how come you never met that deputy before?"

"I dunno," Tiny said, exasperated, really wanting a change of subject. "Maybe he brought him in for extra security, on accounta the bone."

"Brought him in from where?"

"How do I know? Tsergovia, maybe."

"Since we called him?"

Tiny stopped. He frowned at Murch, and Kelp said, "Grijk was a lot happier in that phone call, wasn't he?"

"Well, God damn it.," Tiny said.

They had walked two blocks north on Second Avenue; the return trip was a lot faster. It then took Kelp all of forty seconds to get through the front door. They went down the long, empty front room, the light on Drava's desk still gleaming. They went through the dark and empty office.

Upstairs. Up in the parlor, they found Grijk and Drava and Zara Kotor, all tied and gagged, and lying on the carpets. The bone and the violin case were gone.

27

They were having champagne in the dungeon, admiring the instruments of torture neatly aligned on the refectory table and the realistic chains and shackles fastened to the fake wall, when a servant came in with a cellular phone on a silver salver, bowed with the same obsequiousness that had added such verisimilitude to his downtrodden role in the prisoner game, and said to his employer, millionaire hotelier Harry Hochman, "Excuse me, sir. Telephone for Ambassador Kralowc."

"Thank you," Hradec said, switching his champagne glass to his other hand, and then he spoke Magyar-Croat into the receiver for some time as the others listened without comprehension, these others being Harry Hochman himself, his beloved wife, Adele, and Tatiana Kuzmekistova, a onetime star of Soviet cinema, a tall, slender, sultry brunette now madly studying English with the intention of becoming the next Greta Garbo, unaware there will *be* no more Greta Garbos. (Her research into Western popular culture was unfortunately spotty and incomplete.) Meantime, Tatiana was Hradec's date here at Harry Hochman's Vermont château, for the interrupted charade.

Finishing his conversation, returning the phone to the silver salver (the servant bowed himself out as lugubriously as he'd ever trotted the prisoner's dining table from the prisoner's cell), Hradec smiled at the others and said, "The relic is safely back aboard the embassy."

"Congratulations, Hradec," Harry said, raising his champagne glass.

"I'm so happy for you," said Harry's beloved wife, Adele.

"Of excellence," said Tatiana, whose pronunciation was just about perfect.

They drank to Hradec's good fortune, but then Harry shook his big red head and looked briefly rueful. "It's just a damn shame we didn't get to use this place," he said, waving at their stage set with his half-full glass. (Harry's glasses were always half-full, never half-empty.)

Well, it *was* too bad, really. This space was usually the ground-floor art gallery at the château, with its own wide, wood delivery entrance into the stone foundation of the building, around at the rear, on the downhill side. With the help of the summer theater's set designer and backstage crew, it had been turned into quite a credible torturer's paradise, one that would surely have struck dread into the heart of the unforthcoming Diddums, had he ever seen it.

Here is what they'd done to this windowless and climate-controlled room. The Braque bronzes and third-century Greek torsos had been pushed back out of sight behind drably painted flats placed in front of the walls of Matisses and medieval triptychs. Old barn siding had been laid as an ancient rough floor atop the smooth gray composition modern floor, then lightly sprinkled with stage blood. The nubbly sound-deadening ceiling, overdue for a paint job anyway, had been smeared a dull black, to be restored to its own color after the main event.

But there was to be no main event. First, not daring to stop for gas, and miscalculating how much they'd need, they'd run out, whereon Diddums astonished everybody by rather brutally escaping—he'd been so *lethargic* up till then—and then Hradec had recovered his relic, after all. So all was well that ended well, but it still would have been fun to use this set.

Particularly because of Harry's uniform. Over Hradec's muted doubts, Harry had caused to be flown in from Novi Glad in one of his own planes a Votskojek army general's uniform in 52 short, gaily bedecked with every known Votskojek medal, including those combat medals that, Votskojek's army never having been in actual contention against another army, had never been awarded to anybody.

But they looked swell on Harry Hochman's broad chest, flowing like lava over his broad belly, as well. It had been Harry's intent to be the mutely scowling General Kliebkrecht (Magyar-Croat was not among his accomplishments) in the background of the scene, snarling from time to time as the playlet and his inner sense of drama dictated. Too bad.

Still, he could wear the uniform at the celebratory party, and did. In it, this short, barrely guy in the medal-bedecked dark olive uniform looked like a time-lapse night photograph of traffic going up and down a broad highway on a vast mountain. Fun!

At sixty-six, Harry Hochman was ready for fun. He'd always been a short, barrely guy with a big, fat red face and a lot of silken red hair (then gray hair, then red hair again), who considered himself a self-made man, since, after all, he'd taken his father's minor hotel, motel, and bus-line holdings, worth no more than three or four mil, and had expanded them into this current multi everything—multinational, multimillion, multidirectional. A one-man conglomerate, Harry Hochman *looked* as though he'd swallowed the world and had found it good. His florid face coursed with emotions, all of them operatic—rage, greed, triumph, glee. He was right to wear the uniform; he looked good in it, to the extent that he looked good in anything. (Secretly, he wished he could wear it all the time. But even for a titan such as himself, there still must be unfulfillable desires. Humbling.)

For a man like Harry Hochman, Eastern Europe in its current post-Soviet disarray was a kind of wonderful Christmas present, a model-train set all for him; some assembly required. And Votskojek was the centerpiece. Once it was securely ensconced in its proper traditional United Nations seat, once its economic treaties with its neighbors were in place, that little landlocked barren boulder in the Carpathians would become Harry Hochman's stepping stone to Europe. *All* of Europe.

Soon, Votskojek would join with the other former Comecon nations in a new economic alliance. This refurbished and renamed

Comecon would join the European Community whether France and England liked it or not. And at the end of the day, from the Rockies to the Urals, Harry Hochman would be *the* hotel man. (He'd even suggested that already as a slogan to his advertising agency: "From the Rockies to the Urals, a Hochman pillow will rest your head." The ad guys were thinking about it.)

And of course the hotels were just the beginning. Once established, they would be the base for horizontal expansion into all sorts of industries. Insurance in Holland, television production in France, agriculture in Italy, mortuaries in England; the possibilities were infinite.

That this rosy future for this rosy man had become dependent on a *bone* was so ridiculous as to be infuriating. For the first time in many years, Harry had had to start putting the plastic protector in his mouth at night, to keep from grinding his teeth in his sleep. A *bone*! It's a good thing I'm not a ruthless man, Harry had told himself more than once, I'd just have that senile clot of an archbishop assassinated.

Except, of course, stupid though it might be that the relic of St. Ferghana had become this important in twentieth-century international politics, the fact was that Votskojek did have possession of the little beauty, which gave it a leg up (pardon the pun) on the competition. So. The femur of St. Ferghana fronted the future hopes of Votskojek; Ambassador Hradec Kralowc was responsible for the femur; and Kralowc was in Harry Hochman's pocket. Which was why he'd been so openhanded in setting up his flummery to "gaslight the fella to a fare-thee-well." That, and it was fun.

Harry looked around his converted art gallery, the six-plus millions worth of art now completely out of sight behind the faux dungeon, and he almost wished he could keep the place this way. Come down here in this uniform from time to time, strut around, listen to the hollow thud of these boots on the barn-siding floor. "Damn shame," he said again.

"Harry, you're just a big boy," said his beloved wife, Adele, smiling indulgently upon him. Taller than her husband, and a little younger than he every year, stately as a frigate's figurehead; where he was red, she was black and white all over; hair as black as Ronald Reagan's, skin as white as any golem's. She almost always wore black, under the mistaken assumption that it made her look thinner. What it made her look like, in fact, was Dracula's aunt, but nobody was likely to tell her so.

Harry grinned back at his rather scary but beloved wife. "Admit it, Adele," he said. "You'd have liked to see that fella's face yourself when he walked in here."

"Poor Diddums," Hradec said, and laughed.

Harry's red face turned quizzical, "Poor Diddums? How come?"

"Such a minor cog in the wheel," Hradec explained. "A foot soldier, a nobody. And here he was, at the very center of all this machination. What *I* would like to see is his face when he found out he was in Vermont!"

They all laughed at that idea, Tatiana saying, "Such amusement!" Then they all finished their champagne, and Harry reached into the ice bucket, grabbed the Dom Perignon by the throat, and refilled. "To John Diddums," he said, raising his glass. "The poor schnook."

"Hear hear," said Hradec.

"Of positive!" said Tatiana, and they all drank.

28

When the prowler fell over a chair in the kitchen, May woke up and knew exactly what to do. A woman alone had to be ready to defend herself, and May was ready. The drawer in the bedside table slid noiselessly open. Her hand closed first on the flashlight, which she didn't want, but then she found what she was looking for and slid silently out of bed, holding it out in front of her. In the dark room, she crossed toward the greater darkness of the doorway, hesitated there, and heard the prowler shuffling cautiously in this direction down the hall. She took a breath, held it, turned the corner, and Maced the guy full in the face.

"Holy shit!"

"John?"

"Ow! Ow! Ow!" Crash bang thud bang crash.

Horrified, May backed into the bedroom, frantically feeling along the wall there, finding the light switch, flicking it on, and there was John, all curled up on the hall floor near his spilled beer can, thrashing around like a bug that has just been sprayed with Raid. Which, in a way, he was.

•   •   •

Every time he came up for air, John told her a little more of the story, and May apologized all over again for everything, including having left that chair pulled out too far from the kitchen table. Then, kneeling on the bathroom floor, John would bend forward again like one of those novelty drinking birds and stick his flaming head back into the water-filled bathtub.

And so, piece by piece, May learned of John's capture and imprisonment, his jailer's deception, his own escape, his discovery of the truth, and his long journey home from Vermont in a scattered series of short hops in trucks, truck drivers being the only people in America who aren't afraid to pick up a hitchhiker who looks like John Dortmunder, since most of them look like John Dortmunder themselves.

When at last the stinging abated on John's face and neck and ears, and when he could keep his eyes open without shedding tears all over the place, and when the really *baaaaaddddd* taste in his mouth had to some extent gone away, May left him and went to the kitchen to get them both a fresh beer, plus for him a sliced American cheese sandwich with butter and mayo and mustard and ketchup on white bread nicely quartered into triangles, which she brought to the living room, where John now sat, the white towel around his neck setting off his red skin and red eyeballs, making him look like something that has just been shorn.

He made faces while he ate, the Mace apparently having altered the taste of things he ordinarily liked, but he made no comment beyond one mumbled, "What a homecoming," and he listened quietly while May gave him a report of events here in town while he'd been away up in Vermont on the slippery slopes. How the guys had lost the bone to the DEA but were pretty sure they were off to get it, and probably the Tsergovians even had it by this hour, and Andy Kelp would call tomorrow, probably—no, certainly—with good news, and would be delighted to learn that John was safe, and would bring over his five thousand dollars.

"So. All's well that ends well, then," John said inaccurately, but it was a nice thought to take along to bed, where it helped him sleep right through until Kelp showed up around ten the next morning.

29

Dortmunder looked at the money he'd dumped out of the envelope onto the coffee table. "I don't get it," he said.

Kelp shrugged. "Tiny says it's ours," he said, "and you know how seldom people argue with Tiny. As far as he's concerned, we got the bone and we delivered it. Gave it straight into his cousin's hands, got paid, and that was that. We did what they paid us to do."

"But," Dortmunder objected, "they don't have the bone."

"That's the way it looked to me, too," Kelp agreed, "but Tiny explained it this other way, and Grijk just sat there looking like one of those beached whales you see in the *Post* and said, 'Okay, Diny, okay, Diny,' in that way he has. Tiny told him to go borrow some more from Citibank, he wants us to do it again."

"And what'd Grijk say to that?"

"I think he's discouraged," Kelp said. "That whole crowd over there, I think they got the wind kind of knocked out of their sails."

Dortmunder looked into the coffee cup he'd brought in with him from the kitchen, but it was empty. Shaking his head, he said, "I don't follow the sequence there. Where'd those other people come from?"

163

"What it looks like," Kelp told him, "it looks like the Votskojeks put a tap on the Tsergovians' phone, so when Tiny called to say we had the bone and we're coming over, they went there real quick ahead of us, three of them. Two went upstairs and tied up the people there, and the third one stayed with Grijk to make sure he didn't slip us the high sign, and made Grijk say he was his deputy security guy. So we left the bone and split, and they copped it for themselves."

"That's really irritating," Dortmunder said. He looked in his coffee cup, and it was still empty.

"Water over the bridge," Kelp said. "We did the job, and we got paid."

Dortmunder looked at the money on the coffee table. He looked around the room, but May was off at her cashier job at the Safeway, and there was no one else to consult. "I don't know about this," he said.

Kelp said, "What's not to know? John, this is the most successful job we pulled in recent memory. In even *not* so recent memory. There was something to get, we went out and got it, we got paid for it. Okay, we lost it for a little while—"

"You lost me, too," Dortmunder pointed out.

"John," Kelp said, more in sorrow than in anger, looking at him as though Dortmunder were guilty of some sort of low blow, "John, we said, 'Jump.' You remember that; Stan and me, we both said, 'Jump.'"

"Just pointing out," Dortmunder said. "You said you lost the bone; I'm just pointing out, you also lost me."

"Whatever you want," Kelp said. "We *found* the bone, and you found yourself—"

"In Vermont." (That still griped.)

"—and we got *paid*. Success. Victory. Accomplishment. End of story."

"I don't know," Dortmunder said.

Kelp shook his head. He was getting exasperated. He said, "*What* don't you know?"

For answer, Dortmunder reached for the phone and dialed a number. The phone rang six times, and then there was a click, and then a sound like a bear roused too early from hibernation—part roar, part cough, part gnashing of teeth. "Tiny, it's John," Dortmunder said.

The growl formed itself into words: "I taught you wuh lost."

"I found myself," Dortmunder said. "Tiny, I want to go over to—"

"Don't you know what time it is?"

"What? No, I don't think so, I—Hold on." Dortmunder turned to Kelp, "He wants to know what time it is."

While Kelp vainly searched himself for a watch, Tiny roared in Dortmunder's ear, "I *don't* wanna know what time it is!"

"You don't?"

"I'll find out," Kelp said, getting to his feet and going away to the kitchen.

"*And* I don't care where you been, neither," Tiny said. "If that's what you're calling me about, forget it."

"I been in Vermont," Dortmunder said, "but that isn't the point."

"You been in *Vermont*?"

"But that isn't the point. The point is—"

"*Vermont?*"

"You don't care, Tiny, remember? The reason I'm calling is, I want to go see the Tsergovians, and I thought maybe you could bring me over there."

Tiny muttered a bit, like a subway going by far below ground level, and then he said, "Whadaya wanna go over there for? You got your money, right?"

"I got jerked around, Tiny," Dortmunder said. "I wanna know the story."

"What story? There is no story. You got hired, you did it, you went to Vermont, you got paid. The money's good, right? It isn't draffs, right?"

Kelp came back from the kitchen and said, "It's quarter after ten."

"It's quarter after ten," Dortmunder said into the phone.

There was silence. It stretched on and on. Had Tiny gone back to sleep? Dortmunder said, "Tiny?"

A long sigh came snaking down the phone line. Tiny said, "You wanna go see these people, Dortmunder, whyntcha just go see these people? You need the address?"

"Grijk's the only one I met," Dortmunder reminded him. "You're their cousin; you can like vouch for me."

"I don't do family reunions," Tiny said. "I did what I could for that crowd, and now that's it."

"I don't ask you a lot, Tiny," Dortmunder said, and just let that lie there, and waited.

Long silence, even longer than before. But Tiny hadn't gone back to sleep, Dortmunder knew he hadn't. He waited.

Another long sigh. Tiny said, "All right, Dortmunder, this once."

"Thank you, Tiny."

"I'll call them; I'll call you back."

"Thank you."

"You know, Dortmunder," Tiny said, "you could go too far, you know."

"I wouldn't want to do that, Tiny," Dortmunder said.

"You're right about that," Tiny said.

30

"Zara Kotor," Tiny said, "and Drava Votskonia, this is John Dortmunder and An-*drew* Kelp."

"Hi."

"How are you?"

"Call me Andy."

"Sit down, sit down."

They were in the upstairs parlor at the Tsergovian embassy, amid the tasseled shades and the commemorative plates. All the chairs and sofas up here were deeply stuffed mohair; you sank way down into them, and they itched. Zara Kotor, settling into the big maroon sofa under the ornately framed painting of a corner of a cul-de-sac at midnight during a power failure, patted the mohair seat cushion beside her—puff, puff, the dust lazily rose—for Tiny to come sit beside her, but somehow he managed not to notice and took the settee on the other side of the room. *All* the settee.

It was Kelp who wound up next to Zara on the sofa, but she paid him no attention. Her eyes were on Tiny as she said, "I'm glad you fellows came around. I was afraid we wouldn't be seeing any more of you, lose touch with one another."

Tiny shifted on the settee, which groaned piteously, and said, "It's Dortmunder wants to talk to you. That one there."

"Oh yes," Zara said, eying Dortmunder with wary interest. "You're the one who was captured."

"And given the runaround."

"But you escaped."

"They treated me like a rube," Dortmunder said. He was feeling sullen and embarrassed, having to explain himself this way. Treated like a rube; if he didn't do something about that, then they were right, right?

She looked at his face and nodded, with a little smile of understanding. "You want revenge."

"I want my own back," Dortmunder agreed. "But first I got to know, if you and Votskojek are all so poor, how come they could pull such a major scam?"

"That's an easy one," she said, her smile turning grim. "The answer is Harry Hochman."

"Never heard of him," Dortmunder said.

"He owns hotels," Zara told him. "Happy Hour Inns."

"Oh, them," Kelp said happily. "I've got some of their towels."

"And they've got some of my goat," Dortmunder said. (Grijk looked briefly puzzled.) "But Harry Hochman," Dortmunder went on, "doesn't sound like a Votskojek name."

"He's an American," Zara said. "He came to Novi Glad years ago, with money in both fists, trying to buy people and governments, and when our country split up he decided to put his bets on Votskojek. If they win, he gets richer."

"So he financed it, huh? Running me around in Vermont."

"I think he has a place there." Turning to Grijk, she said, "Get the Hochman file. It's in the black drawer."

As Grijk obediently lumbered away—thud thud thud, down the stairs—Dortmunder said, "You got a whole file on this guy?"

"We keep tabs on our enemies," she said, with a glint in her eye. "When the day comes, we'll get our own revenge."

"If the day comes, you mean."

"When."

Dortmunder nodded, thinking about that. He said, "What are you gonna do next, about the bone?"

"We can't steal it anymore," she said. "They're alerted to that now."

"What else is there?"

Looking very serious and ambassadorial, she said, "We are presenting a formal objection to the General Assembly concerning the makeup of the advisory committee."

"The archbishop, you mean."

"Yes."

"You're saying he's prejudiced or whatever, you want him off your case."

"Yes."

"Isn't it kinda late to make that beef?"

"I'm sorry we didn't do it earlier, yes," she admitted.

Dortmunder nodded again. "And it won't work now, will it? On account of being so late. So then, besides the archbishop's already got a religious thing against you, because of the bone, now he's gonna have a personal thing, because you said he couldn't be fair."

"He *can't* be fair!"

"Less now than before," Dortmunder pointed out.

Zara sighed. She was looking less like an ambassador and more like a Bronx Science student. "We know that," she said. "But we tried the other way, and we failed. Now they're on guard against us, and we don't have any more money...."

"You have a little more," Dortmunder said.

Instantly, she was all suspicion again, gimlet-eyed and stern-jawed, but before she could say anything the thud-thud of Grijk's return sounded, and they all turned to look at the doorway. Grijk stomped in carrying two maroon expansion files with cloth ties in neat bows. He carried these to Zara and she handed one to Kelp, beside her, for safekeeping while untying the other one and fingering through its contents. Meanwhile, Grijk went back to his own mohair seat, passing Dortmunder on the way, pausing to say, with quiet sympathy, "I lost a goat once. It was werry sad."

Dortmunder contemplated that piece of personal history. Grijk resumed his seat, and Zara grunted as she leaned forward to put some papers from the file on the massive dark-wood coffee table, saying, "Mr. Hochman owns a ski resort in Vermont."

"*Does* he." Dortmunder picked up from the coffee table a full-

169

color brochure of the Mount Kinohaha ski resort. Leafing through it, he saw a bright wintertime photo of the shopping area. "The village," he muttered. "That's it right there, the village they ran me through."

Kelp got up to come over and peer past Dortmunder's shoulder at the picture. "Gee, John," he said. "With all those skis and things in the windows? And you didn't catch on?"

"They didn't have skis in the windows," Dortmunder said, with what only looked like patience. "They had food and stuff. And people all dressed in—Ah hah!"

Kelp looked alert. "Ah hah?"

"Summer-stock theater," Dortmunder read from the brochure, and pointed to the phrase. "That's where they got all those goddam villagers and their goddam native goddam garb."

"Boy," Kelp said. "They really put on a whole production for you."

"Sure," Dortmunder said. "So I'd give up and tell them where the bone is, if they'd promise to bring me back to the States. From *Vermont*." Then he frowned over at Zara, who was still frowningly going through the files. "But what about that Dracula's castle place? Where they were taking me when I got away."

"Hochman owns a house near there," she said, "They call it a château. I'm looking for a—Here it is."

This time, what she'd produced out of the file was a bunch of pages cut from a magazine and stapled together in one corner. She held them out, and Kelp came over to take them and deliver them to Dortmunder; except he moved very slowly coming back, leafing through the pages, becoming absorbed in what he saw.

Dortmunder said, "Andy? Do you mind?"

"What? Oh, no, no. Here." And Kelp handed over the pages.

Which were from an architecture magazine; a whole article about Harry Hochman's brand-new château up in the Green Mountains of Vermont. Interior and exterior photos, and gobbledygook copy, leaning heavily on the word *volume,* as in "volume of air," "volume of space," "contrasting volumes of light and darkness." The "volumes flanking the fireplace" turned out to be books, which confused matters.

"Doesn't look like Dracula's castle to me," Kelp said. "Looks kinda pretty good, actually."

Dortmunder pointed to a view of the building from downhill, looking up, the volumes of the design darkly silhouetted against the pale blue volume of the sky. "That's where *I* saw it from," he said. "Okay?"

Kelp squinted, the better to see, and gazed judiciously at the picture for so long that Dortmunder finally, to make a point, turned the page and looked at the rest of the article. He studied it briefly, turned back and forth through the pages, then looked over at Zara Kotor. "Maybe," he said, "we could help each other out here."

When in doubt, Zara Kotor invariably fell back on paranoia: "I don't see how," she said, with a frosty look that somehow exempted Tiny, who was keeping as low a profile as possible, given that he was about the size of a minor Alp. "I don't see it at all."

"Well," Dortmunder said, and patted the magazine article open on his knee, "we both want something, seems to me. You want your UN seat, which means you want that bone, and I want to even the score with some smartass room-renters."

"I told you," she said, "we've given up that approach. Security will be *much* tighter there now. Besides, it's almost too late anyway. They already have photos of the relic, X rays, some test results."

"Not enough to prove it's the right one," Dortmunder said.

"Not yet," she agreed. "But very soon. Then, if we take it, they'll be able to demonstrate they once had it."

"But not yet."

"But soon."

"But not yet. Also, we could lift the test results while we're in the neighborhood."

Zara expelled an exasperated sigh. "All right. Fine. But it isn't going to happen."

"Why not?" Dortmunder asked her. "If we move fast, we can do the whole thing. You can join that club you're so hot for, and I can poke this guy Hochman in the eye. If we move fast, and if we help each other."

"How?"

"I don't have the details worked out yet," he admitted, "but I will, as long as I know I can count on you people."

"For what?"

"Well, you know," Dortmunder said, "behind you, you got a whole country. You got..." he searched for the word "...assets we don't have, being a country."

"Such as?"

"Armies, air forces—"

She recoiled, shocked, bouncing off the sofa-back. "My God, we're not going to *war* with Votskojek! Not here in New York!"

"They'd hardly notice, in this town," Dortmunder told her. "But that isn't what I meant. What I meant was, you could give us like backup support, whatever we decide to do."

"Not necessarily *whatever*," she said, with a very guarded look. "You know," she said, "you're beginning to remind me of those guys in high school, kind of nerdy guys that you didn't notice very much—Bronx Science was full of them—and one day they'd say, 'I have this idea,' and they'd go off, talking to themselves, and the next thing anybody knew, the lab was on fire."

"Not this time," Dortmunder said. "If anything catches fire, it won't be your stuff." Turning to Tiny, he said, "You busy, the next couple of days?"

"Absolutely," Tiny said.

Dortmunder was interested. "Yeah? Doing what?"

"Staying away from you," Tiny said.

Dortmunder nodded. "I understand your feelings," he said.

"Well," Tiny said, "let me express them, anyway. I'm surprised at you, Dortmunder. Maybe *you* can make a nice meal outta revenge, but I'm a meat-and-potatoes man."

"I agree," Dortmunder said.

"So what I'm saying to you now," Tiny said, "is what you said to me before, when I first brought you this bone thing. You remember?"

"My family crest, you mean."

"That's it," Tiny said. "How did that go again?"

"Quid lucrum istic mihi est?"

"Yeah, that was it," Tiny agreed. "'What's in it for me?' Sorry, Dortmunder, I gotta go along with your forebears."

"Don't be sorry, Tiny," Dortmunder said. "Just listen to this." And he bowed his head, to read from the magazine pages on his lap: "'Into its own windowless and climate-controlled gallery space beneath the main building, cut dramatically into the volume of the rock-walled mountain itself on which the château stands, the Hochmans have moved the bulk of their extensive collection of modern and ancient art. Here Matisses and other Impressionists rub shoulders comfortably with Cretan statuary and early Italian church art. In the low-ceilinged and gently lighted volume of this intricate space, far from the prying eyes of the maddening crowd, the Hochmans can be alone with their beloved art, conservatively valued at more than six million dollars.'"

"Holy shit," Tiny said, and Kelp looked extremely happy.

Dortmunder lifted his eyes from the pages. The expression around his mouth was almost a smile. "Turns out," he said, "there's a profit in this thing, after all. My ancestors would be proud."

31

The meeting this time was at Dortmunder's place, which meant May's two grocery bags of fringe benefits from the Safeway this evening had assayed out 90 percent beer, 10 percent potato chips. Squatted around the living room, filling it to overflowing, swigging and chomping, May and Kelp and Tiny and Stan Murch all waited for Dortmunder to say something, but Dortmunder was in a brown study, slumped in his favorite chair, brooding at his beer can, eyes clouded. While waiting for Dortmunder to talk, therefore, everybody else talked.

"I was about ready, with that crowd," Tiny announced, "to see if blood *is* thicker than water, but maybe this way is better. You got a friend at the UN, it could maybe come in helpful sometimes. With airline tickets or like that."

"For myself," Kelp said, "I feel I've got a kind of a personal relationship with that bone now, like I knew the kid, whatsername."

"Ferghana," Tiny reminded him.

"That's her." Kelp raised his palms, as though hefting a watermelon. "I held that bone," he said. "I moved it from place to place. I rescued it from the DEA. I feel involved with it."

"What I'm thinking about," Stan said, "is those Vermont mountains. I understand, the quickest way down those things is, you kick it out of gear and shoot down in neutral."

May said, "Why not just turn the engine off?"

"You could," allowed Stan. "Of course, now and again, you might want your brakes. Power brakes, you know, they need the engine. Of course, maybe not, if you don't have any real *sharp* curves in the real *steep*—"

"The problem is . . ." Dortmunder said.

Everybody shut up and looked at him. But then he didn't say anything else, just sat there and frowned across the room at Kelp's left knee.

The problem was: time. Dortmunder wasn't used to thinking under pressure like this. Usually, you'd decide what you wanted to take, you'd think about where it was and what security you'd find around it, you'd consider the personnel and the geography and maybe the weather and whatever other factors might be involved, and after a while you'd come up with the way to go in and get it and come back out again without stepping in anything. But here in this situation, he'd become annoyed, he'd become irritated at having been treated with such dismissive disdain, and in front of everybody he'd vowed vengeance, and he'd included Tsergovia and their goddam sparerib in the equation, partly for the tactical support they damn well better provide, and that meant a *deadline*. If this thing were gonna get done, it was better that it got itself done soonest. So that was the problem; anybody can think fast, it's how to think fast when you have to.

Dortmunder not expressing any of this aloud—how could he, when it was more mood and feeling than coherent thought?—the others gave up waiting and started to chat again among themselves.

"The nice thing," May said, "is that we don't have to go to Vermont in the winter. I understand it can get brutal up there."

Kelp nodded soberly. "Slipping and sliding down mountains with paintings in our arms," he said. "Not a pretty picture."

"Oh, I don't know," Tiny said. "Some of them modern things are okay. We could use something in our living room, Josie and me, over the sofa. Something in, you know, different shades of green. That's what Josie says. Maybe I'll take part of my piece in a painting."

May said, "You'd better have J.C. pick out the painting herself."

"Oh, yeah," Tiny agreed. "I know that much."

Stan said, "I don't know how my Mom's gonna take to Vermont, should she has to go there. You know how she gets, outside the city. You think we'll need her?"

"No telling," May said.

Kelp said, "If she could look on it like a vacation, maybe—"

"The other problem is," Dortmunder said, and stopped, staring sightlessly at a stain on the opposite wall where an intrusive policeman had once rested the palm of his hand, at a moment when May had been explaining that she had no suggestion to make concerning her consort's then-whereabouts.

The other problem was, this was two jobs in one, and they were two hundred miles apart. Security around the bone was gonna be a lot tighter now than the last time, and who knew what kind of security Harry Hochman had at his château in Vermont? Wasn't there something in history about not opening a war on two fronts? Where's the manpower coming from, just to begin with? And how do you keep control over what's happening in New York and Vermont at the same time?

Do you do them at different times?

Is there any way to tie them together?

The observers waited, and waited, wondering not only what the other problem was but also what the first problem had been, but Dortmunder seemed to have nothing else to say. Then he was seen to sigh, and to drink from his beer can—but not. It was empty. He gave the thing a reproachful look, shook it—no slosh—and got to his feet. He left the room, and Kelp said, "I don't know, May, could be this time John bit off—"

Dortmunder stuck his head back into the room. "Tiny," he said.

"Yeah?"

"Call your people over there, ask them, can they get us a helicopter." And Dortmunder's head retracted from the room again.

"I don't know about that," Tiny said, but he reached for the phone.

With a happy smile, Kelp said, "We haven't been in a helicopter in a long time. Remember that, Stan?"

176

Stan looked a little grumpy. "Probably," he said, "these people would have their own driver."

In the kitchen, Dortmunder stood in front of the open refrigerator, thinking. "And the *other* other problem is," he said aloud, "the UN," finishing a sentence for once.

The problem with the UN was, if the Tsergovians got their bone with any kind of cloud on it, questions about how they happened to have it in their possession, stuff like that, it could make things worse for them instead of better, when it came to influencing people over at the United Nations to give them that seat. So, however the heist was pulled, it had to wind up with the bone clean. Like a stolen car where you've got beautiful paper. Somehow they had to find the equivalent of beautiful paper for a bone.

Dortmunder began to shiver; it was damn cold in here. Then he realized he was still standing in front of the open refrigerator, so he closed the door, turned away, turned back, opened the door, took out a beer, closed the door, opened the beer (bending his thumbnail back so it hurt), and, sucking his thumb, walked thoughtfully back to the living room, where Tiny said, "No helicopter."

"What?"

Tiny shook his head, having expected something like this. "You forgot, huh?"

"Oh, the helicopter," Dortmunder said, and spilled beer on himself while sitting down. Ignoring that, he drank some of the brew and said, "Okay, no helicopter."

Kelp said, "That doesn't louse up your plan?"

"What plan?" Dortmunder asked him; he was really interested.

"I just thought you had something," Kelp explained.

Dortmunder nodded, understanding. Then he went on nodding a while, so the others went back to their conversation, Stan saying to Tiny, "If this country doesn't have any helicopters, what about their boats? Maybe we could disguise an aircraft carrier or something, probably something smaller, sneak up the East River, grapple onto their boat, do it that way."

Tiny shook his head. "They don't have a navy," he said.

Kelp said, "Tiny, everybody has a navy. Every country, I mean."

"Not Tsergovia," Tiny said. "Or the other one, either. Votskojek. They don't have any seacoast, so they don't have a navy."

Disappointed, Stan said, "So they won't have any boats, then."

"Well," Tiny said, "they'd have a hell of a time getting them into the water."

May said, "Maybe that's why the Votskojeks put their embassy on a boat. Maybe to them it's romantic, something different."

"Could be," Tiny said without much interest.

Dortmunder said, "Andy."

Everybody looked at him. Kelp said, "Yes, John?"

"You know a lot of people," Dortmunder told him.

Kelp grinned. "I don't know *everybody*," he said, "but I do know a lot, you're right."

"I'm thinking about fences," Dortmunder said.

Kelp said, "John? That you sell to, or climb over?"

Dortmunder struggled for an answer. "The one with money," he decided.

"Okay."

Tiny said, "Dortmunder, isn't this a little early? Shouldn't we go get the stuff first?"

"Not this time." Dortmunder reached out in front of himself and made little feeble clutching gestures with the fingertips of his right hand. "What I've got," he said, "is I got a corner of something, I *think* I got a corner of something, and if I'm right we got to know we got the fence ahead of time. A very special fence."

Kelp said, "You know the same guys I do, John."

"I hope not," Dortmunder said. "What I hope, I hope you know a guy we wouldn't normally use, that you'd only use if you had a big, major, important big-league haul, a guy that wouldn't be interested in just some little jewelry store."

Nodding, Kelp said, "A conservative estimate six million dollar value fine art collection kind of fence, is that what you mean?"

"Yes," Dortmunder said simply.

"Well, John," Kelp said, "I haven't had that much call in my life for guys like that, but it could happen that I might know guys that know guys. Let me look around, okay?"

"Go ahead," Dortmunder said.

"It's not the kind of question you ask on the phone," Kelp pointed out. "I'd have to go talk to people."

"Fine," Dortmunder said, and sat there looking at him.

Kelp gazed around the room, and now they were all looking at him. He met Dortmunder's eyes again and said, "Oh, you mean now?"

"Couldn't hurt," Dortmunder said.

Kelp had been enjoying the party, sitting with the others around Dortmunder's burning brain, chatting about things. Oh, well. "Sure, John," he said, and got to his feet. "If it won't be too late, I'll come back here."

"It won't be too late," Dortmunder assured him.

"So that's what I'll do," Kelp said, and Dortmunder nodded. But then Dortmunder's head kept slowly bobbing, up and down, up and down, so Kelp knew this latest contact between John Dortmunder and Planet Earth had come to an end for now, so he said so long to the others and left, and six minutes later Dortmunder interrupted general conversation again to say, "Stan."

"Here," Stan announced.

Dortmunder gazed piercingly at him. "Who's a good driver?"

Stan reared up a little. "What kind of question is that? *I'm* a good driver!"

"Another one."

"My Mom!"

Dortmunder sighed a little. He said, "Could we move out beyond you and your family a little?"

Stan said, "How many drivers you gonna need?"

"I don't know yet. Who's good?"

"Well, there's always Fred Lartz," Stan said, and grudgingly added, "He's pretty good."

Dortmunder said, "I thought he gave up driving."

"Well, yeah," Stan said, "but now his wife, Thelma, drives. He kind of just sits beside her."

"So Thelma's the driver."

"In a way. I thought you knew that."

"How is she?"

"Good, John," Stan said with an air of some surprise. "You know, she's better than Fred ever was."

May said, "I never did understand why Fred Lartz gave up driving."

Stan did the explanation, since Dortmunder was getting that faraway look in his eyes again. "Seems like, coming home from a wedding, he took a wrong turn off the Van Wyck, out by Kennedy airport, he wound up on taxiway seventeen, ran into an Eastern Airlines plane out of Miami, spent a couple of months in the hospital, doesn't trust his instincts anymore. So Thelma drives, and Fred sits beside her."

Dortmunder focused again. "Can we get him?"

"Her, you mean," May said.

"Well, both of them."

Stan said, "For when?"

That was the question, wasn't it? Dortmunder looked in absolute agony, as though undergoing some sort of anesthetic-free operation in the area of the lower torso. Finally, he said, "Today is, uhhhhhh . . ."

"Wednesday," May told him.

Dortmunder sighed. Now he looked as though he had a toothache, probably an abscess. "Saturday," he decided.

Everybody was surprised. May said, "That soon?"

"Saturday isn't soon," Dortmunder said. "They've got, uh . . . Is Wednesday the day just finished, or the day just starting?"

"What, today?" May had to think a second. "The day just finished."

"So that gives them two more full days with the bone," Dortmunder said. "To take pictures, measurements, X rays, all this stuff, all this record. It'd be better if we could do it tomorrow, but we can't."

Tiny said, "There you're right."

Stan said, "So, do you want me to get ahold of Fred?"

"Thelma, you mean," May said.

"Well," Stan said, "Fred does the bookings."

"Go see them," Dortmunder said, with unexpected tact, "and ask are they ready Saturday for a maybe."

Stan sat back to think it over. "They moved up to the Bronx to get away from the airport," he mused. "So, with the construction on the Bruckner, I think I'll stay on the Henry Hudson. It's a toll across Spuyten Duyvil, but it's worth it."

"Good," Dortmunder said. He watched Stan, waiting for him to go away.

Stan finished his beer at his leisure, and looked around. "Anybody want a lift?"

"You're the only one going," Dortmunder said.

"Be back," Stan decided, and got to his feet, and left.

Tiny said, "Dortmunder, don't send me nowhere."

But Dortmunder wasn't listening. Instead, spilling a little more beer, he pawed around on the floor beside his chair and came up at last with the torn-out magazine pages he'd borrowed from Zara Kotor. ("Tiny can bring them back," she'd suggested, "when you're done.") Beetling his brow at the pretty color pictures of the interior of Harry Hochman's Vermont château, he said, "Call them, see do they have any spy stuff."

Tiny and May were the only others left in the room, and both guessed it was Tiny that Dortmunder was talking to. Tiny was on much of the sofa, with the phone on the end table perilously close to his right elbow. Picking up the receiver, dialing, he said, "If you had a phone with redial, this would be easier."

"Don't talk like Andy," Dortmunder said.

Apparently, the phone rang a long time. Then Tiny began to talk, and at one point they heard him say, "No, I didn't know it was that late," but not as though he cared. Then he asked his question, and turned to say to Dortmunder, "Grijk says, sure. They got all kinds of spy stuff. What kind of stuff do you need?"

Dortmunder shrugged. "Telephoto lenses," he suggested. "Microphone bugs that you can shoot with arrows. All that James Bond stuff."

James Bond stuff, Tiny said into the phone, and then reported to Dortmunder, "He says they got a ton of that kind of crap. The only thing is, it's thirdhand. They bought it from Pakistan and Cyprus, and *they* bought it from Mexico and Australia and Kuwait."

"Does it still work?"

"Oh, sure. Usually. Except it's long off the warranty, you know."

Dortmunder looked at May. "It's discouraging, sometimes," he said. "Not working with the best equipment. I feel like it's holding me back."

"You'll do the best you can," May assured him.

"Well, yeah, sure." To Tiny, Dortmunder said, "Tell him we'll come around tomorrow—I don't know, eleven o'clock—see what he's got."

"Morning or night?"

181

"What?" Dortmunder worked his way back through the conversation, found the area that matched the question, and said, "Morning. Eleven tomorrow morning."

While Tiny spoke into the phone again, Dortmunder frowned massively at May, and eventually said, "Do we have a map?"

May, used to his behavior under these circumstances, and not fazed by it, said reassuringly, "I'm sure we do. Anything in particular you want to see on it?"

He gestured with both hands, the magazine pages flapping. "You know, here and, uh, there. Vermont."

"Vermont," she said, getting to her feet.

"And here."

She left the room, and Dortmunder looked at the pages in his hand as though they were an anonymous crank letter. After a while, Tiny got off the phone and said, "They'll be waiting for you tomorrow, eleven o'clock, with all the stuff, whatever they got."

"Waiting for *us*," Dortmunder corrected.

But Tiny shook his head, refusing to accept the correction. "Waiting for *you*. Zara already knows, I got this dental appointment tomorrow, just can't break it."

"Oh, I didn't know that," Dortmunder said.

"Now you do," Tiny said with emphasis. He looked around. "Where'd you send May?"

"Vermont."

"What?" Tiny said, but then May came in with the results of her search of the bedroom and kitchen: two roadmaps and a fifteen-year-old almanac. One road map was New York City and environs and the other was New England. The almanac contained maps, though mostly of larger groupings like continents. "The nice thing about the New England map," she said, dumping all this into Dortmunder's lap, "you can see New York City down at the lower left."

Yes, he could. And after a long and irritating search, he could also see Middleville, Vermont, the flyspeck that was the mailing address of Mount Kinohaha Happy Hour Inns Ski Resort and Summer Arts Center, which the Harry Hochman château was somewhere near.

And all of which was quite a ways up this map from New York

City. Dortmunder tried to work out the mileages, point A to point B to point C, and so on, and so on, and finally decided Mount Kinohaha was somewhere between 240 and 320 miles from New York. Say five hours by car. Bennington, Vermont, had an airport—an *international* airport, thank you very much—but, given their travel motivations, maybe they should forget public transportation.

So, you'd go from here to there, and from there to here. . . .

So what?

Dortmunder lifted his head to stare piercingly through Tiny's forehead at something a block away. "Do they have a picture?"

"Sure," Tiny said. "Who, of what?"

"Them," Dortmunder explained. "When it's in the church."

"Oh, you mean the bone? How it's displayed? When it's at home?"

"The Rivers of Blood Cathedral," Dortmunder said, remembering Hradec Kralowc's sales pitch when he'd been Diddums the tourist. "In Novi Glad."

"Grijk's gonna love this," Tiny suggested, and made the call.

Dortmunder looked around the room, but May wasn't there. He was trying to figure that out when she came in with fresh beers for all three of them, already opened. She put Tiny's down next to the phone—he was rumbling at somebody on it, presumably Grijk—hers down next to her chair, and came over to take Dortmunder's empty out of his other hand and insert the fresh one in its place. Now he had maps in one hand, beer in the other, and almanac and magazine pages on his lap. He looked up at her and said, "I forget."

"Forget what?"

He shook his head. "I don't know. Something."

Tiny said, "Grijk says they got lots of pictures."

Dortmunder said, "Have him describe it. Where's the thing kept? Out where people can see it?"

Tiny relayed the question and the answer: "Yeah."

"How? Is it in anything?"

Question; answer. "It's in a glass box, like a little glass coffin, on an altar cloth, on an altar, in one of the side places in the cathedral. Wait a minute." Tiny listened some more, then said, "A glass box vid—*with* jewels on it."

"Can he find out where it is now?"

183

"Dortmunder, why don't you talk to him yourself?"

"He's your cousin," Dortmunder said. "And you're right there with the phone."

Tiny muttered but then asked the question and reported the answer: "He'll call Osigreb in the morning."

"Who's that?"

"It's a what, Dortmunder not a who. It's the capital of Tsergovia."

"Okay."

Tiny listened to the phone, nodded, and said, "Grijk says, you got more questions, why not ask in the morning?"

"Dr. Zorn," Dortmunder said.

Tiny lowered an eyebrow at Dortmunder, but he repeated the name into the phone, then said to Dortmunder, "He's a very bad man. You want a doctor, Grijk'll recommend you a great doctor, official doctor to the Tsergovia Olympic team. You don't want Dr. Zorn; he murders babies."

Dortmunder said, "He doesn't eat them?"

"I was leaving that part out," Tiny explained, "on account of May."

"Thank you, Tiny," May said.

Tiny was still listening to the phone. "He's got no morals, he sells out to the highest bidder." Then he interpolated, hand over mouthpiece, "We're still on Dr. Zorn here."

"I got that," Dortmunder assured him.

"Okay." Into the phone, Tiny said, with surprised interest, "Oh, yeah?" Then he said to Dortmunder, "He lives in a big castle in Votskojek that he bought from the Frankenstein family."

"Sounds like the right guy," Dortmunder said. "Does Grijk know where he is?"

Tiny asked, and answer came there, "In New York. He's working for the UN on famine relief. Grijk says it's a trawisty. What's a trawisty?"

"Something they have in Eastern Europe," Dortmunder told him.

"Oh." Tiny listened to the phone, nodded, looked at Dortmunder again. "Now *he's* got a question for *you*." Listened some more. "He wants to know, can he go to sleep now?"

"Why not?" Dortmunder said.

Tiny gave him a look, then spoke reassuringly into the phone and hung up, and it rang. So he picked it up again, said a very belligerent "Yeah," and looked over at Dortmunder to say, "It's Kelp."

"Good."

Tiny extended the receiver. "You want to take this call?"

But Dortmunder shook his head, saying, "You're right there."

"I may have to move this phone," Tiny said. "In fact, I may have to move the wall." Into the phone, he snarled, "So what's *your* good news?" He listened. "Oh, yeah?" Listened some more. "Okay." Listened some more. "Sure." Listened some more. "Wait, I'll tell him."

"About time," Dortmunder said.

Tiny said, "He says he's got a guy. A fence. He talked to the guy, and the guy is maybe interested, but not without a meet."

"Good," Dortmunder said. "He's coming over to pick me up?"

"Dortmunder," Tiny said, "it's nighttime."

"Oh, right," Dortmunder said. "Late, huh."

"The guy wants to meet you at one o'clock tomorrow," Tiny said. "So Kelp'll come by, twelve-thirty."

"No," Dortmunder said. "He can meet me at the store at eleven."

"It's an embassy, Dortmunder."

"He'll know what I mean."

But when Tiny passed the message on, he used the word *embassy*. Then he hung up and said, "He'll be there. I won't, he will," and the phone rang. Tiny looked at it without love. "I'm gettin tired of this," he said.

May said, "We don't usually get this many calls late at night."

"Nobody does except hospitals," Tiny said, and picked up the phone and bit it in half. Well, not quite; but his *hello* could give you a cauliflower ear. Then he modulated slightly, saying, "Hello, Stan. No, nothing's wrong."

"I knew it was Stan," Dortmunder said.

"I'll tell him," Tiny said, and did: "Fred can do it."

"Thelma, you mean," May said.

"Both of them," Tiny told her. "They're on tap." He listened to the phone again, nodded, and said, "I'll be sure to pass that on." Then he whomped the receiver back onto the hook and said, "He says stay off the Henry Hudson, they're working on the toll-booths."

"I'll remember that," Dortmunder promised.

"Good. And here's another. If this phone rings again, Dortmunder, you're gonna need a new one. You may need a proctologist." However the phone kept silent as Tiny heaved himself to his feet, saying, "We're done for tonight."

"I guess so," Dortmunder said. He had started to look his normal self again, depressed, but not brain damaged.

"I'll walk you out," May told Tiny, and did, while Dortmunder sat drinking beer. When she returned, he had the almanac open and was squinting at it. "You know," he said, "there really are all these weird countries."

"Well, at least now you've got a plan," she said.

He gaped at her. "I do?"

32

"Dod's id," Grijk said.

Dortmunder looked at the top picture of the stack of glossy eight-by-tens. It showed, in brilliant but washed-out color, what was apparently a cathedral niche, an ancient gray stone wall across the back, a crumbly stone arch up above in front. A stone step raised the rear half of the niche's floor, on which stood an altar swathed in cloths of many colors. Centered atop the altar was a glass box edged with gold or brass and surmounted by an elaborately carved golden handle that looked as though it would cut you if you weren't careful. Gleaming dots of red and green and blue and brilliant white were either gemstones fixed to the metal or unwanted light refractions; the lighting of this picture was really very crappy. Inside the glass box lurked something pale and unidentifiable.

"I was hoping," Dortmunder said, "for something a little more clear."

"Looka dee udders."

Kelp said, "Wait a minute, I'm not done."

Kelp and Dortmunder were both standing bent over Grijk's desk in the Tsergovian storefront, looking at this fourth-rate pic ture. To their left, Drava Votskonia, on the telephone, extolled the virtues of Tsergovian rock to an unvisionary new world. Now Dortmunder looked at Kelp's profile and said, "Not *done*? What's there to look at?"

"Okay," Kelp said. "I just wanted to get the picture clear, that's all."

"Too bad the photographer didn't have your attitude," Dortmunder said, and moved that photo out of the way to see what was next.

Another, but closer to the subject. The lighting still washed out some details while making others stand out like 3-D. But at least now anybody who'd ever seen the bone before could recognize it, in there inside the panes of glass and the extraneous highlights and reflections. (The camera itself was faintly visible, reflected in the front of the box.)

Okay, this was at least useful. "That's gold, huh?" Dortmunder said, drawing his finger over the perimeters of the box.

"Oh, sure," Grijk said.

"That's a ruby?"

"Dod one, doo."

"Emeralds here? What are these, sapphires?"

"You know your chools, Chon."

"I've seen a few in my time," Dortmunder said, and looked at the next picture, which was a *long* shot of the cathedral interior, severely underlighted. Grijk pointed at a darkish clump and said, "In dod abse."

"It isn't there *now*," Dortmunder pointed out. "I don't need to see this." Lowering an eyebrow at Kelp, he said, "And you don't need to see it, either."

"I'm not even looking at it," Kelp said.

"Good."

Dortmunder continued through the photos, and the next three were also useless and irrelevant. Then there came a picture of the bone, all by itself, on black velvet.

"There it is, all right," Kelp said.

"Uh-huh." Dortmunder moved on to the next, which showed the glass box all by itself, open, on top of the same or a similar piece of black velvet, the missing bone's indentation visible as a shadow on the rich blue velvet lining the bottom. This was a better picture than most; the old, small, delicate but strong hinges and slender leather straps holding the top open were clearly visible.

"At last," Dortmunder said, bending closer for a better look. But then he frowned, studying the picture. "Where was this taken?"

"In da storage waults a da cathedral. Before da sacred relic come to New York."

Dortmunder said, "But where's the box now? Isn't it here, with the bone?"

"No, no, Chon," Grijk said. "Glass is, you know..."

"Breakable," Kelp suggested.

"Wery."

"Well, hell and damn," Dortmunder said. "I can't do it without the box. Now it's *three* jobs. I don't know, maybe I should just forget the whole thing."

Grijk looked unhappy. "You can'd," he said.

Dortmunder looked at him. "What do you mean, I can't?"

"Zara Kotor," Grijk explained, "she faxed whad you're doing do da government in Osigreb. Only, you know, she made id like id vasn'd our fault da first—"

"Wait a minute," Dortmunder said. "I'm doing this because I feel *responsible,* is that the idea?"

"Dod's id. Nod *my* idea, Chon, you know dod."

"But if I don't pull this off..."

"You god a whole country mad ad you," Grijk said, with a sympathetic nod. "I'm sorry, Chon, but you know Zara Kotor, she's a bureaucrad, she prodects herself."

Kelp said, "A whole country mad at Chon, but so what? I mean, Chon, if you don't ever go there—"

"Nod juss Chon," Grijk said. "D'all of you."

"Aw, hey," Kelp said, finding it a little more serious, after all.

"And ve god, you know, in da Carpathians, a long history of blood feud."

"Now, look," Dortmunder said. "Already we've got two jobs to pull at the same time, one in New York and the other in Vermont. Now we got to also pull one in *Votskojek?*"

"Chon," Grijk said, "you don'd need dod box."

"I need dod box," Dortmunder corrected him. "If I don't get dod box, you don't get dod UN seat. You follow me?"

"No," Grijk said.

Dortmunder thought. His cheeks twitched, his eyes went in and out of focus; his knees sagged a little. He said, "Okay. You got people over there in Tsergovia, they can get into this vault, get this box, get it here?"

"Oh, sure," Grijk said.

"You said that too easy," Dortmunder told him.

"No, no, id *is* easy." Grijk promised. "Dad old cathedral, hundreds of years, rewolts, peasant uprisings, vars, anticlerical riods, all dese dings. Whad you god under dod cathedral, you god so many dunnels, secred endrances, hiding places, false valls, you could pud a whole subway sysdem in dere and lose id. Ve can ged in any time."

"Good," Dortmunder said. "This is Thursday. Can your people get in today, get that box here by Saturday morning?"

"Sure ding, Chon," Grijk aid. "You van em boad?"

Dortmunder and Kelp both looked alert. Kelp said, "Uh-oh."

"You're right," Dortmunder told him, and turned back to Grijk. "There's two of these? Two boxes?"

"Hundred and fifty years ago," Grijk explained, "dey made a fake box, looks just like da real one. For securidy. Bud dey don't use id for fifdy years."

"Is it the same place as the other one?"

"Under da cathedral, ya, bud in a different storage place, you know. Nod so much locked up. Nobody cares aboud dod one, id's all fake chools."

"Okay," Dortmunder said. "I hate to delegate authority, Grijk, because most people don't know how to do anything, but in this case I got to. What I want is, I want your people to sneak in there, put the fake one where the real one is, and bring the real one here, and not get caught, and nobody should know what they did. Okay?"

"Sure," Grijk said.

"The *real* one here," Dortmunder said.

Kelp said, "That's right, Grijk, that's very important. I don't know personally what Chon has in mind, but if he says he wants the real one, he means he can't use the other one."

"Without the real one," Dortmunder said, "we don't pull the job. Have Zara Kotor fax *that*."

"Then it's her fault," Kelp added. "And yours. And your whole country."

"I'm making a node," Grijk said. "Look." And they watched him do so, in ballpoint ink on a white memo pad, and they noticed the Tsergovian alphabet was just close enough to the American alphabet to be maddening. "Okay?" Grijk asked, holding up the memo pad, showing his cipher.

"Good," Dortmunder said. "Now about the spy stuff."

"Sure, Chon."

"It's for the château, up in Vermont. I need to *see* inside, and I need to *hear* inside, before I *go* inside."

"Oh, sure, ve god all dad stuff."

"Fine," Dortmunder said. "And you're head of security around here, so you know how to use it all."

Grijk looked belatedly alert, as though he'd just been blindsided. "Sure, Chon," he said, but a little less forcefully than before.

Dortmunder was not here to take pity on anybody. He said, "Tomorrow, we're going up to Vermont. You're bringing all your spy stuff."

"Okay, Chon," Grijk said, and managed a brave smile, saying, "Be kind of an adventure, huh? Being spies."

"That's right," Dortmunder said. He pointed at the phone. "Okay if I make a call? Local."

"Oh, sure."

Dortmunder made his call, and soon heard Arnie Albright's unpleasant voice saying, "Now what?"

"John Dortmunder."

"Whadaya calling *me* for?"

"I wondered did you have any plastic."

"Oh, sure, a business deal. Nobody calls Arnie Albright just to *chat*."

Dortmunder rolled his eyes. "I would chat, Arnie," he lied, "only I'm in kind of a rush. Maybe I'll chat when I come over, if you got any plastic."

"You'll be in an even bigger rush when you're here," Arnie said. "To listen to me is bad enough. To look at me, you'll run out the door. Sure, I got what you want. Dash by."

"Thanks, Arnie."

Hanging up, Dortmunder said to Kelp, "I know it isn't nice of me, but I wish I didn't have to do business with Arnie Albright."

Kelp said, "So you'll go see Arnie by yourself, right? And I'll meet you at one o'clock at the other guy's place."

"Not a chance," Dortmunder said.

In the subway heading uptown, Kelp said, "What do you think the odds are they'll steal the wrong box?"

Dortmunder thought it over. "Fifty-fifty," he said.

Kelp beamed. "There, see? You're not such a pessimist, after all."

33

Two of you," Arnie Albright said when he opened the door and saw Dortmunder and Kelp both standing there, unnatural smiles on both their faces. "So, Dortmunder, you brought somebody along to talk to so you don't have to talk to me."

"Nah," Dortmunder said, and Kelp said, "I asked to come along, Arnie, I hadn't seen you for such a long time."

"You're lucky you got a nose doesn't grow," Arnie told Kelp, and stepped back to usher them into his smelly apartment.

Arnie's apartment was much like the grizzled, gnarly Arnie himself. Its small rooms had big windows looking out past a black metal fire escape at the stained brown brick back of a parking garage no more than four feet away. For decoration, the walls were covered with part of Arnie's calendar collection. Pretty pictures, sexy pictures, dumb pictures, all over an infinity of Januaries, Januaries starting on every possible day of the week, under pictures of automobiles from every automotive era, pinups from every era of permissiveness, plus enough cuddly puppies, kittens, foals, and ducklings to induce diabetes. Just to keep interest alive, the occasional calendar began with October or March.

In front of the parking garage-view windows was an old library table, on the surface of which Arnie had laminated several of his less valuable half-year calendars—duplicates and drugstore displays and those on which pencil additions graced the girls. On this table now was also a small brown paper bag, toward which Arnie gestured, saying, "That's what you came here for. Not to see *me*. People don't ever want to see *me*, you can take my word on that."

"You're too hard on yourself, Arnie," Dortmunder assured him as he moved toward the table and the paper bag.

Seating himself at the table, Arnie said, "Save your breath, Dortmunder, I know what a scumbag I am. People in this town, they call a restaurant, before they make the reservation they say, 'Is Arnie Albright gonna be there?' I know these things, Dortmunder."

It was so hard to talk with Arnie. How could you agree with him, but on the other hand how could you not agree with him? Avoiding the issue entirely, Dortmunder said, "So you've got plastic, huh?"

"Sit down, Dortmunder," Arnie offered. "If you can bear to be that close to me, with the smell."

Dortmunder and Kelp took the other two chairs at the table, Dortmunder trying to look nothing but businesslike, Kelp with a manic bright expression of camaraderie and fellow-feeling. "Okay," Dortmunder said, "here we are."

"It's my stomach," Arnie said. "My own stomach hates me; it's so aggravated it gives me this breath. Well, you can smell it for yourself; I smell like a toilet."

"It's not that bad, Arnie," Dortmunder said. It was, in fact, worse.

Kelp, talking through that Kabuki mask of palship, said, "You got some cards for us, huh, Arnie?"

"That's why you're here," Arnie said, and dumped out of the paper bag half a dozen batches of credit cards, each held by a rubber band, each with its own scrawled note on a scrap of paper on top. "There you are," he said.

Dortmunder said, "How much?"

"Depends how long you need it, and for what," Arnie said. "You need a card you can go on using for six months, rock-solid, take it overseas, that gets expensive."

"Don't need anything that good."

"Three months is—"

"Not that long, either."

Arnie nodded. "The big deals don't come to me," he said. "All I get's the penny-ante stuff. People know I gotta carry junk, because otherwise who'd come to a shithole like this to see a shithole like me? Anything decent, they go right to Stoon. To buy, to sell, Stoon's their man."

Dortmunder said, "Oh? Is he out of jail?" And he couldn't keep the interest out of his voice.

"You, too, Dortmunder," Arnie said. "Don't tell me different. You, too, would rather deal with Stoon than put up with the piece of crap I am."

"Arnie," Dortmunder said, "you know I always come straight to you first. What have you got for me here, Arnie?"

"So what are you talking? Just a dirty weekend?"

"This weekend."

"Well, sure, what other weekend?" Arnie scooped all but one of the stacks of credit cards back into the bag, then pointed at the remaining stack. "These are good until Tuesday."

"Fine. That's all we need."

"But I mean Tuesday," Arnie said. "Up till then, they're fine, give you no trouble. Tuesday, you try to pass one of these, sparks are gonna come from it, smoke, a stink worse than this joint here."

"By Tuesday, I'm done with them," Dortmunder said. "How much?"

"How many you need?"

"Two."

Arnie nodded. "Fifty apiece," he said.

"Arnie," Dortmunder said, "you yourself just said these things die on Tuesday. How many customers you gonna get between now and then?"

Arnie considered that. Then he said, "Dortmunder, let me put it to you this way. Would you rather spend half an hour here, arguing with me, being around me, being around this septic tank of an apartment, all to save twenty bucks, or would you rather pay the hundred dollars?"

34

Ahundred bucks isn't bad for a weekend in the mountains," Kelp said as they walked through Central Park, watching each other's back. "Everything considered."

"Arnie Albright considered," Dortmunder said.

"Well, that."

"Tell me about this guy we're going to see," Dortmunder said.

"Well, I heard about him from a guy that knew a guy," Kelp began.

"I figured it was something like that."

"This guy," Kelp said, "will not touch anything that Interpol isn't looking for. This guy deals only with what you call your major commissions."

"That's what I need, all right," Dortmunder agreed. "Will he deal with us?"

"That's what the meeting's about. Eyeball each other, see do we call the preacher or forget it."

"What about the guy personally?"

"That I don't know," Kelp said. "On the phone, he sounded like an actor."

"An actor."

"You know, those English actors, come on the talk shows late at night cause they got a movie out you never heard of."

"I don't know them," Dortmunder said. It wasn't that he didn't watch television; it was that television didn't stick in his brain; it washed through like sterile water through a chrome pipe, leaving nothing and taking nothing away. It kept his eyes open till bedtime.

"Anyway," Kelp went on, "the arrangement is, we're pretending to be the carpenters."

"With the guy?" This made no sense that Dortmunder could see. "He thinks we're carpenters? How we gonna talk to him about a robbery if he thinks we're carpenters?"

"No, no, his *office* thinks we're carpenters. You know, on account of how we look, there's got to be an explanation why we're there."

"I don't even know this guy," Dortmunder said, "already he's insulting me."

"John, you want a careful guy, am I right? So this guy is a careful guy. So for the moment we can be carpenters."

Dortmunder held up his right hand as they walked through the dogs off leashes, the infants off leashes, the maniacs off leashes, all rollicking together in the park in the bright spring sun. He studied his palm. It had a pleasing softness and smoothness to it. The tools a burglar holds are delicate tools, gentlemanly tools; they leave the operator's hands pleasant to be around. Nothing like carpenters and *their* tools. "Well," he decided, "I'll do my best. But I won't do any demonstrations."

"No, no, this is just the cover story for the staff."

Dortmunder said, "This is a fence with a staff?" The kind of fence he was used to was more of a fella like Arnie Albright, or a guy named Morris Morrison who scratched himself all the time and had a big warehouse building full of dubious goods over in Long Island City before he retired to jail in Florida.

"John," Kelp said, "this is a fence with an eight hundred number. This is a fence with offices in London and Paris. This is a fence with the Getty Museum's unlisted number."

"I dunno, then," Dortmunder said. "Maybe he *won't* deal with us."

"All we can do is present ourselves, honestly and straightforward."

"Oh, we don't have to go that far," Dortmunder said. "What's the guy's name?"

"Guy."

"Yeah. What's his name?"

"Guy Claverack," Kelp expanded.

Dortmunder said, "The guy's name is *Guy?*"

"It happens," Kelp said. "There's also guys named Hugh."

"Like me, for instance," Dortmunder said.

"No, I— Never mind. Don't get hit by that bus," Kelp suggested and, having left the park, they now successfully crossed Fifth Avenue.

"Funny to be in this neighborhood in the daytime," Dortmunder commented.

35

I am afraid I will have to interrupt lunch at one point," Guy Claverack apologized to his guests as they placed themselves at table. "Carpenters are coming to discuss some renovations back in the storage area."

"Not at all."

"Quite understand."

"Poor Guy."

This was, of course, not just any lunch. This was lunch with Guy Claverack, premier art dealer to what is left of the aristocracy in this plebeian world. Guy Claverack was the man to see if the exigencies of fate required you to sell off that fourteen-foot-by-forty-three-foot arras portraying the Battle of Tronfahrt that had been in your family since 1486 and in which your own forebear Murphyn the Unrepentant is clearly visible in the center right, just beyond those massed bowmen.

Conversely, Guy Claverack was also the man to see if the tables at Monte Carlo had been good to one—well, Lord, it does happen from time to time—and one was prepared to purchase a fourteen-foot-by-forty-three-foot arras of somebody else's ancestors in noble battle for that drafty blank spot on one's own castle wall.

199

In short, to have Guy Claverack answer one's phone call was as important in the world of pretenders to long-gone thrones, as emblematic of acceptance, as, in a crasser world, it would be to have your phone call returned by your senator, your banker, your agent.

It also didn't hurt Guy Claverack that he was, in addition to being rich and powerful and important, also handsome and mysterious. Handsome in a large and bearish way, six feet six inches in height, with a high, broad forehead, clear brown eyes, thick, wavy brown hair, and a full, rich brown beard neatly topiaried into an oval cupping his well-fed face. And mysterious in a rather thrilling way; known to have associates in the louche world of thieves and forgers and confidence men, confidantes among the police, connections with smugglers, to be in fact a sort of Raffles, for those who've never read Raffles, which by now is almost everybody. Stolen artworks could very often be reacquisitioned, at of course a fee, through the efforts and contacts of Guy Claverack. He was known, to put it another way, to be a fence, though only in the nicest and most acceptable way, and no one would ever have associated his name with such a beggarly word.

Guy was also known to be an arbiter of social acceptance in his narrow world. Whenever those who thought of themselves as insiders—big-ticket art world insiders, or bearers of the blood when 'tis blue—found themselves in New York, they invariably phoned Guy, and if he invited them to lunch their bona fides were accepted, they could believe they were believed to be, in the outer world, who they believed themselves to be at home. (If—shocking thought—they were *not* invited to lunch, they skulked from the city at the earliest opportunity, hoping no one would ever learn they'd been there.)

In addition to its status-side meaning, the Guy Claverack lunch was also a culinary experience not to be missed. It took place in the small dining room at the rear of his office suite on East Sixty-eighth Street near Madison, and it was catered by the four-star French restaurant down the block (in which Guy held a small interest). The food was invariably delicious, the gossip frequently so, and the experience generally as satisfying and ego-fulfilling as a good facial.

Today's guests, three in number, were something of a mixed

bag. Commercially, the most interesting was Mavis, Princess Orfizzi, fresh from her divorce from the repellent Prince Elector Otto of Tuscan-Bavaria, flush with marriage loot to dispose of. Most useful in the long haul was no doubt young Alex Leamery of the London home office of Parkeby-South, the world's most prestigious auction house. Parkeby-South maintained offices and auction galleries in New York and Paris and Zurich, but the twits of its London office were the only ones who actually mattered, and of them the willowy Leamery was perhaps the most promising.

The third guest, Leopold Grindle, came closest to that mysterious other side of Guy's life. An expert art appraiser, a bent, chunky man with unruly gray hair and thick eyeglasses, Grindle was on retainer to any number of museums, sheikhdoms, banks, and private purchasers the world around, to authenticate or dismiss their purchases. Very rarely were his attributions reversed. And yet, if the circumstances or the money was right, as Guy well knew, Leopold could rise above accuracy. A fine quality, at times.

Lunch was delivered by deft, dwarfish Hispanics—there are fewer and fewer fine French waiters in New York every day, alas—whose chief quality, apart from the silent skill of their serving, was that they spoke no known language other than, among themselves, some mongoloid cousin of Spanish, which meant that gossip at Guy's table—and what other reason was there to get together?—would stay at his table, and not find its way either to the burning ears of the subjects or the open maw of the public prints.

Gossip at table today centered mostly on the goatish, mulish, and piggish qualities of Prince Elector Otto, Mavis's recent ex, the pretender to a throne so obscure that not even Otto himself claimed to know precisely where it was or who his subjects would be were they ever unwise enough to accept his credentials. Beyond his amusement at the missing Otto, Guy had yet another reason to indulge Mavis's evident desire to dish her obnoxious former spouse. Among the art treasures she had made off with from the wrecked sloop of their marriage were two pieces in which he had a particular interest, both having kicked around the art world from buyer to buyer the last few years, both the work of major figures, and both with pedigrees just clouded enough to make negotiations interesting. One was a Veenbes, that early

Flemish master, a contemporary of Brueghel, if somewhat darker in his view and in his work; his *Folly Leads Man to Ruin* was now in Mavis's possession. As was also a Rodin bronze, four feet tall, a young ballerina seated on a tree stump. Neither item would be so much as mentioned during lunch, of course, but a discreet form of preliminary negotiation was nevertheless under way.

Today's simple sole had just been completed, and the Hispanics were wafting around a heavenly salad of seven kinds of immature lettuce leaf when the small phone on the delicate Chippendale candlestick table behind Guy made its merry little tinkle. Reaching back for the receiver, placing it to his head, Guy said, "Guy," and listened to his secretary say, "The carpenters are here."

"Oh, good, have them go down to delivery." Hanging up, "Duty calls, it's the carpenters," he told his guests, dabbed his lips with white linen, took just a sip of the Sancerre, and left the room.

Guy Claverack & Co. occupied a town house on the north side of the street, with well-tended flower boxes at the streetward windows and only the discreet gold-lettered name on the leaded glass of the front door to suggest this house was a center of trade. One reached that door by climbing a broad but steep flight of scenically crumbling brownstone steps, flanked by intricate wrought-iron railings. Guy's offices and dining room were at this level, display rooms one flight up, his private quarters on the top two floors above.

There was, however, another street entrance to the building, marked by a white-enamel-lettered iron sign affixed to the right-hand staircase railing. DELIVERIES, it read, with an arrow angling steeply down. On this side, next to the main broad brownstone steps climbing up, more plebeian slate steps clomped down, made a sharp turn, and finished beneath the main steps at a windowless gray metal door. Beyond this door lay a beehive basement of stone and concrete, composing many small cells filled with unsold arts and crafts, all bisected by a front-to-back central low-ceilinged corridor.

Along this corridor Guy now made his way, his black shadow in the fluorescent overhead lights sweeping around him like a cape. He undid the several locks that would release the gray metal door—gray metal within, as well, niceties of decoration being unknown at this level—and opened it, to reveal two men waiting out there who, if in fact they had really been carpenters, Guy wouldn't have let work on a bird cage.

But they weren't carpenters, were they? Sloping, suspicious, dubious, ramshackle people, dressed as though for a long bus ride somewhere in the Third World, they were about as far from the general idea of Raffles, the gentleman thief, as one could get without actually entering prison. "Come in, gentlemen," Guy said, which was his idea of a joke. He stepped back, with a sweeping gesture, like Errol Flynn taking off Robin Hood's hat. "Come in."

One was taller and gloomier, the other sharper-featured and brighter-eyed. It was the bright-eyed one who said, as he crossed the threshold, "We were sent by—"

"I know who sent you," Guy cut in, smoothly but firmly slicing off the naming of any names. "The *construction* work is back this way," he went on, and shut the door, and retraced his steps down the bare, bright corridor, trusting them to follow (but not trusting them much farther than that).

Midway along the corridor, Guy paused to unlock a door on the left, pulled it open, reached in to switch on the overhead fluorescent, and gestured his guests to go on in. They did, Guy followed, and all found themselves in a square concrete box, harshly lighted by long white tubes from above, and overly full of Victorian sofas with disintegrating velvet upholstery in many once-rich jeweled colors, rubies and emeralds and sapphires all now sun-bleached and time-stained, with dark wood crest rails and scrolled arms and feet all dinged and dented and deeply scratched, as though they'd been used at one time in a Gay Nineties dodgem car concession.

Many sofas in here. Sofas sat on sofas, with sofas atop. Some sofas tilted upside down, stubby feet in the air, as though hurling themselves into oblivion. Two sofas, however, nearest the door, stood unencumbered, and it was to one of these, after closing the door, that Guy next gestured, then, while they sat obediently side by side, settled himself on the other.

"Now," he said. "I understand you might have use of my services." He did his best to keep a faint note of incredulity out of his voice but didn't entirely succeed.

The bright-eyed one spoke again. "We're gonna have some stuff to sell. Morry said you—"

"Yes, yes," Guy said, preferring to put the case in his own words. "As I understand the situation from our mutual friend," he said delicately, "someone has suffered a loss, and you are in a position to believe I may be instrumental in helping the owner reclaim his property."

"Something like that."

"Except," the gloomy one added, in a gloomy voice, "this particular loss hasn't happened yet."

Guy didn't like that, not a bit. "Oh, dear," he said. "If you two are going to invite me to participate in anything illegal, I'm afraid I must—"

The gloomy one held up a hand for Guy to stop, and Guy surprised himself by stopping. Using the same hand, the gloomy one took something from his interior jacket pocket and extended it.

Paper, some sort of papers. Curious, cautious, Guy took the papers and saw they were color photographs cut without their captions from a magazine, showing the interior of some sort of museum or private collection. Hard to tell exactly what or where, but some of those pieces, well, if they were really what they appeared to be, he could already see they were extremely valuable.

Where was this place? What or whose was it? Well, whatever was on the back of these clippings should give him some hint as to what magazine they'd been cut from, and then he'd easily track down the right issue. So he turned them over, and what was on their backs was masking tape.

Guy looked up and saw the gloomy one watching him with gloomy satisfaction, having guessed ahead of time what his reactions would be. So, do not underestimate these people. Reaching forward, extending the bits of paper, he said, "You'll want these back."

"Right," the gloomy one said, and took them, and made them disappear.

The bright-eyed one said, "So? You're interested?"

"I'm not sure," Guy told him. "It's very unusual to be approached *before* the unhappy event. The ethics of the situation leave me at a bit of a loss."

"What we'll do," the gloomy one said, ignoring Guy's ethical quandary, "on Monday we'll bring you some more pictures. Better ones than these. Close-ups, so you'll know it's the real stuff. Pictures where they are now, and pictures where they get moved to. You give those pictures to the insurance company—"

Guy said, "Not the owner? Sometimes, an owner can—"

"Not this time. This time, it's the insurance company, nobody else."

"Very well," Guy said. "*If* we go forward."

The bright-eyed one said, "Oh, sure. *If* we go forward."

The gloomy one nodded that away. He said, "You give them all the pictures we give you, all of them, and you dicker like you do, and you keep half of what you get, and we give the stuff back."

Guy felt increasingly alert. Was this entrapment, somehow? Half was more than he would normally expect in a circumstance like this; his commission—that's the word he used—was usually between a quarter and a third of whatever the owner or his representative paid for the return of the stolen objects. Were these people ignorant, or baiting him, or what? "I see," he said carefully.

The gloomy one watched him with an unnervingly bleak eye. "Half okay?" he asked.

Say something, or not? "If we go forward," Guy said, temporizing. Then, remembering his recent decision not to underestimate these people, he said, "It's higher than usual."

Was that a smile on the gloomy one's face? If so, it did nothing to relieve the gloom, as the fellow said, "We know it's high. It's so you should do what we ask, and don't do anything else."

Not entrapment. These two were offering Guy no details, asking him to offer them no encouragement. Most likely, they were working for the owner himself, and this was a false robbery for the insurance money; not the first time that ploy's been pulled in this old world. Feeling on surer ground, and wanting to test this theory, he said, "Not do anything else, like for instance warn the victim, should I happen to know who it is."

The gloomy one gave him nothing. "Like anything," he said, deadpan. "Just take the pictures on Monday and give them to the insurance company, and dicker, and then we'll contact you, and, when the price is right, you collect, we'll tell you where the stuff is, and we'll come get our half of the money."

Half. Half of what? Judging from Guy's previous experience, the insurance company couldn't be expected to come up with better than 20 percent of the established value of the pieces, particularly if they were valuable enough or well known enough to make resale difficult. Guy's portion, then, if he chose to go forward, would be in the vicinity of 10 percent. Of what?

Elaborately casual, Guy sat back on the sofa. "Do you have an estimate of the value of the items in that lot?"

"Six mil," said the gloomy one.

Guy was a trader; he knew how to keep a poker face. Ten percent of 6 mil is $600,000. "What time Monday," he asked, "can I expect the new pictures?"

36

Walking westward again through Central Park, back toward more familiar territory, Dortmunder and Kelp shared a companionable silence until Kelp said, "So. Whadaya think?"

"I'm thinking," Dortmunder said.

Kelp said, "I'll tell you what *I* think. I think *that* place is a pipe. Full a valuable stuff; we could break in there with a spoon handle, back up your borrowed truck—"

"You don't heist a guy you're dealing with," Dortmunder said, not without reproach in his tone.

"Not *now*," Kelp explained. "After, I meant."

Dortmunder nodded, accepting that revision, and they continued to walk through the sunshine and the greenery here in the lungs of the city until Kelp said, "Does that mean yes?"

"Does what mean yes?"

"We're dealing with him. Are we dealing with him?"

"Who, Claverack?" Dortmunder was surprised. "Why, you got a better idea?"

"I thought," Kelp said, "you were thinking about it."

"What's to think about? He's the right fence for the job. I knew you'd know the guy, and you know the guy."

"Thank you," Kelp said modestly, but then went back to the point. "John," he said, "if whether or not we deal with that guy, Guy—you know what I mean, that guy. If that isn't what you're thinking about, what are you thinking about?"

"The string," Dortmunder said. "This time, we gotta build a long string."

"We can do that, you and me," Kelp said. "With all the people we know? Easy."

"Except," Dortmunder said, "I gotta do something else. And this is already Thursday, and we got to pull the job Saturday night. So you and me and Tiny have to get together, right now, and then I have to work out stuff with Grijk, and then—"

"You know," Kelp said, "I think that *is* the way he says his name. Very good."

"Thank you. Anyway, I'll go get him, or however it works, and then we're off, and you and Tiny are gonna have to collect the people we need, for a meet tomorrow night at the OJ. I'll be back by then."

"Back? You and Grijk? Where you going?"

"Skiing," Dortmunder said.

Kelp looked around at grass and sun and people in shirt sleeves. "I think," he said carefully, "it's the wrong time of year."

"Not the way I ski," Dortmunder said.

37

"Well," May said, "it's really kind of nice, isn't it?"

"It's like a motel," Dortmunder said.

"That's what's nice about it," May told him, looking around at the rose-pink wall-to-wall carpet, the beige fabric-covered walls, the Mediterranean-style wood-veneer furniture with the drawers that slid very easily in and out, the two giant beds with their pale cream covers stretched flat across their surfaces, the wall sconces and the swag light with the dull gold chain, the big TV in the top part of a tall cabinet that you could hide behind cabinet doors that looked as though they'd come from a cathedral somewhere. A very shiny cathedral. "It's not at all like home, that's what I meant," May explained.

Dortmunder stood over by the sliding glass door, looking through the glass and out over the balcony—their very own balcony, with a Lucite-topped table and two white lawn chairs—at the green hills of Vermont, with the long vertical meadows that he now recognized as off-season ski trails. "Grijk oughta be here by now," he said.

"Relax, John," May suggested. "You don't want him to get in touch with you when he gets here, and you can't do anything about anything until tonight, anyway."

209

Dortmunder nodded. Looking out at the view, he said, "There's just so much about this I don't like, you know?"

Under the swag light was a round dark wood-veneer table, flanked by two chairs with cushioned seats. Settling into one of these and finding it less comfortable than it looked, May said, "Do you want to talk about it, John?"

Did he? There was a little silence while he contemplated that question, and then he sighed and shook his head. "The first thing," he said, now looking at his own dim green reflection in the glass, "is the rush to do it, the pressure, the deadline."

"But you've got it all organized, don't you?"

"How do I know? I'm not even there. Two places at once, that's another problem. And also, May," he added, turning away from the glass and his own cheerless image to the more cheerful view of her seated there with one forearm on the table, fingers hardly twitching at all for a nonexistent cigarette, "also beyond that," he said, "I've always believed, and I've always said, you shouldn't get too complicated with a piece of work."

"That's right," she agreed.

"If a job can't be done with five men," he said, "it isn't worth doing. That's what I've always said."

"I've heard you say it," she confirmed.

"And now here we are, and here's this thing, it's in two places at once—no, *three,* we got a bunch, who knows how many or if they know what they're doing, going into the bottom of that church over there, that Rivers of Blood place to get the glass box—and we got what, hundreds of guys?"

"Oh, not that many," May said.

"Not five, either." Dortmunder turned back to the sliding glass door, decided he didn't want to look through his own reflection anymore, grabbed the door's handle, yanked, felt several sharp pains in his hand and wrist, figured out how to unlock the door, yanked harder than before, and the door zipped away along its well-oiled track, *boinked* off the end piece, and came demurely rolling back in front of him again. He gently moved it out of the way, then at last looked out unencumbered at all that scenery, and felt that real mountain air on his face, and said, "And I still got to find Hochman's place."

"You'll find it," May assured him. "Hasn't it been easy up till now?"

Well, sure; because up to now all it consisted of was an 800 number. Having left his instructions with Tiny and Kelp, having made last-minute arrangements with Grijk, all Dortmunder'd had to do was dial 800 HAPHOUR and book himself and May into Kinohaha for tonight, including the special hotel-operated bus—they called it a jitney, for some reason—that left the Port Authority at 2:00 P.M. and arrived at the hotel door at 6:15. Meanwhile, May had packed for them both, had taken a cab to the Port Authority, and they'd connected there at two minutes to two, "*Plenty* of time," as May had pointed out, to catch the nearly-empty bus. They even got to sit in the front row on the right, where you can see where you're going.

Figuring that anybody who drove this round-trip twice a day to make a living probably knew the quickest routes, Dortmunder kept track of the roads the bus driver chose, jotting them down on a scrap of paper, even while knowing Stan Murch would argue with every decision along the way. Still, he was doing his part. And he didn't lose the paper, either.

And now it was 6:30, the long June day continuing undiminished outside, they were here in room 1202 on one of Arnie Albright's good-till-Tuesday credit cards, and it was time for Dortmunder to do his next part. He took a deep inhale of pure country air, coughed, turned away from the view, and said, "You want this open or closed?"

"Oh, open," May said. "I love the air."

"Yeah, it's okay. I'll go out, see what I can get."

"I'll be in the tub," said May, who, unlike Dortmunder, knew how to be on vacation.

Dortmunder nodded vaguely, searched his pockets, found the room key, and left.

The lobby was *huge*. Not high-ceilinged, just long and wide and spread out, with acres of neutral carpeting and lots of conversational groups of empty sofas and big free-form-shaped roped-off areas of tropical plants. Vast stretches of this lobby were just wasted, lying fallow, and the reason is, most destination resorts built since World War II have been designed with the idea that someday, someday, the particular state in which this particular resort is located just *might* legalize gambling; and whadaya know? Right here's where we'll put the slots.

All unknowing, Dortmunder walked through several ranks of ghost slot machines, looking around. But not for Grijk. The deal there was, Grijk would drive himself up, by himself, in an embassy car, with all the embassy spy stuff in the trunk, and would find a bed-and-breakfast somewhere in this general neighborhood—Vermont, it's full of cute little bed-and-breakfast places with interesting histories and authentic architectural details and amiable current owners and fairly solid antique furnishings and Laura Ashley *everywhere,* check it out—and find his own dinner somewhere, while Dortmunder and May planned to eat at Kinohaha the dinner they were already paying for (or not paying for, given the method of payment) in the package they'd agreed to. Then, after dinner, Grijk would drive over to Kinohaha and wander around the lobby—this big lobby here—until he and Dortmunder caught sight of each other. Then, without either acknowledging awareness or knowledge of the other, Dortmunder would follow Grijk out to his car, they would both board it, and they would drive over to . . .

Where? That's what Dortmunder was here to find out. Where is Harry Hochman's château? And what is the clever, subtle, indirect, fiendishly cunning method by which Dortmunder would ferret out its location? Time would tell.

Over there. Over there, in a lobby corner that now, in its pre-gambling phase, was rather out of the way and forlorn, stood a small, ornate desk at which sat a small, ornate woman trying to look as though she weren't bored out of her mind. GUEST SERVICES, read the brass sign on the desk, and if you think that means she's here to service the guests, you're wrong, mister, and you're out of line, and, if you don't move along this *instant,* it may become necessary to call for the bell captain. Huh!

"Excuse me," Dortmunder said.

The small, ornate woman gave him an extremely skeptical look, but no words.

There was a small, ornate chair in front of the s. o. desk and woman, but Dortmunder somehow didn't feel he ought to sit in it. Standing beside this chair, not touching it at all, bent slightly forward at the waist, he said, "My wife and I, uh . . ."

And the sun broke through the clouds! Perking right up, the guest servitor said, "Yes, *sir!* Do sit down, sit down!" And she waved many scarlet false nails in the direction of the chair.

So Dortmunder sat down. "We just got here," he explained, "and we thought we'd like to maybe, uh, take a little trip around, see some stuff in the uh, uh, uh . . ."

"Neighborhood," she suggested. "Area. Environs."

"Yeah, like that," Dortmunder agreed. "We figured, we don't want to spend all our time in the uh, uh, uh . . ."

"Hotel," she offered. "Grounds. Compound."

"That's it." Dortmunder rested a palm on the desk, next to the dangerous brass sign. "So something away from here," he said. "Something, uh, uh, uh . . ."

"Interesting," she concluded. "Different. Unusual."

"Yeah."

She pointed one of the scarlet nails off thataway, saying, "You saw all of our, uh . . ."

"Information?" he wondered. "Brochures? Pamphlets?" He hadn't. "Yeah," he lied, "but they're all uh, uh, uh . . ."

"Expected," she finished. "Standard. Uninspiring."

"Yeah."

She smiled brightly. "How about Harry Hochman's château?"

He gaped at her.

She said, "Do you know who Harry Hochman is? He's the owner of Kinohaha. Do you know what his company is? It's the third-largest hotel chain in the world. Do you know what he has only eleven miles from this very spot? A beautiful château that he built personally, under his own direction, just for himself and his beloved wife, Adele."

"Whadaya know," Dortmunder said.

"No one is permitted inside, of course," she said, "not even when it's empty, like now—"

"Oh, it's empty?"

"Yes, but still no one is permitted inside," she said, with a sympathetic little smile. "But we're encouraged to encourage the guests to drive over there and take a look at the place, just to admire Mr. Hochman's, uh . . ."

"Taste," guessed Dortmunder. "Skill. Money."

She was absolutely beaming at him by now. "Would you like to see the château?"

"Yes."

"Do you know where it is?"

"No."

So she opened a drawer and whipped out a little map, and drew a circle around the hotel and another circle around the château, and drew a line showing the best route between the two. Then she handed Dortmunder this map, and a big smile, and a wish he should have a nice day.

"Thank you," Dortmunder said.

38

In the amber glow of the Hyundai's dashboard lights, Grijk stared pop-eyed at the map. "You even god a map," he said.

"Sure," Dortmunder agreed.

"You pwofessionals," Grijk said, his deep voice deeper with admiration. "I don't know how you do such a ting."

"You learn this stuff, over the years," Dortmunder told him, with a modest little shrug. "How to find out what you gotta know, if you're gonna do the job."

Grijk just couldn't get over it. "You found oud vhere id is," he said, "you god da vay ve ged dere, you even goddida place is empty."

"Tricks of the trade," Dortmunder said. "So why don't we head on over there now, okay?"

"Sure, Chon."

"It's John."

Starting the Hyundai's washing-machine motor, Grijk said mournfully, "I vish I could say yours so good like you could say mine."

"Yeah, well."

Shaking his head, Grijk put the Hyundai into a loud gear and

215

drove shakily out of Kinohaha's huge parking area—almost as big as the lobby—and out to the empty public highway.

Empty. Not even eleven o'clock, and all Vermonters and their summertime visitors were well tucked in for the night. This was an early-fading part of the world, all right. In fact, when Dortmunder and May had drifted down to the dining room for dinner at 8:30, it turned out the kitchen was just getting ready to close, and it had been made pretty plain that upright people were *done* with dinner by 8:30, not starting it. Feeling the pressure all around him to gulp down his chicken and peas and mashed potatoes and clear out of this bright, ugly dining room so the staff could go home, Dortmunder had slowed his intake so much, he ate as though he had the metabolism of a king cobra, and even May began to get nervous at the general chill in the air hovering over all these empty tables, and said, "Maybe we shouldn't have dessert."

"Oh, yes, we should," Dortmunder said.

Dortmunder had the pecan pie with the vanilla ice cream, and it was pretty damn good. It was, in fact, sitting quite comfortably inside Dortmunder right now as he rode beside Grijk through the green darkness of Vermont in the orange embassy Hyundai, a car that, wearing diplomat plates, looked like a little girl in her mother's high heels.

Though they would never learn who specifically had been responsible, the truth is, it was a third-generation Dartmouth student who had taken as a design touch for his dormitory room that one crucial road sign that caused Dortmunder and Grijk to wander irrelevant portions of Vermont for an extra twenty minutes before finally getting back on track, but except for this one glancing nod from the Ivy League, molders of America's leaders, the journey was uneventful, and soon enough they found themselves at the front side of the château.

Even at night, even from uphill, the château was impressive, a sprawling, turreted, gabled, lofty folly that fit with this mountain scenery without at all blending in; like a black beauty mark on the cheek of a cancan dancer, it augmented the surrounding niceness without ever for a second appearing natural.

And the other thing about the château, which became immediately apparent, was that when the small, ornate woman had described the place as "empty" she had not meant that as a synonym for *alone*. The château was not actually one building but three, the central magnificence being flanked by two outrider buildings, both pocket versions of the same architectural style, the one on the left appearing to be a combination garage/storage/ utility structure, and the one on the right a fairly modest but nevertheless roomy house, two stories high plus attic, and occupied.

Very occupied. Scattered out front of this appendage building were a pickup, a station wagon, a dirt bike, three bicycles, a tricycle, and a stroller. Lights were on in two upstairs rooms, and blue television light flickered in a couple of adjoining downstairs windows.

Of course. Naturally. People like the Hochmans would have a staff in residence, a large family to take care of the place while they're away and see to it no vandals break in. Or others.

"Well, let's put it this way," Dortmunder said. "If they made it too easy, I'd probably get bored and not even want to go on with it."

Grijk gave him a funny look. "Chon? Is dat true?"

"No," Dortmunder said.

"Okay."

"Let's find a place to hide the car."

The château and its auxiliary buildings stood at the nadir of a wide, winding blacktop driveway down through evergreens from a two-lane country road. The blacktop drive flowed into spreading rivulets of vowel at the bottom, making an O at the château entrance, an I across the second residence, and an E abutting the garage.

Beyond the château was a steep climb, providing the view. To left and right were tumbled mounds of scenery, tree-covered. With only the Hyundai's parking lights for illumination, Grijk drove them over to the far end of the utility building, the extreme end of E, which put them as far as possible from the occupied portion of the complex, and there they got out to look things over.

Grijk's spy equipment included a flashlight, and by its beam they saw a dirt road meander off into the forest from the top of the E, at the farthest corner of the utility building, heading away from

217

all the structures. They followed it, shining the light this way and that, and soon came upon the Hochmans's illegal dump. (Why aren't we surprised?) Stacks of newspapers, cartons of empty bottles, plastic bags of junk, bunches of rags, all the usual detritus drooling down a declivity, a slope full of slops. The dirt road, no more than a pair of tire tracks, meandered past the upper edge of this effluvium, then faded away into a footpath that headed morosely downhill.

Dortmunder looked it over. "Okay," he said. "Bring the car in here."

"Okay, Chon."

"It's John."

"I know id is," Grijk said hopelessly, and went away with the flashlight, leaving Dortmunder alone in the dark, to be comforted only by the faint downhill chomping of rats and raccoons and squirrels and other denizens of the natural world as they worked their slow, persistent transmogrification on the Hochmans's dump.

Ah, but here came the faint Hyundai lights, followed by the faint Hyundai. With many hand gestures and other encouragements, Dortmunder had Grijk park the beast as close to the edge as possible, over by the far side, where it tilted downward a bit, almost as though about to fall in. Then, as Grijk climbed out of the car, Dortmunder said, "Before we do anything else, we take off the license plates."

"Ve do?"

"We do."

"I don't ged id, Chon, but okay."

The trunk was nicely equipped with spy stuff, including all the screwdrivers and pliers you could possibly want. Lickety-split, the license plates were removed—rust was no match for Grijk's upper-body strength—and stowed in the trunk with the tools. Then Dortmunder and Grijk walked back behind the moving pool of flashlight gleam to the buildings, where they found that the blacktop made one consonant as well; a J that sliced between main house and utility building and curled around to the broad door in the stone wall at the rear, one level below the front.

This, according to the magazine article, would be the entrance to Harry Hochman's art gallery. Dortmunder didn't actually *do* anything to this door yet, but he studied it a lot, and then he said, "Okay. Now let's see if they left an unlocked window."

"Chon, they're gonna have alarms."

"You know it. Let's see how good they are, and how good the response is."

"Is dis a good idea, Chon?"

"It's the best, Grijk."

So they circled the house, moving slowly, using the flashlight sparingly, and at last found a small window to a downstairs powder room that had not been locked. "Okay," Dortmunder said. "What time is it?"

Grijk's spy stuff included a glow-in-the-dark watch. "Eleven fordy-do," he said.

"Good." Dortmunder opened the small window, counted slowly to five, and closed it again. "Now we go over there," he said, pointing toward the utility building, "and see the response."

"Okay, Chon."

The response was quite good, really. Dortmunder and Grijk had barely concealed themselves at the far end of the utility building when two guys holding their shotguns up one-handed while they struggled their other arms into their coats came boiling out of the residence on the other side and trotted to the building. Also, a dog started barking; interesting that it hadn't barked while they were spooking around. But that's the way it is with dogs, anyway. They don't bark as a warning or communication; they just bark because something exciting's happening. Still, it was nice to know about the dog.

So the unofficial response to the breaking of the alarm's zone was less than a minute, from the house next door. The official response—three sheriff's department cars with flashing lights and yowling sirens—took eleven minutes longer. As those three vehicles screamed their way up and over the mountain, Dortmunder said, "Time to go hide," which he and Grijk then did, trotting down the dirt road, past the dump and the Hyundai, then veering off into the trees, where their erratic flashlight beam was insufficient protection against low branches and high roots. The second time they both fell, they stayed there.

Five minutes later, they had to hunker down even lower when

one of the sheriff's men, following the dirt road, came along with the flashlight, shone it on the dump, shone it briefly into the abandoned old car, and went back the way he'd come.

The search of the empty château was long and thorough, and Dortmunder and Grijk watched most of it from the far end of the utility building. They saw the flashlights moving around inside the darkened château, bobbing from window to window. They saw one of the sheriff's men come out and speak earnestly for a long while into his radio. And at last, thirty-five minutes after Dortmunder had raised and lowered that window, the sheriff's cars drove away again, more quietly than they'd arrived, the two shotgun-armed guys went back to their TV watching in the other house, and peace and quiet descended once more on the landscape.

It was now 12:17. "Let me know," Dortmunder said, "when it's ten minutes to one."

"Vha'd ve do in the meandime, Chon?"

"I'm gonna nap," Dortmunder said, and went back to the Hyundai, and was just settling into some nice soothing sleep when Grijk knocked on his knee and said, "Den minudes do one."

"Okay," Dortmunder said, sitting up, yawning. "Let's go do it again."

"Da same ding?"

"The same thing," Dortmunder agreed, and led the way back to that unlocked window—still unlocked, they hadn't found it—where he did it again.

Second go-round, response time from the house even shorter, almost down to thirty seconds. Sheriff response also shorter, nine minutes.

Ah, but the search of the château was also shorter than before, nor was there any eyeballing this time of the Hyundai and the dump.

"Good," Dortmunder said when everything was quiet once more. "Before we do it again—"

"Ve gonna do id again, Chon?"

"That's why we're here, Grijk."

"Id is?"

"It is. But before we do it again, let's use some of that spy stuff of yours."

So this time, while wandering around the buildings, they used some of the spy stuff. Grijk had brought along, for instance, little microphones with suction cups. You stuck one of these in an inconspicuous spot on a window, and your radio, once you tuned it to the right frequency, would play for you every sound taking place in that room.

For the art gallery, a windowless room, there was an even more sensitive and powerful microphone that attached with two sharp—"Ouch!"—talons to the wood of the door. Other equipment hooked into the four phone lines emerging from the château and the residence. All of this stuff was twinned to radio equipment stuffed into the trunk of the Hyundai. Everything was old and used and thirdhand, like the Hyundai itself, but everything had just been tested by Grijk, back in New York, and it all still worked.

It was five minutes after two when they were finished. By now, all the lights were out and the TV switched off over in the occupied residence. This was a very quiet and peaceful mountain when Dortmunder headed for that unlocked window to do it again . . . and found it locked. "They got it this time," he said.

Grijk had been yawning and yawning. "So now ve go home?" he asked.

"Not yet."

Dortmunder tromped around to the front of the house, used his own square of flexible metal to open the main door there without leaving any marks, counted slowly to five, then shut the door and strolled away with Grijk as, behind them, lights popped on in the other building.

Slowing down now. Almost two minutes response time from the two armed guys next door, and sixteen minutes for the sheriff's three cars. A very brief inspection of the château, this time listened to by Dortmunder and Grijk, moving from frequency to frequency, microphone to microphone, as the searchers moved from room to room.

The searchers were getting irritated. "It's just *gotta* be a short," they kept telling one another, and the guys from next door kept assuring the sheriff's men they'd phone the alarm service first thing in the morning.

Dortmunder was most interested to hear what they had to say

when they reached the art gallery. "Wait a minute, there, let me turn off the other one," said a voice he recognized by now as one of the locals.

"Shit," said a deputy's voice, "I can see in there from the doorway; there's nothing and nobody in there. It's *gotta* be a short."

"Well, do you want me to turn it off or not? I got the picture down already."

"Nah, the hell with it."

"If you say so."

It was a brisk walk the searchers took through the château this time, scanning most of the rooms merely from the doorway, as they'd done with the art gallery. In hardly any time at all, they were through and outside and saying good night to one another.

Once the crowd of them were out, and the front door had been slammed shut, Dortmunder and Grijk shut off the radios to the château but kept the telephone intercepts alive. "They should be about due to make a phone call now," he said, and as he said so the sound began: the beeps and quinks of an outbound long-distance call.

There were half a dozen rings before a sleepy male voice somewhere else in the world said, "Hochman residence."

"Simmons again," said the local voice, and it sounded really annoyed. "The damn alarm system just keeps going off and going off. There's nobody there, there's nothing—"

"Well, what do you want *me* to do about it?" demanded the long-distanced voice, also sounding irritated. "I'm certainly not going to wake Mr. Hochman at this—"

"Just tell him, in the morning, the system's—"

"I said I would, the last time you called."

"He's gotta get them on it, first thing."

"He *will*, Simmons, all right?"

"It just keeps going off."

"You need not," said the long-distance voice in a very frosty manner, "report it to me if it does so again. Not tonight. Good night, Simmons." And the phone went bang.

"Good," Dortmunder said. "We can shut all this stuff down now."

They did, and closed the Hyundai trunk, and Grijk said, "Vhat now, Chon?"

"Now," Dortmunder said, "we give them a quick one." And he walked briskly up the dirt road and over to the château to open and close the front door, then retired to the usual vantage point.

The response this time was pathetic; one guy without his shotgun but with his flashlight came clumping across, a full three minutes after Dortmunder had tripped the alarm. One sheriff's car, no sirens, no flashing lights, showed up five minutes later, but of course he wouldn't even have been back to headquarters yet when the new call had come in; and his two pals had continued on, not bothering to come back.

This time, there appeared to be some sort of heated words expelled into the night air in front of the château, between local and deputy, before the sheriff's car peeled off over the mountain, burning rubber, and the unarmed resident stomped back home and slammed his door.

"What time is it?" Dortmunder asked.

"Den minudes do dree. In da morning."

"Wake me," Dortmunder said, "at five after four."

"Chon? Vad am I supposed to do vile you're sleeping?"

"Bring back all your spy stuff. We don't need it anymore." And, ignoring Grijk's wounded eyes, Dortmunder curled up on the backseat of the Hyundai, snoozed very satisfactorily for over an hour, and got up with hardly any aches or spasms when Grijk awoke him at five after four.

Dortmunder scratched and stretched in front of the sagging Grijk. "This one should do it," he predicted, and went cheerily off to open and close the château's front door.

That one did it. Not a light went on in the other house. No sheriff's car showed up. "Now," Dortmunder said, "we can go home and get some sleep."

39

The last time the back room at the OJ had been this crowded was when everybody was trying to figure out who among them had stolen the Byzantine Fire, a priceless ruby belonging to Turkey or the United States or somebody, the lifting of which had caused such official wrath, such unrelenting heat, there were *still* people serving sentences upstate only because they were holding the wrong items at the moment they happened to be dredged up in the sweep. Many people then had blamed Dortmunder for the situation, until the true culprit had been exposed. A peaceful person, Dortmunder had long since forgiven everybody.

But there was still a little pang of remembered terror when he found himself once again in this setting with all these people. Fortunately, he was fresh and rested from his vacation yesterday and this morning in the mountains, and he knew nobody here harbored any more suspicion concerning him and that miserable ruby, so he could rise above his instinctive fears and chair the meeting. "Tiny Bulcher and Andy Kelp gave you all the rundown on what we're doing here, right?" he asked, and looked around to receive general agreement from all these familiar faces.

DON'T ASK

Familiar faces. Over there was Wally Whistler, tanned and ready, back from a long stay in Brazil. A longer stay than he'd planned, in fact. Usually, the way Wally Whistler traveled was by extradition; confess to the local police a crime you claim to have committed in the country to which you wish to travel, then retract the confession and demonstrate your ironclad alibi once the extradition is complete. Unfortunately, between Brazil and the United States there is no extradition treaty, a fact Wally had learned only too late. It had galled him, but finally he'd admitted defeat and performed enough burglaries around São Paulo to buy a first-class ticket home. The worst of it, he now said, wasn't spending the money; it was the traveling alone, without the accompanying police escort who usually helped so accommodatingly to while away the time.

And there was Jim O'Hara, out of prison again, skin still pale and gray-looking. It seemed to Dortmunder that every time he saw Jim O'Hara, the guy was either going into prison or coming out. Their last encounter, a few years ago, had ended on a rooftop downtown, when Jim had made the error of taking a fire escape down into the arms of the waiting police while Dortmunder had more sensibly legged it the other way.

And over there was Fred Lartz, the driver, almost as good as Stan Murch (but don't tell Stan that). Of course, Fred's wife, Thelma, did all the actual driving these days, but Fred was still the one who made the meetings.

And here's Gus Brock, sitting blunt and four-square, with a grim expression on his face, as though his mustache was too heavy. And Harry Matlock and Ralph Demrovsky, a burglary tag team so proficient and persistent, they always traveled by van, just in case they happened across something too heavy to carry. And Ralph Winslow, debonair lockman, who always had a glass in his hand with ice cubes cheerfully tinkling, which meant he'd by necessity become adept at stripping locks one-handed.

"What we're doing here," Dortmunder told all these people, "is two different jobs. Well, no, it's three, but we're not doing the third one; a bunch of people over in Europe are doing that. In fact, the word is, they already did it. Right, Grijk?"

Grijk grinned and held up his massive left fist, around which was curled a sheet of slippery, shiny, crappy paper. "Ve god a fax," he announced. "Ve incurzed da Rivers a Blood Catedral; ve god da box; id's flyin here righd now on a Coca-Cola plane."

Dortmunder frowned. "I thought you said Pepsi-Cola."

"Vun a dem," Grijk said, and waved a dismissive hand, the one with the fax wrapped around it. Because, after all, to an Eastern European, all American logos look alike.

Here's the situation: As major American corporations rush to bring Western culture to the opening markets of Eastern Europe—Pizza Hut, Kleenex, Budweiser—there's a certain amount of quidding taking place among all the quo. (Not necessarily to the extent that Harry Hochman and Hradec Kralowc were fondling one another, but still.) Corporate jets traverse the globe all the time, bearing vitally important executives to vitally important meetings, and there's always room aboard for a diplomatic courier from a recently friendly—that is, profitable—nation. The soft-drink Lockheed currently skying NYward would not be subjected to any customs and immigration indignities upon landing in New York, nor would the courier riding it, bringing with him the medium-size pet carrier labeled:

MITZI

Ambassador Zara Kotor's Pomeranian

Beware of Dog

Extremely Dangerous

Extremely quiet, too, as it happened.

"Okay," Dortmunder said. "Part one is taken care of. Now, part two, I've got to tell you, and I'm sorry about this, but part two is ridiculous. Part two is, we steal a bone. It isn't worth anything to you and me, but it's worth something to Grijk there and the people from his country, so we're doing it for them. *Because,* part three is where we get our own. Part three is rare and valuable art, worth more than six mil, and Grijk and his country are gonna help us lift it. Right, Grijk?"

"Right!" Grijk flew his fax again briefly and beamed around at the mob.

Harry Matlock, speaking for himself and his partner, Ralph Demrovsky, said, "Dortmunder? Six mil, you say."

"Around that."

"What's in it for us?"

"We got a very high-powered fence," Dortmunder told him. "Not like the usual run of guy. He's gonna dicker with the insurance company for us."

Gus Brock said, "But..." and looked alert.

"But he gets half."

Nobody in the room liked that. That is, those who'd been aboard this thing from the beginning—Tiny Bulcher, Andy Kelp, and Stan Murch—understood the situation and didn't bother to like it or dislike it, but the seven new guys all didn't like it, and made that clear with grunts, body language, and the shaking of heads. Ralph Winslow cleared his throat, clattered the ice cubes in his glass, and said, "Does he get half of a bigger pie? Is that why he's worth it?"

"We hope so," Dortmunder said. "But for now, let's say it winds up he gets a million."

"He should do better than that," Ralph said.

"Probably he will," Dortmunder agreed. "But we're doing worst-case here. Worst-case, he gets a mil, he keeps half, we split half a mil about eleven ways, that's—"

"Forty-five thousand," Ralph Demrovsky said, "four hundred fifty-four bucks. More or less."

"So that isn't bad," Dortmunder pointed out, "for a weekend's work."

"It should be more," Ralph Winslow said, and Ralph Demrovsky said, "Ralph's right," and Ralph Winslow said, "Ralphs are always right," and Ralph Winslow and Ralph Demrovsky smiled at one another in perfect convivial understanding.

Dortmunder said, "So that means you two are out?"

The Ralphs stopped smiling. Ralph Demrovsky said, "Who said such a thing? Did I?"

Ralph Winslow said, "John, if you can renegotiate with this amazing fence, I know you'll do it. If you can't, and what we get is what we get, then that's what we get. I'm in."

"Naturally," Ralph Demrovsky said.

Dortmunder looked around the room. "Everybody?"

There was more shuffling, there was more body language, there was more grunting of discontent, but in the end everybody agreed with the Ralphs; they were in. "Good," Dortmunder said.

Then Harry Matlock said, "You say a weekend's work, and you say two jobs. When do we do all this?"

"Well," Dortmunder told him, "the main stuff is tomorrow night, but there's some setting up first. We need places to stash some stuff, and vehicles, and like that. Also, tonight we got to send a team up to Vermont, with Grijk here in charge, to keep the burglar alarm active."

Fred Lartz said, "That's sounding like a job for me."

"It is," Dortmunder agreed. "I'll give you a credit card; you and Thelma might as well stay at the ski place up there. I can recommend it."

Wally Whistler, who seemed to speak now with a faint Portuguese accent, after his long stay in Brazil, said, "You got something now in Vermont. Nothing in New York? That's it for tonight?"

"Well, no," Dortmunder said. "Like I say, the main robbery's tomorrow night, but tonight we got to do a little preliminary something here in town."

"What?"

"A kidnapping," Dortmunder said.

40

Karver Zorn, M.D., F.A.C.S., F.R.C.S., P.C., R.N., C.N.M., D.D.S., D.M.D. (all disputed), sat at the old organ in the chancel of the deconsecrated church he called home and played an execrable version of *Also Spracht Zarathustra*. Well, in the first place, it's getting harder and harder these days to find a competent organ tuner; in fact, in some parts of the world, it's just about impossible. So when Dr. Zorn's scrubbed fingertip pressed upon a particular stained ivory key, the note that groaned or squawked out of the mighty machine curving all around him like an Art Deco half-moon was not necessarily the note that was *supposed* to emanate at that moment. In the second place, Dr. Zorn was a pretty miserable musician, and the key his scrubbed fingertip pressed upon was just as likely to be the wrong one. But none of that mattered, really, because, in the third place, Dr. Zorn was tone-deaf.

Given all of the above, it was fortunate for Dr. Zorn's neighbors that he didn't have any. The slum clearance project that had made this church de trop had swept through this once-bustling and -vibrant community in the South Bronx like the twentieth century's version of the black plague, but had done it a full genera tion ago, demolishing, leveling, razing, pounding everything flat and then pulverizing the remains beneath the treads of mighty yellow machines as intelligent as their masters.

And why didn't St. Crispinian succumb when all about it fell to the planners' scythe? The building had to be deconsecrated before it could be destroyed, an arcane ritual that causes no harm to the structure but the lack of which can cause political harm in the general area. By the time the two bureaucracies, divine and mundane, had completed all their mumbo jumbo, yet another of society's agonizing reappraisals had taken place, it had belatedly been realized that the wanton destruction of living communities for the sake of the erection of dead projects was wrong, and the whole plan had been scrapped. A chain-link fence was put around the area, and the planners all turned their serious, busy, college-trained numskulls to the next corner they could brighten.

Leaving St. Crispinian. The Church didn't want the church back, having deconsecrated it and it having been stripped of its entire congregation. The city didn't want to know about it—though the city owned it now—because past errors are not merely embarrassing but are also uncomfortable hints that present schemes might also be imperfect. Yet leaving it there, all alone for blocks and blocks in every direction, boarded up however efficiently, was an open invitation to vandals, druggies, general criminals, cultists, and all sorts of undesirables.

Many are the small accommodations that take place between the United Nations headquarters apparat in Manhattan and the city government of New York. Each finds the other irritating but indispensable, and each occasionally finds the other useful. And so it was that the UN, once upon a time, took over control of St. Crispinian from the City of New York on a long-term no-cash lease, in aid of some forgotten scheme put forward by a Third World representative, whose government, unluckily, was overthrown, boiled, and eaten before the scheme, whatever it had been, got any further than the signing of the lease. Since when, the UN struggled to return the church to the city, which refused to take it, and in the meantime the world body tried everything—guard dogs, private security, blue-helmeted soldiers from Sweden and Finland—to keep those aforementioned undesirables away from St. Crispinian, but nothing *really* worked until Dr. Zorn.

DON'T ASK

It wasn't only his musicianship that kept Dr. Zorn's surroundings pest-free. There was also something about his personality; for some reason, people didn't seem to warm to him, not even truly scuzzy people of the sort who might break into a deconsecrated church late at night in hopes of finding some leftover religious artifact they could pawn for drug money. And beyond that, there was his work for the UN.

Famine relief. Let others concentrate on moving food around the world from where it is to where it's needed. Let others do long-term planning, with crop rotation, flood control, population density, and all that. Dr. Zorn had set himself a simpler and more basic question to answer: What could people eat, if there wasn't any food?

The apse, and apsidal chapels, of the former church, arched and rounded stone recesses in the final wall beyond the altar, had been converted now to something that was a cross between a kitchen and a laboratory, with beakers and retorts steaming away, foul liquids bubbling, electric arcs coursing between points, strings of lights flashing on and off, great coils of tubing that arced and swooped like carnival rides for roaches, plus high shelves full of glass jars containing strangely warped items that might have been—and sometimes were—diseased tennis balls. Here Dr. Zorn experimented with the food potential of things not usually though of as edible: socks, grass, filing cabinets, fingernail clippings. (To solve the problems of human hunger and waste management at one fell swoop; wouldn't *that* be a coup, worthy of the Nobel Prize!)

Of course, the other indispensable element in all this experimentation was some actual humans. *Someone* had to eat all these outpourings from Dr. Zorn's kitchen. In the early days, the neighborhood provided a sufficiency of laboratory humans for the purpose, people who entered the church with agendas of their own but stayed to assist the good doctor in his Nobel work. (Various traps and pitfalls he'd installed around the narthex, assisted by tranquilizer darts and other mood-altering devices, ensured that his guests did not make untimely departures.)

More recently, however, as the doctor's reputation had spread among the underclass, pickings had become rather more slim, and he was beginning to contemplate the idea of placing some sort of

231

ad in the less prestigious public prints, if only he could figure out the precise wording. So difficult to describe scientific undertakings to the layman.

What made the setup here so perfect for Dr. Zorn's work, in addition to the church itself and the nearby supply of experimental persons, was the block on which the structure stood. Everything else had been reduced to a pink rubble, its color prettily tinged by brick dust, and then the entire block had been sheathed in an eight-foot-high chain-link fence. Originally meant to keep people out, it worked just as well to keep people in, particularly once Dr. Zorn had electrified it. Oh, not with a lethal jolt, certainly not; just enough to discourage premature departure.

How pleasant it could be, on a moonlit night, to climb into the belfry and gaze down at the current herd, moving slowly about on the rubble below. It was even fun sometimes to take the BB gun up there and do a little plinking into the herd down below, keep them moving; good for the digestion.

At the moment, though, unfortunately, there was no herd. He having as yet found no really adequate substitute for food, Dr. Zorn's assistants tended to reach a point of emaciation at which their responses to stimuli were no longer adequate to his purpose, at which time he would permit them to crawl away (or would wheelbarrow them away on foggy nights, if it came to that).

Also Spracht Zarathustra rolled on, magnificent in its awfulness. Dr. Zorn was so caught up in the sheer mass and complexity of what he was creating here, the volume of it, the rich confusion of cascading chords, that he barely noticed the white light mounted high on the stone column to his left when it began to blink.

He'd installed that light some time ago, since he couldn't hear anything else while playing the organ and so wouldn't know when the narthex had snared another customer. The blinking light meant something had just entered one of the traps; good. There were a number of nonfoods he was eager to try out on fresh subjects.

But there was no hurry. The visitor or visitors—the equipment in the narthex could capture and hold up to four newcomers at a time—would wait. He could finish his playing.

And did. And sighed with satisfaction as the last sprung chord clanged about the upper reaches of the structure. And turned about on the organ bench to gaze into the eyes of eight grim-looking individuals.

Oh, dear. They'd never shown up in this quantity before. The narthex would have snared the first four, but then the next four would have released them while the good doctor had all-unknowingly played on.

And now all eight were here, in the chancel, gazing at him without love. From afar came the sound of slow dripping, a leak in the columbarium he'd never bothered to do anything about. Other than that, there was not a sound as they stood and gazed at him, apparently waiting for the final echoes of *Zarathustra* to fade inside their skulls before trying to move or to speak.

What now? These would be simple creatures. Negotiate with them, find out what they want, either send them on their way or somehow turn the tables on them. Dr. Zorn pondered, in the few seconds of silence he had for planning, on the arsenal of medicines and laboratory equipment at his command, and he tried to think how he might turn the tables on eight people all by himself, and while musing on that question he suddenly realized that one of those grim faces was somehow familiar.

Diddums! John Diddums, from the Votskojek mission!

Dr. Zorn was lithe and fast. He was off the organ bench like a shot, and halfway around the ambulatory before they laid hands on him. Many hands. Many hard hands.

The person who sat on Dr. Zorn was immense. In a different context, the doctor would have been happy to have this fellow as a research assistant out there in the rubble; such a monster would survive on nonfoods for *months*. Unfortunately, this was not a different context, this was *this* context, and in *this* context the many hands had grabbed Dr. Zorn and picked him up and carried him back to the chancel and stretched him facedown on one of the remaining side pews originally meant for the choir. Then this huge one had sat upon him, quite effectively holding him in place while the others searched the church.

For what? What did Diddums want, beyond simple revenge? Clearly it wasn't merely simple revenge the man had in mind, or he wouldn't have shown up with seven friends. In fact, if Did-

dums was here because he wanted something, that was more or
less good news for Dr. Zorn, because it meant there was some
probability he would survive this encounter.

Whatever it was Diddums wanted, Zorn decided, he would
give to the man, at once and without equivocation. Betray Hradec
Kralowc? Done. Assist in some new scheme of Diddums' own?
No problem. Provide poisons or a weapon or an alibi or anything
at all? Just ask. Thy will, as they used to say in this building, be
done.

From some distance away, some large, heavy wooden object
was dragged across the stone floor of the nave with a sound that
even Dr. Zorn could tell was unpleasant. The sound continued, at
first advancing and then retreating, and at last it came to a stop,
leaving once again only that irregular drip, drip, drip from the
columbarium.

Were they merely here to rob him? To pry through his delicate experiments with their unlettered fingers? Though breathing was difficult, though movement was virtually impossible,
the eternal verities of science called, and Dr. Zorn struggled to
lift his head, to warn them to leave his laboratory alone!
"Don't—!"

The man monster seated on the doctor's back whomped him
across the top of his head. "Sharrap," he said, and shifted position.

Oh! No! Don't do that! Dr. Zorn sharrapped; he lowered his
aching head; he remained very still and obedient; he did absolutely nothing that might cause this huge creature on top of him
to shift position any more. Don't shift position!

"Okay," said Diddums's voice from somewhere, and the
monster climbed off, leaving a somewhat-pressed Dr. Zorn
prone on the pew. Did they want him to go somewhere? He
didn't think he could move; certainly couldn't stand; beyond
possibility to walk.

But that didn't matter. Hard hands gripped him by the elbows
and knees, he was lifted from the pew, and he was carried in that
prone position across the chancel and nave, head drooping, eyes
blearily watching the movement of the stone floor beneath him
and the scissoring of legs all around.

Into the columbarium. The recesses for the ashes of the dead
were empty now, and Dr. Zorn had found no other use for the

high-ceilinged, bare stone room. The sound of the drip was louder here, echoing faintly against the stone. There was a pause, with Dr. Zorn continuing to hang like a canopy in the middle of them all, seeing nothing, smelling damp stone, tasting dinner—he personally still ate food—and then he was flipped like a pancake, dropped onto a long wooden bench—*that's* what they'd been dragging!—and tied with many ropes and extension cords.

Off to the side, Diddums watched with gloomy satisfaction. Ask me, Dr. Zorn telepathed at that bony brow, ask me anything and I'll do it. Just ask!

But, no. The bench was picked up with him on it, now supine and strapped. It was carried across the room and put down, then shifted this way and that until it was just so. With his forehead under the leak. Drip, went a drop of cold water on his pale brow. Drip.

Diddums came over and looked down at him. "See you later," he said.

It took Dr. Zorn, distracted by the dripping water, a second too long to realize what was happening. They were all going away! "Wait!" he cried. "I'll do it! Whatever it is, I'll do it!"

But they were gone. Drip.

Oh, this is ridiculous, he thought, struggling against his bonds, twisting his head back and forth. I'm just going to get wet here, cold and wet, the Chinese water torture doesn't—drip—actually work, you're wasting your time, Diddums, you could—drip—merely ask me.

The drips are not—drip—rhythmic, they do not fall—drip—to any pattern, you can never guess when the next one will land. Drip.

Daylight stained the stained-glass windows, and still he was alone. Dr. Zorn had yelled himself hoarse, and then grown silent, and then yelled again, and then grown quiet again, merely whimpering from time to time. He'd turned his head this way and that, filling his ears with water, to no effect. He'd struggled against the ropes and extension cords. He'd grown convinced *this* was the revenge; they would never come back.

Capillary action is what makes water spread from where it is to where you are. Dr. Zorn was soaked. His clothing was soaked. His head seemed to burn with an ice-cold burn wherever the drips touched. The squlsh of water when it struck his flesh sounded through his brain, dissolved his brain, dropped his brain into an acid bath. He shivered, his breathing was irregular, he was exhausted but couldn't— drip —sleep.

And you never knew when it would drip again; you'd wait and tense and wait and nothing and then *drip* and you'd think *at last* and *drip* immediately and you'd be even more tense than before, and on and on and on....

"How you doing, Doctor?"

This was one of the periods when the doctor's eyes were squeezed tight shut, because water spraying in them had made them ache with cold. Now his eyes popped open—DRIP!—and there was Diddums. "Please," the doctor whispered.

"What we want you to do," Diddums said.

"Yes, I will."

"Isn't gonna be that hard."

"I'll do it."

"The hypodermic needle full of stuff you shot into me that time—"

"I'm sorry, Diddums, I'm heartily sorry."

"I want you to make up some more hypodermic needles just like that."

"I will. Absolutely."

"Don't do anything different."

"No, no."

"Just do like you did before."

"Yes! Yes!"

"And a couple other little tasks along the way. Easy ones."

"Anything! Anything!"

Diddums stood there, frowning down at the wide-eyed Dr. Zorn, and another droplet of water came and went, shattering the doctor's brain, permitting him just time enough to gather again the shattered pieces when another droplet—

A second person came and stood beside Diddums and looked down at the doctor. This was a sharp-nosed fellow with a bright and amiable eye. "You know, John," he said, "I think he's ready."

My benefactor! Dr. Zorn loved this person; he admired and esteemed and trusted him; he would follow this person to the gates of hell; he would never never fail this godlike person. "Oh, yes," he whispered. Drip. "I'm ready."

41

CONTINENTAL

DETECTIVE

AGENCY

it said, on the side of the blue-gray van driven by stout ex-cop Joe Mulligan and containing the rest of the seven-man guard team: Fenton, the wiry little old head of the crew, perched on the only good seat in the van, next to the driver; Garfield and Morrison in the row behind that; Block and Fox next; and Dresner spreading out (but taking the bumps) at the rear.

They were the graveyard shift, midnight to eight, on yet another miserable, insulting third-rate assignment; when, oh when, would the perfectly understandable lapses of the past be forgotten so they could relax into the *good* life again, out on Long Island? The construction company owner weddings, the rock impresario's daughter's high school graduation party, the shopping center openings, the accountancy firm cruises on the Great South Bay. Jobs a man could be proud of, jobs completely free of peril or complication, jobs with some meat and potatoes to them.

But, no. The seven bouncing down Second Avenue in this van, on their way to some kind of kooky Eastern European embassy on a *boat,* if you could believe it, these seven able men, all ex-cops or ex-MPs, all perfectly qualified for a job of contented ease amid the good citizens of Long Island—far from the Boschian hell of New York City—had run into a string of bad luck, that's all, could have happened to anybody, and now look. Siberia.

They *used* to work on Long Island, this same crew of seven. But then, one night, they lost a bank. Well, nobody'd *ever* found it, not the combined police forces of Nassau and Suffolk counties, not the feds, not anybody, so why did opprobrium have to land so heavily and exclusively on Sergeant Fenton's team, from the Continental?

Well, it did, that's all. And life hadn't been improved a couple of years after that, either, when the team had been guarding a rich man's party at a town house on the East Side—the wealthy East Side—and the place was broken into by a whole lot of robbers, extremely armed robbers, who took everything in sight, locked the guards in closets, and got away clean. (The party host, some nasty snob named Chauncey, had refused to pay the agency for the guards; can you believe it?)

So here they were, still at the bottom of the bottom. Working Manhattan, dangerous, crummy Manhattan, where a fellow in a uniform could get hurt real bad real fast, instead of being out in the lush Eden of Long Island. *And* working graveyard shifts.

Saturday night; the hairiest night of the week. At least it wasn't the full moon. They were taking over for the original crew on this shift, who would be off now till Wednesday, so tonight they were to arrive a few minutes early for orientation from the four-to-midnight guys.

According to the clock on the van's dash, they'd make it in plenty of time, even though Second Avenue was littered with traffic pouring in on the Fifty-ninth Street Bridge and through the Midtown Tunnel from Queens and Brooklyn and (admit it) Long Island. (Traffic outbound to those calmer climes clogged the cross streets.) Stately, plump Joe Mulligan steered the company van carefully through the cluttered traffic, and took it easy. No more screwups.

He made the turn onto East Twenty-eighth Street with no trouble, proceeded eastward according to directions all the way to the FDR Drive and on under the Drive and beyond, and there, on its far side, was the chain-link fence he was to park beside. He did, and said, "Here we are."

"All out, boys," Fenton said, unnecessarily, since everybody was already clambering toward the sliding door in the van's side. But Fenton liked being the fellow in charge, and kept making little fellow-in-charge noises, which were generally ignored. He would have liked it, too, if the crew were to call him Chief, but they never did.

The guys from the four-to-midnight shift were there, inside the fence, waiting. The two groups were dressed alike, in dark blue policelike uniforms, with the triangular badge on the left shoulder echoing the one on the van door. Policelike shields over their hearts were embossed CDI, plus a number, and to complete the look they all wore gun belts and holsters containing .38-caliber Smith & Wesson Police Positive revolvers.

The sergeant of the earlier shift was a comfortable fat man named Edwards, who unlocked the gate for them, locked it again behind them, and said, "Well, boys, it's a piece of cake."

"Good," Fenton said. "I like a quiet tour myself. Leave the excitement to the paratroops, that's what I say."

"Amen to that," Edwards agreed. "Come along, let me show you what we've got."

All seven crew members went along, and what Edwards showed them did indeed look like a piece of cake. A ship and an old ferry slip. Access through the gate in the chain-link fence on the landward side. Theoretical access by boat from the East River. The crew would divide into three pairs, one at the gate, one out at the river end of the slip, and one inside the access door in the hull. Comfortable-looking folding chairs were set out for them at all three locations so they wouldn't have to spend the entire eight-hour shift on their feet. Fenton, in charge, would move among the three groups, seeing to it that everything remained calm.

Edwards turned over to Fenton his clipboard, saying, "Nothing to it. There's only three residents in the ship, and you've got their photos right there. That's the two clerks, Lusk and Terment, and they're already in for the night; you won't be seeing them anymore. That's the ambassador there. His name is Hradec Kralowc; he's a bit of a rake, you know. He'll come rolling in around one in the morning with something very delectable on his arm. Remember her going in, you'll probably see her going out."

Fenton took the clipboard and said, "What's it all about, then? This is more security than you'd be likely to give an outfit like this."

"They've got something in there," Edwards said. "Don't ask me what it is; I don't know and I don't care. It's valuable, that's all I know about it."

"Then that's all *I* need to know," Fenton said. (Pity; Mulligan would have liked to know more.)

"Apparently," Edwards went on, "there was some sort of run at it once before, and they're afraid the same bunch might try again."

"Not while we're on," Fenton said firmly, and Mulligan fervently hoped he was right.

"The ambassador's the only one you take orders from," Edwards said. "Nobody in or out without him saying yes."

"I like it simple," Fenton said.

"Then you're gonna like it here," Edwards told him.

Mulligan handed over the van keys to his opposite number on the other crew, a tall, bony Jamaican named Kingsbury, and then the four-to-midnight guys drove away back to headquarters uptown while Fenton dished out assignments; Block and Fox out at the watery end of the slip; Morrison and Garfield inside the entrance to the hull; and Mulligan and Dresner on the gate.

"Keep a sharp eye out," Fenton said, unnecessarily. "Though I don't suppose you'll see much."

Which, for the first fifteen minutes, was absolutely true. Seated on the folding chairs by the locked gate, Mulligan and Dresner could look up and catch glimpses of the traffic hurtling by up there on the FDR Drive, but no traffic at all came to this dead end down here. Nor was it a spot likely to attract pedestrian traffic after dark. A quiet night, then; exactly what the doctor ordered. Mulligan and Dresner sat at their ease on the folding chairs and whiled away the time with Superghost.

Headlights. Approaching; stopping. Would this be the ambassador coming home? Mulligan looked forward to eyeballing the good-looking girl who would allegedly be with him.

But, no, this was not the ambassador, unless the ambassador moonlighted delivering pizzas. That out there was a white with red trim Dominick's Pizza truck, a famous national brand, and here came a cheerful-looking, narrow-nosed guy in the white Dominick's delivery uniform, carrying what looked like *two* pizza boxes.

Careful, Mulligan told himself. This could be a trick. Or a trap. Or trouble. He and Dresner both rose, both stood warily, hands on holstered guns, as the cheerful-looking guy approached and said, "This the Votskojek embassy?"

Mulligan and Dresner looked at one another. Votskojek? Was it? Temporizing, Mulligan said to the delivery guy, "It's the embassy."

"Right," said the guy. "And this is the pizza. It's a treat from the ambassador, uh, wait a minute, wait a minute—" He turned the boxes around until he could read the delivery slip taped on top. "What kinda name is *that?*" he wanted to know. "Hradec Kralowc." Bright-eyed, he looked at them through the fence. "That's your guy, right?"

It was indeed. Mulligan remembered the name and remembered looking at a photo of the guy on the clipboard Fenton was now carrying in this direction. "That's right," Mulligan said, and Fenton arrived to say, "What's this?"

"Pizza," Dresner told him, while Mulligan said to the delivery guy, "The pizza's for the ambassador?"

"No no no no no," the guy said. "The pizza's *from* the ambassador, for you guys. To welcome you—what's he say?—aboard. Because it's your first night, right?"

The smell of pizza wafted through the chain-link fence. It smelled great. Dresner said, "Now *that's* what I call a boss."

"Things are looking up, boys," Fenton said, and told Mulligan, "Open up, Joe, we'll watch your back."

"Right." Mulligan unlocked the gate and opened it, while Dresner and Fenton peered into the darkness, alert to any opponent who might suddenly rush the fence, and the delivery guy stepped through all alone, grinning. He put the two boxes on one of the folding chairs, looking brightly at them all, and said, "Enjoy your pizzas."

"We will," Mulligan assured him, standing there by the open gate.

When the delivery guy made no move to leave, when he went on standing there, bright-eyed, expectantly smiling, Mulligan tensed up for a second, thinking, *It is a trap!* But then Fenton caught on, and dug into his hip pocket. Dragging out his skinny old wallet, he slipped a couple bucks out of it and passed them to the delivery guy, saying, "Thanks, pal."

"Anytime, sport," the delivery guy said, and went grinning through the gate. While Mulligan relocked, the delivery guy hopped in his truck and drove away, and Fenton and Dresner checked out the boxes. "Both the same," Dresner announced. "Sausage and cheese."

"Not a bad thing, sausage and cheese," Mulligan allowed.

Fenton picked up one of the boxes. "I'll distribute this one," He said. "You guys start on that. Don't eat the whole thing, though, the two of you."

"Who, us?" Mulligan said, and chortled, because he could probably get through that entire pizza all by himself with no help from Dresner at all.

It was nice, though, a nice way to start the job. Mulligan put the pizza box on the ground between himself and Dresner, and they each pulled out slices and started to eat. It was excellent. They had no reason to be suspicious at all.

42

The fourth time Hradec saw *Nana: The Musical,* it still didn't make any sense, but by now he was used to that. The British import was a Broadway sellout, in more ways than one, but who knew what the Broadway audience was anymore or what that audience thought made sense? The green-tinged lighting, the smoke and mirrors, the gritty evocation of low Parisian dives, the all-singing, all-dancing, all-gyrating sansculottes, the coloratura climaxes, the utter Technicolor despair at the curtain, it was all loud and spectacular and expensive, with every penny of expense visible right there onstage in the whirling sets and lunatic effects, and that's what it presumably was all about. The audience applauded the sets and came out humming nothing, and seemed to believe it was having a good time.

As for Hradec, he contented himself with watching the fourth sansculottes from the left. Krystal Kerrin, she klaimed her name to be, and what shapely yet powerful legs she possessed! To think that, in just a few hours, those legs would be wrapped around *him*. While Nana's bleak history was baroquely told, Hradec Kralowc sat in the house seat his pony Krystal had obtained for him—fourth row, a bit to the left of center—and watched her trot.

244

And then it was over, and like legions of stage-door johnnies before him Hradec trooped around to the stage-door alley, where very quickly Krystal came tripping into view, powerful legs twinkling silver below a short black skirt. Soon, over lobster and pouilly-fuissé at Bernardin, she was bubbling on about her recent activities —tryouts, costumings, classes (sword fighting was going particular well), hairstylists, agent troubles, backbiting backstage at *Nana: The Musical*—through all of which Hradec sat in shadows across from her, a half-smile of inattention on his face. Her mouth was lovely, and had its uses, but what he mostly thought about was her legs.

And then the taxi to the embassy, arriving a bit after one in the morning, to find all was well. There was a new team of guards on tonight, confidence-inspiring in their policelike getups. The pair at the gate were Laurel and Hardyish, in that they were fat and thin, but otherwise appeared not to have much of a bent for the comical, unless one counted the length of time it took Hardy to compare Hradec's self with the photo of himself on the man's clipboard. But Hradec didn't mind; total security may take a little longer, but it's worth it in the long run. Yes indeed.

When Hardy at last felt he could live with the idea that the man before him and the photograph were both references to the same individual, and Laurel at his instructions unlocked the gate, it was Hardy who offered an oily smile and gestured to some trash on the ground as he said, "Appreciate it, sir."

Whatever that might mean. Hradec's thoughts were all of Krystal's nether pins. "Very good," he responded, and took his lady of this evening by the elbow and steered her toward the embassy.

En route, they passed this team's sergeant, a skinny little geezer who walked with them briefly, started to say, "Even—" then had to stifle a mammoth yawn. Eyes watering, he tried again. "Evening, Ambassador. I'm Fenton. Everything's quiet."

"Good," Hradec said. "Carry on."

"The boys appreciated the thoughtfulness, sir," Fenton said, stopping in Hradec's wake and tossing off a semiofficial kind of salute.

"Yes, yes," Hradec said, not listening, moving on. Those silver legs whipsawed along beside him in the soft darkness toward the ship.

The two guards just inside the entrance rose from their folding chairs as Hradec and Krystal boarded. Both smiled and nodded their greetings, and one of them abruptly covered his mouth, segments of a yawn appearing around the perimeter of his hand. Hradec found himself about to yawn in sympathy but forced himself to stop. Can't have any of that. There's much to be done before sleep tonight, much, oh, much to be done.

And was. The clock read well after two when at last Hradec switched off the light and settled down to a much-needed rest in dear Krystal's arms, and it read not yet three when rough hands switched the lights back on and poked at Hradec's shoulder and head, and a rough voice said, "Rise and shine, you."

Hradec's eyes popped open. Beside him, Krystal's mouth popped open and a scream began to emerge, but then yet another rough hand clamped down over her face and the scream went back inside. That hand held a white cloth; the tang of chloroform prickled the air, and Krystal's eyes glazed o'er.

The room was full of men wearing ski masks. In June? Hradec, still fighting free of a silver-legged dream, stared around and saw only one familiar uncovered face. "Karver!" he cried at the cringing figure of Dr. Zorn over by the door.

Zorn refused to look up. His hands miserably washed one another at his waist. He twitched all over.

"Karver!" Hradec cried, to his onetime classmate at Osigreb Polytechnic. "What's going on?"

But it wasn't his old friend Karver Zorn who answered his plea. No, Zorn was now blinking pathetically at the array of hypodermic syringes in the small carrying case being presented to him by the largest and meanest-looking of the invaders. No, it was another one, the nearest of the interlopers, a slope-shouldered fellow whose features were hidden behind a ghastly purple ski mask blotched with hideous green snowflakes, who said, "We've taken over the ship."

Diddums! Hradec had sense enough not to blurt the name out loud. Instead, staring at the syringe as it approached, "This is piracy!" he cried.

"Good," said the phlegmatic Diddums, behind his mask. "I never did that before."

43

By Saturday night, when Stan Murch and the burglar team of Harry Matlock and Ralph Demrovsky arrived in Vermont, the château was as ready as a fifteen-year-old boy after two hours of foreplay. The château had had two *nights* of foreplay, and was just begging to be robbed.

Grijk Krugnk was having an awful lot of fun here. He'd driven up yesterday, Friday, leading the driver team of Fred Lartz and, at the wheel, his wife, Thelma, plus lockman Ralph Winslow, who even carried a glass with tinkling ice cubes in the car, and heavy-mustached utility man Gus Brock. Fred and Thelma stayed in the Dortmunder room at Kinohaha, Grijk reclaimed his room at the bed-and-breakfast place, and Ralph and Gus made arrangements at a motel down the mountain, using the other one of Arnie Albright's ticking credit cards. Friday night at the château, while they'd triggered alarms and watched reactions, they'd also installed a lot of Grijk's spy stuff, both in the château and in the other house, and had done some of the preliminary work on removing alarm systems entirely.

While this group was thus hard at work up in New England, back in New York Dr. Zorn had been strapped to a bench in his

247

church, studying hydrodynamics. Around the time Andy Kelp was testing the doctor and declaring him ready, Grijk and Fred and Thelma and Ralph and Gus were settling into their beds in Vermont for a good day's sleep.

With dark on Saturday came more fun at the château. The telephone lines they'd tapped into were blue with the smoke of furious phone calls. The TV monitors they'd installed in both buildings showed the protectors of the estate running in increasingly smaller circles, going *out* of their minds. The alarm systems that had already been removed now rusted quietly at the bottom of Harry Hochman's illegal dump. Total and productive quiet would soon arrive.

Meanwhile, down in New York City, Dr. Zorn doctored pizza, and Andy Kelp delivered it. Then Kelp searched several hospital parking lots and parking buildings before he found what he wanted: a large van with fold-down seats and M.D. plates. Firmly believing that doctors understand comfort and discomfort better than anyone else, Kelp always based his automotive choices on medical opinion. And as usual, he was right; the van drove well, its interior was soft and well appointed, and it would very easily transport eight, three of them unconscious.

Timing is all. The guards were sleepy, but not yet asleep, when Hradec Kralowc and his lady friend returned to the embassy a little after one in the morning, just around the same time that Stan Murch was backing his borrowed truck down the curving driveway beside the château and halting at the wide door that led to the Hochmans's art gallery. Ralph Winslow, one-handed, sipping from his drink, opened that door just a short time before, down in New York, the other expert lockman in the crew, Wally Whistler, passed his hand over the gate leading to Votskojek territory, and the gate sagged open with a little sigh.

Wally, Dortmunder, Kelp, Tiny, Jim O'Hara, and the subdued Dr. Zorn entered that sovereignty, strolled past the guards all of a heap in their folding chairs, and made their presence known—and felt—to the ambassador and his friend. Zorn put up no resistance when they had him inoculate against consciousness first Kralowc and then the already-chloroformed young lady. Since Zorn was giving no trouble, they permitted him to walk to the van under his own power, where he made absolutely no complaint about dosing himself with the same sleepy juice.

Up in the Green Mountains, certain adjustments of placement and position had been made to the treasures of Harry Hochman's art collection. Grijk Krugnk, walking as delicately as an elephant in a room full of mice, carried into the gallery the jewel-encrusted glass box that had been flown across the Atlantic from the Rivers of Blood Cathedral and placed it on the pedestal that had been made available for it when a Brancusi torso was relegated to a lesser position.

Moving quietly but efficiently, Thelma Lartz, still wearing her hat, started taking Polaroid pictures of the collection in situ; so far, the glass box either didn't appear in the pictures or was merely a small feature of the background. In any case, as Thelma finished exhaustive pictorial documentation of each section of the gallery, Harry Matlock and Ralph Demrovsky and Ralph Winslow and Gus Brock and Grijk Krugnk carried the pieces out and stowed them carefully in the truck. (Drivers don't do heavy lifting.) At each stage of the operation, Thelma would also take a couple of pictures of the interior of the truck, being careful not to show any human beings or license plates.

Back on the *Pride of Votskojek*, Wally Whistler moved like a ghost through several locks, leaving no traces, and making it possible for Andy Kelp once more to lay felonious hands on the femur of St. Ferghana.

Gotcha.

44

False dawn haloed the mountains, and *still* they were driving north. "I don't see why," Dortmunder groused, "they couldn't put their ski hotels and their châteaus down by the city."

"There aren't any mountains down by the city, John," Kelp explained. He was doing all the driving, because he liked to do all the driving, when it was a doctor's car. "It's all flat down there," he explained further. "Near the coast."

"Better," Dortmunder said. "Safer skiing that way."

Kelp nodded. "I never thought about it in exactly that light," he admitted.

These two shared the bench-style front seat of the doctor's car, with the magic bone seat-belted into place between them. Tiny basked in spread-out splendor alone on the seat behind them, with Jim O'Hara and Wally Whistler on the seat back of that, and the three sleeping travelers stretched out on the padded surface at the rear that had been created when the rear seat was folded down. These sleepers bounced sometimes, when there was a rough spot on the road, but mostly the road was a good smooth one, and they lay as quietly back there as the pods in *Invasion of the Body Snatchers*—the real one, the first one.

250

DON'T ASK

There's *always* traffic in the vicinity of New York City, but once they got about a half hour north that all thinned out and they mostly had the road to themselves. Kelp stayed within a few miles of the speed limit, not wanting to have to explain to any inquiring state trooper that those three passengers in the back were not drunk or stoned, merely sleeping. Sleeping *hard*. Kelp drove sanely and sensibly.

South of Rutland, north of Bennington, in the general vicinity of Mount Tabor and Weston and Peru (no, a different Peru), sprawling into the Green Mountain National Forest from a base just outside the forest perimeter, stands the Mount Kinohaha Happy Hour Inns ski resort. The nearest town is Middleville, but what Middleville might be in the middle of nobody any longer knows. Nowhere, basically.

But it was in Middleville that Dortmunder told Kelp to make the turn; not the well-marked, well-signed come-on-over turn toward Kinohaha, but the other way, up a steep dark asphalt road that quartered and strayed and goofed around but kept more or less tending upward until Dortmunder pointed out the next turn, which was the dead-end road up to the château. "From here on," Dortmunder said, "we gotta be silent, and we gotta be dark."

Kelp switched off the headlights and came to a complete stop, and he and Dortmunder peered through the windshield at the world. At first, neither of them could see a thing, until their eyes adjusted to life without headlights, and then Kelp said, "There it is."

Dortmunder still couldn't see anything: "Are you sure?"

"John, John," Kelp said. "Have some faith."

"One time," Tiny rumbled from the seat behind them, "you drove us into the reservoir."

"I never did," Kelp said as he put the van in gear.

The outside environment was in shades of black: deep black with some deep green mixed into it on both sides of their vehicle, paler black tinged with blue and pink up above, and flat gray-black in a ribbon out front. The last one was the road, and Kelp steered along it uphill until they came over a rise to some great knobby black mounds, with glints in them; that was the château and its outbuildings.

Following Dortmunder's whispered directions, Kelp angled

around to the left, away from the second residence and toward the long garage, where he almost, but not quite, ran into Stan and Fred, hunkered over the open trunk of Grijk's Hyundai, monitoring the video and audio spy stuff. Fortunately, blue TV light glinted off Fred's high forehead just in time for Kelp to hit the brakes, causing the sleeping logs in back to roll half over and then back.

Something made Fred lose concentration on the tiny TV screens lined up on the floor of the trunk. He turned his head, he saw the chrome front bumper of the van immediately beside his right elbow, and he jumped a foot—*four* feet—knocking over Stan in the process.

Before it was all over, a lot of shrill whispering went over the dam, with a repeated refrain being Fred's "You don't sneak *up* on people like that!" counterpointed by Kelp's "We're being *silent,* Fred, that's the whole *point.*" "You aren't being silent now" was Dortmunder's contribution.

Finally everybody calmed down. A glim at the TV screens and a hark at the radios reassured them that no one over at the residence had been disturbed, and they all got back to business. While Kelp picked up the blessed bone and carried it away downslope to the art gallery, Tiny picked up Ambassador Kralowc, Wally Whistler picked up the girl, and Dortmunder and Jim O'Hara picked up Dr. Zorn. Dortmunder led the way around to the main front door of the château, he being the one who'd been to this place before.

Down in the art gallery, the movers, having gone as far as they could without the bone, were taking it easy, sitting around on the floor in the faint illumination from one set of indirect lights at a very low dimmer setting. Harry, the two Ralphs, Gus, Grijk, and Thelma, still wearing her hat, all perked up when Kelp came in through the open doorway, carrying the sacred object. They all rose and stretched and whispered greetings, and Thelma picked up her Polaroid, saying, "Let's get this show on the road." Thelma'd become more aggressive since she'd taken over as the active driver in the partnership.

Kelp nestled the bone into the glass box, fitting it precisely to the indentations already existing in the felt. He and the others stepped out of the way, and Thelma took half a dozen pictures, all clearly showing the bone in the box in the art gallery, amid the rest of the collection.

Meantime, upstairs, Wally Whistler gently laid the girl onto the small bed in a ground-floor guest bedroom and covered her with the down comforter, while Tiny and Dortmunder and Jim O'Hara carried Kralowc and Zorn up the broad main staircase and into the master bedroom. A few arrangements were completed, and the sleepers were left there as Dortmunder and the others went back downstairs and out the front door and around to the art gallery entrance just in time to watch Thelma's latest round of pictures of the interior of the now nearly full truck, with the bone in the glass box prominent.

(Down in New York, in and about the Votskojek embassy, seven guards severally awoke from their naps, feeling rested and content. Fenton, the oldest of them, who'd slept curled up on the carpeted staircase half a flight up from the entrance, was the last to awaken, and the most disconcerted. How long had he been asleep? He wasn't sure. Had the others noticed his absence? Quickly adjusting his uniform, swallowing the taste of old pizza in his mouth, he hurried down the stairs, to find Garfield and Morrison alertly on duty at the door, the others all bright-eyed and at their posts. Fenton, like the other six, believed he was the only one who'd fallen asleep, which he would certainly not verify with self-exposing comments to the rest of the crew. He was just relieved that nothing untoward had happened during his momentary lapse, that everything was still all right aboard the embassy. Whew!)

Up in Vermont, there was little left to do. A couple of minor torsos and a Dine oil were stowed in the now-full truck, which was then shut up. All spy stuff was removed from both buildings and stashed any which way in Grijk's Hyundai, which Grijk then drove off, headed for New York. Stan, with Jim O'Hara riding shotgun, steered the truck up and over and out of there. Fred, with Thelma at the wheel, drove Ralph Winslow and Gus Brock away in the same car they'd come up in. And Kelp, back at the wheel of the doctor's van, had for his passengers Dortmunder, Tiny, Wally Whistler, Harry Matlock, and Ralph Demrovsky.

Real dawn painted the sky in faint pastels as the four vehicles fled away from the mountain, leaving a temporary peace in their wake.

Now all that was left was the anonymous phone call.

45

Silver legs, silver legs. No, loud noises. Bright lights, crashing around, heavy feet on stairs. What stairs? Headache. Mouth dry, nose clogged. Silver legs?

Rising reluctantly from blissful sleep, Hradec frowned; he frowned against the noise and the aches and the light pressing insistently on his eyelids; he frowned against consciousness entirely. Straining to dive back down into dear oblivion, he snuggled against Krystal, nose moving against her hairy shoulder, arm around her—

What?

As horrified as any Stephen King character, Hradec jolted awake, to stare at Karver Zorn's unlovely sleeping profile, four inches away. Mouth open, small snores emerging. I'm naked, Hradec thought, I'm in bed with Karver and I'm naked. And so is he!

"Agh!" Hradec recoiled to a sitting position, arms protectively about himself, just as the room filled with uniformed men pointing guns. At him.

Horror on horror! Which horror to be appalled by first?

"Hold it right there!" said a lot of the uniformed men.

DON'T ASK

Hold it! Right *here*? In this bed, with this, this *person*?

Memory swooped back, like a giant hawk with poisoned talons.

Diddums! What *is* this place? What has he done to me?

Somewhere, a girl screamed.

46

Guy Claverack usually started his day with the *New York Times,* but this Monday morning was different. Having seen the early reports of the Hochman art collection robbery on the television news last night, and having understood immediately that this was the job his carpenters had been planning, he wanted to know more about what had actually happened. Much more. He wanted to know everything there was to know, in fact, and somehow it seemed to him that with this particular kind of story the tabloids would be far likelier to squeeze out of it all the juice it might contain. Lack of journalistic restraint, that's what he craved this morning, and so he sent his secretary out first thing for the *Daily News,* the *Post,* and *Newsday,* and they did not disappoint.

The *Post*:

GAY LOVE NEST STRIPPED OF 6 MIL ART

Newsday:

THEY SLEPT
THROUGH IT

DON'T ASK

Hotelier's Guests
Unaware of Robbery

The *Daily News*:

TWO MEN, SNEERING WOMAN
SLEEP THROUGH ART HEIST
She Slept Alone

The stories below these headlines read something like this:

Following an anonymous phone tip, Vermont
State Police and Windham County Sheriff's Department deputies yesterday morning searched the supposedly empty mountain retreat of multimillionaire
hotelier Harry Hochman, to find a scene described by
Deputy Buell Rondike as "like nothing I ever seen
before in my life."

Downstairs in the plush châteaulike building,
police found that the Hochmans's world-renowned
art collection, valued at more than $6 million, had
been cleaned out, down to the bare walls. Upstairs,
police and deputies discovered an Eastern European
diplomat, Hradec Kralowc, ambassador to the
United States from the recently formed nation of
Votskojek, asleep in bed with another Votskojek
national, a United Nations Famine Relief researcher,
Dr. Karver Zorn. The two men claimed to have no
knowledge of the robbery, and to have slept through
it.

In another part of the building, police found
Broadway actress Krystal Kerrin (see accompanying
photo), currently featured in *Nana: The Musical* at
the Mark Time Theater. Miss Kerrin's claim to have
been forcibly abducted and drugged by a large group
of homosexual men has been hotly denied by the two
Eastern Europeans.

As to their own version of events, Ambassador
Kralowc is said by police sources to be claiming dip

257

lomatic privilege, although, "I don't believe there is
any such thing as diplomatic privilege in a situation
like this," said State Department spokesman Rondike
Buell in Washington last night.

Guy was still wallowing through this stuff—the *Post* gave
greatest emphasis to the homosexual angle and *Newsday* to the
value of the stolen art, while the *Daily News* went with Hochman's wealth, Krystal's show biz link, and Kralowc's upper-crust
social standing (posh, posh, and posh)—when his secretary
buzzed him to say, "The carpenter's calling."

"I thought he might." Guy switched over to the outside line
and said. "That's some letter of recommendation."

"We stand behind our work," said the phlegmatic voice on the
phone, though with an understandable hint of pride. "We
thought we'd come by today, show you some pictures of stuff
we've done."

"Come ahead," Guy urged him. "I'm looking forward to seeing
them."

47

Dortmunder and Kelp let Claverack drool over the pictures as long as he wanted. They were back in the basement storage cubicle with all the imprisoned Victorian sofas, and they spent the time looking the place over for a possible future visit.

At last, Claverack sighed, and the eye he turned on his guests was shiny with emotion. "Beautiful," he said. "Beautiful objects. Beautiful work. Beautiful documentation."

"Thanks," Dortmunder said.

"We aim to please," Kelp added.

"And these other photos, as the truck is being loaded," Claverack said, fanning out the pictures in his hands. "Is that where the material is now? Still in this truck? Or did you move it somewhere else?"

"It's safe," Dortmunder said.

"Yes, of course."

Safe? Dortmunder certainly hoped so. He didn't see any reason why it wouldn't be safe, given the decision they'd made. Keep the goods in the truck so they're easily movable, and keep the truck where nobody will pay any attention to it.

Therefore, when they'd left the scene of the crime early Sunday morning, Stan and Murch and Jim O'Hara had run at first along back roads eastward to Interstate 91, then took that south past Brattleboro and out of Vermont into Massachusetts. They'd dropped through Massachusetts from north to south, on into Connecticut, and finally left 91 at Hartford, taking Route 2 southeast to the Connecticut Turnpike, then south on the Pike to the coast at New London in plenty of time for the noon ferry across Long Island Sound to Orient Point, the eastern tip of Long Island's more expensive and more residential north shore. Then at last they'd turned west toward New York but angled down along local streets to the island's less expensive and more industrial south shore. Finding a commercial area full of parked trucks, within walking distance of a Long Island Railroad station, Stan had parked their truck in among all the others on a warehouse block, and he and Jim had taken the train to New York, calling Dortmunder at home a little after six to report the job was done. Every couple of days, until the deal was complete with the insurance company, Stan would take the train back out to the island and move the truck a town or two, to keep it from becoming noticeable. Being a big, boxy, gray-bodied, green-cabbed, anonymous International Harvester of a certain age, with J & L CARTING hand-stenciled in black on both doors, it would take a *lot* to make that truck noticeable. Safe? Yeah.

"I should think," Claverack said at last, "there shouldn't be too much difficulty with the insurance company. These photos pretty well establish you people as the perpetrators, the ones with actual possession of the collection. We'll simply dicker a bit, I think. How will I get in touch with you?" he finished, and started to put the thick stack of photos into his inside jacket pocket.

"Hold it," Dortmunder said, pointing at the pictures. "You don't get those yet."

"I don't?" Confused, Claverack stopped putting the pictures away. Instead, he looked down at them, looked up at Dortmunder, and said, "I can hardly negotiate without them, you know."

"I know that," Dortmunder agreed. "Give em here."

"Whatever you say."

A bit miffed, Claverack handed back the pictures, and Dortmunder put them away in his own inside jacket pocket, saying, "The thing is, it took a bunch of us to do this, and we're out certain expenses here."

Claverack looked wary. Carefully, he said, "I don't see what that has to do with *me*."

"What we estimated, when we talked about this before, you remember that time—"

"Of course I remember."

"What we estimated, we estimated twenty percent of value from the insurance company, right?"

"That's correct."

"Half for you," Dortmunder said, "and half for us."

"That's what we agreed, yes."

"Now, normally," Dortmunder reminded him, "you'd get maybe a quarter, maybe a little more than that. But this time, you're getting half, on accounta you're doing it exactly like we want you to do it, right?"

"Certainly," Claverack said. "We've already agreed to that. I show those photos to no one but the insurance company—or companies, I suppose, unlikely to be just one of them at this level of valuation—the companies involved."

"And you give us an advance," Dortmunder said. Beside him, Kelp smiled.

Claverack didn't smile. "You never said this before."

"There was nothing to talk about before," Dortmunder pointed out. Patting the pocket with the pictures, he said, "Now it's real, now we got something, now we can talk it over. So far, we're out all these expenses and travel and trouble and all this, and we're taking half. So far, all we get from you is you nod and smile and say that sounds nice, and you're getting half. So what we figure, we need you to contribute."

Claverack nodded, but he didn't smile and he didn't say that sounds nice. Instead, he said, "How much?"

"We figure," Dortmunder said, "five percent. Our piece ought to be, minimum, six hundred grand, though we'd like more, you know."

"I'll do my best, for both of us," Claverack said rather stiffly.

"I know you will," Dortmunder agreed. "And five percent of six hundred grand is thirty."

Claverack gazed at him, absorbing that. "Thirty thousand dollars? Is that what you want?"

"An advance," Dortmunder repeated. "You take it outta our half when the insurance people pay."

"Thirty thousand dollars is, well, uh . . ."

"Nonnegotiable."

"Mm." Claverack shook his head. "Do you expect me," he said, "to have thirty thousand dollars in *cash,* just lying around? I presume you wouldn't take a check."

"What I expect," Dortmunder said, "I'll call you tomorrow, unless that's too soon, you tell me, and if you got the thirty we'll come back and we'll give you the pictures and you'll give us the cash."

Kelp had been quiet up till now, letting Dortmunder do the haggling, but now he played good cop a little, saying, "If tomorrow's too soon, that's okay. We don't want to rush you."

Claverack brooded. He chewed a bit on a thumb knuckle. He sighed. He said, "Tomorrow's not too soon."

48

Home at last, in a false beard and turban, surrounded by blue-uniformed Continental rent-a-cops, all to avoid the ravening press. Reporters squealed and squirmed around the *Pride of Votskojek* like dogs around carrion, the landward contingent buttressed by seagoing journalists in every kind of boat they could rent or steal; and a helicopter from the *Star* hovered overhead.

But the press wasn't Hradec's main concern, and he knew it; though they were certainly pestiferous. And the blow to his manly reputation wasn't his main concern, either, though the newspaper accounts had wounded him deeply, where he lived. Since Harry Hochman's lightning trip to Vermont, verifying Hradec's hastily concocted claim to have been a legitimately invited houseguest— "Hradec, do you know where my shit is?" *"No!"* "Your word's good enough for me"—neither legal action nor Harry's mistrust was anymore an overriding consideration.

As to the faxes and telegrams and telephone messages that were surely awaiting him aboard the embassy from his wife back home in Novi Glad, wanting to know who and what is this Krystal Kerrin (because *she* would have no doubt as to his sexual orientation), they were a mere dermatitis in the array of his afflictions.

263

No, his main concern, his main problem, the main disaster he knew still faced him was . . . the relic.

The sacred femur of St. Ferghana. Somehow, some way, it was gone. Hradec knew that as well as he knew that Votskojek's future, Harry Hochman's future, and his own future depended on the relic's presence. But it was not going to be present; he knew that. There wasn't a chance of it, despite the assurances of the Continental security people that Saturday night had passed without an incident of any kind aboard the *Pride of Votskojek*.

Well. Here he was aboard at last, though hardly alone. A helicopter loudly coughed overhead, zoom lenses were aimed at every porthole, and reporters were being repulsed in every direction. (Oh, for the days of boiling oil!) Tearing off the turban, flinging it at the useless Terment, beaning Lusk with the beard, Hradec strode to the lab, used his keys, threw open the door, and . . .

"You fainted, sir," Lusk said.

"What? Of course I did!"

Hradec sat up. Lusk and Terment stooped with concern at the foot of his bed. They had carried him here to his bedroom, where the iron storm panels had been closed over every window and every light had been switched on. Midnight at noon, the perfect metaphor. Hradec's dark midnight.

I can't report the theft, not with seven guards, my own employees, who insist that nothing went wrong. A simple wiretap won't get the relic back to me like last time; the Tsergovians aren't that stupid. Where is it? Can I get it back without the outer world being the wiser? Can I get it back at *all*? There isn't a clue, a hint, a single thread to follow. Like Harry's art collection, and just as impossibly, the relic has simply vanished into thin air.

That fiend Diddums! He's my Moriarty, Hradec thought, but Hradec had never particularly *wanted* a foeman worthy of his steel. All he'd ever wanted was a life of ease and comfort, that's all, to be his nation's representative at the United Nations and in Washington, to be Harry Hochman's friend, to be escort of an endless supply of sweet young things. Was that too much to ask?

Apparently. The revenge of Diddums; the phrase ought to have more of a ring to it.

Think, Hradec, think. It isn't over. What's Diddums up to? What happens next?

"Sir?"

He glowered at his faithful servants. The only thing in the world he had to rely on, and it was *them*. "Leave me," he said. "I must think."

"Sir," they murmured, and bowed themselves from the room, snicking the door shut after themselves.

"And no phone calls!" he screamed at the door.

"No, sir," wafted the faint reply.

Hradec adjusted the pillows and reclined to muse. The theft of the relic and the theft of Harry Hochman's art, it was all connected somehow. And Diddums's revenge isn't complete yet, is it?

Of course not.

What next?

49

What I think you ought to do," Dortmunder said to Zara Kotor, back in their upstairs living room over the embassy, "if you don't mind me giving you a little advice—"

"I don't mind," Zara said, though brusquely. "I see these pictures of the sacred relic, I see you've apparently done what you set out to do, and even more, so I don't mind at all if you give me advice. What I *wish* you'd give me, though, is the relic."

Present for this meeting, in addition to Dortmunder and Zara, were Grijk and Andy Kelp. (Once again, Tiny had been unavoidably tied up elsewhere, though Zara had asked specifically that he be along, and some of her present bad temper was probably a result of his absence. Dortmunder didn't know what Tiny's problem was with these people—they were *his* relatives, after all, and nobody else's—but he was sorry the big man wasn't here, if only so Dortmunder didn't have to keep repeating himself to the mulish Zara all the time.) "If I give you the bone," he said, demonstrating a patience he didn't feel, "what are you gonna do with it? You can't show it to anybody or admit you got it, or they're gonna ask you where you got it from, how long you had it, how come you never showed it before, how'd it get to the States, all these

266

questions. The main thing about this bone is, when you claim it, your hands have got to be clean, or this archbishop's gonna take against you. Am I right?"

"Conceivably," Zara admitted.

"Good," Dortmunder said. "So conceive it. Now, here's my advice. Today, this afternoon, you do a press release or a press conference or however you work it, and you announce you've privately had tests done on your own St. Ferghana bone, the one you've been claiming all along you've got, the one that made Votskojek have to test *theirs* all this time, and the tests you did on your own prove conclusively it's a fake. You apologize to Votskojek—"

"Never!" Zara cried, and Grijk actually jumped to his feet and looked around for a pike or a halberd.

"Just wait for it, okay?" Dortmunder said. "Sit down, Grijk, it comes out okay at the end."

Frowning like an avalanche, Grijk resumed his seat while Zara said, "I will never apologize to Votskojek for anything."

"Okay, fine," Dortmunder said. "Apologize to the UN instead; that's even better. You apologize to the world, okay? Sorry to cause this delay and trouble, but you always believed you had the right bone, but now you have to admit Votskojek has it, so all they have to do is show it in public and you'll withdraw your application to join the UN."

Zara stared at him in wide-eyed disbelief. "And what do I get out of that?"

"Your seat at the UN," Dortmunder told her.

50

"Well, well," said the archbishop.

Having come here to his office at the United Nations building on New York's First Avenue directly from yet another memorial service, the archbishop was outfitted in full funereal vestments, with the purple cassock and purple cope piping nicely setting off the dazzling white linen of the stole and cope, the whole ensemble belted and sashed with an array of cinctures. The lacy rochet below the stole contrasted with the massive, dark—and heavy—mahogany pectoral cross lying on his sunken chest like the stone before the grave at Gethsemane. He had removed the tall white miter from his head and placed it on a corner of his desk, and had then dropped like last year's leaf into his swivel chair, just to get a few minutes rest. And he was no sooner settled, a scrawny little old guy gasping for air inside all the panoply, when one of his clerical clerks brought in a fax, uncurled it like the scroll it was, and held it up for the archbishop to read. Which was when the archbishop said, "Well, well."

"Yes, Your Grace," said the clerk.

"Call, um, er, umm, that fellow, you know, the fellow we don't call."

268

The clerk nodded, looking thoughtful. After the briefest of pauses, he said, "Would you mean the Votskojek embassy, Your Grace?"

"Can't call them," the archbishop said, laying a scrawny finger aside his scrawny nose to indicate slyness. "Can't indicate bias. Not a hint of bias."

"Of course not, Your Grace."

"Not an issue now, eh? Get him for me, that, uh, umm..."

"I believe, Your Grace, his name is Ambassador Kralowc."

"That's the fellow. Ring him up."

"At once, Your Grace."

As the clerk turned away, still holding the fax in both hands, the archbishop waggled bony fingers at him. "And leave that."

"Yes, Your Grace."

The clerk let go of the fax with one hand, and it flexed shut like a clam. He handed this tube to the archbishop, then retired to his outer office while the archbishop spread the fax faceup on the desk, weighing the corners with a stapler, a Scotch tape dispenser, a pocket calculator, and a small plaster statue of the Infant Jesus of Prague. Making these moves, grunting with the effort of shifting around inside all his vestments as he reached out across the gleaming teak surface of his desk, he looked like some major chess player of mythology, losing another big one to the devil.

The archbishop read the fax again, savoring it, and then the phone at his right elbow rang, and he disrupted the whole construct in his effort to swivel around and pick the damn thing up. "*What!*"

"Ambassador Kralowc, Your Grace."

"What? *Here?*"

"On line one, Your Grace. I rang him for you."

"Oh! Right!" The archbishop punched a button and then another button and said, "Hello?"

"Archbishop?"

"Yes, of course. What did you want?"

"Archbishop, this is Hradec Kralowc, from Votskojek, you remember me, your clerk said you wanted to—"

"Yes! Yes, of course! Well, my boy, are you relishing the good news?"

"Good news, Archbishop?" Kralowc didn't sound like a man who believed in good news.

"The press release. Didn't those people send you the press release?"

"Who, Archbishop?"

"Who? *Them!* Those upstart pretenders at the, over there in the, *you* know, the competition."

"Tsergovia?"

"*That's* the place. They didn't send you the press release?"

"No one has sent me anything, Archbishop," the ambassador said, but the tone of self-pity in his voice was lost on the archbishop, who was distracted at that moment by his struggle to recapture all the corners of the fax without losing the telephone. Slamming the Infant Jesus of Prague onto the final corner, he said, "There! Now *stay* there!"

"Archbishop?"

"Wait, I'll read it to you," the archbishop said. "Are you there?"

"Yes."

"Good. Listen. Are you listening?"

"*Yes*, Archbishop. I'm here, and I'm listening."

"Good. Listen, now." Squinting through his wire-framed spectacles and down past his pale, old, narrow hawk nose, the archbishop read, "'Immediate release. Major General Zara Kotor, Ambassadress to the United States from the free and sovereign state of Tsergovia, has received today permission from her government at Osigreb to announce the result of certain tests made at Osigreb Polytechnic, in Osigreb, Tsergovia, in an effort to authenticate a certain relic, known as the Relic of St. Ferghana, consisting of a thighbone purporting to be the thighbone of the martyred St. Ferghana of Carpathia. Knowing that a similar relic has existed for some time at the Rivers of Blood Cathedral in Novi Glad in our sister republic of Votsko-jek, and knowing further that the question of the authenticity of these two supposed relics has served to complicate and exacerbate the relations between these two sister republics, and to further complicate and exacerbate the question of the successor seat available to one but not to the other of our nations at the United Nations in New York City, United States of America, it is our sad duty to announce that the result of our scientific investigation of the Relic of St. Ferghana in our possession at Osigreb is that it is, in fact, false. We no longer—'"

"*What?*"

"There, now, you see, my boy?" the archbishop said, chortling and wheezing over the fax. "Good news comes unexpectedly, does it not? Let me go on," he said, and, not hearing the long, low moan that then emanated from the throat of Ambassador Kralowc into the telephone system known as NYNEX because it is run by Venusians, he continued to read:

"'We no longer make any claim toward the authenticity of the relic in our possession, nor do we demand of Votskojek that she produce any evidence, scientific or historical or otherwise, in support of the claim that the relic in her possession is the true relic. It is our understanding that the true relic is currently in New York City, under the protection and in the care of the government of Votskojek on behalf of the people of Votskojek. When the government of Votskojek, or its representatives, shall present this relic to the General Assembly at the United Nations in New York City, United States of America, we, the sovereign state of Tsergovia, will give up, cede, and relinquish for all time from this moment until the end of the world any and all claims we might have had to the successor seat at the United Nations. We would pray to that august body that we be considered for a new seat, at the earliest opportunity. By the grace of God and the order of the freely elected and democratic government seated at Osigreb, sovereign state of Tsergovia. Signed, Zara Kotor, Major General.'"

Chuckling and panting, the archbishop said, "Well, Ambassador, what do you think of that?" He waited. "Ambassador? Ambassador?"

Very faintly came the voice of the ambassador: "It's wonderful, Archbishop."

"Overcome, are you? Well, I don't blame you, my boy; it's been a long struggle and those Tsergovians didn't mind fighting dirty, I can tell you that, and I can tell you now it's a great relief to me to have this matter resolved, because it was, I'll admit it now, it *was* difficult not to show bias toward those sneaking, underhanded, sacrilegious—"

"Archbishop?"

"Yes?"

"Was that release sent to anyone else?"

"*Anyone* else? My boy, it was faxed to *everyone*. Down at the bottom here, wait just a minute, here's a list, it's—Yes, every United Nations member—"

"Every one?"

"Every one. All major news media, the Roman Catholic Archdiocese of New York—Ambassador? Was that a moan?"

"No, no, Archbishop, I was merely clearing my throat. Uh, this *is* wonderful news, as you say. I can hardly wait to tell my superiors back in Novi Glad. Archbishop, uh, would you mind faxing me that fax?"

"Not at all," the archbishop said. "Delighted to be the bearer of good tidings. I'll fax the fax at once. I have your fax number?"

"Your people have my fax number."

"As long as they have your fax number, there's no problem. We'll fax the fax in just a moment."

"Fax you—uh, I mean, thank you, Archbishop."

"My pleasure," the archbishop said; which was more accurate than he knew.

51

Hradec had barely hung up from talking with Archbishop Minkokus, that doddering old fool, when Lusk came in to say, "Sir, the president is on the phone."

"The president?" As weighed down by worry and care as he was, it took a few seconds to work that one out. "*My* president?"

"Our president, yes, sir," Lusk agreed. "On the phone from Novi Glad."

"Oh, God." Bad news travels fast. Or, that is, good news travels fast. Whatever. That damn *helicopter;* why wasn't this ship equipped with antiaircraft weapons? That's Votskojek airspace you're violating up there, pal, I'd have every legal right to shoot you down, blow you away, knock you out of the sky.

"Sir?"

Reality calls; that is to say, the president calls. "What time is it in Novi Glad?"

Lusk consulted a wristwatch, made a calculation, said, "Quarter after six, sir. P.M."

"Did he sound drunk?"

"No, sir."

More's the pity. What to do? Impossible to tell the president the truth; that would lead to immediate recall, dismissal, public shame, and possible dismemberment. Was there still a way out of this mess? Temporize, Hradec, temporize. "Leave me," he said.

"Sir." Lusk bowed, departed, and Hradec painted a huge smile on his face, breathed rapidly three times, picked up the phone, and said into it, at top speed, "Isn't that wonderful news? I just heard it myself this minute from the arch—"

"What? What? What's all that?"

It was only when he heard the president's gravelly voice yelling Magyar-Croat in his ear that Hradec realized he'd been speaking in English. Will *nothing* go right? Switching at once to his native tongue, Hradec said, "Oh, Your Excellency, I'm sorry, I thought I was speaking to the *New York Times*. The entire city is agog at the news."

"Of course they are," said His Excellency. "What sort of ceremony do you plan for the occasion?"

"Ceremony, Your Excellency?"

"Of course, ceremony," grated the voice that used to bring a chill to many a heart and a confession to many a lip in the old days when His Excellency was a hands-on head of the VIA, the Votskojek Intelligence Agency. (From leading the nation's spies to leading the nation is a rather common route to power these days; Andropov in the former Soviet Union, for instance. Other examples come to mind.) "You'll want to give the relic a first-rate ceremony at the United Nations," this terror-striking voice went on. "Votskojek expects it of you. The *world* expects it of you. I expect it of you."

"Yes, Your Excellency, of course."

"You aren't going to just walk over there and *flash* it at them like a ticket of admission to a film show."

"No, of course not, Your Excellency. But," as a ray of hope seemed to gleam before him, a tiny ray, a temporary ray, but still a ray, "a ceremony will take a little while to organize, Your Excellency, to arrange. This won't be immediate."

"No one expects it to be immediate," His Excellency snarled. "Let them wait a little."

"Your wish is my command, Excellency."

"The waiting game, Kralowc," that voice purred, heavy with awful memories, "it has its uses in many departments of life."

If he ever finds out, Hradec thought, if this brute of a president ever finds out, he'll restore flaying to the Votskojek code of justice, just for me. "I'll let them wait, Your Excellency," he promised, his voice hardly trembling at all. "I'll drag it out, I promise you, just as long as I can."

52

Somehow, Guy just didn't like having these carpenters in his house. They kept looking *around* all the time; it was unnerving.

That may be why he didn't bargain with them, haggle them down from their arbitrary thirty thou. Not that he didn't have the money, or the reasonable assurance he would get it back and tenfold, but merely that it wasn't his nature, under any circumstances, to accept the first number he heard. But with these two, playing the game was somehow just not worth it. Get them in, get them out, get it over with.

And so he did, early Tuesday morning. They went away from his basement with thirty thousand dollars in cash tucked away in their pockets, looking around at everything on their way out, heads turning back and forth, eyes glancing off locks, windows, electric outlets, who knew what. Guy, in relief, shut and locked the basement door on them, hurried upstairs to his office, and phoned Perly.

Jacques Perly was an old associate, a known quantity. A private investigator by trade, his specialty was art theft and his employers usually insurance companies or banks—those who had to pay for insured losses, those who had to absorb uninsured losses. As Guy had supposed, there was more than one insurance company involved in the Harry Hochman art collection; there were three, and Jacques Perly represented them all. Guy had phoned him yesterday to say he might be of use in the present instance—"I rather thought you might," Perly had answered, a bit too dryly for Guy's taste—and now today Guy phoned to say he'd made contact with the thieves and was prepared to be the go-between.

"Fine," Perly said. "Lunch? Or are you doing one of your own today?"

"Not today, or at all this week. I've cleared the decks for this, Jacques."

"Lunch, then," Perly decided, and they met at one o'clock at Tre Mafiosi on Park Avenue, a smooth, hushed place in white and green and gold, with yellow flowers. Perly had arrived first, and he rose with a smile and an outstretched hand when Tony the maître d' escorted Guy to the table. A round, stuffed Cornish game hen of a man, Jacques Perly retained a slight hint of his original Parisian accent. A onetime art student, a failed artist, he viewed the world with a benign pessimism, the mournful good humor of a rich, unmarried uncle, who expects nothing and accepts everything.

"Good afternoon," Guy said as Tony seated him and Angelo distributed menus and Kwa Hong Yo brought rolls, butter, and water. "You're looking well."

"And you."

Menus were consulted, food and wine were ordered, and then Guy took the bulky envelope from his inner pocket and, without a word, handed it over. Perly raised an eyebrow, removed the photos from the envelope, leafed through them, and smiled dolefully as he said, "A well-documented felony."

"These are professionals," Guy assured him. "We don't have to worry about any of the works being harmed."

"No, I suppose not. May I keep these?"

"Of course."

Food and wine arrived and were consumed, with small talk about the city, the weather, the disappointing Broadway season— "Although *Nana: The Musical* isn't bad," Perly suggested—and one's plans for the summer. Then, over espresso and raspberries, Perly said, "Honestly, Guy, the *extreme* professionalism of these people, with all these Polaroid prints, gives me pause. Are we creating this monster, you and I?"

Guy looked askance. "Which monster is that, Jacques?"

"These thieves," Perly explained. "If they were to steal a loaf of bread, it would be to eat. If they steal money, it's to spend; jewelry, to pawn. But when they steal an art collection like this"—*tap-tap* on the envelope of photos—"it is only to *sell it back.* And how could they do that, if it were not for you and me? We are certainly collaborators in their crimes, but are we more? Do we encourage the commission of these crimes, by our very existence? Do we *instigate* them?"

"Nonsense," Guy said in automatic disagreement. "People will steal anything; you know that as well as I do. We don't encourage the theft; we encourage the recovery."

"Without the punishment of the perpetrators."

"With or without," Guy said, dismissing that. "Capturing is the police's job. Recovery is ours."

"But if we didn't exist, Guy, you and I, what would these very professional thieves do with all these paintings and sculptures they've just loaded so precisely into their truck? Would they present their demands direct to Harry Hochman? He'd set the dogs on them."

Guy smiled faintly. "Or the shotguns, more likely."

"Exactly. We are the go-betweens, and necessary, if anything useful is to be done. But in this instance, don't the go-betweens create the very condition they're supposed to be alleviating?"

Guy shook his head, irritated by this conversation and surprised that a man like Jacques Perly would demonstrate such compunction. "The thieves will sell Hochman's art to the insurance companies, through us. You want to know what they would do without us? Or without the insurance companies, who, after all, put up the money, so maybe *they* create the monster."

"Very possible," Perly said, nodding.

Guy didn't need that particular agreement. "Without any of us," he said, "the thieves would find a way to make contact with art dealers in Europe. Switzerland, for instance, or Holland. Or maybe South America. The dealers would buy, no questions asked. The dealers—some of the dealers, anyway, and you know a number of them yourself, Jacques—those dealers would be happy to cobble together brand-new authentication and sell the works to collectors anywhere. There's a market beyond us, Jacques, and you're just being provocative to suggest there isn't, and you know it. What *we* do is keep the collection together, no small consideration, and in the rightful owner's hands."

Eyes twinkling, Perly sipped espresso, bit delicately into a raspberry, and said, "So, Guy. You mean we are without guilt?"

"Absolutely," Guy said. Blotches of red stood on his cheeks.

"Such a relief," Perly murmured.

53

When Dortmunder walked into the OJ Bar & Grill, the regulars were discussing why cable television needs wires. "It's because of the vibrations," one of them was saying. "They send these vibrations down the wire, and that tells the TV what to show."

"How?" asked a second regular.

The first regular stared at him. "Whadaya mean, how? I just told you how. With vibrations."

A third regular weighed in. "That's a load of crap," he announced, and gestured forcefully with his beer glass.

The second regular adapted his question to the new circumstances: "How come?"

"If a TV's gotta have vibrations to tell it what to show," the third regular belligerently reasoned, "how come *regular* TV don't need it?"

Here came a fourth regular, saying, "That's easy, pal. Regular TV works like radio, without wires."

"How?" asked the second regular, but the first regular overrode him, saying, "Without wires? *Radio* works without wires? Whadaya think that dark brown cord is, comes outta the back, goes into the wall?"

"It ain't cable," said the fourth regular with supreme confidence.

The first regular glared at him. "It's a *wire!*"

The second regular, building strongly on his original base, said, "How about portables?"

The third regular banged his beer glass on the table. "I can't stand them," he announced. "Boom boxes. The only stations you can get on those things is brain damage."

"They *cause* brain damage," said the fourth regular, being positive on a whole new subject.

"How?" asked the second regular, returning to the basics.

"Vibrations," said the first regular, also returning to basics.

But the third regular rounded on the fourth and said, "How can you be sure it isn't the other way around?"

"*What* isn't the other way around?"

"They were already brain-damaged to begin with; that's why they bought the boom boxes."

"No no no," said the positive fourth regular. "They *used* to have enough brains to walk into a store, hand over the money, walk out with the radio."

"Can't stand those things."

"But you look at them now," the fourth regular persisted, "walking around with those boxes, you can *see* they don't have enough brain left to close their mouths."

The others, establishing a certain level of brainpower, closed their mouths to mull that one over, while Dortmunder approached Rollo the bartender, snoozing against the cash register, and said, "Anybody back there?"

Rollo's eyes focused. "I would say," he answered, "*everybody's* back there. The other bourbon's got your glass."

"Thanks."

Dortmunder nodded to Rollo, who'd drifted off again, then he walked past the regulars, who were all blinking and frowning, trying to remember what they'd been talking about, and headed for the back room.

Which, as Rollo had suggested, was full. With Dortmunder, all eleven from the caper were here: Kelp, Tiny, Stan Murch, Gus Brock, Fred Lartz, Harry Matlock, Ralph Demrovsky, Ralph Winslow, Jim O'Hara, and Wally Whistler. All of the chairs were occupied except the one with its back to the door, and a few of the guys were sitting around on upended wooden liquor cases.

Dortmunder upended a liquor case, sat on it, and Gus Brock said, "Dortmunder, we got three cents left over."

Dortmunder wasn't ready for this. "How come?"

Gus said, "We got eleven guys, we got thirty grand. That comes out twenty-seven hundred bucks a man, but with three hundred bucks left over. So we split that, and it's twenty-seven bucks a man, but with three bucks left over. So we split that, and it's twenty-seven cents a man, but with three cents left over, for eleven guys."

Dortmunder nodded. Somehow, he felt as though he were still out front with the regulars. He said, "We'll give it to Tiny; he didn't get anything the first time around."

Everybody agreed that was fair, especially Tiny, and then everybody wanted to know what was going to happen next.

"Nothing," Dortmunder said. "We'll give this guy Guy Claverack, this guy Clav—Guy—Him. We'll give him two days to meet some people, talk it over, start the negotiation. Thursday we'll give him a call. Meanwhile," turning to Stan, "how's the truck doing?"

"Fine," Stan said. "I went out there today and moved it to a different town. Every six blocks out there, it's a different town with different cops, so all I have to do is keep it moving; no police force is gonna notice they got this same truck all the time."

Gus Brock said, "How long is this two thousand seven hundred twenty-seven dollars and twenty-seven cents supposed to last us? In other words, when can we expect something from your guy?"

"You mean Guy?" But then Dortmunder waved a hand in the air, saying, "No, forget that, I know who you mean. And the way I figure, it's going to have to be at least a week, so they can all negotiate, and maybe a month, but it can't be any longer than that."

Stan said, "I'm gonna take the train out to Long Island and bop that truck around every other day for a *month*?"

"I hope not that long," Dortmunder said.

Harry Matlock said, "Me and Ralph got a suggestion." Meaning his partner, Ralph Demrovsky.

Dortmunder wasn't sure he was in the market for suggestions—they were already moving forward on the agreed-upon plan here, after all—but he said, "Sure. What is it?"

"Just in case there's a problem with your guy," Harry said, "in case it looks like there's a problem, or there could be a problem, or whatever, Ralph and me a few years ago made contact with a couple people that move art to Europe. First to Canada, and then to Europe. We could slip that truck into Canada, get some people in Europe that buy that kind of stuff. Dealers, you know."

"That's a possibility," Dortmunder agreed. "It's less money, because they pay less, and you got more people along the route with their hand out that they got to have a little piece, but if the first plan falls through, that's good you've got those contacts."

"When?" Harry said.

"You mean, when do you call your contact? When do we figure things aren't working out? Is that what you mean?"

"Yes," Harry said.

Stan said, "I don't feature taking that train every other day for a *month*, I'll tell you that."

Dortmunder considered. The essence of leadership is compromise. That, and sensing the needs of your people. That, and remaining confident on the surface. And some other stuff. "Two weeks," he said. "How's that?"

Everybody agreed two weeks was fine. It was long enough to know if the negotiation with the insurance company was going to come to anything, but not so long as to drive everybody, and especially Stan, crazy.

"Fine," Dortmunder said. "When I call this guy Guy on Thursday, I'll tell him the deadline. In the meantime, we already got a little taste, almost three grand apiece."

"And me," Tiny said, deadpan, "I got three cents for the first caper. Things are lookin up."

54

Harry Hochman was not a detail man. The kind of man Harry was, he *hired* detail men, and they took care of the details, while Harry kept his mind and eye on the big picture. What Harry Hochman was was a big-picture man.

Which was what made it so goddam irritating to be in this hotel room with these people, listening to *details*. The room itself was all right, but it damn well better be, it was his. But really *his*. This was the living room of the Imperial Dragon Suite on the top floor of the Dragon Host Hotel on Park Avenue in New York City, just north of Grand Central Station and south of the Crispinite monastery, and this was the flagship of a chain of seventeen Dragon Host hotels Harry owned in partnership with the Japs, because the only way to get into the Japs' pants was to let them get into yours. So Dragon Host ran hotels in New York and Washington and Chicago and San Francisco and Los Angeles, plus a few in Canada and South America, but it *also* ran hotels in Tokyo and Osaka and Kyoto and Otaru and Yokohama and Nagoya and Kobe, and that's what Harry Hochman meant by the big picture. Not these goddam details about insurance and art thieves and private eyes. Why couldn't he just hire somebody to handle all these details and give him a call when everything was straightened out and the art was back where it belonged and Harry could go visit the Vermont château once more?

But, no. Outside, if a person had the leisure to stand up and look out a window, was all of Manhattan Island, or at least all of Manhattan Island that a big-picture man like Harry Hochman needed to look at, but could he go look at it? No. He had to sit here in the living room of the Imperial Dragon Suite with a lot of detail men and converse with them about *details*.

Like these Polaroid pictures of his art collection. Pictures showing it where it belonged, and then pictures of it in some goddam truck. "Do you recognize these, Mr. Hochman?" asked one of the detail men. Perly, his name was, Jacques Perly. He was the private eye, though in his blue suit and round plumpness he looked to Harry more like an untrustworthy doctor. Didn't look like any private eye *Harry* had ever seen.

"Of course I recognize them," he snapped, leafing rapidly through the pictures, barely concentrating at all, for so many reasons. Details, for one. And the fact all this stuff was gone, stolen, for another. And that the thieves took the photos, for a third.

If that pissant little faggot Hradec had only torn himself out of the embraces of his smarmy little lover—talk about your untrustworthy doctors!—long enough to hear an entire moving van being filled with paintings and statuary, none of this would be happening, and Harry would be comfortably concerning himself with some big picture somewhere, instead of looking at these little pictures in his hands here. (Since Harry wasn't taking any of Hradec's constant phone calls, he was unaware of Hradec's theory that the whole thing was the work of Diddums, nor was he aware of Hradec's contention that he and the ungood doctor had been drugged and were not sexually involved with one another, but, even if he'd heard all that, he wouldn't have believed it, mostly because he was too irritated.)

The private eye, Perly, said, "The reason we need your positive identification, Mr. Hochman, is because your insurance companies are uninterested in paying for works that you don't own."

"Well, they damn well better pay for the works I *do* own," Harry snarled, and glared around generally at the four men and two women here representing the insurance companies. More detail people, as were the two lawyers, the accountant, and the two men in wrinkled neckties from the New York Police Department. (How do people wrinkle *neckties?*) The NYPD men were here because, even though the theft had taken place in Vermont, and everybody's best guess was that it was a Boston gang that had pulled the job and they were hiding the loot somewhere in Boston, the *extortion* attempt was taking place in New York. The reason the Vermont police and the Boston police weren't here was because they were searching Boston for Harry Hochman's stolen art, and fat chance they had of finding it, is what Harry thought. Fat chance. *He* thought it was all in Canada.

This detail man, this private eye, Perly, wasn't finished with him yet. "Sir," he said, "could you take a look at the photographs? Just identify one or two items for me, sir, if you would."

Details; you could drown in details. "Very well," Harry said with bad grace, and peered at one of the photographs. "There," he said. "Leaning against the side of the truck there, that's a Botticelli, two angels with one ribbon around their necks, bought that eleven, no, twelve, no eleven, I think maybe twelve, years ago in Geneva. Then here—"

"Thank you, sir. Something from one of the other photos would be good."

Harry sighed long and loud to let them know what he thought of this pecksniffery. Lotta crap. "Here we are," he said. "That's a de Chirico. You see the little white Doric column, the blue sky?"

"Yes, sir, Mr. Hochman, thank you."

Harry, with the feeling of an adult dragooned into a child's game, put that photo at the bottom of the stack in his hands and looked at the next one. He blinked. "Now," he said, "what the hell is *that?*"

Nobody in the room had expected such a reaction. This was a simple cut-and-dried procedure, legally necessary but not normally full of surprises; the victim identifies the stolen insured items. The whole crowd in the room tensed up, detail people realizing that a detail was wrong.

Jacques Perly, already leaning solicitously over Harry to guide him through the identification process, said, "What's that you say, Mr. Hochman?"

"This damn thing," Harry said, pointing at the damn thing, prominent in the photograph. "What the hell is *this* supposed to be?"

"Don't you know, sir?"

"How the hell am I supposed to know? What *is* this?"

"You mean, sir," Perly asked, bending down even closer to Harry and the photo, "that glass chest or coffer there? That small casket? No, let me see . . . reliquary, I would say."

"Don't be stupid," Harry said. "I don't own any reliquary."

"Are you sure, sir?"

Harry did not believe his ears. In his own suite, in his own hotel, in his own nation, on his own planet, he was being insulted to his face. "Am I *sure*?"

Perly withdrew his objectionable head somewhat from Harry's lap but held out his hand instead, saying, "May I see that photo, sir? If I may?"

"You can keep it," Harry said, and slapped the damn thing into the damn man's damn hand.

Perly, unruffled, studied the photo. "These other objects visible here," he said. "You do recognize these, don't you? Isn't this the de Chirico you mentioned before, in the background here?"

"Don't show me that damn thing," Harry said, waving it away. "I didn't say the rest of it isn't mine, the rest of it is mine. I'm saying, what the hell is that glass box doing there?"

"With something in it," Perly said, peering closely at the photograph.

"And that isn't mine, either," Harry said. "Whatever the hell it is."

One of the insurance munchkins said, "Mr. Hochman, isn't it possible, with everything you own, I mean, with all your possessions, isn't it, that you might have, uh, have, uh . . ."

It was Harry's fierce eye that ground the fellow to a stop, and Harry's pointing finger that pinned him in his place. "Say the next word," Harry said, "and you're looking for a job."

There was a long silence in the suite. Everyone but Harry was too uncomfortable to move; Harry was too irritated to move. When he'd established that the insurance company clown was *not* going to say the dread word, Harry answered it, anyway: "I know every piece of art I own. And I do not own that glass box. And I do not own whatever is inside it."

Perly cleared his throat. "Excuse me, Mr. Hochman," he said.

Harry bent his fierce eye on Perly, who, being an independent subcontractor, was less intimidated by it. "What," Harry said.

"I believe, Mr. Hochman," Perly said, pointing at the photos in Harry's hands, "if you'll look through those, you'll see some showing the box in your gallery, on a pedestal."

"Bullshit," Harry said.

"If you would look, sir . . ."

Harry looked. Harry's eyes widened. There it was. There the damn thing was, by God. And there it was again. And, tucked away in the background, there it was yet again. "Well, what the hell is *this?*" Harry demanded.

"It's a pity, Mr. Hochman," Perly said, "that your collection was never catalogued."

"What's the point in that? I'm always buying or selling; it changes all the time. We just did some painting down there, moved things around. But this glass box is not mine."

"It appears to be, sir," Perly dared to say. "It very strongly appears to be."

Harry had had enough of this. This goddam glass box was one detail too many, the detail that right this minute was breaking the camel's back. Glowering once more at Perly, Harry said, "You're the private eye, aren't you?"

"We prefer private investigator, Mr. Hochman," Perly said.

"Oh, do you. Well, *I* prefer to know what's going on, and it seems to me it's your job to *tell* me what's going on. Here's a picture of this glass box for you, Mr. Private Investigator. Investigate. When you've got it figured out, let me know." He strafed the room with his glare. "When you've *all* got it figured out, let me know," he said. "This meeting is over. Good-bye."

55

Perly turned the Lamborghini onto Gansevoort Street, thumbing the beeper on his visor as he did so, and down the block, amid the warehouses and the few remaining elements of the meat-packing industry, his battered old green garage door lifted out of the way. Perly steered into the building, beeped the door shut behind him, and drove up the concrete ramp.

The conversion didn't start until the second floor, where the high stone block walls were painted a creamy off-white and spotlights mounted high in the metal ceiling beams pinpointed the potted evergreens in front of his office door. Perly parked in his spot—the other was for the occasional client—crossed to the faux Tudor interior wall, handprinted the door open, and stepped into his reception room, where Della looked up from her typing to say, "Hi, Chief. How'd it go?"

"Weird one this time, Della," Perly said, skimming his hat across the room to a perfect ringer on the hat rack.

"They're all weird, Chief," Della reminded him. "What's the story this time?"

Sitting with one heavy hip cocked on the corner of Della's desk, Perly said, "Rich guy, Harry Hochman, hotels. Art collection

289

stolen up in Vermont. Thieves took pictures of the loot, prove they've got it." He took several photos from his inner jacket pocket, hefted them. "Did the standard ID with Hochman, showed him the pictures." He put a photo on the desk in front of Della, pointed. "See that reliquary?"

"It's a beauty, Chief."

"Hochman says it isn't his."

"He does?"

Perly spread the rest of the photos in front of Della. She looked at them, photo after photo of Harry Hochman's art collection, with the glass box. She did her soundless whistle. "Wow, Chief," she said. "Why would he say a thing like that?"

"That's the question all right, Della." Perly stood from her desk, brushed the seat of his trousers, shot his cuffs, and said, "I told you, Della, it's a weird one this time. Call Fritz, tell him I need blowups of the best pix of the box, soonest. Then call Margo, Jerry, and Herkimer. Meeting here at four o'clock."

"High gear, eh, Chief?" said Della.

"You've got it, Della," Perly said. "I want to know what that box is, and I want to know what that thing inside it is, and I want to know what it's all worth, and I want to know why Harry Hochman's so shy all of a sudden. And I want it all yesterday."

"Consider it done, Chief," Della said, and reached for the phone.

56

Archbishop Minkokus rarely if ever read the lay press. It was so full of discomforting information. "In order to hold your faith intact/Be sure it's kept unsullied by fact." Therefore, he had not known, when he'd phoned Hradec Kralowc on Monday about Tsergovia's wondrous abdication by fax, about the Votskojek ambassador's other problems, the robbery in Vermont and the sudden public doubts about his sleeping patterns and sleeping partners. It wasn't until Wednesday morning, when one of his clerks brought him the anonymous letter and the photograph that had just been hand-delivered to the guard desk by the UN building's main entrance down below, that the archbishop began to learn what had been going on in the mundane world while he'd been concentrating on the eternal.

The photograph, a Polaroid shot, placed neatly on the desk in front of him, was clearly a picture of the sacred relic of St. Ferghana—he recognized the reliquary—supposedly in the care and safekeeping of the Votskojek authorities in Novi Glad, but apparently in some sort of underlit art gallery somewhere. Naked statues and paintings of naked women were discomfitably visible in the photo, causing the archbishop to look hastily away and to stare at his

291

clerk instead, saying, "Father? Why are you showing me this?"

"The letter explains, Your Grace."

The letter. The first draft of this letter had been written personally by John Dortmunder, by hand, on Sunday night. It had been read, on Monday and Tuesday, by Dortmunder's faithful companion, May, by Andy Kelp, by Tiny Bulcher, and by Grijk Krugnk, all of whom pronounced it wonderful, and all of whom knew how to fix it. Statements were altered by this editorial staff, emphasis was shifted, entire sentences were moved from place to place, additional thoughts were inserted (some of them later to be removed again), and eventually a letter was produced that everybody but Dortmunder found satisfactory. He still preferred his first draft.

But the letter the archbishop now held was far from that first draft. Handwritten by May on typewriter paper from the Safeway, it read:

Dear Archbishop Minkokus.

I am a disgruntled employee of Mr. and Mrs. Hochman, the hotel people. They think their better than anybody. So I helped steal all their art. But I am a devout person, I pray to Saint Dismas all the time, and I was shocked when I saw this sacred relic in among all the profane and filthy art that people like those people like. Naked pictures, and pictures that hold the Church up to scorn. Mr. and Mrs. Hochman are doing many dirty deals with Ambassador Hradec Kralowc of Votskojek, like him helping them get around the tax laws in this country and Europe. They paid to fix up a love nest apartment in that Votskojek ship for the Ambassador. And now he gives them this sacred relic, for them to pretend it is "art" like all that corrupt filth they have their, I say their going too far. Archbishop, the people that stole all that "art" may be thieves, but they have got more respect than that. They will treat the sacred relic like it should be treated, and when the insurance company pays and the art goes back I hope you will see to it that the sacred relic is treated decent and like it ought to be from now on.

Sincerely,

A Sinner but not a Total Loss

"Absurd," the archbishop said when he'd finished this group effort. "Ridiculous. I don't even understand most of it."

"Your Grace," said the clerk diffidently, "I took the liberty of bringing along these recent articles from the *New York Times*. If you'd look at these two reports, Your Grace, you'll see what the letter writer is talking about."

The archbishop viewed the papers in the clerk's hands with deep mistrust. "It isn't about world population growth, is it?"

"No, Your Grace. It's about the art theft referred to in that letter."

"I hate all that anticlerical stuff about world population growth."

"This is something else entirely, Your Grace," the clerk assured him.

Still dubious, prepared to clamp his eyelids shut at the first sign of an uncomfortable reality, the archbishop took the papers and began to read. When, four minutes later, he raised his head, he was a changed man, though not on the subject of world population growth. "Get me," he said coldly, "that man. On the telephone."

"Yes, Your Grace."

The clerk started to leave, but the archbishop said, "Take these things with you," waggling bony fingers over the newspaper articles and the letter.

"Yes, Your Grace." The clerk picked up the papers, saying, "Should I turn the letter over to the police?"

The archbishop stared. "Whatever for? To have this shameful revelation in the newspapers?"

"I only thought, Your Grace, the police might think it was evidence or some such thing. Concerning the crime."

"Temporal laws are not our concern," the archbishop instructed. "We have the Church to consider. File that letter under miscellaneous correspondence."

"Yes, Your Grace."

"I'll keep this photo a while."

"Yes, Your Grace."

The clerk bowed himself out, and the archbishop brooded at the photograph, observing this treatment of the relic of St. Ferghana, until the clerk buzzed him that he had the ambassador on the phone. The archbishop pressed the button. "Hello."

"Hello, Archbishop, how are you today?" There was a nasty homosexual nasal quality to the ambassador's voice that the archbishop had never noticed before. If there was one thing the archbishop hated more than normal sex, it was abnormal sex. His own voice, usually thin and gravelly and harsh, became colder and more forbidding than ever as he said, "It doesn't matter how I am today, Ambassador. When do you intend to bring the relic of St. Ferghana over here to the UN and present it to the General Assembly?"

There was a brief startled silence at the other end of the line, punctuated by little coughs and grunts. Then the ambassador said, "Well, Archbishop, I was on the phone yesterday with President Ka—"

"I want to know," the archbishop said, "when we'll be seeing the relic over here at the UN."

"Well, there should be, you know, Archbishop, a certain ceremony in connection with—"

"When."

"I had thought, well, uh, you know, a few weeks—"

"Tomorrow," the archbishop said.

The silence this time was stunned, and profound. "Tomorrow, Archbishop?"

"Tomorrow."

"But my president wants a ceremonial occa—"

"You may have your ceremony whenever you want it," the archbishop said. "Whatever sort of *ceremony* a fellow like you might devise. But the relic is to be in this building, in my office, for safekeeping, tomorrow."

"Archbishop," the miserable invert stammered, "I don't see how I can, uh, uh, uh . . ."

The archbishop hung up.

57

It turned out, Guy could host a lunch on Thursday, after all. There happened to be a few people in town who could be useful or amusing when put together at his table, at least two of whom immediately broke other appointments when they received his invitation, which was highly gratifying. The lunch went as well as Guy had expected, and after it, after seeing his guests out at the front door to their limousines waiting on East Sixty-eighth Street—Guy did prefer guests who departed by limo rather than by cab—he returned to his office, to learn that two calls had come in while he'd been lounging upstairs: Jacques Perly and the carpenters.

"Ah," Guy said, standing over his secretary's desk, holding the two "While you were out" slips. "No number for the carpenters?"

"They said they were on a job site without a phone," she explained, "and would call back after three. It sounded as though they were at a pay phone."

The pay phone is to the telephone as the taxicab is to the limousine. "Get Jacques for me, then," Guy said, "and put the carpenters through when they call back."

"Yes, sir."

Guy moved on into his own office, and beyond, to his bathroom, where he dropped two Alka-Seltzer into a glass of cold water. Carrying it back, listening to the fizz, feeling the faint shower of bursting bubbles on the hand holding the glass, anticipating the relief just ahead, he sat at his desk as the intercom said, "Mr. Perly on one."

"Hello, Jacques." Guy sipped Alka-Seltzer. "How are we coming along?"

"Slow and steady," Perly answered. "This situation, Guy, I'm afraid it isn't quite as simple as you and I, in our own simplicity, assumed."

"Were we assuming that?"

"Well, I was assuming it," Perly said, "and I suppose I was assuming you were assuming it, as well. But you already knew this affair was complicated?"

"Well, no," Guy said. He felt his feet weren't quite touching bottom in this conversation. "I wouldn't say I thought it was *complicated.*"

"Because if there's anything I should know . . ."

"No, no, no," Guy said. "I merely meant, I never assume any situation is *simple.*"

"Ah. A wise philosophy. This situation is quite other than simple. I'm having to run down a few leads here and there."

"Leads?" Guy drained the Alka-Seltzer, suddenly needing it more. "You mean to *find* the collection, rather than buy it?" Thirty thousand down instead of a million up; a hell of a thought.

But Perly said, "Not precisely. In a way, I think what we're dealing with here is an inside job."

"Fascinating," Guy said. "Anyone I know?"

"I'll be happy to chat about it once I've cracked it," Perly said. "But what I need now is time."

"Oh, dear." Guy was sorry the Alka-Seltzer was all gone. "You don't want me to stall these people, do you? Desperate criminals like these?"

"Frankly, yes."

"We discussed at lunch, Jacques, you know we did, the alternatives they *do* have. Europe, South America. To be just as frank as you are, I'm already out-of-pocket in this situation, to keep them contented—"

"That's up to you, of course."

"I know it is; I'm not complaining. But to stall? They already phoned once today, while I was out; they'll be calling back after three."

"All I want," Perly said, "is two weeks."

"*What?* Impossible. How can I ask these people to wait two weeks, when they know any second they could be exposed, arrested?"

"What can you do for me, Guy? I need time. Ten days, can you do that much?"

"One week," Guy said firmly. "In good conscience, that's all I could even try for."

Perly sighed. "Well," he said, "then it's up to me, that's all. Work faster, that's all."

Which was when Guy realized one week was how long Perly had hoped for from the beginning. To be negotiated with, *and not notice;* the Alka-Seltzer turned to gall and wormwood in Guy's stomach. "I'm sure," he said acidly, and burped, "you'll find the way. You're very resourceful, after all." And he hung up on Perly's suave good-bye.

By one minute past three, when the carpenter called, Guy was feeling better about life, mostly because of other business dealings that had occupied his time. Now, hearing the gloomy tones of the chief carpenter in his ear, he was positively cheerful when he said, "No news yet, I'm sorry to say."

"That's okay," the carpenter said. "For now, it's okay. Pretty soon, though, it's not gonna be okay."

"I understand."

"We're hanging out here in the wind, you know."

"I perfectly sympathize."

"The longer it takes, the more chance something goes wrong, one of us gets nabbed, the whole deal goes south."

"I couldn't agree more."

"We got other things we could do with this stuff."

"Everyone is aware of that, I assure you."

"So we gotta have a deadline here, and then after that we're gonna have to go and *do* other things. Some one other thing."

Here was the sticking point. Gripping the phone, speaking carefully, Guy said, "I don't know how much I can rush the process here. We're dealing, after all, with insurance companies and so on."

"That's okay. You just tell them the deadline, if they ever want to see this stuff again. Or, if they'd like to pay a hundred cents on the dollar to the guy in Vermont, they could do that, too."

"I'm sure they'd rather not."

"So they'll meet the deadline."

"I don't know how rapidly we could all—"

"Two weeks."

. . .

"You there?"

"Oh, yes," Guy said.

"You heard me?"

"I heard you. Two weeks, you said."

"And not a minute more."

Guy smiled all over his face. "My friend," he said, "I think I can assure you, it might even be a few minutes less."

58

The storm came out of nowhere, whipping northward up the Atlantic Coast, swamping small boats, eroding beaches, exposing the frenzied ocean waves to the lurid glare of its lightning bolts. Wind rammed the rain before it, sweeping across the bare decks of the Staten Island ferries as they wallowed in the heaving harbor and waddled slowly toward shore. Sheets of rain flung themselves up Broadway, drumming on taxi roofs, theater marquees, closed newspaper kiosks. Skyscrapers ran with fat tears of water; the gutters boiled; trees in the parks bent and trembled before the fury of the elements. Far up in the Bronx, the storm raged and shrieked around the black bell tower of St. Crispinian, where pale arching currents of electricity feebly echoed the jolts of lightning from above, and where Hradec Kralowc's faint voice, torn by the wind, was heard to cry, "We *can't* give up! Not now!"

Electric power had not failed, at least there was that. Round light globes beneath circular tin reflectors hung on long black wires from the shadowy stone ceiling high above Dr. Zorn's laboratory. The globes swayed in the air as crooked fingers of wind reached in through cracks in the church walls, making shadows twist and writhe in all the corners, but at least the lights stayed on. The experiment could continue.

There was to be *no* defeatism. They *were* winning, they *were*! Hadn't Hradec succeeded in quitting the *Pride of Votskojek* unobserved, eluding the press by wearing the uniform of a Continental Detective Agency guard and exiting with the eight-to-four shift? Hadn't he brought his cellular phone with him, and hadn't he used it, right here in this former church yesterday afternoon, to convince Archbishop Minkokus, that fiend from Hell, that he needed twenty-four more hours before he could bring the sacred relic to the archbishop's office in the United Nations building? Hadn't he done so by claiming he couldn't move the relic without permission from his president back in Novi Glad, which permission had not as yet come through but would surely come through at any moment, once the situation had been sufficiently explained to the president? And hadn't that persuaded the archbishop to say, "Very well. Friday. By noon"?

Friday, by noon. That was hours from now. Hradec had been here for more than twenty-four wakeful hours so far, spurring Dr. Zorn to greater heights of experimentation, *demanding* success, and they still had until noon tomorrow, nearly eleven hours. Surely, surely, *surely* by then they could fake a bone!

"We won't fool *any*one!" Zorn insisted, that defeatist, that miserable mewling swine. "This doesn't even look like a femur!" he cried, pointing at the bone they were working with, brought here by Hradec from a butcher shop in Chinatown, the closest thing he could find to his memory of the stolen relic.

"We don't have to fool anyone," Hradec argued. "The only person who is going to see this bone is Archbishop Minkokus, that senile, old, doddering fool. This is only to buy time, Karver, only to buy a little time."

"Defrauding an archbishop," Zorn wailed. "They'll lock us up forever!"

"No one will know! The archbishop's half-blind!"

"The *other* half will see this bone doesn't even come from a human being!"

"How do you know? Maybe it does! No one knows what goes on in Chinatown!"

Dr. Zorn picked up the bone in question and banged it on the autopsy table. "This is *not* a human bone."

"How would the archbishop know such a thing? What does he know of the inside of the human body?"

The argument raged on within as the storm raged on without. They shaved the bone; they painted it; they surged powerful beams of electric energy through it; they lowered it into various solutions; they exposed it to the storm; they radiated it; they boiled it but didn't keep the soup; they froze it. On and on the work continued, without pause or rest.

Around the church, the storm keened and crashed, but the two within remained bent over their experiments. The storm abated, its cruel teeth withdrew, the storm fled away northward to exhaust itself on the upland slopes, and still Hradec and Zorn labored on. Morning came, and with it the sun, and still they did not rest.

And then the phone rang.

Hradec looked up from the container of dry ice. Smoke and steam enveloped his head. He listened to the tone of the ring. "That's my phone," he said. "It must be Lusk or Terment, from the embassy; no one else has my cellular phone number."

"You'd better answer it," Dr. Zorn suggested. He was haggard from lack of sleep, his reddened eyes behind the thick lenses looking this morning like targets.

"Oh, God," Hradec moaned, turning unwillingly toward his briefcase, where the ominous phone shrilled once more. "What now?" And he fished it out.

It was, as Hradec had supposed, Lusk or Terment; he himself didn't care which. "I am not to be disturbed," he barked, his voice hoarse and ragged.

"A Mr. Perly called. He's investigating Mr. Hochman's theft."

"I don't care about that."

"He says he wants you at Mr. Hochman's suite in the Dragon Host Hotel at ten o'clock this morning."

"What? For God's sake, why?"

"He didn't say. He just said Mr. Hochman will be there, and everyone else concerned will be there, and it would be better for you if *you* were there."

Outraged through his exhaustion, fitting the tattered cloak of diplomatic immunity about himself, Hradec said, "Are you implying he *threatened* me?"

"It sounded that way, sir. I told him you'd be there."

"You take a lot on yourself!" Hradec cried, but Lusk or Terment had hung up.

Across the way, a beaker exploded.

59

Pacing, Perly prowled the luxurious parlor of Harry Hochman's suite, while in the room the tension mounted. The eight people he'd assembled here did not include any of the lawyers or insurance executives who so cluttered this case; one way and another, these people here were all principals. And Jacques Perly, with their help—witting or unwitting—was about to crack this case wide open.

He was, in fact, about to speak, to open the meeting, when Harry Hochman abruptly said, "Well? Are we all here?"

Perly took a moment to answer. Hochman, because this was his suite, was attempting to direct the agenda of the meeting, but Perly had other ideas. "Yes, Mr. Hochman," he said eventually, "we're all assembled."

"Then get on with it," Hochman said, either displaying irritability or revealing nervousness; hard to tell. "I'm a busy man."

"We're all busy men, Mr. Hochman," Perly said. "The question is, Busy at what? May I turn to you, sir," he said to another of the invited guests. "Would you tell the group your name and occupation?"

The tall, slender, white-haired man recrossed his legs. Calm, self-confident, he sat comfortably in an uncomfortable chair, arms folded, and said, "Name's Hammond Cash. I'm regional manager for CDA."

"Continental Detective Agency."

"Yes, sir."

"You have had the contract to provide security for the Votsko-jek embassy for some months now, is that correct?"

"Yes, sir."

"And there was a robbery at the embassy some little time ago?"

The thin man smiled thinly. "It looked like a robbery, yes, sir."

Perly was gratified to see, from the corner of his eye, Hradec Kralowc's sudden spasm of shock at that sentence, but he pretended for the moment not to have noticed. Concentrating on Cash, he said, "*Looked* like a robbery? Could you describe the event, Mr. Cash?"

"Certainly." Cash had a battered old briefcase on the floor beside his chair. Reaching into it, bringing out a sheaf of papers, he said, "I have here the affidavits of the security men on duty at the time, but to sum it up, Ambassador Kralowc there had two guests aboard the ship, one of whom created a diversion at the gate while the other one scampered about, waving something that was supposed to be the relic of St. Ferghana—"

"Supposed to be!"

"One moment, Ambassador," Perly said. "You'll get your chance. Mr. Cash?"

"Having made sure my men saw this artifact," Cash continued, "the accomplice made his escape in a powerboat operated by a third member of the group."

"Quite elaborate," Perly suggested.

"Yes, sir, very." Cash chuckled, then sobered and said, "My men naturally suggested phoning the police, but the ambassador wouldn't hear of it."

"You mean, this relic was apparently stolen in front of the eyes of your security men, and Ambassador Kralowc refused to make a police report?"

"Yes, sir. He apparently released the first man as well."

Kralowc was on his feet, yowling: "What? What are you suggesting? What are you trying to imply?"

"All in good time, Ambassador," Perly told him. "If you'll just be seated—"

"I want to know what you think you're—"

"Sit down, Hradec," Harry Hochman said with such cold distaste in his gruff voice that Kralowc dropped back into his seat as though he'd been hit by an air bag.

Perly turned back to Cash. "Could you tell us what happened next?"

"They shut the embassy," Cash replied. "We stayed on the job, but they shut the place down and all the Votskojek nationals left the country."

"I see." Perly turned to another of his guests, a thoughtful, pipe-smoking man. "Sir, would you tell us your name and occupation?"

"John McIntire," the thoughtful man said, sucking on his unlighted pipe. "Johns Hopkins. Forensic science."

"And have you had occasion to spend time on the *Pride of Votskojek,* the Votskojek embassy?"

"Quite a lot of time, in fact."

"For what purpose, sir?"

"There was some question raised about the authenticity of a certain relic, a femur, this bone along here." He indicated by running the wet end of his pipe along his left pants leg.

"And on the day of the alleged robbery, were you—"

"Alleged!"

Many people glared at Ambassador Kralowc this time, and he subsided after that one word. Perly turned back to McIntire. "Were you contacted by Ambassador Kralowc later that same day?"

"One of his people, I believe. Lusk or Terment. They called to say they were shutting the place down for a while, I wasn't to continue my work. That situation maintained until very recently, when my fellow investigators and I were permitted to study the relic once more. Or *a* relic; no telling if it's the same one."

"No," Perly agreed. "No telling. Do you know why doubt had been raised about the relic to begin with?"

"Some sort of dispute," McIntire suggested, "with Votskojek's neighbor over there, another little country. Sorry, don't know the name."

"Tsergovia," Perly supplied, and turned to the bulldog-shaped woman in the olive green uniform. "You are Ambassador Kotor of Tsergovia, are you not?"

"Yes, I am."

"Could you tell us why you raised this doubt about authenticity?"

"We possessed a similar sacred relic ourselves," she said. "Until very recently, we thought ours was the real one and theirs the imitation. But we tested ours, and were embarrassed to learn we had the fake."

"Why was this an issue?"

"There were political considerations," the ambassadress said. "At least, we thought so."

Perly turned to the scrawny old man in the clerical black and the red beanie. "You are Archbishop Minkokus, are you not?"

"I am."

"You head a commission concerning the future UN seats of both Votskojek and Tsergovia?"

"I do."

"Has there been a rumor that, because of religious bias, you intended to give favorable consideration to whichever country possessed the true relic?"

"Scurrilous!"

"But the rumor existed. Was it false?"

"Of course! What an idea!" The old archbishop grew quite pink in the face.

"Of course," Perly agreed, sympathetically. "But foolish ideas sometimes are believed." He turned to Ambassadress Kotor: "Did you believe the rumor?"

"I'm sorry to say we did, for a while. Until we got to know the archbishop and found out what a fair and sensible man he was."

"Thank you, my dear," said the archbishop, bowing in her direction his beanied head.

Perly turned to Kralowc. "And did *you* believe the rumor?"

"Of course not!"

"No, you didn't," Perly said, and bore in. "You proved you didn't believe the rumor, by giving that relic to Harry Hochman!"

Kralowc's eyes bugged out. "*What?*"

"You and Harry Hochman," Perly pursued, "have been

engaged in influence peddling, both here and in Europe, for some time. I have signed statements gathered by Interpol in Europe."

"Now, wait a minute," Hochman said. "Just a damn minute here."

"No, sir, *Mr.* Hochman," Perly said, turning on the financier. "You think of yourself as an art lover, an art collector, as well as a captain of industry."

"I am," Hochman said, as though it were obvious, "that's what I am. I'm all of those things."

"An art lover to the extent," Perly said, "that you would try anything, do anything, to get a work of art you loved."

Too late cautious, "I certainly wouldn't say that," Hochman said.

"*I* would," Perly told him. "I have affidavits concerning unethical and illegal activities you hired others to engage in, in Geneva and Rotterdam and Buenos Aires, to obtain certain works you coveted."

"Oh, balderdash," Hochman said. "The art world is a very special—That's Guy Claverack sitting right there; he's a dealer in— you just ask him!"

"We'll get to Mr. Claverack in due course," Perly said. "Suffice it to say, for now, you have been known to go to extreme lengths to get a work of art you desired."

"No more than anyone else in the field who—"

"Considerably more, I would say, Mr. Hochman. Not many art lovers would resort to blackmail!"

Hochman screwed up his captain of industry face into shocked disbelief. "Are you *out* of your *mind*?"

"I don't believe so." Perly took a folded sheet of paper from his inside jacket pocket, opened it, and handed it to Kralowc, who seemed stunned by events. "Ambassador, this is a list of women you have dated in New York City in the last twelve months. There are forty-nine names on this list."

Kralowc gazed dully at the list. He shook his head. "If you say so."

"We left three names *off* the list," Perly said. "Could you fill them in?"

"Of course not," Kralowc said. "How am I supposed to remember?"

"Three women you dated within the last year. Three women you spent time and money on. Three women you went to bed with. But you have no memory of them."

"I don't know, I mean, I don't see the, what's the *point* in all this?"

"They remember you," Perly said. "They and several of the others. I have affidavits concerning their sexual experiences with you. None of them felt you were, shall we say, highly motivated. Their general impression was that you hadn't much real interest in heterosexual experience."

"I don't believe you," Kralowc said. "Where are these affidavits?"

Perly pointed at a gruff-looking, gray-mustached, athletic man across the room. "In the possession of Bill Karnitz over there. He's a detective with the Fraud Squad of the New York Police Department."

"Fraud!"

"I suggest, Ambassador," Perly said, "that you and Dr. Karver Zorn have been lovers ever since you shared a room in your undergraduate days at Osigreb Polytechnic, that you married to hide this relationship, that you parade with attractive women in New York for the same reason, because you know exposure would ruin your diplomatic career."

"That's ridiculous," Kralowc sputtered, "the UN is crawling with—"

"You were followed, Ambassador," Perly interrupted, "when you left the embassy in disguise two days ago. You spent all of the last two nights at the home of Dr. Zorn in the Bronx. Why?"

"I can explain!"

"Go ahead, Ambassador."

Kralowc stared, thought, started several sentences, moaned, closed his eyes, put his head in his hands.

Now Perly had him, and he knew it. "I *further* suggest," he suggested, pointing a rigid finger at the top of Kralowc's head, "that Harry Hochman told you he wanted the relic of St. Ferghana, as well as the jewel-encrusted sarcophagus in which it was—"

"Reliquary," Guy Claverack said.

"I beg your pardon," Perly said; "you're absolutely right; I was carried away. Reliquary. It was the reliquary he *really* wanted, wasn't it? And threatened to expose your affair with Dr. Zorn if he didn't get it. And how did he know about that affair? Because he had loaned you his Vermont château as a secure love nest for you and your doctor friend!"

Hochman surged to his feet: "This is outrageous! To sit here, in my own hotel, and listen to this absurd string of ridiculous—"

"You think it's ridiculous, Mr. Hochman?" Perly pointed toward Bill Karnitz, the Fraud Squad cop. "After our meeting here, you'll be able to discuss this ridiculous story with Detective Karnitz."

Hochman blanched. "I don't know why you're trying to frame me with all this, Perly," he said, "but I never knew Hradec Kralowc was a faggot until—"

"I'm not! I'm not!"

"I *never* let him use that place! He broke in there! He's probably in league with the thieves; I wouldn't put it past him. Question *him*!"

Bill Karnitz spoke quietly from his corner. "We will, Mr. Hochman. We'll question everybody."

"And if you have nothing to hide," Perly said, with a faint sneer, "you'll be all right."

Hochman could be seen adding up the things he had to hide. Silent, no longer full of braggadocio, he sat down.

Perly turned to the group. "To sum up. Ambassador Kralowc faked a theft of the relic, but didn't report it to the police, because they would uncover the fraud at once. But the record would exist in the Continental Detective Agency files, if and when the question ever arose as to what had happened to the relic. Having established this false robbery, the ambassador closed the embassy, turned relic and reliquary over to Harry Hochman, obtained a false relic from somewhere, then reopened the embassy. All would have gone well except that, on an occasion when he and his lover Zorn were in residence in their love nest provided by Harry Hochman at his château, thieves broke in and stole the entire art collection, including the relic and reliquary. Even then, no one would have been likely to search for the truth behind appearances if Harry Hochman, in panic, had not denied ever having had the relic and reliquary in his possession. But now we know why he told that lie, as we know why the ambassador who was supposed to be guarding the relic in New York was in fact asleep in Vermont when that very same relic was being stolen right out from under him... *in Vermont.*"

"Amazing deduction," the archbishop murmured.

Perly smiled, pleased with himself. "A tricky little case," he said, "but I think that wraps it up."

Guy Claverack, looking bewildered, said, "Jacques? I thought we were here because of the theft. What happened to the stolen art?"

Perly looked at him in surprise. "The stolen art? I suppose the thieves still have it, until the insurance company pays off. This isn't about stolen art, Guy. Stolen-art cases are a dime a dozen. This is the case of the orphaned reliquary."

60

For weeks the neighborhood had been complaining about the smell. State and federal offices, county offices, even town offices had been deluged with calls. Children on the way to school were getting sick and housewives in a several block radius were blacking out, especially on warm, sunny days. "It's like all the dead fish in the world, all in one place," people said.

Nothing did any good. EPA vans went by, registering the air. OSHA inspectors closed down two dry-cleaning plants and a bowling alley. State police ticketed a record number of motorists. But still the smell hung over the neighborhood, a curse that would not lift.

Finally, several of the neighborhood men got together and spent an entire weekend searching for several blocks in every direction, until at last they found the center of the stink, its fetid core. The smell was coming from a truck parked in the middle of the neighborhood on a commercial block. It even *said* it was a fish truck.

Calls were made. More calls were made. "Come take this stinking truck away!" Weeks went by; the smell got worse; real estate values in the entire community were beginning to slide.

And then, at last, a police tow vehicle arrived. And wouldn't you know it? Took the wrong truck.

311

61

Monday morning, Guy received a phone call from Jacques Perly, saying, "When do you expect to hear from your people?"

"Probably today sometime. Why? What can I tell them? I haven't heard any numbers yet."

"Tell them we need more pictures," Perly said. "One of the insurance companies is holding out; they want to be sure your people haven't *already* moved the goods offshore. You know, paying the ransom and not getting anything for it."

"Jacques, what are you talking about? Of course they've still got it."

"I'm just telling you what the insurance company says. A picture of the loot, or at least some of it, with a copy of today's newspaper showing so they know it's a new picture."

"What if they say no?"

"Then this one insurance company isn't going to pay, and that's a big chunk of it gone."

"Jacques, this doesn't make sense, but I'll do what I can."

"I'm sure you will, Guy. As you say, you're already out-of-pocket."

"And getting less pleased about it every second."

"We'll laugh about this when it's over."

"I'm glad to hear that."

Monday afternoon, fresh from an entertaining lunch in his upstairs dining room, Guy received a phone call from the carpenters. First, he explained the negotiations were still in an early stage, and then he said, "They want another picture."

There was a pause, and the gloomy-voiced carpenter said, "Oh, yeah?"

"They're just dragging their feet, if you want my opinion, but there's nothing I can do about it. One of the insurance companies, they insist on proof you haven't already gotten rid of the collection somewhere else. They want a picture of it, some part of it, with a copy of today's newspaper visible, to show it's a new photograph."

"Uh-huh. Do they care which newspaper?"

"I'm sorry?"

"Never mind."

"Was that a serious question?"

"Who knows what's serious, Mr. Claverack?"

When Guy hung up, the sound in his ears was the fluttering of many dollar bills, flying away.

Monday evening, Grijk Krugnk got a call from a friend, who said, "No names."

"Oh, hello, Chon."

"I said no names!"

"Oh. Vhy?"

"In case anyone's listening on this line."

"Your line, or my line?"

"Any line. Listen, I want you to do me a favor."

"Sure ding, Cho—Oh. Zorry."

"Don't worry about it. In the morning, I have to go out to where we left the truck with all the stuff in it; you know the stuff I mean. Don't mention it!"

"Oh, no, I vouldn't."

313

"We don't have a car now, so could you drive me out?"

"Vad, are you giving id back?"

"No, they need another picture, don't ask me why."

"Oh. Hokay."

"It's out on Long Island, in Farport, on Merrick Avenue, in a big gray truck that says J & L CARTING on the doors."

"You're comin vid me, aren'd choo?"

"Sure, me or somebody with a camera. I just want you to know where it is. I'll come to your place around eight in the morning."

"I'll be here, Chon. Oo! Zorry."

"S'okay."

62

The neighborhood was a lot more bearable now that they'd taken the right truck away at last. On the other hand, it was a lot more populated after they brought the wrong truck and very carefully parked it exactly where it had been parked before.

There were vans, with men in the back, parked now at both ends of that block. Even after the video store in the middle of the block closed for the night, there were still people faintly visible moving around inside there. There were also people moving around on the roof of a two-story warehouse very near where the truck had been reparked. There was more traffic in the area than usual, and a lot of it consisted of slow-moving, plain four-door sedans with two burly guys in front. Pedestrians also made more of a presence than was usual at night in a Long Island commercial/ suburban south shore community. It kind of made you wonder, in a way.

It was a little after one in the morning, and the active population of the neighborhood was still surprisingly high, though maintaining a rather low profile, when a vehicle with diplomat license plates and two occupants drove slowly down that block, braked slightly beside the returned truck, then drove on. Eight

315

minutes later, it drove by once more, even slower than last time. And seventeen minutes after that, according to several videotaped records of the incident then being taken, the same vehicle appeared again, inched past the truck, pulled in behind it, and parked. Its lights switched off. Silence and darkness ensued for another three minutes.

The passenger door of the new arrival opened, and a figure dressed in black emerged. He moved forward cautiously to the rear of the truck, which was closed with a segmented metal door that would slide up to open. He reached out and grasped the handle of this door, and as his fingers closed around it a million floodlights suddenly flashed on, aimed directly at him, and a million voices shouted, "Freeze! Police!"

Like a rabbit in headlights, Hradec Kralowc spun about and pressed his back against the truck. "Diddums!" he wailed, voice cracking. "It's Diddums!"

In the car, the Lada with diplomat plates, Dr. Karver Zorn lowered his forehead to the steering wheel and wished himself dead. Unfortunately, it didn't work.

"Diddums," Hradec mumbled brokenly, over and over, as they handcuffed him and read him his rights and stuffed him into a squad car. "Diddums. Diddums. It's Diddums."

"Going for an insanity defense," the cops told one another. And with these lousy liberal judges, they figured, he'd probably get away with it, too.

63

So that's that," Dortmunder said, watching from the window of a darkened, closed laundromat a block away as Kralowc and Dr. Zorn were arrested in a blaze of light. Handing the binoculars to Kelp, he said, "He doesn't look happy."

"None of us look happy, John," Kelp said, and peered into the binoculars.

"The cops do."

What had happened was, the instant Guy Claverack said, "They want another picture," Dortmunder knew what it meant: The cops had found the truck, and were staked out all around it. He *knew* that, as clearly and instinctively as you know how to scratch where it itches, but of course instinctive knowledge always has to be verified scientifically, or it isn't worth anything, so the question was how to put some other puppy's paw in the snare and see if it went *spannnggg*.

It was Tiny who remembered that Kralowc had at one time put a bug on the Tsergovian embassy's phones, a fact that still stuck in Tiny's craw. "Maybe it's still there," he said.

Turns out, it was.

Dortmunder and Kelp had come out to Farport by themselves,

317

much earlier today, to see what happened to their puppy, and now, while waiting for the massive police presence to dissipate, they sat on adjoining driers with their feet swinging and discussed whether or not Guy Claverack knew he was sending them into a trap. Kelp kind of thought he did, and felt they should avenge themselves by visiting Mr. Claverack's storage rooms, but Dortmunder disagreed. "You didn't talk to him on the phone, I did. He didn't sound sly or guilty or nervous or anything like that; he just sounded irritated, like he wanted to get this show on the road and didn't see why there had to be all these delays."

"I still think we oughta visit him."

"Maybe," Dortmunder agreed. "Later on. But maybe not to burn our bridges there. It could be, down the road, we could do business with Claverack again."

"I don't think I could afford it," Kelp said.

The cops took quite a while to vacate the field of play, long enough for Kelp, having no choice, to become philosophic. "There are some bright sides to this," he announced.

"Oh, yeah?"

"Well, we didn't get nabbed, that's one thing."

"True."

"And you and me and Stan, we come out about eight grand ahead. Almost."

"Not the numbers we had in mind."

"No, but it's *some*thing."

"And the other guys got less than three."

"Don't forget the extra three cents to Tiny."

By the light of departing police cars, Dortmunder looked at his friend. "You gonna mention that to Tiny, when we get back?"

"Maybe not," Kelp said.

64

Zara, Grijk, and the archbishop stood admiring the sacred relic of St. Ferghana, gleaming inside its jewel-encrusted glass reliquary, standing atop a marble and iron fourteenth-century table, originally a side altar in a long-ago-sacked Moravian or Moldavian church, now given pride of place in the archbishop's office in the United Nations building, centered on the wall directly opposite the archbishop's desk, so that every time he looked up from his heavy labors, there it would be, safe and sound.

For the foreseeable future, this would be the femur's home, that having been agreed to three weeks ago, once the relic and all the rest of Harry Hochman's art collection had been recovered out there on Long Island. Those involved, being the Tsergovian government, the United Nations secretariat, and the archbishop himself (but not Votskojek), had agreed that not only was this the safest location for the holy artifact under present unsettled global conditions but that it was only justice that the archbishop, who had worked so diligently to protect the saint's remain, should have her care put into his palsied yet capable hands.

The new friends had come here after Zara Kotor's investiture as delegate to the United Nations from that body's newest member, Tsergovia, assuming the seat of the no-longer-extant nation of which at one time it had formed a part. The archbishop provided sherry, in *very* small glasses, they drank to their new understanding, and then they admired the relic a while.

"It's hard to believe depravity like Kralowc's," the archbishop commented. "To hand over this symbol of purity and beauty and eternal truth to a mere temporal prince. The dear St. Ferghana is not to *be* of the mundane things of this mundane world."

"I couldn't agree more," Zara said, and smiled upon the archbishop.

Who smiled back, saying, "Well, at least we know we shan't have the unspeakable Kralowc to worry about anymore. Though it's a pity he didn't get his just desserts."

"You mean," Zara said, "the punishment he so richly deserved?"

"That's it exactly."

"Not that he got off scot-free," Zara acknowledged.

In fact, Kralowc had escaped by the skin of his teeth, having plea-bargained his way onto a one-way flight out of America forever and back to Novi Glad (and Mrs. Kralowc) permanently. The videotaped confession he'd made in exchange for his freedom, in which he'd outlined his part in Harry Hochman's scheme to bilk the insurance companies of $6 million—a scheme carefully described to him beforehand by the federal prosecutors—was expected to feature prominently in Hochman's trial, upcoming in just a few months, once his lawyers' delaying tactics were exhausted, despite Kralowc's craven refutation of the confession once he was beyond the reach of American justice.

"Id looks bigger in daydime," Grijk said, frowning through the glass at the bone.

The archbishop said, "Eh?"

Grijk abruptly looked terrified, but Zara distracted the archbishop's attention by grasping the elderly prelate's forearm and saying, "I was just thinking the same thing. You know, for people like Grijk and me, the only time we could ever see the holy relic of St. Ferghana was in the cathedral in Novi Glad, where they kept it in such a *dark* little corner."

"*Dod*'s righd," Grijk said, bobbing his head. "*Dod*'s vhad I meand."

"Well, the Votskojeks won't be getting their hands on this precious relic again anytime soon," the archbishop said with unsaintly satisfaction.

Zara said, "Once they get into the UN, though, won't they petition for its return?"

Chuckling deep inside his Adam's apple, the archbishop said, "That won't be for some little time, I'm afraid. There's a certain protocol to these things, you know, a certain dignity and ceremony; only one new nation's application would normally be considered at a time. You have come in ahead of Votskojek, and I believe next there will be some small island nation in the Atlantic, Maylohda, I believe, a former colony, and then . . . oh, someone. It's a changing world, you know."

"Well, Archbishop," Zara said, "the nicest change is how we're all getting along."

The archbishop agreed with that and pressed another eighth of an ounce of sherry on them, but Zara felt she shouldn't take up any more of his valuable time, and so they made their escape, and when they were out on First Avenue, with 163 flags flapping in the breeze and the UN building glinting over their shoulders in the sunlight, Zara said, as though she'd just thought of it that second, "I tell you what. Let's see your cousin!"

"You mean Diny?" Grijk was dubious. "I don't know, he's maybe—"

"It'll be a nice surprise," Zara predicted. "Come on."

65

Tiny had called Dortmunder and Kelp and said, "J.C.'s back; there's something she wants to talk to us about; come on over," so they went over, and they were all there, greeting one another, when the doorbell rang. "We're all here," Tiny pointed out.

"So it's somebody else," said J.C., who hadn't gotten to her subject matter yet and so was a little irritated by the interruption. "Come on, Tiny, get em in and get em out."

"You got it."

Tiny buzzed for the downstairs door, then opened to the upstairs bell, and here came Zara Kotor and Grijk Krugnk, Zara beaming a big wide dolphin smile at Tiny, saying "Tchotchkus!" while Grijk grinned uneasily and said, "Hi, Diny."

Kelp said, "Who?"

"I brought champagne!" Zara announced, and held it up like a flag on the barricades. Smiling coquettishly at Tiny, she said, "You've been avoiding me, you bad boy."

"Aw, naw, Zara," Tiny said. "I just been busy. Especially since Josie here come back." He gestured at J.C., who smiled like a shark and said, "Hi-i."

Grijk, extremely uncomfortable, said, "Hi, J.Z."

"Hi, Grijk."

"Chon's still d'only one can pronounce id."

Zara looked at J.C., and the champagne went to half-mast. "Hello?" she asked.

Tiny made the introductions: "Zara, this is my roommate, Josie. Most people call her J.C. Josie, this is Zara Kotor; she went to Bronx Science."

"Did she?" J.C. smiled on Zara. "I bet you were good at it, too."

"Zara's," Tiny explained, "ambassador of Grijk's country, Tsergovia."

"And today," Zara said, getting some of her wind back at the thought, "we are a member of the community of nations!"

"No kidding," J.C. said. "So am I."

"What I mean," Zara said, "today we are a member of the *United* Nations."

"That, I'm not," J.C. said.

"Congratulations!" Kelp said, and Dortmunder chimed in, "That's great news."

"Though I've got my application in," J.C. said.

"And we owe it *all*," Zara proclaimed, "to you guys!"

J.C. said, "Tiny? Do we still have champagne glasses? Or did you bust them all while I was away?"

"Josie, you can believe me," Tiny said, crossing the room to the nice glass-doored cabinet, "I never once *touched* your champagne glasses while you were gone."

"I believe you," J.C. said.

While Tiny got out the glasses, Kelp sidled over to Zara, pointed his thumb over his shoulder at Tiny, and murmured, "*What* was that you called him?"

Zara was about to answer when Grijk, with abrupt, unexpected forcefulness, said, "She called him Diny, same like you and me."

Zara thought about it. Kelp watched her. Zara's expression cleared. "That's right. I called him Tiny."

Tiny brought over the glasses, Grijk wrung the bottle's neck, and they toasted the newest member of the world's least exclusive club. Then Kelp said, "J.C. had something she wanted to talk about," and Dortmunder said, "Maybe she just wanted to talk to a couple of us," and Zara said, "That's okay, we'll go; we just wanted you to know, you can always count on Tsergovia."

"In da schoolbooks!" Grijk promised. "Anonymous, bud in da schoolbooks."

"That's right," Zara said. "Well, we'll be off."

"Hold it a second," J.C. said. "You people feel grateful to these guys?"

"Forever!"

"So they could trust you."

"Vid dere lifes!"

"Well, it won't come to that," J.C. said, "but why don't you two sit down? Let me tell my story."

So they all sat down, and some of the group switched to beer, and others stuck to champagne, and J.C. said, "When Grijk was here the last time, and I saw the advantage in being a country, I figured, Why not? So I've got my own country now, and I'm ready to cash in."

Tiny said, "Josie? Whadaya mean, you got your own country?"

"I've got consular agency offices set up in Geneva and Amsterdam and Nairobi and Tokyo, and now I'm setting up the commercial attaché's office here in New York, and then the embassy in Washington, that's next."

Zara was frowning like a steam engine. She said, "Excuse me. You and what army? Who are all these people?"

"What people?"

"The offices in all those cities."

"Mail drops," J.C. said. "All forwarded here to the commercial attaché. You'd be surprised how many little countries do business by mail drop in different parts of the world."

"No, I wouldn't," Zara said. "The world is an expensive place."

"Exactly. Mail order has been my business for more years than I'm gonna tell you, and if I can be a songwriter and a police chief and a wife by mail order, I can be a country."

Grijk said, "J.Z., vere is dis country?"

J.C. airily waved the hand not holding champagne. "Somewhere in the Atlantic," she said.

"Vad's ids poppalation?"

"Well, you know," J.C. said, "if truth be told, since it doesn't have any landmass, it really can't support that much of a population. The population's pretty much me."

324

Dortmunder said, "J.C., you're gonna get caught."

J.C. looked at him. "Who's gonna catch me? All the countries there are in the world, and more every day, and the old ones breaking up into smaller and smaller independent pieces, who's to say Maylohda isn't a legitimate country?"

Zara said, "What was that? What do you call it?"

"Maylohda," J.C. repeated, and explained, "You know, with my New York accent, it's how I say mail order."

"Me, too!" Zara cried, and laughed, and said, "You're ahead of Votskojek! You're applying to the UN!"

"Sure. It's part of the legitimacy, but, you know, that's gonna string out for *years*. Cause I don't really want to belong, too much trouble. I'd have to hire a whole diplomatic staff, maybe even find an actual island somewhere. I'm better off just being a lot of commercial consular offices, and a lot of brochures. See, here they are."

She brought out and distributed nice four-color brochures, describing the wonders, natural attractions, scenic beauty, history, and economic potential of Maylohda, former colony (under other names, of course) of the Netherlands, Great Britain, and Spain. "This stuff was a lot easier to write than the how-to-be-a-detective book," she said. "I used the same printer as always. With this stuff, I can get seed money for feasibility studies of joint ventures in tourism, development of natural resources, and expansion of infrastructure. I can deal with banks, governments, trade associations, the UN, and the IMF. It's harder now at the beginning because there isn't any track record, which is why I was going to ask the guys to travel to some other countries and send me back orders and commissions and stuff, but maybe me and you people could trade somehow. Sell me something, or buy something from me. Maybe you'd like a million copies of the detective book, or some national anthems."

Sounding mournful, Grijk said, "If only you could be a customer for our rocks."

"Oh, I remember your rocks," J.C. said. "Sure, I'll buy them."

Zara was never far from suspicion. Squinting at J.C., she said, "How?"

"We're a low-lying island nation," J.C. explained; "you have

325

no idea *how* low-lying. Like Holland, we want to expand our landmass, build acreage out into the sea. We'll buy your rocks to build up our coastline. What you do, you put together a proposal; you inflate the price a little so I can skim for myself; I put it together with *my* proposal for new acreage; I take it to one of the development commissions, maybe straight to the IMF. We do feasibility studies—"

Dortmunder said, "Don't they go look at the place?"

"They look at me," J.C. said. "I'm a registered lobbyist for the nation of Maylohda; I already took care of that. I show them pictures, I write up my proposals, I talk cute, I cross my legs, I say we've almost got malaria licked out there, and dengue fever, and when would you boys like to go visit. Okay?"

"Okay," Dortmunder said.

Zara said, "But if you work the deal, and you buy the rocks, what then?"

"You deliver."

"Ve're landlocked," Grijk pointed out. "Ve god no ships."

"Good," J.C. said. "We'll find a country with ships and some economic problems of their own. One of the Baltics or the Balkans, maybe. There'll be one official that'll be happy to go along with us, and now Maylohda *must* be real, it's dealing with *two* other countries."

Zara said, "But *where* do they deliver the rocks?"

"To these certain coordinates in the ocean."

"And just dump them?"

"Who knows," J.C. said. "With enough deliveries, maybe we'll *make* an island there. Anyway, it's a start."

Zara looked at the brochures. "This is exactly what such paperwork looks like," she said.

"Naturally."

"Only . . . If you don't mind."

"Productive criticism from a real country," J.C. said, "can only help."

"This state seal here," Zara said. "It's nice, with the lions and all, but shouldn't it say something on this ribbon across the bottom?"

"That's what I said, too," Tiny agreed. "Liberty and truth, or one of those."

"I don't like any of those mottoes," J.C. said. "They don't seem to cover the situation."

Kelp said, "What about that line from John's family crest? John? How'd that go?"

"*Quid lucrum istic mihi est?*" Dortmunder quoted, and explained to J.C., "It means, 'What's in it for me?'"

J.C. smiled. "Can I use it?"

"Be my guest."

Tiny said, "Dortmunder, I've just got to ask you this."

"Yeah?"

"You were an orphan, right?"

"Right."

"Brought up in an orphanage in Dead Indian, Illinois, right?"

"Right."

"What was it, an orphanage run by the Bleeding Heart Sisters of Eternal Misery, am I right?"

"You're right, you're right," Dortmunder said. "So what?"

"So what are you doing with a family crest?"

Dortmunder looked at him with disbelief. He spread his hands. "I stole it," he said.